Miami Confidential

Meredith Ward

Fisher,

thanks for being such a great friend & coworker! VP wouldn't be the same without your cheery attitude every morning! Seriously, give me some of that coffee. :) I hope you enjoy reading it!!!

-♡-

MIAMI CONFIDENTIAL

Copyright 2014 Meredith Ward

All rights reserved.

ISBN: 1497580897
ISBN-13: 978-1497580893

MEREDITH WARD

Table of Contents

Chapter One

Chapter Two

Chapter Three

Chapter Four

Chapter Five

Chapter Six

Chapter Seven

Chapter Eight

Chapter Nine

Chapter Ten

Chapter Eleven

Chapter Twelve

Chapter Thirteen

Chapter Fourteen

Chapter Fifteen

Chapter Sixteen

Chapter Seventeen

Chapter Eighteen

Acknowledgements

About the Author

Dedication

To my family. My dreams would still be collecting dust if it weren't for your continued love and encouragement. Love you always and forever.

MEREDITH WARD

CHAPTER ONE

"¡Aye caramba, it's hot!" Juanita wheezed in her Cuban accent as she plopped into a chair next to me behind the front desk. Her arm was working overtime trying to fashion a limp piece of folded paper into a high-speed propeller.

I peeked over my shoulder and scowled.

"Oh, quit your whining. You just think it's hot because you've been on the go all day. Honestly, the only complaints I've heard around here are from you and the rest of the cleaning staff."

"Nu-uh, Señora Nicole. It's hotter than balls in here. I thinks chu raised the temperature in the hotel again."

She distastefully raised an arm above her head and gave the exposed armpit a whiff. "Got me sweatin' like a goat in here. Must be at least eighty-five degrees."

Sweating like a goat? I presumed she meant pig. Juanita never did get the American sayings right the first time around.

My face scrunched in disgust at her cave man gesture. Smelling armpit sweat. Was it really necessary? As if the mere odor from her underarms was equivalent to the role of a thermostat that would conclusively report the exact temperature of the hotel lobby.

"Juanita, I set the general area for eighty-one, and I'm not lowering the temperature anymore. The cost of electricity last month was the highest yet, and besides, the customers crank down the A/C in their rooms anyways. I'm sorry but you're going to have to make due like the rest of us."

"Mhmm," she glowered at me. "Well don't chu come complaining to me when chur customers begin to flee to other hotels 'cause they don't wanna catch a heatstroke. I'm just sayin!" She innocently pulled her hands back, adding, "It's bad for the customers, too, chu know?"

I rolled my eyes. I still had no intentions of budging. I was the Money Nazi when it came to the hotel's budget and expenses. We could not afford to pay another electric bill like we did in April. Juanita and the other hospitality workers could fuss all they want, but ultimately the financial decisions were my responsibility. I'm the manager. I pay the bills. And yes, I'll admit the rumors are true that I am a cheapskate.

Then again, I was able to rationalize my prudent spending tendencies since I did have a valid reason for being tight with the hotel money. The economy wasn't at its strongest point. Being that our hotel was dependent on tourism, matter of fact, the majority of Miami was dependent on tourism, this was unfortunately one of the first areas to fluctuate when the economy hit a rough patch. We weren't receiving the same booming headcount that we used to have several years ago. I imagine this was mostly due to the financial state our country was in, but I'd also bet that the recent *incidents* in the area didn't contribute positively to our track flow either.

The need for customers was evident when balancing our check book. Between the costs associated to run this place and to pay the staff on hand, there wasn't much margin for profit on our off seasons. To embrace the silver lining, at least we were quickly approaching our busy season of the year. We should be able to cover some ground that we lost from earlier in the year over the next few months.

I clicked through one of the computers at the front desk. "Room 437 needs a thorough standard cleaning. The couple checked out early this morning and it's ready for you," I announced to Juanita.

"Ay, ay, ay." Juanita shook her head and stomped off toward the elevator. She'd be back again with more complaining, I'm sure of it. I could always count on her for that.

As she headed in the other direction I watched her smack the elevator button and tap her foot impatiently while she waited for the elevator to arrive. Juanita was barely over five-feet tall. Her round, plump body sat heartily on her stumpy legs.

Although she came to work with her black, curly hair in a tight, slicked back, low bun, in less than a few hours it never failed to transform into a mane of black frizzy fly-aways. Somehow her hair managed to convert itself into an uneven pair of horns protruding from the top corners of her head. I felt the symbolism was appropriate.

Juanita had a pair of dark chocolate brown eyes which were usually wide-eyed and alert because of something she heard about in the daily gossip. Then when she discovered something really worth gossiping about, her all-too-enthusiastic, gap-toothed smile would expand from ear to ear.

Yes, indeed. Juanita loves the gossip. When it's especially juicy, she'll chatter faster than an auction spokesman with a bad case of diarrhea. Her words practically pile on top of one another with her thick Cuban accent. In addition to that, her tongue will engage in a game of peek-a-boo between her two front teeth. She really is a sight to see when she gets all wound up.

I finished dabbling on the computer and left the front desk to Rose and Valerie, the two teenage employees who work as Front Desk/Member Services Representatives. Half of the staff around here were disrespectful, midriff-flashing, teeny boppers just trying to earn some extra spending money for their next adventure with "Puff the Magic Dragon." Oh, I was well aware of their extra-curricular activities since kids these days apparently think it is OK to talk about their Mary Jane trips within earshot distance of their boss. How quickly they forget that adults have a hearing range of a distance greater than three feet. Oye. Teens. They aren't so bright sometimes.

I shook my head free of the pessimistic thoughts and dismissed myself from the front desk. I strolled over toward my separate office on the opposite end of the lobby where I could take refuge from the gossiping Hollister groupies.

Once I closed the office door behind me, I flopped onto my bright orange leather chair. It was stiff and awkward, and much too loud for my taste, but according to our overly priced interior decorator, 'exuberantly festive modern designs are the only way to go.' The rest of the hotel was decorated to the max with vivid, tropical colors accented by a certain appeal of modern sleekness. The hotel is beachfront property, smack dab in the middle of the Double Tree and Courtyard Marriott on South Beach Miami.

I leaned across and opened the wooden plantation blinds to look out the window. A turquoise blue pool lay atop the creamy-colored ceramic stone, and toward the end of the pool lay a tiki hut where drinks were served on the back patio. Follow the patio but a few feet further down the steps and your toes would instantly emerge into the warm sand of the beach. From there it's a clear shot to the shoreline.

The ocean was reflecting small slivers from the glistening sun, beckoning me to strip off my suit and dive into the cool water. I snapped the blinds shut, deciding it best not to entertain the idea. When I plopped back into my seat at my desk, a mountaintop of papers impatiently awaited me. It consisted of bills, finances, inventory checklists, bills, room reports, bills, scheduling changes, advertising proposals…oh, did I mention bills?

Simply thinking about the numerous tasks left for me to handle sent me into an uncontrollable spiral of anxiety. I smacked my hand to my chest and clenched my suit jacket in a cold ninja grip. My breathing became short and jagged while my heart began to bounce out of control within my ribcage.

"Goddamnit!" I gasped in between painful breaths. Where's my chocolate?

Scouting the room, I didn't see any more Dove chocolates in my candy bowl. So I straightened up and began searching through my purse. Surely there was a spare chocolate somewhere in here.

Since the search was proving to be unsuccessful, I did what any other woman would do with a tote-sized purse, and turned the bag inside out to dump all of its contents out. There beneath the receipts I found them, two foil-wrapped pieces of Dove dark chocolates. Chocolates and sex were the only two things that truly helped me de-stress. I could be plopped in the middle of Running of the Bulls in Spain, a bull's-eye tacked to my ass, all the while sporting a red cape and I'd be hunky dory so long as I had some chocolate. Now, I don't think sex given that particular situation would be plausible, but in many other situations sex worked just as well, too.

I peeled back the foil wrapping and chomped down on the chocolatey goodness. Deliciousness filled my insides and my body started to ease up. My breathing eventually returned to normal and my muscles began to relax. The overwhelming feeling that had come over me regarding my To Do List alas subsided.

Much better.

When I balled up the wrapping and tossed it in the trash can against the far wall, I caught a glimpse of my reflection in the hanging mirror.

"Whoa." My eyes widened then zoned in on my hair which was now protruding in all different directions from my mini anxiety attack. I skirted over toward the mirror on the wall and licked my fingers before I smoothed my hair back into its rightful place.

As I wiped away black residue from my eyeliner, I locked eyes with mine in the mirror for a split second too long. My eyes were a soft green, the same color as my sister's, but unlike hers, mine seemed to constantly display signs of exhaustion. My hair, which was now slicked back into its rightful place, was the color of dark coffee and was tied into a low, professional bun. Once in a blue moon when I actually let my hair down, it was easily to the middle of my back. However, it has become such a pain in the ass to fix that I hardly ever bothered with it anymore.

I brushed my fingers beneath my eyes in attempt to magically force the dark circles under my eyes to disappear. Eh. Oh well. It's not like I am trying to impress anyone anyways.

My cheekbones were high and distinctive, definitely from my dad's genetics. I could say with confidence that my cheekbones were probably my best physical attribute. As for the rest of me, I'd consider myself...average. About five-feet-seven, natural curves, decent weight depending on my stress-induced chocolate intake. It'll fluctuate like most others.

Turning sideways at the mirror I gave myself the once over. I was probably pushing around a few extra pounds these days. I sighed. It must have been those donuts on the way to work this morning. No, wait. Maybe my dryer just shrunk my clothes a little? I preferred the latter excuse, so I decided to roll with it instead.

My skin tone appeared drained of color. Most wouldn't have guessed I was full-blown Italian because of my paleness. If I actually have some spare time I'll catch a few rays down on the beach to rejuvenate my dormant tan. That's if, a very big if.

Before I parted with the mirror, I tugged my navy blue suit jacket back into alignment and flattened a crinkle out of my skirt. There.

Suddenly the office phone rang which sprung my attention back to work. I answered, "Sunset Cove Hotel and Resorts, this is Nicole, how may I assist you?"

"Yes, I'd like to book a room for you and your future lover boy, please. The one I just set you up on a blind date with," his voice snapped with a hint of sassiness. Clearly it was Landon, my flamboyantly gay best friend. 'Loud and proud,' as he puts it with the snap of his fingers and a chicken head wobble to go with it. Such the diva.

"Landon, don't tell me you set me up on another one of your blind dates again. The last guy you tried to hook me up with was a body builder only interested in the tape measurement size for the circumference around his biceps. Not what you'd call much of a conversationalist." Not much of anything going on upstairs either, if you asked me.

"Oh come on Nicky, he was supposed to be for sex only. He pays the dinner bill, gives a good screw, and ditches after a steamy one-night stand. You don't actually try to have a conversation with him. The only words you'd need to exchange would be trampy little phrases, like 'Ay, Papi' in between orgasms." He sighed. "Hell, honey, if you don't know what to do with a man, just pass him over to me. I'll show you."

And I didn't doubt him.

"Well considering the fact that a woman's orgasm is ninety percent mental, if we weren't even connecting on a basic level of common brain waves, then I wouldn't be screaming, 'Hallelujah' to the gods above my bed anyways. I'll take my chances that he just wasn't for me."

"OK, OK, so maybe he wasn't the best match, but this guy I met outside of Jamba Juice is absolutely perf for you."

"Details?" I can't believe I'm getting sucked into another one of these.

"His name is Marco. He is six-foot, good looking, single, early thirties, and enjoys long walks on the beach." Great. Another closet homo who has yet to emerge from secrecy. Landon just wants me to turn him gay like that Frank guy he tried to set me up on a date with. I believe he goes by the name Franquito now.

"Uh-huh," I mumbled.

"Anyways, I already gave him your number, so you should be expecting—"

"Hold on a minute," my brows furrowed. "You already gave him my number, without asking me? What if I had said no?"

"I know you too well. You wouldn't pass up the opportunity to meet a potential romance. You, my dear girl, are a hopeless romantic. And a desperate one at that."

I rolled my eyes. This was true. I was getting desperate. Already twenty-seven and still no prospects in sight. I was acting against Mother Nature by remaining unmarried this long. Speaking of mother…

"Crap, I'm late," I jumped. "Landon, I have to go. Ma ordered me over for an early dinner tonight. I need to get moving, so give me the remaining details in under sixty."

"Ugh, you know I hate to be rushed. It gets me all stressed out and flustered. I feel like I'm—"

"Focus, Landon!"

"Right. Marco will call you in a few days, more than likely. It's only Wednesday, but by Friday you should have heard something from him. He likes sushi. So grin and bear it if need be."

Disgusting. Sushi has never been a favorite of mine. I could tell Marco and I were already off to a clean, honest start.

"Marco. Sushi. Friday. Got it. Call you later?"

"Ciao, Ciao love," he sighed.

Once I hung up the phone, I rushed to collect the contents of my purse that were still sprawled out on my desktop and shoved them back into my purse. I quickly organized the papers and bills on my desk into two piles: first priority and second.

As I slung my purse over my shoulder, I estimated the amount of time it would take to reach Ma's house across town. If I showed a little leg to the taxi drivers, I could probably land a ride in under twenty seconds, plus the twenty minute drive. I glanced at the clock in the lobby before I rushed through the entrance doors. 5:46 p.m. I'd never make it there by six, which meant I'd never hear the end of it from Ma. Great.

Just outside the steps, I whipped my fingers into my mouth and gave a sharp whistle as I waved my other hand at the swarm of taxis on the street. One immediately pulled up in front of me, and I hopped in the back seat.

"Where to, lady?" the cab driver grunted across the seat. He had a three-day stubble beard growing in and sported a pair of plastic orange sunglasses. He was sweating and his hair was slicked back with what I assumed was grease from his lack of showering. At least I'm guessing he didn't shower, maybe ever, because the entire cab smelled like grunge with a body odor so pungent it burned my nostrils.

I hurriedly shouted Ma's address while I checked my purse for some kind of body mist; if the cab's stench was this strong there was no way the scent wouldn't follow me around for the rest of the evening. "And I'll tip you ten if you can make it there by six," I added with a shred of hope.

"Make it twenty."

Damn. Guess it wouldn't be America if someone wasn't taking advantage of another's desperation. "Fifteen," I bargained.

What can I say? I own up to my legacy as a tight wad.

That seemed to do it because he took off like a bat out of hell. I was clenching onto the seat for dear life to the point that I nearly broke my nails.

As I peeked around the cab I noticed several interesting pieces of décor. An adorable childhood nursery rhyme was scratched into the seat that read:

Roses are red,
Violets are blue,
Open your legs wide,
And I'll show you a thing or two.

Oh. That's nice. Must have been another teeny bopper who came up with that ingenious rhyme. On the floor I saw an old, grimy tennis shoe that was covered in filth and simply oozed of some kind of bacterial fungus. Just above that, on the seat, I discovered some kind of elastic thing. Looked like a popped balloon or something. Maybe some little kid got their white birthday balloon stuck in the taxi door.

I leaned over to see what other magical treasures I could discover in the back seat, but as I neared what I thought was a balloon, I found out that it was, in fact, a condom. A used one. Yum. I was definitely hungry to go eat dinner now.

"Christ! A used condom, really? When was the last time you cleaned your cab? I feel like I'm obligated to contact the CDC to have this thing quarantined."

He shrugged nonchalantly, clearly a fan of his own filth.

I sat upright in my seat, veering as far away from the disgusting thing as possible. I reached into my purse and fished out my hand sanitizer. After I squirted half the bottle in my hand, I began to scrub down my hands as well as any exposed glimpse of skin.

When he pulled to an abrupt stop in front of Ma's house, I checked the clock on the dashboard. I threw the money at him and hurried onto the sidewalk.

"Hey lady," he shouted out the window. "Where's the fifteen dollar tip?"

"I said six o'clock, not six o'three."

"Cheap ass," he added before he peeled off. Yeah, I got that sometimes.

I almost leapt to Ma's back door, still trying to sneak in without hearing her psychobabble about my tardiness resulting in her near heart attack. She'd go on about how she was just about to call the police because she was worried that something happened to me. I don't think I could stand to listen to another fifteen minute speech about skipping out on a lousy three minutes. Not worth it.

After I located the spare key from under the flower pot, I unlocked the door and slipped right into the laundry room. The dryer was booming away, so I prayed she didn't hear me.

I tiptoed into the kitchen and sat down at the table. Just then Ma stomped through the kitchen to the oven. "Nicole Marie D'Angelo."

The full name is never a good sign.

"Yes, Ma?" I hesitated.

"Where have you been? I've been worried sick about you. I thought you could have been kidnapped or something. You know, like those adult kidnappers who prey on single, vulnerable women. Why are you so late? What were you doing?" She shot an array of questions at me.

"Ma," I began. "I was only three minutes late. Don't work yourself into heart palpitations or anything. I came straight from work. No kidnappers."

"Nicole," she placed the hot quesadillas onto the island counter top. "Being late is a reflection of bad character."

I slumped down into my chair, preparing for the next wretched fifteen minutes of my life that I'd never get back. Just as she was beginning to jump into her spiel, my sister bounced into the kitchen. My little nuisance of a sister proved herself good for something for once since her entrance distracted Ma from her train of thought.

"Mmmm," my sister was nearly drooling over the plate of food. "That smells delicious, Ma." With that she got out a plate for herself, piled some quesadillas onto it, and plopped onto the kitchen chair.

I rolled my eyes and stood up. I took out two plates, one for Ma and me, and served us both. We wandered over to the table where Vi had already dug into her mountain pile of food.

"Nice Vi," I smirked. "Who taught you those table manners?"

She sat back in her chair and stared for a long second. "And who did you sit next to? Ugh. You smell like a dirty cab."

Stupid taxi ride.

I self-consciously snuck a whiff at my blouse. A shower when I got home was a must. I glared across at Vi. I wanted to make a snide remark back, but she didn't smell like dirty cab, more like Dior perfume. Quickly I did a glance over. Let's face it. There was nothing I could poke fun at concerning her looks. She was perfect down to her nails, which were long, trimmed, and painted a sheer peach. It was very flattering with her sun-kiss tanned skin.

My sister, Violeta, or Vi as everyone calls her, was the beautiful one out of us. She had legs for days, which were thin and toned, any other woman's worst nightmare. Vi had the same light green eyes as me.

Her hair was trimmed into a stylish bob cut, longer in the front and shorter in the back. Her hair was a lighter shade than my deep brown, and she had natural sun-streaked highlights in her hair from being out on the beach during the day. I'd regrettably admit that my sister has the looks of a goddess. As irritating as it was to be compared looks-wise to her, at least I knew that I had her beat in other areas of the gene pool.

For starters, I had actually finished college, and she dropped out halfway through. Not that college was anything I held over her head, but it did irk her to know that school was something that came much easier to me. As far as careers go, Vi found herself working from one local bar to the next. Meanwhile, I've maintained the managerial position at the same beach front property hotel for the past several years. Where Vi had the looks of the family, I had the stability.

I raised a brow patiently waiting for her to finish the forkful of quesadillas she recently shoveled in her mouth. "So Vi, how are things at work?" I drew a dramatic sigh. "I just couldn't imagine working night shifts like that." I took pleasure knowing how much she hated working nights since it imposed on her nightlife style.

Vi forcefully shoveled some more guacamole onto her quesadilla. "You couldn't imagine working nights because you are in bed every night by nine-thirty, old lady," she tilted her head to the side.

I felt the blood start to boil beneath my skin. She knew age was a sensitive subject for me. She was only twenty-three, still practically a child. Meanwhile I'm twenty-seven, going on forty. Well I mean, at least I will be forty soon.

I shoved my food aside and was about to stand up from the table when Ma began to shout, "Oh Nicky, sit your bony ass back down." I plopped back down in my seat. "Damnit Vi." Ma shook her head, "We are going to enjoy our dinner for once. No screaming, no arguing, and none of that passive aggressive bullshit you girls are so fond of."

We were silent, both of us deciding not to tick Ma off any more than she already was. Though she was known for her motherly nagging and long winded tangents, in general, she was the laid back type.

So laid back, in fact, that as kids she was usually late to pick us up from school, and couldn't care less about what time we stayed up to on a school night. In high school, she would buy us a bottle of booze on our birthdays and we'd celebrate by drowning ourselves in it as we sang 'Coconut' by Harry Nilsson.

Over the past decade I've analyzed to death this so-called 'family unit' that we have going on here. I think I've finally come to the conclusion that Ma is the reason I turned out to be the reserved and reliable one in the family. Seriously though, there at least has to be one responsible person in every family. If Ma wasn't sneaking a smoke or downing a drink out next to the garage, then she was at the races, betting away our money for next month's electric bill on some losing horse. She still has issues with gambling, the horse races being her weakness, though she will never admit it. As a result I've had to step in from time to time to pay Ma's debts to keep her out of trouble.

I know what shrinks would say about me, that I'm an enabler. It's probably true, but what else am I supposed to do? I can't just let her work herself into a situation where some guy is about to bust her knee caps in over a few grand.

So I'm kind of like her babysitter when things go wrong at the tracks. I bail her out, so her electricity isn't shut off. Of course, as a result of her costly bad habit, I'm twenty-seven years old and still without a car. Vi has even tried to bum off of my own place, but that's where I drew the line. Vi plus me…it's like oil and water, matches and fuel, Walmart and Prada. Simply a no-go.

Therefore in an attempt to prevent such a catastrophe, Ma's letting Vi live under her roof instead. This is the same house we moved to when Dad passed away. We packed all of our belongings and left New York for Miami.

I glanced back over at Ma. "So what's new with the Delightful Daisies this week?"

Ma was a member of her neighborhood book club which consisted of all sorts of elderly, suburban women. And yes, they actually called themselves the Delightful Daisies. They even have a specially designed badge to wear at their meetings and important events. Ma claims it is a badge of honor. Vi and I agree it is a badge of shame and embarrassment.

"It's my turn to be the host for next week's meeting and, well, you know Martha," Ma snorted. "She wants me to make some complex Japanese dish and serve elaborately stuffed spring rolls as a side. She mistakes me for someone who cares."

Ma was a good cook. Her kitchen probably ranked in the top three of my favorite restaurants. But being that she was a true, native New Yorker at heart, she didn't bother with some of the Southern hospitality and hoorah her fellow neighbors put into house gatherings.

"Sushi," Vi interrupted. "Martha just wants you to make a few sushi rolls. They aren't that difficult, Ma."

"Well, then, why don't you make them?" Ma raised her eyebrows.

Vi and I both looked at each other in horror. The last time Vi tried to cook—which wasn't even cooking, more like microwaving—she tried to heat up a piece of pizza for ten minutes, so that it would be hot by the time lunch rolled around. Yeah, not the sharpest tool in the shed, that one. That little fiasco ended with the microwave catching fire and the house smelling of a burnt aroma for the following two weeks.

"I have a better idea," I suggested. "Why don't you buy a bulk amount of sushi from the store, throw away evidence of the purchase, and serve it to the Daisies as if you made it yourself?"

"Because it's the principle of the matter!" Ma never fails to revert back to that excuse. Her argument will not be a situation, but the very principle of the situation. "Martha always expects me to go above and beyond. What do I look like...Betty fuckin' Crocker?"

I personally didn't think sushi was above and beyond, but I wasn't about to say anything with her face turning that shade of fire engine red.

"Well, maybe she has a problem with you," I offered instead. Or more so, maybe Martha has a problem with her husband openly checking out Ma. Really, the man had no shame.

"Yeah," Ma nodded. She fancied that rationalization. "She's probably just jealous of my body."

I stared at her from across the table. Pushing sixty and she thinks she's still a fox. Originally a brunette, Ma dyed her hair bleach platinum blonde. However, her dark roots had the habit of sticking out like an eye sore when she neglected a trip to the hair salon. Her hair style was fierce with the short gelled spikes which strongly contrasted her soft hazel eyes. Her skin was darkly tanned, partly thanks to her full Italian genes, but also due to spending so much time out in the sun.

Ma was shorter than me, by a few inches, but she always stood tall and proud; no doubt a trait of that New Yorker, self-importance mindset. In spite of all the time we've resided in Miami, she has yet to kick that Yankee accent of hers.

I looked down at my watch and sighed. It was time for me to go home and get ready for, what seemed like, my one hundredth first date. "I need to get out of here, so I can get ready for my date tonight."

Vi took our plates from the table and walked over toward the kitchen sink. "Oh? Another blind date?"

"Geez, Nicole," Ma shook her head. "Why does a woman like you need to go on so many blind dates? You know how to cook, you have an education, and you're easy on the eyes. Why can't you date the old fashion way?"

"First of all Ma, it's slim pickens out there. The dating world is not what it used to be. And secondly, FYI, it is not a blind date. The guy I'm meeting tonight is an old college buddy of mine who happened to move into town recently." My smile was smug. I decided it was better not to mention that, however, Landon was also trying to set me up on another blind date with Marco. She would do the whole see-I-told-you-so-look thing. Very annoying.

"Who is this guy?" Vi pried in interest.

"Benny Casen."

Vi was stumped trying to picture him.

"I don't think you met this one before. He moved up to Idaho for some time after we graduated, but he moved here several months ago. We happened to bump into each other on the strip."

"On the strip? So Benny likes to go out?" Vi began to unconsciously rub her legs together. She loved studs. She loved sex. She loved to party. Put all three together, and she could hardly control herself.

"No, not really," I thought back to the time I bumped into him. He was a little on the conservative side as far as I could tell. "He said he was just checking out the sights."

"Oh," Vi frowned. "He's a nerd."

Hardly. He just wasn't the party type, which happened to be right up my alley.

"I'll let you know how it goes." I pecked Ma on the cheek and exchanged good-byes.

The cab picked me up and dropped me off at my place. I hurried along the sidewalk and passed through the bare front yard of my town home. I've been meaning to do something with the landscaping and plant some flowers or perky shrubbery, but I haven't had time lately.

After I opened my front door, I slung my purse onto the entry table and locked the door behind me. The entry area opened up to the living room which flowed into the kitchen. Dark wooden floors covered every inch of the place, but it was that special, naturalistic kind of wood, you know, the ones with lumps and scratches that are purposely added. I still can't believe I paid extra to have someone come in here and install scratched up floors.

My entire house swam in beige. Beige couches, beige pillows, beige walls, beige-speckled granite counters, beige bed spreads. Yeah, I'm not much of the type to step outside of my comfort box. Beige is simple, It's neat. A lot like me.

I darted up the stairs to my bedroom, first door on the right. It too was drowned in beige and browns with my California king sized bed plopped against the wall. Two walls were covered in ceiling to floor windows with—surprise, surprise—beige curtains. A pair of French doors would open the room to a much neglected, empty balcony.

Immediately I began to unbutton my navy blue suit. I untucked my white button down shirt and tossed it onto the edge of the bed, kicked off my heels, and made my way to the bathroom. Once my shower cap was in place, I hopped into the shower and rinsed off the stench from the cab ride.

Looking at my reflection after I emerged from the tub, I shuddered. I absolutely had to do something about my hair. If I went on a date with my hair still pulled tight in the low bun from work, my date would probably run for the hills in the opposing direction. I kind of resembled a stuck-up librarian. Then again, some guys do find that kinky.

After heating up the straightening iron, I smoothed over my hair until it was straight and under control. Quickly I looped in my black chandelier earrings and reapplied a fresh layer of makeup.

Ta-da. I looked semi-attractive. There was definitely a transition between my work look versus my date look. The latter, of course, being easier on the eyes.

Now for the lingerie. I tapped my fingers along the entry doorway of my closet as I stared at my options. I guess matching bra and panties aren't so important on the first date, considering I don't commonly practice the one-night stand deal.

On the other hand, I honestly can't remember the last time I had sex.

I pondered my standards a while longer. Well technically, if Benny and I did the deed, it wouldn't be a one-night stand since I have known him since college. I debated with myself for a few more minutes until I finally decided.

Matching panties it is!

I thought I felt my boobs perk for joy at the mere thought of finally getting laid. Yup! I definitely needed to get some.

I slipped into my bright pink push-up bra and matching lace panties before stepping into my black, slinky dress. I laced up a sexy pair of strapped stilettos.

Shoes. They are not only the number one priority when it comes to wardrobe necessities, but they're also my established key to confidence. You could not touch my esteem in a pair of F-Me pumps for the life of you.

As I was rubbing lotion onto my smooth, freshly-shaven legs, my phone chirped downstairs. Wasting zero time, I jumped off the bed and fumbled down the stairs to reach my phone before it went to voicemail.

"Nicole?" It was Benny.

"Benny, hey, I was just finishing getting ready. What's up?"

"How are we going to do this?" He sounded stiff and a little awkward, and I assumed it was nerves since it was our first date.

"Well, we could meet up at the restaurant in say, thirty minutes if you'd like? I was thinking somewhere casual like Rusty's or Jullian's Grill?"

"Actually, I was more in the mood for Prime 112, and I'd be more than happy to swing by to pick you up."

Prime's? A tad pricey, but hey, if that's what the guy wants, and it's not on my dime…then by all means. "That's fine with me, but really I don't mind driving to meet you up there—"

"I'll pick you up. I insist." He seemed pretty adamant about it, so I caved and gave him my address.

When we hung up I was confused as to why he wanted to pick me up. I've always been told to drive to the first date in case things didn't turn out well and you have that option for a quick escape.

I shrugged it off. I've known Benny all throughout college, though never in a romantic sense. We were study buddies for several of our overlapping courses.

To my recollection during those college classes, I thought of him as a genius. Whenever we had our study groups, it was always him carrying me in the study sessions. Side thought: I wonder if he's a genius in the sack, too. Guess there's only one way to find out.

I rushed around the house tidying up little tidbits here and there. In general, I was pretty much a neat freak as it was, so there was only so much straightening up to do. Vi insists I have OCD, but I think cleanliness is a good trait to have.

Once the dishes were put away in the kitchen and the pillows were realigned on the living room couches, I hurried to my bedroom for some finishing touches. I tossed my beautification utensils, as Vi calls it, into the makeup bag and slipped it underneath my bathroom counter. Then I strolled down the hallway into my guest bedroom and did some light dusting. There, my house was spick and span.

The doorbell rang and I sped to open the front door just in time to catch Benny Casen finger deep, picking his nose. And when I say finger deep, I do mean digging-for-gold, attempting-to-scratch-his-brain, picking-his-nose finger deep. Quite attractive, I must say.

"Benny!" I probably sounded a little more disgusted than excited to see him, and he instantly whipped his finger out of his nose. Quickly I recovered my composure. "Thanks for coming to pick me up, you're too thoughtful."

"Not a problem," he kind of managed a goofy grin. "My mom raised me to be a gentleman."

Did she raise you without a proper introduction to the concept of tissues, as well? Besides, who mentions their mom on a first date? I had to stop myself from being a Negative Nancy and skimmed over the mental trash talk. "Give her my thanks," I plastered a half-assed smile on my face.

"Shall we?" He motioned with one hand out the door and placed the other hand on my back. I prayed he wasn't touching me with the boogie hand.

I skirted out the door and locked up my house once he was out. It was a short drive to Prime's and when we arrived outside the restaurant, he pulled into the valet parking area. We stepped out of his Volkswagen van—that's right, a Volkswagen van—and he tipped the valet attendant a quarter. Not at all embarrassing.

Once we were seated inside a dim lit corner booth, I ordered a glass of wine while he ordered chocolate milk in a glass with a straw. Ma has always said any man that drinks out of a straw is a sissy.

Looking at Benny Casen tonight, I'd have to agree with her conclusion. As I stared at Benny slurping through his straw, draining his glass of chocolate milk, I came to the realization that Benny was indeed a nerd.

I had already made up my mind that after this date I would purposely never see Benny again.

"So Benny," I tried to make some small talk. "Tell me what you think about Miami so far?"

Little did I know that minor question would result in the telling of his entire life's story. From the time he was six and used to be chased around by his older brothers with Nerf machine guns to the very moment before he picked me up at my house this evening. It was no short story, to say the least.

For dinner, I only had a loaded baked potato since I was still pretty full from the quesadillas I had earlier at Ma's house. Though I did have a few more glasses of wine as I impatiently waited for this miserable date to be over. Meanwhile, Benny was busy multi-tasking between shoveling chunks of meat into his mouth and monopolizing the conversation, too preoccupied to notice my unreserved frustration. Finally, when he stopped to take a breath for air, he ended up choking on his mouthful of food.

I'll admit I was debating whether I should take advantage of this moment to flee from the table and hitch hike a ride home, or whether I should perform the Heimlich and save this man's life at the expense of my poor ears.

Damn my conscience.

I reached across the table and started slapping his shoulder forcefully, maybe with a little more force than necessary. Turned out I don't actually know the Heimlich, but I do know how to smack the shit out of someone. His face began to turn different shades of blue and I began to smack harder to the point that the chunk of meat lodged within his throat, flew across the table and slapped me right on the forehead.

I leaned back in my chair and calmly remained seated as the lump of half-masticated meat covered in saliva slowly slid down my forehead and dropped into my lap. I didn't scream, I didn't cuss, surprisingly I didn't retch. I just stared directly at Benny as I pursed my lips in disbelief.

The waiter, who could stand to work on his timing, rushed over and asked if everything was alright.

"Everything's. Just. Peachy." I glowered up at him. "I do believe we're ready for the check."

Benny looked appalled, "But we haven't even had dessert yet."

CHAPTER TWO

Juanita was bent over, trembling with laughter. Usually I'd be laughing with her, but this time I was just too pissed off to join in. I could not believe I wasted my time with that loser. I'm fed up to my eyeballs with these dead end first dates. In fact, I'm almost to the point where I'm done with men, in general. Kaput. Finito. Sayanara.

"I'm telling chu, Señora, chu should have left his blue ass choking on his meat. Just hit the road, and don't look back." She had been laughing so hard a tear started to roll down her cheek. "Shoot, that's what I would've done."

I cracked a smile at the thought of that. "Would I be an awful person if I told you I considered it?"

We were both still giggling when a tall man suddenly entered the front entrance of the hotel lobby.

Juanita and I froze. The instant he strolled into the lobby a breath of cool, fresh air brushed right along in with him. Everything around him moved in slow motion. That or my brain was just moving in slow-mo at the mere sight of him. His body was drenched in perfection from head to toe.

He was my ultimate favorite client to look at, particularly from behind, and fortunately for me he was also a regular client of ours. Every other week, if not every week, he has stayed at our hotel.

His name is Rafael. Rafael Mancini. He was absolutely, mouth-wateringly, down-right scrumptious. A towering six-foot plus Italian with dark brown hair effortlessly tossed in a carefree style. His eyes were a piercing soft gray which, when locked with my eyes, caused my mouth to fumble. He had a strong and toned build with big…feet. And we all know what that means. Not to mention those tight buns. Goodness, I could bounce a quarter off of them.

Juanita nudged me a little with her elbow and I managed a resistant shove back at her. I knew exactly what she was thinking.

In response to my reluctance she stomped her heel on my foot which nearly sent me to tears.

"Alright, alright," I whispered under my breath.

"Back again, Mr. Mancini?" I threw my best controlled smile at him considering that I was still holding back the pain inflicted by Juanita.

"Yeah, afraid so," he leaned against the front desk on his elbow, cracking that beautiful grin of his.

"Guess that means business is good?" I innocently pried. I still wasn't exactly sure what it was that he did for a living.

His grin widened at that. "Sure, you could put it that way. How is this weekend looking?"

Same question, different week. "The weather should be bright and sunny. A scorcher for sure this Friday. Do you plan on mixing a little pleasure with business this weekend?"

"You never know," he winked as I slid him his hotel key.

"You'll be in your usual room. Don't hesitate to call if you need anything." I was beaming with sheer stupidity.

Anything at all. Like towels, several additional pillow chocolate mints, room service, fresh bed linens fully equipped with a naked me tucked in between.

"I'll be sure to let you know." He made his way toward the elevator and glanced over his shoulder once before he disappeared behind the elevator doors.

Juanita reached over and snapped my jaw shut. "Chu are catching birds, sweetie."

I rolled my eyes. "Flies. Catching flies, Juanita."

"Well, whatever it is that chu are catching, chu are also drooling all over my clean counters in the process. Geez. I just wiped this."

She brushed over the area with her wash cloth and tossed it into her cleaning bucket before she plopped down into the chair.

"My knees are starting to act up again," she sighed, rubbing her pudgy knee caps.

"Why don't you get those looked at? I told you that I'd give you a paid day off to visit the doctor."

"Nah," she straightened up out of her chair. "I don't need no doctor to tell me to stay off my feet for a few days. I may be small, but I am mighty."

There wasn't too much that was small about Juanita's figure, apart from her height, but I nodded anyways.

"What room chu got for me next?"

After I clicked through the system I found the next available room. "721 needs some cleaning. The Galloway's sent a request for fresh towels and a quick run through. Would you mind making one last run before your lunch break, or should I page Stacey instead?"

"No, no Señora, I handle this one. No problema."

"It shouldn't take but fifteen minutes or so."

"Si claro." Her lips curled into a very mischievous grin and was gone before I could stop her. For someone who is having so much trouble with her knees, she sure can book it when she wants to.

I left the front desk and meandered over toward the dimly lit bar on the opposing side of the lobby. There, Toni stood nonchalantly behind the polished granite counter tops, already pouring a tequila sunrise as I neared the bar.

"Drinking on the job?" I teased as I sat on the bar stool and propped up on my elbows.

He slid the drink over on a cocktail napkin to a middle-aged woman and wandered over toward me. He grinned. "What'll it be? Nicks? An appletini? Cosmo? Daiquiri?"

"Nope, not today. I haven't had much trouble yet, so I don't think that'll be necessary."

"Well, you know, the day is still young." He poured a glass of cold water and slid it toward me.

Toni is kind of like that. A tall glass of cold water. Sheepishly, I'll admit it's the main reason I hired him on in the first place. He is definitely easy on the eyes and as a token of my stressful hard work, I decided to treat myself to a daily piece of eye candy. I did a once over on Toni. Any girl would boldly bat their eyelashes at him.

He was just shy of six feet, jet black hair styled in a short buzz cut. His arms were big and bulky as they bulged from beneath his tight black tee. A small shell necklace hung from his neck hinting that given the opportunity he'd throw down his bar rag and tail it to the ocean for a quick surf.

Toni is Caucasian, though you'd hardly know it because of his deep-set tan from riding the waves, day in and day out.

His eyes were a crystal blue, which paired perfectly with his broad, white smile. Could break a girl's heart with a smile like that. Self included. But I decided long ago to never mix business with pleasure.

I took a swig of water and closed my eyes for a quick minute.

"Something the matter?" Toni wrapped his fingers around my shoulder and gave me a light squeeze. "You seem…tense."

"Toni," I peered over at him, "when am I not tense?"

"Maybe I could help you out?" He began to lightly massage my shoulder and my body involuntarily moved with the motion of his hand. A hushed moan accidentally slipped out and instantly I straightened up causing his hand to let go of my shoulder.

Definitely crossing the line of professionalism. "Ah, thanks." I smiled. "I'd better get back to my priority stack of tasks in the office. I'll see you around."

Urgently, I skedaddled back to my office before I was further tempted to reach across the bar and rip off Toni's clothes. No ma'am. He was the hotel bartender for God's sake. Get a grip!

Back at my office I tackled about half of the first-priority stack, and by the time I glanced up at the clock, it was almost time to call it a day. I packed up and locked the office door behind me. When I entered the lobby, the television mounted above the bar caught my attention. It was typically set to a sports station, but this afternoon it was switched to the news.

I strolled over and plopped my bags on the bar stool next to me. The news reporter was replaying the images from the two tourists that had gone missing a few weeks back. The two girls came to Miami on a mini weekend vacation and never returned to their rooms at the hotel just down the street from us. They looked like they were fairly young, in their early twenties. Cute little things. Last seen on the hotel footage with them calling a cab at the valet service in front of the hotel.

"Toni, change the channel to sports. Hell, you can turn it to Sponge Bob Square Pants for all I care, just get it off the news. We don't need to remind our customers of these recent events. We want to keep things light around here."

Toni picked up the remote and changed the channel to golf. I nodded in satisfaction. Juanita pranced over next to the bar area. She looked happy…almost a little too happy.

I tapped Juanita on the shoulder. "Well aren't you little Miss Ball of Sunshine?"

Juanita straightened up and managed a muffled cough. "Oh, uh, hola Señora. Chu looks fabulous. Did chu do something to chur hair since I last saw it?"

I glanced at Toni who raised his hands as if to suggest 'I don't know.' And then I stepped closer to her and stared directly into her eyes. "What are you talking about? I just saw you this morning. You feeling alright?"

She giggled. "Si claro! Of course!"

I nodded still a little confused and was about to head for the lobby door when I caught a whiff of something.

At first I couldn't identify it, though it smelled vaguely familiar. I took another sharp inhale trying to pin point it. Almost smelled kind of like, like…pot?

I studied her face a moment longer. Juanita's eyes were red and watery. I took a deliberate sniff. Fantastic.

"Juanita! Have you been smoking?" I glanced around to make sure the other guests didn't hear our conversation.

"Señora Nicole, chu know I dun smoke cigarettes. That stuff will kill chu."

"Not cigarettes, Juanita. Pot! Have you been smoking pot at my hotel?" I could feel the veins in my neck emerge and my face flushed with heat.

"Pot?" Her eyes darted around the room. Focusing on everything but me. "Ah. Well, chu see, what had happened was…"

You know something worse is yet to come when someone starts off a story with 'well you see what had happened was…'

"I was replacing the Galloway's towels and changing their trash bins when I stumbled across a little package of these errbs."

"Herbs?" I raised a brow.

"Si, si. Errbs. That's what the baggie said. So I says to myself, 'Self, chu gots to make sure these errbs are appropriately prepared for the Galloway's.' I mean, the last thing we want is for them to be unsatisfied with their stay here, right?"

Uh huh. I folded my arms still listening. "And just how were you planning on making their stay successful with a bag of 'herbs?'"

She was smiling now that she reeled me in. "Well, I was cleaning up and organizing their things so I decided to organize their errbs too, chu know, like the rest of the room. I was moving the bag out of their suitcase and into the—"

"Wait a minute!" I shouted, louder than I intended. Toni's eyes widened as he watched with pure entertainment. "You took belongings out of someone's suitcase?"

"Well, I maybe, kinda, accidentally stumbled over their suitcase and it happened to open on its own."

"The suitcase opened on its own? It just magically opened on its own? Like 'POOF' the zipper unzipped itself?" I could hear my pulse inside my own head.

"Ah…no. No. Not quite like that. Chu see, my fingers tangled up with the zipper and the zipper opened up. It was almost like I was supposed to uncover these errbs."

I blew a big gust of air out of my cheeks and closed my eyes. "Alright Juanita. Let's just pretend you were actually cleaning. And let's make believe that your fingers innocently entangled with the suitcase zipper and that it, in fact, opened on its own. Say that you truly were 'organizing' the herbs to benefit our guests. What exactly happened as you were organizing these herbs?"

She stared down at her white sneakers and rocked back and forth a bit. "Now this is the crazy part. I sort of tripped again—"

"Wow, you're one hell of a klutz," Toni smirked.

"It's these damn outfits," Juanita looked down. "I'd be able to sneak around easier without this stupid cleaning skirt."

Sneak around, huh? Juanita ratted herself out, but I continued to listen without pointing this out.

"Anyways, I ended up spilling all the errbs on the floor. I couldn't have the Galloway's using unsanitary errbs so I took them out back next to the garbage cans and lit them on fire." She was near gleaming at this point.

"Why would you light them on fire?"

"Well I read in the Reader's Digestive that germs die at a certain point of heat, like boiling water."

I smacked my forehead with my hand. Reader's Digestive? It's Digest. Reader's Digest. Whatever, that's the least of our worries.

"Juanita, did you notice that everything around you started getting hazy? And suddenly you found yourself feeling rather, stress-free?"

"Si!" she laughed. "Chu are verrry smart, Señora Nicole."

Toni chuckled and patted me on the back. "Look at the bright side, Nicks, you could have Juanita fill out a satisfactory report about your management rating while she's feeling so high...spirited."

True. "Juanita. Grab the managerial report packet from underneath the front desk. Fill it out."

She nodded and fluttered off to the front desk. "That woman," I shook my head.

"Martini?" Toni suggested.

"Hardly. I'll take a shot of the hard stuff, make it a double." I should've known better. I'd never make it through a day of work without a drink. Juanita would see to it, I swear.

After Toni urgently poured my source of serenity, he slid the glass to me, where I enthusiastically downed it. I made a sour face as I felt the heat trickle down my throat. "What are you going to do when the Galloways discover their stash of weed is missing?"

He was busy putting up the bottle before he noticed my face of pure horror. "Shit! I didn't think of that. Did Juanita finish it all?"

"You saw her eyes," he grinned and did a minor shrug.

"Yeah," I slumped in my seat. "They were pretty red, huh?"

"Bloodshot."

"Where the hell am I going to find some riff raff that sells dope?" I shook my head in my hands.

"Are you kiddin'? Ask any beach bum. They eat, sleep, and breathe that stuff."

I looked at him questioningly, "Do you?"

"I'm offended," he faked a hurt look. "I may be a beach bum, but I strictly hit the beach for the waves. Drug dealing isn't really my thing." He said. I blushed, ashamed I stereotyped him. "I could help you find a bum in a sec though if you can wait until Dylan takes over his shift."

A minor sigh escaped my mouth. "Yeah, I'd appreciate that. Thanks, Toni. Who would have thought that purchasing drugs would fall under the hotel manager's job responsibilities?"

"It's no prob. Got to adapt to survive." He threw a smile at me and I could have sworn I glimpsed a flash of light reflect off his teeth.

Oh, the things I'd like to do to you, Toni Versalies.

When Dylan emerged from the front doors, Toni swung his gym bag across his shoulder and wiggled his hand on top of my head; completely messing up my slicked back hair. "Let's hit the beach."

"Ah 'come on Toni." I frowned as I tried to smooth back my hair.

"Why don't you ever let your hair down? Literally and figuratively-speaking," He said as we left the lobby and ventured toward the beach. "The up-tight bun look doesn't flatter you."

"Blunt much?" I managed to say as I tried to balance myself in the sand while still wearing my heels. I definitely was not prepared to dress for an emergency stroll on the beach in search of a pothead to refill a client's stash. I just didn't see it coming.

"Now, how do you know which one of these guys is packing?" I nervously observed the other people around us.

He chuckled. "Packing? These people are hardly drug lords. It's easy to spot them though; they're the ones with squinty eyes and big smiles."

"There," I shouted as I pointed at some guy waxing his surf board.

As soon as I said this, the man perked up and stopped smiling. He threw down his bar of wax and bolted to the ocean where he disappeared amongst the waves. That was strange.

"Nicole," Toni placed a hand on each shoulder and stooped down to look me in the eyes. "There's a system. You can't just point at some guy who is doped up and shout 'THERE,' you'll scare them off. Matter of fact, your outfit is all wrong for buying."

"I'm sorry, Toni. Generally I don't wake up each morning and pack an extra outfit that will be utilized to purchase marijuana. Lesson learned." I crossed my arms. "So what would you propose I do?"

"Change it up a bit," His hands were quick to slip out my hair band and as a result my hair immediately spilt down in a rush of full, thick, waves. "Better," he smiled, "but we've got to do something about your wardrobe. You look like an undercover cop or something."

I took off my suit jacket and laid it down on a random beach towel. "Ok, I'm ready," I started to march toward the next squinty eyed, smiling fool.

"Hold on a minute," Toni's hand gently gripped the back of my neck. "Your blouse. Undo a button or two."

Since my blouse was button all the way up to my neck, it wasn't such a big deal. Until he reached up and undid three more.

"Hey, hey now!" I shouted. It was below my bra line.

"Oops, I only meant to do two extra. Butterfingers." He winked.

Yeah, yeah, butterfingers my ass. I buttoned one more up so there was just enough cleavage showing. "Anything else I should be changing?"

"That skirt could stand to be a little shorter, but I don't see how we could manage that." He was studying every curve of my figure without reservation.

"You could always rip it up the seams. Maybe I should show some more leg too?" I said sarcastically.

"That could be arranged," His head was tilted as he stared me up and down, practically stripping me to my birthday suit with his eyes.

"Let's go." I rolled my eyes and started to walk away. After a minute or two we finally came across a dealer. "Alright, how should I approach him?" I whispered.

"Put a little limp in you walk, speak either surfer or street lingo, and whatever you do, keep a relaxed composure. You don't want to frighten him off." He slapped my ass and pushed me forward toward the guy.

I gathered some spit and attempted to spit it to the side, but it backfired and kind of dribbled down my chin. "Yo, pimpin." I added a head nod as I half galloped, half limped over toward him. "How's it hangin' bra?"

The man sort of leaned back and stared at me like I was a nut. That's probably because I couldn't decide which lingo to go with, gangsta or surfer. I finally decided gangsta. "Wuzup mayne?"

"Uh, dudette, are you talking to me?" He glanced to either side of him.

I did a nod that said yes.

"Nothin spectacular. Just enjoying the sounds of the waves. What's wrong with your leg? Surfing accident?"

At this, I gave up the thug façade and just used my natural given gifts, my feminine curves. I don't know why I didn't think of that earlier. "Say, you wouldn't happen to have anything on you by any chance, would you? I'm dying to have a little fun around here." I batted my lashes and leaned over just the slightest bit to give him a glimpse of my girls.

He was fumbling over his words in no time. "I-I-I've got a little something. What's on your mind?" His eyes never met with mine after that.

"Just a bit of God's natural herbs. I just need a little something to get my spirits up." I smiled my biggest smile, but it's not like he'd notice.

"S-s-s-ure," he mumbled as he reached into his bathing trunks. Wait a minute, he's wasn't going for the pockets. I think, I think that he's—yup. He's actually digging around inside his bathing suit. Nice.

When he pulled the bag of weed and waved it around, I was just thankful it wasn't in his water proof compartment. It was simply in his shorts. Whatever, it's not my problem. The Galloways would never know the difference anyways. I leaned over and gave him a peck on the cheek and snatched the bag.

"Thanks hun," I grinned and headed back to hotel with Toni.

"That was interesting."

"You did that on purpose," I gave him a light shove. "Telling me to be gangsta or surfer dude when all I had to do was just be a vixen."

He threw his head back and laughed, "Well it was amusing to watch you impersonate the two. Nice swagger by the way. It was definitely...creative."

Jerk off. I shot him a bitch look and continued on into the hotel lobby. When I spotted Juanita slumped over at the bar shoving peanuts into her mouth like they were going out of style, I grabbed her by the arm and hastily led her to the elevator.

With her mouth full of peanuts, Juanita asked, "Mmm, Señora Nicole, have chu tried these peanuts before? My God, they're amazing. I've been eating these by the handful. Chu've got to try some. Here." She dug out a handful of peanuts from her pockets. When did she even have time to stuff her pockets?

"No! I don't want any damn peanuts. I want you to go back to the Galloway's room and replace their belongings." I directed her into the elevator, and Toni followed us in, tapping the seventh floor button.

"Do you know what I had to go through to get this?" I shoved the weed four inches from her face, not wanting to bring it much closer considering it had been in some fool's jock strap.

She stared up at me hopelessly, like sad puppy dog eyes. Great, I mean, who could honestly be mad at a face like that? I released my head and let out another sigh.

"So what's the game plan?" Toni had his arms folded as he rested against the elevator walls.

"I'll unlock the door; Juanita will sneak in and put the goods back where they belong." I repeated that for her to hear, "Back-where-they-belong."

"Good plan, good plan." Juanita was crouched low to the ground as if waiting for a whistle to blow on a football field. The elevator bell dinged and she bolted from the doors to room 721. There's no denying it, the woman was fast.

I tip toed over, unlocked the door, and creaked it open. Juanita peeped her head in, saw that the coast was all clear, and snuck into the bedroom. While she was completing her dirty business, Toni and I waited outside the door. I was on the brink of a panic attack and Toni was still openly checking out my girls in my unbuttoned shirt from his bird's eye view.

I fastened the buttons back to normal and was about to call him a pervert when an elderly couple strolled out of the elevator. My heart skipped a few beats but calmed at the belief that the elderly couple had to be from another room on the floor. They looked too sweet to be secretly puffing on weed. At that my heart calmed, and I waited from them to surpass the room.

Low and behold, the couple slowed near the entrance of the very same door and the man pulled out his room key card. As luck would have it, the couple was Mr. and Mrs. Galloway. My eyes widened and jaw dropped as I felt the air rush out of my lungs. Toni could tell by my apparent expression that it was them without even turning around.

"Just play along," He whispered to me before he swung me around and gently plopped me on the floor. Then he yelled, "I think she's having a heart attack!"

I closed my eyes once I caught on to what he was doing. The Galloway's inched closer and his hand went up. "Stand back, stand back. You two go to the lobby and get the manager. Tell her it's a code red."

Mr. Galloway started to say something, but Toni spoke again, more demandingly. "GO! NOW!"

The couple skirted toward the elevator and frantically waited until the elevator arrived. When I heard the sound of the elevator doors close, I assumed they were out of sight and tried to get up, but Toni pushed my shoulder back down. "There are some bystanders still," he whispered. "Stay put."

I immediately closed my eyes and felt the pretend gentle staccato pulsing on my chest until suddenly Toni's lips were locked on mine.

Whoa. Hello.

He acted like he was blowing air into my mouth at first. Then he carefully opened my mouth with his and I felt a wave of heat ripple through my body as his tongue moved softly with mine. His hands lightly cradled my face, and then I felt his body lean into mine.

That body of his was strong, powerful, and forceful, but most of all, his body was hot. And I do also mean hot, temperature wise. Or maybe it was just my body; there were surges of warmth pulsating through every inch of my skin. I could feel a buildup of energy burning within me. I had been without this kind of touch for so long, I think my body took on a will of its own.

Involuntarily my hands reached up to the underneath of his ears and I lightly dug my finger-nails into his scalp. I was soaking up as much of this moment as humanly possible, enjoying even the slightest movement. His mouth moved from mine down the base of my jaw and along the crevices of my neck. Those pouting lips felt excellent as they skimmed across my smooth skin. I had completely forgotten everything and anything, for all I could think about was that I wanted more. And I wanted it now.

His kisses continued down my neck. Through my partially opened eyes I caught Juanita standing over us, covering her mouth with her hands, wide eyed in shock. Moment over.

"Toni!" I yanked him back. "You manipulated me!"

OK. So maybe I sort of allowed him to manipulate me, but if he wasn't so incredibly sexy I'd be able to control myself a little more. It's that smile. And those eyes. Not to mention his marvelously sculpted, broad chest...I could just lick chocolate right off of it. Mmm, and his lips.

I found myself unconsciously sucking my bottom lip simply thinking about him. Toni smiled and raised a brow. See, that's the smile I'm talking about.

"Oooo, wee," Juanita licked her lips. "Who needs HBO when chu've got access to a live showing right here?"

"Please, grab a bucket of popcorn while you're at it." I smacked Toni's hands back and stood up to straighten myself out.

Toni stood up too, leaned in, and snuck a quick peck on the cheek. "Hey, I was just trying to save your life. This is the kind of thanks I get?"

And I'm a monkey's uncle. I looked around nervous about the other bystanders Toni mentioned earlier until I realized that I had been bamboozled. There was nobody except the three of us in the deserted hallway.

Juanita's eyes were lit up like a Christmas tree. "Toni, Toni. Chu can save my life any day of the week. Come to think of it, I'm kinda feeling a little weak." She held her hand to her forehead and closed her eyes. Oh brother.

"And what would your husband Alonzo say?" He patted her hand. "You're a married woman. And your husband's prison term is almost up." He plotted a kiss on her hand and then shook his head. "I'm not that crazy."

She folded her arms, "Well, we could always fix that."

The elevator door dinged and we rushed to the stairs at the end of the hall. At the bottom of the seven flights, we panted and wheezed uncontrollably. Toni, of course, looked as though he was ready to take on another couple hundred flights. Gym rat.

Once we collected ourselves, the three of us headed in different directions. After we split up, I made my way to the street out front and hailed a cab to take me home.

On the cab ride home, my phone rang. Unknown number.

"Hello?" I answered cautiously.

"Hi, is there a Nicole D'Angelo there?" A heavy, raspy voice answered.

A little hesitant I responded, "Um...yes. This is she. Who is this?"

"It's Marco."

Marco, Marco, Marco. Hmm, where have I heard that name before? I tried to pull the name out of my pea-sized memory, but turned up empty. "I'm sorry, could you refresh my memory?"

"I ran into a friend of yours, Lance or Landon, something like that, down at Jamba Juice the other day. He suggested some kind of blind date?"

"Right! Marco. I remember Landon mentioning your name before. Yes, so a date? Any places in mind?"

"Well, your friend mentioned that you like sushi."

Well, my friend's a damn liar. I hate sushi.

"Absolutely," I cheesed. "Love it."

"Good. How about Kona? 8 o'clock tonight. On the strip." He sounded a little pushy, but I guess that just meant he didn't like to beat around the bush.

"Sounds good. I'll meet you there."

"Nah, I'll swing by and pick you up." Not again.

"I mean, I'd actually prefer to meet you there, if that's alright?"

"It's no biggie. Give me your address; I'm picking you up."

I gave him my address. Note to self: learn to say no. And I'm not so sure how I feel about all these first daters having my home address in the first place. What if they all merged together and created a union against me? Torch down my house or something crazy like that?

The taxi dropped me off at the front of my house and after I paid the fare I jumped out of the cab and rushed inside. I glanced at my phone to check the time. 7:18? I did a double take. Yep. I read the time right, which meant I had less than an hour to get primped up.

After I fumbled up the stairs and unzipped my makeup bag to reapply the beautifications, I wondered just what kind of fella this Marco character was? What did Landon see in this guy at the line for Jamba Juice?

Of course, knowing Landon, I'm sure it was his looks. He was never able to pass up a hottie with a great ass—even if the guy wasn't gay.

I shimmied out of my work clothes and tossed them into the dirty hamper. For a few wasted minutes, I switched back and forth between a red slinky dress that hugged every nook and cranny of my curves, versus a simple white, plain-Jane-type summer dress. Going against my better judgment I selected the red one. Today, my sister would be proud. And I'm sure my mother would have a stroke.

I decided to wear my hair up, in a style of loose curls with several strands that occasionally drooped down. I applied some clear lip gloss to my plump lips and made a smacking noise as I finished up at the mirror. I was ready to go.

I started out my bedroom until I remembered my shoes! How could I forget my favorite part of dressing up for a date? My stilettos.

Back in my closet I was stumped, contemplating a pair of red heels with thick straps and another pair of black, peep-toe heels. Hmm…decisions, decisions. If I went with the red shoes, I wouldn't have to match shoes with accessories; if I went with the black shoes, it attracted more attention to my curves. Eh, but I didn't feel like carrying around a purse tonight. Inevitably the red shoes won.

I was pulling out my ID and cash from my wallet, when the doorbell rang. I hurried to the front and swept open the door.

In walked Marco. Señor Marco. Mr. Hottie-with-a-Body Marco. He was so steamy I thought my windows were going to fog.

Instinctively I licked my lips. Landon, my friend, you did good.

"Hi," I managed to squeak out. "Marco?"

"One and only," he grinned and my knees buckled out from underneath me.

He was tall, at least six-foot-three, maybe four, with dark bedroom eyes. His jet black hair was cropped short and off his neck. His skin was a smooth caramel coloring, and I figured he was mixed with African American and some kind of Asian blend. Maybe Japanese? The body of a Greek god and the smile of Denzel Washington, what more could a girl want?

"Good to finally meet you face-to-face," I was positively beaming as we shook hands.

"Hot outfit," He looked me over for a while, obviously pausing somewhere lower than my eyes. I got the feeling he wasn't staring at my necklace though. "You ready to bounce?"

"All set!" I stashed the money and ID deep in my cleavage.

"Wow, that's a first," he snickered. "You women are never ready on time. Always gotta make a man wait."

I take it he's bitter from previous experience. Awkwardly I laughed it off. "Well, guess I'm a rare breed. Let's go get some sushi. I'm starving." No, not really; I purposely scrounged down some left over pizza as I got ready so I wouldn't have to stuff anymore sushi rolls down my throat than necessary.

He reached across and pinched my belly. "You obviously can't be starving too badly." He winked and turned out the door for me to follow.

No, this son-of-a-bitch did not.

After I squeezed an imaginary stress ball, I warily stepped outside. I locked the door behind us and was still trying to shake off his inconsiderate remark. Was he calling me fat? No. Surely he was not that stupid.

As I whirled around to follow him to his car, I stopped short. My face contorted into one of confoundment as I stood frozen there on the front porch steps.

"It seems that your car is missing two wheels, a passenger's seat, and an air conditioning unit." My head tilted to the side.

He stared at me like I was a dumbstruck blonde. "It's a bike." He pointed to his motorcycle. "Haven't you ever seen a cruiser before?" He wasn't picking up on the sarcasm.

I mentally rolled my eyes. "I've seen bike's before. What I seem to be having trouble with is imagining how I'm going to mount that thing in this tight ass dress." Not to mention my heels.

"You women," he grunted, "so damn high maintenance." I thought I heard him mutter something about me being a pampered princess, but I disregarded his annoying utterances.

"Alright, you first," I pointed to the cruiser and he slid on with ease. Now, I know I won't look as graceful at straddling the bike as him, but hell, he isn't the one wearing four inch heels.

I steadied one foot on the curb and tried to swing my leg up and over the seat on the other side, but the skin-tight dress wouldn't allow it. Maybe if I used just a little more oomph to the swing, I would be able to—

RIPPP.

My eyes closed as I exhaled. The side seam ripped wide open, not only ruining my dress, but it also amped up my already-hoochie-mama wardrobe a few notches on the slut-o-meter, if that was even possible.

Marco's eyebrows just about touched the clouds as he stared at the spread eagle view of my turquoise blue lace thong. I instantly slumped onto the bike and muttered, "Just drive."

On our way to Kona, I self-consciously re-adjusted my dress so that it wouldn't keep flapping open in the wind every time Marco accelerated. Pretty much the majority of Miami was getting a shot of my woo-hoo. I was beginning to feel like Britney Spears.

Once we arrived at the restaurant I shakily managed off the bike and followed him toward the front entrance. It seemed that apparently Marco was not one for well-mannered gestures as he has yet to help me on or off the bike, and I seem to find myself trailing after him when he marches off without waiting for me. I already picked up on a chauvinist vibe, but I'd try to disregard the feeling since I have been known to be a little over-analytical when it comes to dating.

At the front door, he walked in first and nearly closed the door on me in the process, which merely reconfirmed my initial accusations. Considerate? Negative.

The host led us to a seat in the bar area and divvied out two pairs of chopsticks. As soon as the waiter appeared to introduce himself, I immediately asked for two ladies' margaritas. Pronto. If

I was going to enjoy his company, I would need to be heavily intoxicated.

The song "Red, Red Wine" was blasting in the restaurant speakers and there was an assortment of diverse people filling the space around the bar. Some dressed in shorts and sandals, others in sexy little numbers similar to my own outfit.

"So how long have you been in Miami?" he asked before he took a swig of his drink.

"I moved here when I was fourteen and I've been here ever since, well, minus college." I smiled finding a flicker of hope in that he wasn't one hundred percent preoccupied with himself.

"Oh?" He seemed indifferent. "From where, and what brought you down here?"

"Moved here from the Bronx," I said. "Truthfully, we moved here because my mom wanted to get as far away from New York as possible after my dad died."

When Dad died, Ma didn't take it too well. She literally packed up our minimal belongings, buckled me and Vi in the back seat, and drove. She drove and drove until she couldn't drive south anymore and we started our lives over in the sunny, and humid, city of Miami. We've never looked back since then.

"Huh," he grunted. "Did your dad leave you a lot of money or something?"

"No," I shrugged.

"Oh. Did your mom re-marry then?"

"No. Why?" I wasn't quite following his line of questioning.

"Well, how did your family manage to survive without a man around the house? I mean who paid the bills?"

I felt my face slump into a stupor. He couldn't possibly be suggesting that women can't fend for themselves or make their own money could he? I decided to ask, just to clarify. I was probably making assumptions again. "Um, what, what do you mean Marco?"

He shifted around in his seat, "Men are the breadwinners. We bring home the bacon and women are the ones who cook it. I don't see how your mom could afford to live in Miami if she didn't have a man to take the reins, no offense."

I turned my head from side to side to see if anyone else heard his ridiculously sexist and offending remarks, and to my surprise, there were a couple other women staring at him with utter disgust. OK. I was justified in my reaction.

"I would laugh, but your ignorance really isn't a laughing matter."

Marco's jaw tensed and his eyes nearly pierced through me. "Ignorance!" he snarled. "I guess I gave you too much credit if you really think you women can amount to much without us. Women don't even belong in the workplace as it is, unless it has to do with cooking us food or patching up clothes," he paused, deep in thought before he added, "or as strippers. World wouldn't be the same without strippers, so you can add that to the list, too," he chuckled, clearly amused with himself.

Obviously we would be as perfect together as Marilyn Manson and Mother Teresa. Even if I hadn't made up my mind within the first five minutes of meeting him, his poorly established philosophy on life was enough to ensure that this was going nowhere. If we didn't drive each other crazy, one of us would probably end up behind bars on account of murder.

Since I knew this was a done deal and we now had an accumulation of fellow bystanders blatantly eavesdropping on our conversation, I decided to take this opportunity and throw in a little theatrics. What can I say? After being friends with Landon for so many years, his dramatic tendencies were bound to rub off on me eventually.

I abruptly rose from the bar stool, dramatically whipped my head in his direction, and pointed a stern finger in his face. "You, Marco, are an insult to the modern society. How dare you accuse women of being inferior subjects to men when your little, pathetic idea of reality so accurately represents the 'intelligence' you so clearly lack."

I pulled back my hands and dramatically thrashed my head from side to side. Then I yelled, much louder than necessary, "You disgust me!"

By now the few surrounding bystanders extended further out so that nearly all the customers in the bar area were fixated on our argument. Their eyes felt heavy on my skin. The margaritas I drank dulled the effects of the adrenaline, but my stomach was still doing flips of excitement. For the final touch, I snatched the drink and splashed the remainder of my margarita on the rocks in his face, hoping the ice cubes stung like a bitch, while I proudly marched out the restaurant.

Asshole.

Once I was outside I felt a surge of rejuvenation. Of course I didn't have to be so dramatic with my exit, but I was on a roll once I got started. Now I see why Landon loves the theatrics; it's quite liberating. There could have been some displaced anger there, but what the hell, the guy was a jerk anyways.

I glanced around the parking lot and the light bulb lit up. I arrived here with Marco and I purposely wore my red shoes so I didn't have to carry a purse with me. This is my life.

Oh, wait! I almost forgot about the mad money stashed between my boobs. I pulled it out and kissed the wad, thankful for my girls.

I waved down a taxi and hastily gave him my address. The sooner out of that parking lot, the better. As we pulled up to the curb I gave him some cash and went inside.

The first thing to do on my list: extract these clothes—now. After I finished, I called Landon. Oh yes, we needed to talk.

"Who's your best friend?" Landon answered the call with smug pride. "I picked a winner, huh?"

"Sure Landon. A real winner." I growled as I shimmied on my loose sweats and rolled on a pair of ankle socks. "He was easy on the eyes, but a complete asshole. Did you know that he thought women couldn't take care of themselves? He thought we needed a man for financial survival. Psh! Get real. I bet I make more money in one paycheck than he does in a year." I'm sure it wasn't true, but when venting it's therapeutic to elaborate.

"Aw honey, I'm sorry. Did you manage to find out if he has any gay, available friends?" Landon asked. His S's were drawn out and sounded more like "ssssss."

"No Landon, I was too busy finding the nearest object to throw at him."

"Ooo! Please tell me you threw your stiletto again. You did, didn't you? Oh you're such a bad girl!" He was giggling like a little school girl.

"Not this time. Although now that I think about it, it may have caused more damage if I threw a shoe at him instead." Rewind button, anyone?

He sighed. "Well, I wish the evening went a little smoother for you, I really do, but I'm kind of in the middle of something right now—"

"Gotcha," I puffed out air in frustration. "I'll talk to you later."

"I have something important to show you; want to meet up at Quella's tomorrow? Say six-ish?"

Quella's is the best ice cream joint in town, which only the locals know about. I agreed, a little skeptical about this thing he had to show me. "Sure, whatever."

"Great! Love ya, toodles!" He hung up.

Toodles. I sat in my bed for a little while toying with my hair contemplating what Landon seemed so excited about when my doorbell rang. Three times in a row. Who could that be at this hour?

I wobbled down the stairs and flung the front door open.

Mrs. Guerreza blinked up at me with big gray eyes. She was just shy of five feet, by several inches and her silver hair was bundled into a high bun. She was wearing what looked like a maroon carpet, which was desperately trying to pass as clothing. It was hideous, but I suppose to each their own. I shifted my gaze down and saw that her hands were holding a rather large bird cage and a parrot was staring up at me curiously.

"Mrs. Guerreza," my mouth remained open for a second or two. "Good to see you and your…"

"Trixie. This here is Trixie." She shoved the cage at me so I was left holding it. "Would you be a dear and watch over her while Mr. Guerreza and I go out of town on our cruise?"

"Umm…"

"It will only be for a couple days. The cruise is just a seven day one. Trixie really is a sweetheart and low maintenance. All you have to do is refill her water and food tray. That's it." She was turning around and half way back to her side of the town house.

"But, but, Mrs. Guerreza," I called out to her.

"Thanks Nicole, you're such a doll. The food is on your step. See you in a week."

I stood there slack-jawed, parrot in hand, unsure of what just happened. One minute I'm sitting on my bed minding my own business, next I'm at the front door, babysitting a molting, nearly bald parrot for the next week. Did I miss a step?

Reluctantly I picked up the bird food with my other hand and carried the bird cage inside. As soon as I closed the door the bird began to squawk and frantically flap its wings. I carried her to the corner of my kitchen and tried to soothe her. "Trixie, Trixie, calm down. Shh. Chill out!"

But little miss Trixie didn't stop. So I tried another approach "I'm not going to eat you. Promise! In fact, I don't even eat chicken." I crossed my fingers behind my back.

She continued screeching and flapping around so I checked her food and water, both were full. What the hell is the matter with this thing? Is it defective or something? Maybe she wanted people food.

I dug around in the refrigerator and came up empty. Well, actually, I came across some left over carrot cake, but Trixie would have to pry it from my cold, dead fingers before I willingly gave that up.

Then I remembered in the movies people always gave parrots crackers. "Polly want a cracker?" I said aloud, but the bird didn't stop. I tried feeding Trixie a cracker but she didn't budge, so I tried the next best thing to food. Jose Cuervo.

At first I poured just a little in her water cup, but simply decided to dump the water and fill it with booze. To my surprise the house was restored to its natural order and peace resided once again. Write that down: Trixie's a drunk.

I crept up the stairs and back into bed where I collapsed. This babysitting-parenting stuff was hard. I've come to this conclusion after a full twenty minutes of babysitting a bird. This is likely a sign from God himself that I should avoid procreation.

CHAPTER THREE

I hailed a cab to work—again—and on the ride there I wondered why I hadn't bought a car to call my own yet. Then that annoying, nagging, inescapable voice in the back of my mind pulled me back to reality, the permeating reminder of my everlasting financial responsibility for my mother. Oye.

If it weren't for her ridiculous gambling habits, I would not be here to cover two mortgages and two different sets of bills. When it's all said and done, I barely have enough money left to buy toilet paper to wipe my own ass, let alone afford a car deposit and monthly note.

Vi is no better either, living with Ma and barely contributing to any of the bills. She earned her income in tips at the bar and then turned right around to spend it at the bar. Vi, Miss Social Butterfly. She's in with all the hot spots and VIP invites. She enjoys mingling with the other club junkies. She is a permanent member of the nightlife society.

Whatever, though, she can do what she likes with her life. I honestly don't care, but she shouldn't be the leech stuck to the bottom of my wallet, draining my pockets dry. That kid drives me nuts. She's irresponsible, immature, an impulsive spender, boy crazed, and unbearable to live with, but what I am I going to do? She's still my sister.

I shrugged the thought off, and with this motion noticed my clothes fit a bit snug today. I peeked down at my belly. Maybe I should hit the gym. Nah, when my clothes don't zip up all the way then I'll make my way to the gym. Feeling satisfied about my success in avoiding physical punishment, I smiled to myself and enjoyed the scenery on the way to the hotel.

Arriving at work, I was instantly thrown into a chaotic mess of landscape designs and lay out arrangements with our primary landscaping architect and his team of workers. This being just one of the many neglected projects stacked mile high on my desk of things to do.

"Mrs. D'Angelo—"

"Ah, ah, ah, Pierre. It's Ms. D'Angelo." I corrected him.

"Of course, forgive me." Pierre, our leading landscaping architect, made an apologetic smile. "We have much to do today. The assortments you selected prior to are waiting in the trucks. My men are ready to lay out the assortments and plant the back patio area given your signature." He pointed to the contract with the signature fields tagged for me to sign.

"And the front?" I asked as I signed my approvals.

"Ms. D'Angelo, there is no way we can complete the entire proximity of the hotel in one day, but we could complete the front tomorrow if we finish the back today."

I waved my hand in a carefree motion. What would I know about adequate landscaping schedules, it's not like I've done much work with my own yard at home. "Sure, go ahead and get started on the back. When the work is done come to my office and we'll complete the payment. Thanks, Pierre."

"Yes, of course." He nodded and turned back toward his workers where he began to administer a slew of commands.

I continued walking into the lobby where a wave of cool air invitingly welcomed me. It was a scorcher out there and the hotel felt crisp and cool in comparison. However, Juanita stomped toward me in a desperate manner, hair wild and eyes wide with rage. Apparently to some people, the air conditioning settings did not feel as cool to them.

"My goodness, Señora Nicole, me and the rest of the girls are burnin' up in here," she fanned herself and wiped the sweat off her brow. "Please, turn the A/C just the teeniest bit down. I think the new girl, Jessie, is gonna pass out. Do it for her sake, por favor!"

I contemplated this. A lawsuit due to hazardous working conditions sounded expensive. "Fine." I snapped. If the employees were this uncomfortable, then they aren't being efficient anyways. If they're not of full efficiency, then they're costing me money and I hate losing money. "I will lower it, so it is in the seventies." More like seventy-nine.

"Thanks," she said flatly and then pivoted on her heel, moving toward the hospitality desk. She softly mumbled under her breath in Spanish.

"What was that?" I shouted across the lobby to her. "This is a single lingual facility, none of that bilingual stuff."

She turned to display an angelic smile. "Señora Nicole, I only said how beautiful chu look today."

Something told me that's not at all what she said.

I was rubbing my temples trying to drive out my negative assumptions about her Spanish translation, when Toni crept up behind me and slung an arm over my shoulder. "Rough day already? You haven't even made it to lunch hour yet."

He smelled delicious, his cologne completely easing the tension away. It was a heavenly aroma consisting of a mixture of midnight air and the ocean breeze. I peered up into his crystal blue eyes encroached in a few natural creases from so many years of smiling. He had a warm smile stretched across his face and his laughing lines looked charming and humble on him.

"Story of my life," I said with a small smile. "Fortunately I get to leave early today. Ma asked me to help her with the Delightful Daisies meeting this afternoon."

"Oh, those Delightful Daisies. That's one hell of a crowd."

And I couldn't agree more. "Yeah, Ma is the host this week and well…you know how she is. She's kind of lacking in the—"

"Responsibility department?"

"I was going to say hospitality realm, but I suppose that would be a plausible suggestion."

He sighed. "Hun, when are you going to start taking care of yourself first? I've been working with you for how many years now, and not once have you taken time for yourself. If you aren't helping with your mom, then it's your sister. If it's not Vi, then it's the hotel."

I decided not to mention Trixie, the parrot, since that would only prove his point further. "Huh. Well, I'll be in my office. I need to speak with headquarters in Vegas about our current advertising arrangements."

"There you go again." He sighed and nudged me in the direction of the office.

"It's my j-o-b." I huffed as I stormed toward my office.

I melted into the office chair where I remained throughout lunch, making phone calls and calculating the available wiggle room in our budget. Capacity wise, we weren't doing *that* bad. Typically, the spring and summer seasons were our best times of the year, but due to the bad publicity from the recently missing tourists, our tourist numbers were at an all-time low. The spring season has seemed to leave most businesses with a pinch in their pockets as the city thrives predominantly on tourism. Secondly, on crime.

Apparently, the advertising of special packages helped generate some traffic flow through the hotel again. While this is a welcomed site, it still does nothing to ease my nerves about the financial hole on which we're teetering. Corporate is well aware of the situation and has been closely monitoring the profit margins of my site. They are trigger happy on the thought of cutting staff to decrease their costs. I, on the other hand, work with these people every day and am doing everything in my power to keep food on their tables. I've managed to negotiate a deal with corporate to extend the deadline through the end of the year. If I'm unable to increase profitability by the end of the year, we can re-visit their idea of letting some staff go.

Of course no one knows of this aside from corporate and me. The last thing we need is a company-wide drop in morale or for employees to start jumping ship. If there's a chance to turn this thing around, I'll do my absolute best to make it happen. I rubbed my temples and went back to the work in front of me.

By about two o'clock, I was packed up and headed for the front door when Juanita pulled me aside to the counter at the bar and perched me up on a stool. She struggled lifting her short chubby legs onto the ledge and with great effort fought to lift herself onto the elevated barstool. She seemed urgent, and I was impatient, so after about two minutes of painfully watching her try to get up, I grabbed her under the arms and lifted her onto the seat.

"You had something you wanted to say?" I presumed.

"Señora Nicole," she was panting. "I just found out the most terrid—horror—terrible or is it horrid...?"

My eyes widened. "Terrible, horrid, horrible. They're all possibilities. I won't know until you tell me the news!" I said perturbed. I don't like bad news.

"Si. Terrible is good. Well, I don't mean terrible means good. Actually terrible as in the situation, meaning the situation is supposed to be malo, or bad."

"Get on with it." I squeezed my temples.

"Well, I found out the most terrible news. I was cleaning in room 405 when I heard voices from the next room over, 407. Anyways I says to myself, 'Self. Chu've got to listen to what these people are saying because they could be asking for help, and I wouldn't even know it if I was too selfish not to listen closely.' So I listened with my ear pressed to the wall, but couldn't make out clear screams for help, so I pressed an empty glass to the wall and listened harder because chu know, they may need me."

"Of course. Heaven forbid if someone wasn't listening to their conversation through the wall with a glass pressed to their ear."

"Exactly!" Her eyes were wide with enthusiasm. "So while I was listening I heard two girls talking about their other two friends that didn't return to the room last night. They sounded very worried. One of the girls was contemplating calling the local police."

"Uh-huh. And when you heard the possibility of a sex scandal, naturally you listened harder?"

"Oh, Señora Nicole, chu are very smart." She winked at me. Toni had been casually wiping down the counter nearby, but Juanita caught his attention and was now leaning on the counter right beside me. I tried to concentrate on Juanita's story, but Toni's presence was causing my body to have trouble remaining cool and collected.

"Any-y-y-y ways." She took a deep breath to emphasize the important information she was about to tell us. "As I was listening to them, I heard them say they were out at that new nightclub, Chic, last night. They all took a cab there together and two of their friends went to the bar with some strangers. That was the last they saw them."

"At Chic?" Toni raised a brow. "Isn't that the same place..."

"Exactly." Juanita nodded her head with a grave expression on her face. "The same one."

"Oh for heaven's sake!" I tossed my hands in the air. "Quit being so melodramatic. Just because Chic is where the last group of girls went missing does not mean the two girls who went MIA for a night were abducted too."

"You think it's just a coincidence?" Toni asked in a serious tone.

"I think two of the girls probably left their friends to go have an all-nighter, or at least have some fun with some guys they thought were attractive. Wouldn't be the first. They are probably hailing a cab back now in their walk-of-shame attire from last night as we speak."

"And if that's not the case?" Toni asked.

"Yeah, if chu're wrong…then what are we gonna do?"

"What? Juanita, no! We are not going to do a damn thing. It's not our job to keep track of promiscuous college girls. They come here to get away from their mothers. We certainly aren't going to substitute their mother's place while they're here. Let them have their indiscretions as they wish. We don't pass judgment, and we definitely don't intervene."

"But Señora Nicole—"

"No 'but's' this time. It is not our place to interfere in the customers' personal business. In fact, by interfering you're ensuring that you'll lose their business in the future. They can spend their spare time doing whatever their heart desires. We're not going to be the ones to lecture them about it."

"She's right, babe." Toni stared down at me. "If it turns out they've gone missing like the incident from earlier this spring, then this will not only look bad for the hotel, but it also wouldn't be right if we did nothing to help. Don't you think it would be better to try to get ahead of this thing in the event it really is another incident?"

I sighed. They had a point, but it was too premature to jump to any kind of conclusion. "Look, it is too early to start playing amateur detective. It hasn't even been 48 hours. Why don't we just wait to see if they come back this evening? Juanita, I have to get going, but if you want to keep an eye on their status until your shift ends tonight, we can recap in the morning and take it from there. When I say keep an eye on it, I mean a very inconspicuous eye. For the love of God, do not interfere in the customers' lives," I demanded. "That's an order."

Juanita and Toni looked relieved that I was at least taking this into consideration.

I hopped down from my stool and rushed outside to hail a cab. As I walked away the two of them were shaking their heads and whispering to one another. I didn't like the looks of their sneaky exchange, but I had to go. I was now in a time crunch to get to Ma's house and help her prepare before the Daisies arrived.

When I finally pulled up at Ma's house, smoke was being fanned outside of the kitchen window. I opened the back door to see Ma frantically flapping her kitchen rag toward the opened window, simultaneously smearing sweat from her forehead with her right arm. To say she appeared flustered would be an understatement.

"Ma, what in God's name are you doing? I thought you were supposed to make sushi."

Her eyes were wild and her nostrils flared, never a good sign. "That's what I'm doing! I'm tryin' to cook this damn sushi and I guess the seaweed wraps caught fire somehow. This is a nightmare!"

"Isn't sushi usually raw though?" I asked.

"Well, I didn't want to be responsible for giving Janice food poisoning because the meat wasn't cooked all the way. You know how much she hates me. At the first chance she gets, she's going to have me shunned from the group." In other words, expelled from her little gossip circle.

She plopped a hand on her hip and looked wonderingly out of the corner of her eye. "Of course, then again if Janice just so happened to be mysteriously food poisoned, and suppose it got so bad that she rolled over and croaked, I wouldn't have to put up with her whiny, passive-aggressive remarks anymore."

Uh-oh.

Before she contemplated premeditated murder for Janice Hartwicker any further, I decided to chime in and interrupt her hazardous train of thought. "Give me your cookbook," I demanded. She passed it to me and together we went to work on some shrimp and crab-stuffed sushi rolls.

While the frozen package of egg rolls Ma bought were heating up, Ma and I began to catch up. "So," Ma leaned against the counter and lit up a cigarette. "How are the men?"

By 'men' she was referring to the slew of first daters. I've gone on so many first dates, I actually lost count over the years. I don't know. There was just always something missing with them. Maybe I'm a snob. Maybe I don't know what I want. But what I do know is that whatever it is, I just haven't found it yet.

"Eh, same ol' same ol.' You'll be the first to know when I find the guy." Although I wouldn't hold my breath if I were her.

I was beginning to accept the idea that I'd die alone. I would have eleven cats, and I would end up having conversations with them because no one else would be around for companionship. Inevitably I'd be known as the cat lady.

She blew out a stream of smoke from the corner of her mouth and relished in a moment of pure satisfaction.

"I thought you said you were going to quit smoking." I snatched away her cig and disposed of it down the sink's drain. For extra effect, I turn the garbage disposal on and smiled as it ate away the remains of her smoke.

Ma's face curled into one of hostility by the time I turned the disposal off. "What was that for? I stop tomorrow. Cold turkey. No more smoking ever again."

Right. I've never heard that one before.

"Uh-huh," I rolled my eyes. "You need to quit this junk." I held up her packet of cigs and tossed it back onto the counter. "You're going to kill yourself, and then who is going to be the rebellious troublemaker in the Delightful Daisies. You can't leave them high and dry."

She rubbed her chin deep in thought. "Yeah, I suppose you're right. What would they do without me?"

Well, for starters, Janice could sleep in peace at night knowing she isn't going to be 'unintentionally' food poisoned by a fellow Daisy member. And Martha, the president of the Daisies, could probably get off that medication she had to start taking to lower her blood pressure.

"They'd be bored without you." I said, knowing Ma kept things interesting.

"Speaking of bored, what have you been up to these days? I noticed the flowers in the backyard were wilting from neglect, and usually that's what you do all day. Tend to your gardens and collect neighborhood gossip to exchange with the Daisies. You aren't hanging around the tracks again, are you?" I'm sure my face displayed a contortion of anger, fear, and pain, so I tried to conform it into one of pure curiosity.

Suddenly Vi swung into the kitchen in her bare feet, dressed in a pair of little white shorts and a loose turquoise tank top. The color blend was fantastic with her summer tan. She smelled of Japanese Cherry Blossom lotion and already had her little grabby hands on our freshly stuffed sushi rolls.

"Put that down Violeta D'Angelo or so help me!" Ma had a butcher knife in her hand, so naturally Vi put it down before it ever reached her mouth.

"What?" She threw a pair of innocent puppy dog eyes her way. "I was just going to taste test it for you. Make sure it tasted OK." She took a whiff of the air and her nose twisted in revulsion. "Maybe it really does need a taste test by the smell of it in here. Did the oven catch fire or something?"

Ma's grip tightened a fraction on the butcher knife. "The oven and the sushi are just fine." The vein in her neck pulsed in annoyance.

"There are only enough for the Daisies." I muttered, trying to veer us away from the subject which was obviously an agitation for Ma.

"If anyone is going to test taste the sushi, the honors will go to Janice Hartwicker." A dark smile crossed her face. Oh, brother.

The doorbell rang and Vi fluttered over to open the front door. She flung the door open, welcomed the Daisies into the foyer and asked them to join Ma in the kitchen.

Shortly after, a bundle of seven…ahem…elderly women—who dare not be called 'old'—came bursting into Ma's tiny kitchen. Ma instantly grabbed the evidence of the frozen egg roll box and tossed it into a cabinet under the sink. Before I knew it, the gossip session had begun, with but only a pause of a breath.

Cynthia was the first to crack, "Daisies, you're not going to believe what I heard about Mr. Hoonagan and Mrs. Galawazky."

Robin chimed in, "Let me guess. They had an affair?" Her face was stuck in a permanent frown. Given that I have yet to see her with a different facial expression, I was beginning to wonder if she was born with that look. What an ugly baby she must have been. Her attitude was no better either.

Just then I did something no one outside the Daisies circle would ever venture to do. I spoke. "Isn't Mrs. Galawazky a widow though? And Mr. Hoonagan, has he ever been married? I don't see what the fuss is all about."

The seven women in the kitchen, excluding Ma, stared at me with vicious eyes and lips pressed tightly together. Ma just shook her head in embarrassment. They weren't happy that I intruded in their little circle's discussion. Apparently I made a whoopsie.

Martha Collins stepped forward with a superior air. "I'm sorry, my dear, but where is your Daisy badge?"

"Uh," I glanced down at my daisy-less, white blouse and back up to Martha's inquiring eyes. "I've a pair of underwear with daisies on it back at the house, if that counts for anything."

"Hah! A Daisy wannabe," Janice lunged. It was an ironic accusation when truth of the matter was I felt quite the opposite.

"No Daisy badge, no invite," Janice sneered. "This is privileged information for Delightful Daisies only."

Martha, the president of the club, shot Janice a look of death and Janice knowingly stepped back to her place. They operated like a cult keeping the in-group isolated from the out-group.

I took the hint and nodded. "Sorry, I didn't mean to intrude. You ladies have a nice meeting."

As I hurried through the Daisies, Wanda grabbed my shoulder and said, "It was good to see you again. I'll have to come by later and tell you of an interesting young man I met."

"Mrs. Wanda," I was about to tell her that I wasn't accepting blind dates anymore, but Martha Collins was headed straight toward me to kick me out the back door.

"Excuse us, Nicole," Martha gave me little shove, and I fumbled out the back steps. The door slammed shut behind me.

Well, that was nice.

I straightened up and dusted off my blouse. Outside I could hear Ma threatening Janice Hartwicker to mind her tone when she speaks to her daughter. Her heart was in the right place.

"They're vicious when they get together, aren't they?" Vi said, from beneath a pair of Aviator sunglasses. "I've learned to get the hell out of there when they arrive."

"Yeah thanks for the heads up." I sneered. "I almost got ripped apart."

"Animals, they are."

"Oh shit. Animals! I completely forgot about Trixie. I need to give her some more tequila before she runs out." I was frantic. I couldn't handle that ear piercing squawking when I got home. Last night, I thought my ear drums were going to burst.

"Who is Trixie? Are you babysitting an old lady again? I told you already, you can't give old people alcohol. It messes with their medications and shit."

"Trixie is a bird."

She raised her lip and slightly resembled Elvis. Before she could ask questions I asked, "Where's your car? I need to borrow it for the evening."

She paused, "Well, you see what had happened was—"

"Please don't tell me you sold your car. How the hell do you get to and from work?"

"I sold the car because there was this really cute dress I wanted, and it was designer. Of course, I had to buy it. So, I sold the clunker and bought a fuel-efficient scooter." She was smiling, quite proud of her purchase.

"A scooter." I said with an expressionless tone.

"Not the kind that you push around with your feet. You know, it's an automated scooter. Goes up to 40 miles an hour which is more speed than I need here on the strip."

"So it's a moped then? I suppose that could work. Would you mind if I borrowed it for the evening?"

"Yeah, sure the keys are just inside the back door, if you're willing to risk going back in there?"

She had a point. "Maybe if I'm quiet enough I can get in and out without being recognized."

"It's your neck," she laughed.

I crept to the back door, quietly cracked it open, and reached as far as my hand would extend, shooting for the keys in the basket. I blindly fumbled around until I finally grabbed a hold of the keys. Then a broom came down and smacked my knuckles.

"YOW!" I yelled and retrieved my hand still clutching the keys. "Someone whacked me with a broom!"

Vi was laughing. "I bet it was that Janice Hartwicker."

Next thing I know, a roar of women are screaming, "SPIES! There are undercover spies after us. Get your kitchen utensils Daisies, they must not escape!"

"Dear Lord!" I gasped as I hopped on the moped and revved up the engine. Vi scrambled out of her plastic lawn chair and up to her feet.

"Take me with you. I don't want to be here when they get out that back door!" She hopped on the back and she strapped on the helmet as we flew out of there.

The moped took off with speed and force, making a kiddy toy VRRRROOM sound as we peeled out of the driveway. The wind was whipping my hair around and I felt like my cheeks were doing a rippling effect from the wind speed. I imagine I looked like one of those animated characters straight out of a cartoon.

"Isn't this great?" Vi was yelling over the wind.

"What?" I couldn't quite make out what she was trying to say.

"I SAID, ISN'T THIS GREAT?!"

"Oh! Yeah, I feel so free!" I lifted an arm to emphasize my statement. Just as we cleared Ma's neighborhood, the moped coughed and choked until it quickly began to decrease its speed despite my attempt to accelerate.

"What the—" I was confused as we came to a halt. "What's wrong with this thing? We couldn't have exceeded the weight maximum."

Vi curled her lips in and looked down. "Actually, I may have forgotten to put gas in it last night. That's my bad."

She 'may' have forgotten to put gas in it last night? Life with this woman would never be simple. Now was not the time to be running out of gas, in the midst of a getaway. I glanced around and spotted a gas station not but a football-field length away.

"Come on," I sighed. "At least we can push it to the station. Get off and take the right handle bar. I'll take the left."

Vi made a grunting noise. "Aw, man."

"Don't you even start with me," I glared at her. "You're the one who forgot to re-fill the tank in the first place."

After that, she was silent, and we pushed the moped to the gas station together. When the tank was refilled we jumped on the moped and started up the engine to continue our much delayed getaway. The mob of Daisies had yet to drive out of the neighborhood, so I'm going with the risky assumption that we were safe from the savages.

I drove to my townhouse and parked the moped along the side of the street. Once inside, Trixie was flapping and screeching at the top of her lungs, just having a nasty bitch fit.

"So this must be Trixie?" Vi asked. "Goodness, fill up her cup of booze already. She's giving me a headache."

I was already working on it, with the Cuervo in hand. When I poured it into her cup and refilled her food bowl, she was instantly silenced. If I were ever one to believe in magic, now would be the time.

I went upstairs to my bedroom and Vi followed behind me.

"So what are your plans tonight?" she asked, as she started to browse through my shades of nail polish.

"Landon and I are going to Quella's for some ice cream. Apparently he has some big news to tell me."

"Oh?" She raised a brow. "Do you think he found the one?"

"It's possible," I thought. "Who knows? I think he enjoys the single life too much to give it up for good though."

I changed out of my work clothes and into a pair of denim cut-off shorts and a yellow, off-the-shoulder top. I stepped into a pair of thin-strapped yellow sandals and went to the bathroom to secure my hair into a ponytail.

"Let me do your hair," Vi snatched the brush from the counter and began to work on my hair. "You have such beautiful hair, Nicky, why don't you wear it down occasionally?"

"I don't know. It just takes so long," I shrugged. "You want the straightening iron too?"

"Of course," she grinned. "We can't have you bopping around town with a frizzed Afro. This isn't the eighties."

CHAPTER FOUR

I dropped Vi off at the bar for her evening shift on my way to meet Landon at Quella's for ice cream. After I parked the moped and dislodged the helmet borrowed from Vi, I wandered up to the front counter and ordered a triple scoop of mint chocolate ice cream in a waffle cone. At the picnic tables under the trees, I took a seat and waited for Landon to arrive. He had a knack for grand entrances.

"Hold it right there. Step away from the ice cream."

I jumped a little in surprise, his loud voice interrupting the silence. When I turned around I found Landon there with a sassy hand on his hip, face contorted into one of judgment.

"Hey Landon," I looked at him curiously. "Why are you giving me that look?"

"Because you're about to chow down on a serving of ice cream that could feed a third-world country. You may be young honey, but your metabolism…not so much. You only need about a fraction of that cone."

I rolled my eyes and brought it closer to mouth.

"Don't do it Nicky!" He stepped forward and snatched the cone away from me before I could bite down. "I want you to know that I'm doing this because I love you." With that he peeled off the top two scoops of ice cream and tossed it on the ground.

"What the hell, Landon! What do you want from me?" I shouted.

He handed me the significantly reduced remnants of my ice cream cone and wiped the residue from his fingers on a napkin. "I want you to find happiness, love."

"And you think taking away my ice cream is going to make me happy?" I challenged.

He did the European cheek kissing thing to me and smiled.

"I think drowning yourself in comfort food instead of drowning yourself in endless sex will be considerably less satisfying. Like I said, I'm telling you this because I love you, and as your gay best friend I have the right to be frank." He tapped my behind with a few quick smacks. "Let's keep these tight for the fellas, shall we?"

My jaw was still in my lap by the time he came back from getting his ice cream at the counter. I suppose my butt did jiggle a bit like Jell-O when I shook it. My line of thought was interrupted when I saw him carrying a banana split sundae caked in chocolate syrup, bing cherries, whipped cream, and sprinkles.

"Are you shittin' me? You're going to give me a lecture about my eating habits, and you come over here with a heart attack served in a bowl?" I growled. "Hypocrite."

"What?" He dug into his sundae with an oversized spoonful.

"I hope your love handles get love handles." I muttered, knowing this was highly unlikely. He couldn't gain weight if he tried. A six-foot-one bean pole with toned arms and six-pack abs…I envied his genetics.

On the bench next to him, I noticed his Dolce and Gabbana hand bag and wondered when Landon started carrying a purse around. Well, it was big enough to be considered a suitcase, but for argument's sake, I deemed it a purse.

His hair was bleach-blonde, parted, and smoothed to one side. His eyes were an artic blue and slightly dilated. He had a little bit of a tan, and dressed his body from head to toe in designer clothes. In a way, he kind of reminded me of the preppy men you see at country clubs playing tennis with their business partners, some spring afternoon. Landon would only been seen in public on a date with guys of a certain status or level of sophistication. He was a bit of a reputation snob.

He absentmindedly shoveled another spoonful of ice cream into his mouth.

We chatted away as our ice cream disappeared before our own eyes. When I was finished, I placed my elbows on the table and sighed in excitement. "So, enough of the small talk, what's this big news you had to tell me?"

"Well, the news is about someone big in my life. Although, he isn't particularly big, actually he is rather quite small—"

"You aren't going to go into detail about your sex life again are you? I don't want to hear about the measurements of his—"

"Good heavens, no!" He looked baffled.

Hallelujah. "Wait. Do you mean you're dating a little person?"

"What, like a midget?" His brows nearly touched his hair line.

"I believe they prefer to be called 'little people,'" I corrected.

"For the love of God, please stop guessing." He rolled his eyes and unzipped his D&G bag. Out popped a little head.

I screamed. "Ah! It's a rat! Kill it, kill it!" And I took off my shoe to smash it.

"Nicky!" Landon yelled. "This is Tito, my new dog." I stared from him to Tito then back to Landon. "I bought him this week," he smiled, "isn't he just the cutest?"

"He's balding." I said.

"No, that's just how his breed looks. It's a Hairless Chinese Crested. They're very upscale."

"Tito more so resembles a rodent than a dog." I reached over to try to play with his few strands of hair on top of his head, but he growled and snapped at my fingers.

"He tried to bite me!" I gasped. "I take it back. He's half rodent, half piranha."

"Tito doesn't like to be teased," he said as he bundled him closer to his chest. "Now, I can be just like Paris Hilton."

"Doesn't she carry a Chihuahua around? Whatever it is, I think it has more hair than that thing you picked out of a dumpster."

"Please, they're the hottest thing in the fashion industry right now."

I wonder what would happen to poor Tito next month when he was no longer the hype of the fashion world. He'd probably wind up at the pound or SPCA. Living creatures should probably be banned as fashion statements, because the instant they're outdated – badda-bing! – their ass is out on the street.

"Whatever you say, Landon," I shrugged. Landon's ringtone suddenly blasted 'Girls Just Wanna Have Fun' and he reached for the phone in his man-purse.

"Whoops, I'm getting a call," he shoved Tito into my arms. "Hold him while I take this."

"Uh, sure," I muttered. I held Tito away at arm's length to observe this alien life form at a safe distance. I'm no dog whisperer or anything, but I imagine my disgusted facial expression wasn't much of a comfort to him.

Landon pressed the phone to his chest and said, "I've got to take this, it's one of our delivery vendors from work. It may be awhile. Is that OK?" I nodded yes. "Take him for a walk or something, he loves the beach. The leash is in the bag."

Landon waltzed back to his car and I looked back at Tito. Great. "It's just you and me kid. I don't want any trouble, you hear?"

He blinked. I took this as a mutual agreement and held him a little closer. I grabbed the leash from his bag and held it with the other hand until we reached the sidewalk parallel to the sand. As I walked with Tito still in my arms, we took in the sights, sounds, and smells of our surroundings.

It was dark outside now and the streetlights were on. The local bars and restaurants were buzzing with loud, Bohemian music and laughter. The night was significantly cooler than the day, and there was a light, refreshing breeze blowing from the ocean, which carried with it the blended scent of salt and seaweed.

After a few minutes of walking alongside the beach, Tito became too squirmy to keep in my arms. I set Tito down on the ground and unraveled the leash from my other hand. Once I clasped the leash to his collar, Tito bolted in the opposing direction of Quella's with his leash taut to its furthest extension.

"Woah!" I shouted in shock as I allowed him to pull me rapidly down the sidewalk. Absolutely no idea what he was so eager to get to.

Quickly I discovered that Tito was an Olympic sprinter, and that I was desperately out of shape. Tito wound in and out of the side streets off the strip. We treaded further and further away from Quella's as he intertwined deeper into the slums of South Beach.

Generally, I felt pretty safe in South Beach, but that's not say there aren't some shady hangouts in the area. In assessing Tito's speed and focus he seemed bound and determined to investigate some creepy looking abandoned warehouse. I paused a moment to weigh my options: follow Tito into another dimension of the unknown, or return to Landon and wait another half hour for him to get off his business call. I figured Tito had a strong dislike for me from the get-go, so chances were that he was trying to lead me to an abandoned warehouse so that I could get chopped into tiny pieces by an ax murderer. No thanks!

"Tito! You must've lost your marbles if you think I'm going near that place. Come on. We're going back." I pulled on his leash and dragged him in the opposite direction. I rounded the corner of the neighboring building, dragging Tito behind me as he made heaving noises resisting the direction change. When we passed the garbage cans, I smacked into another person. A head-on collision. There was a booming sound, one that reminded me of a bowling ball obliterating a bowling pin. The two of us toppled over to the ground. By the time my brain had fully caught up to what just happened, I was yanked off the ground and shoved up against a wall. My feet dangled a good few inches off the ground, and by looking down, I discovered my unknown fear of heights. I dropped the leash in a moment of blind panic. Tito bolted in the direction of the warehouse.

"What do you want?" my voice accidently cracked of desperation. The hands dug deeper into my collar bone.

The man's voice was low and harsh, "Who are you?"

The light was dim, and I could barely make out his face, so I'm assuming he couldn't see mine too clearly either.

"N-N-Nicole D'Angelo." I gulped. Should I have even told him my real name? I was silently cursing myself to hell after I said it. I should have come up with a good false identity name. Like Ki Ki, or Penelope. Actually, I don't really know if I could get away with those names, but I'm sure that giving my actual name was a stupid move.

"Nicky?" The hands quickly lowered me to the ground. "What are you doing here? I-I'm sorry; I thought you were someone coming at us."

He gently touched my arm and I flinched away. "Nicky, it's me, Toni."

"And Juanita," Juanita grunted as she stood up from the ground.

"What in the world?" I huffed as I rubbed the sore place on my collar bone where Toni pinned me to the wall. "What are you guys doing out here?"

Toni flipped his flashlight on and my eyes squinted until they adjusted more to the light.

Juanita shifted her weight from foot to foot. She looked at the ground as she kicked a small pebble from the loose pavement.

"Chu see what had happened was... we was only tryin' to look into the missing tourist situation. We wanted to see if we could connect a link between the last abduction and the one from the girls at the hotel."

Toni interjected, "Something just doesn't feel right about this, Nicky. We had to at least see if there was a link."

"Didn't you both hear me when I specifically said not to interfere? You never listen. It's like you both secretly conspire all kinds of ways to raise my blood pressure by doing the exact opposite of what I ask you to do. What is it with you people?"

"You people?" Juanita raised a brow. "Are chu speaking about my Cuban peeps? Don't chu get racist on me."

"What? No! I was referring to you and Toni... you people. Don't try to pull out the racial card. That's not going to get you out of this one."

Juanita muttered something under her breath, but I ignored it.

"Well..." I tapped my foot on the ground like a mother scolding her kids for being out past curfew. "What are you doing skulking in the dark allies on this side of town? Listening for any street talk about two missing girls from Sunset Cove? Please enlighten me on what your game plan was exactly."

"Well Toni thought we should start at the scene of the crime, or at least where the girls were last spotted. From there we were going to scout a five mile radius from Chic."

"So you're trying to solve the first mystery from months ago in addition to the 'situation' that is supposedly occurring as we speak. If the police couldn't solve the case with all the resources they have backing up their investigations, what makes you think you would be able to solve it with your detective skills?"

"Well, we know about the most recent abduction in advance, so we can, at least, see if the security at Chic caught anything on the strangers last seen with the girls," said Juanita.

"Tell me, how do the girls look?" I asked. "Juanita heard two of the four talking by eavesdropping from the room over. So how are you going to be able to spot them on camera footage if you don't know what they look like? Not to mention, how do you think you're going to gain access to their security cameras? Tell me that, genius."

"Well...I know I was planning to bribe Chic's bouncers and security into letting me view the tapes from the night using only my killer smile and my seductive body." Juanita placed a hand on her hip and cradled her figure down to her thigh. " Toni, what was chur plan for spotting them on the tapes?" She asked innocently.

"What?" Toni sounded bewildered. "I thought you would at least be able to identify two of the four girls. You're the one who said we should look for them on the tapes. You mean you haven't even seen what they look like?"

I shook my head. "Well thought out plan, guys."

Toni shook his head. "Guess this was a bust." He kicked his duffle bag from the shadows in frustration. I looked quizzically at him. "Smoke bombs." He replied.

I still wasn't picturing how smoke bombs would play a part in the plan.

"In case Junaita's body failed at persuading security."

Mhmm. "There are so many flaws with your plan, I can't even take you two seriously. You may want to start by identifying the girls in question. We know what room the four are staying in, so if I were you I'd look into their time of check in and then review the security cameras at the hotel to see what they looked like."

Juanita and Toni's eyes lit up in excitement. Something that never crossed their minds, apparently.

"And instead of using Juanita's...body or smoke bombs as method of persuasion with Chic, I'd network. Use someone who could easily pull strings there. Someone like Vi, who is on the inside of the Miami nightlife. I'm sure she knows some crooked professionals there who would be willing to do her a favor."

"Can we have your sister's number?" Toni asked bringing out his phone.

"What?!" I shouted. "No, absolutely not. I said someone *like* Vi, not to actually get her involved. She doesn't need to be involved in any of this. She's my sister for crying out loud."

"But—" Toni, started.

"But, nothing. Shame on you for trying to drag my little sister into this. I still can't believe how recklessly you're both pursuing this little investigation of yours. You haven't even done your homework, and now you want to involve my sister in something that could lead to physical harm if there was any real connection with the abductions."

Juanita and Toni looked apologetically at their hands.

"Now, go home and stay away from Chic. We don't even know if the two girls came back this evening. This may have all been in vain. I have to take Tito back to Landon at—" I froze mid-sentence. "Oh my God. Tito!" I looked around. I dropped the leash and he ran off for that damn warehouse when I initially ran into Toni and Juanita.

"Who is Tito?" Juanita asked.

"Landon's dog. I took him for a mini walk and now he's run off. Ugh! I can't believe I let go of his leash."

"We'll help you find him." Toni offered. "This isn't particularly a safe part of town. I wouldn't want you wandering these streets by yourself."

"Of course. Did chu see where he took off?" Juanita asked looking around.

"He seemed especially interested in a dank, abandoned warehouse the block over. Maybe he went for it again?"

Toni picked up his bag and we hurriedly rushed toward the building. At the entrance I tried the front door. Locked, go figure.

"Well that's a good and bad sign, right?" I muttered. Good as in a locked door means Tito couldn't have gone in, but bad as in I have no idea where he ran off to. Landon is going to murder me.

Skirting the outer premises, I found a thick metal door propped open a few feet. Great…guess that means we should scout the inside a bit.

I pointed to the door. "Alright, you first big guy." Lightly I shoved Toni first.

"Oh, thanks Nicky."

"I'm a woman of tradition. And traditionally men put their lives at stake before endangering a woman." I plastered an innocent smile on my face.

As he entered the door he reached for his flashlight and switched it on. Scoping the general area I could see rusted pipes and cement walls wet with humidity. I had no doubt we were breathing black mold-infested air molecules. There were several piles near the outskirts of the open space where cement debris was collected hazardously in unbalanced mountains. This place had obviously been neglected for years.

I turned on the flashlight from my phone as did Juanita.

"Ok, we should probably split up to cover more ground," I suggested.

"What?" Juanita's eyes practically fell out of her head. "No, no, we should definitely not split up. Are chu kidding? That's exactly what the dumb blonde says in horror movies before she gets viciously murdered by an angry demon."

"Yeah, I don't care for that plan," Toni says cautiously while still scoping the layout of the warehouse.

"Ok, well Landon will be done with his call in a little while I'm sure, and if I don't have Tito by that time, you can already start planning funeral arrangements for me. I'm going to take the rooms under the stairs over there. You guys can cover this area together. Remember, Tito is basically a hairless rat, but for some reason has been categorized under the canine species. Call me if you find him."

I left the two and headed off in the direct of the stairs. The sooner we found Tito, the sooner we could get out of this gloomy, doomsday, horror-house scene.

When I reached the first room I found nothing but some grungy cans and buckets of unknown substances. I didn't see Tito anywhere, but I did see a few rats scatter along the edge of the room. An involuntary shiver ran the length of my body.

"Tito," I whispered at the entry of the other rooms. Nothing. The last door led to a small corridor with multiple rooms linked to the hallway. A subtle glow shined out the cracked door at the end.

Hmm...perhaps the abandoned warehouse was not so abandoned after all?

I slowly made my way toward the glow when my leg brushed against a furry object. I jumped back a few feet and held in an incredibly girlish squeak. My hands pressed to my mouth muffled the sound from echoing on the bare walls. When I shined my light on the object, I let out a sigh in relief.

"Tito," I half cried, half whispered. He was curled up against the wall shaking like a leaf, with his leash caught on a jagged rod protruding from the cracked cement wall. I untangled his leash and swooped him into my arms. "Poor baby."

When he was tucked in my arms, I hesitated. The door with the light tugged at my curiosity. Who could possibly be here in a place like this? I crept closer to the door in silence. My neck stretched out, I craned my head, so I could peek into the room through the cracked door.

A man with a blonde ponytail was facing away from me with several other men in the room. They were sitting around a table with the stench of cigars and filth seeping through the opening. Against my better instincts to turn and haul ass, I held my breath and listened closer.

"I'm not going to tell you again. The boss said no. So no is the final answer."

"And why would my partner and I want to go into business if we can't assure our product is being produced according to our standards."

"Because it's a lucrative business. There's no need to question something that's already generating as much income as it currently is. Either you want in on the deal with no strings, or you can walk."

"Will it ever be revealed? I understand wanting to protect the product, but surely there comes a point when we will gain full access to our portion of the business."

"Depends on what the boss man makes of you. He will let you know."

"Let me know? Humph," the man with the ponytail sounded frustrated. "And what about the boss himself? When will we get an audience with him directly?"

"He will let you know that, too, when you prove yourselves."

"After we introduce the next customer, we're meeting with Diego. Once I nail down this next client, I assure you he will prove to be a big source of income for your line of work. Trust me; I've worked with him for years. So after I land this deal, I'm demanding to meet the boss. No exceptions, or the deal is off, and I'll pull every client I've ever arranged with you."

"I can tell you this much, the boss doesn't take too kindly to threats, Mr. Jenkins, if that's what you're suggesting."

"I'm suggesting he extend the same professional courtesy as we've shown him throughout our arrangement. And—"

Suddenly my phone blasted the ringtone "Fashion" by Lady GaGa, which meant Landon was calling. The men immediately stopped talking and turned to glare in my general direction.

"Shit." I muttered under my breath and shot down the corridor in the direction of the exit.

I heard an assortment of shouting and shuffling feet heading toward the door. I held Tito tighter to my chest and pumped the air as forcefully as I could while I aimed for the opening. The voices and footsteps grew closer and closer until I felt a pair of hands snag the back of my shirt and snatch me backwards. I fell back against the cement floor and coughed as the air swept out of my lungs.

Instantly a bright light was turned to my face. "Well, well, well…what do we have here?" A low cool voice slipped through the darkness. "Did the mouse find its way into the cat's den on its own? This must be our lucky day, boys."

"Yeah, check out that figure." Another voice chuckled and reached for my hips. "She would be a lovely asset to my personal collection."

I swat his hands away and struggled to get off the floor. Another pair of hands pinned me down. I couldn't see any faces, but I noticed a particular skull tattoo encased in a heart on the inside of one wrist with the words "Love Kills" written in cursive beneath it.

"We don't know who she is," one voice cautioned. "Don't do anything stupid that could put everything in jeopardy."

"Yeah? And you think letting a snitch on the loose won't complicate things?" Another voice answered in a sharp tone. "Why don't you and your partner stick to your sales end of the business, and I'll handle my end. You may not be able to stomach much, but cleaning up the messy end of things is what I do best."

I struggled further and screamed, "I-I-I don't even know what you're talking about, I swear. I was just looking for my dog." I held up the leash to the blinding light. "Please," I started to sob. "Please just let me go."

One hand involuntarily made a trail down my curves, when another hand swept it away from my body.

"That's enough. I don't think she knows anything. We can keep an eye on her, and if she says a word about this to anyone we'll slit the throats of everyone in her family."

I trembled at the thought.

"Not good enough. Boss would want us to take care of it here and now. So I say we—"

Suddenly the sound of three metal cans connected with the concrete ground, and a cloud of gas dispersed across my already hindered line of vision. The hands released me, and I heard a slew of cursing and loud coughing. I closed my eyes and grab my last breath of air before I aimlessly tried for an escape route.

On hands and knees I crawled for a few yards and then climb to my feet. Met with a pair of warm hands, Toni whispers to follow his lead.

I scrambled alongside him and trusted that he was able to guide me through the smoky darkness. Tito whimpered as I pulled him with me. Poor thing. He'd never be acclimated to Aunt Nicky after this adventure.

When we reached the exit door, Toni shoved me in front of him and tossed his duffle bag over his shoulder. Juanita was already out the door ahead of us, barricading through the alley in attempts to flee the trouble we were running from.

"Keep running, Nicky. Do not slow down until I say we're clear."

"Where do we go?" I panted in between pants, my eyes still adjusting to the scene. "Do we go back to Quella's?"

"Yes, go and I'll meet you there." Toni took off in the other direction, toward the perimeter of the abandoned warehouse. You couldn't get me back in there if it were my last option to survive on Earth.

My body shivered in disgust. What were they going to do in there? Rape me then murder me? That guy was going to add me to his collection of women he'd raped? My heart raced with shock and adrenaline. I was so close to an irreversible catastrophe. I was in some serious danger back there…shit, I still am. Those guys wanted to kill me. Me!

The thought was haunting. If it wasn't for Toni's bag of smoke bombs, I don't think I would've made it out of there alive. Mental note: thank Toni when I next see him. Scratch that, praise him with gratitude and shower him with gifts next time I see him. He undoubtedly saved my life back there.

The thought made me wonder, when would I see Toni again? Why did he run back toward the warehouse? He wasn't going after them alone was he?

My head began to fill with worrisome thoughts and negative images of Toni getting caught and beaten up by those thugs. My phone rang. It was Landon calling yet again. I glanced at the distance and saw Quella's in view. I'd explain to him when I got there.

Finally, Juanita and I arrived at Quella's, bent over, panting and heaving as we tried to gulp in more oxygen. Landon skittered over to us with a look of perplexity.

"Oh my God, Nicky. Are you alright? I tried calling you several times and you didn't pick up. I was starting to get worried." When he witnessed the fear in my eyes, he added, "and maybe I was right to be worried…What happened?"

I glanced around in terror. After what the guys in there said about slitting my family's throats if I said anything, I didn't want to share the details in public.

"Not here." I breathed.

"Ok, honey. Not here. Let's get you home then."

"What about Toni?" Juanita added. "He's meeting us here, isn't he?"

I pulled out my phone and dialed Toni. Straight to voicemail.

Just then my phone lit up with his number; we must have been calling each other at the same time. "Oh, thank heavens," I answered with a half cry. "Are you ok? Where are you?"

"I'm on my way there now. Are you and Juanita ok?"

"Yes, we're fine. Where did you go?"

"I'll explain later."

"Well, I can't stand to be in public right now. I just, I just need to get back to the comfort of my own home. I think the shock is starting to wear off now. I have to get out of here." I started rubbing my thigh in nervousness.

"Do you have a ride home? I can take you."

"No, I've got a ride." I looked at Landon. "Landon, will you ride home with me tonight? I don't feel like being alone."

"Of course," Landon sweetly patted my back.

"Landon will see that I get home, OK. Can you make sure Juanita gets home safely?" I asked glancing over at Juanita.

"Let her know I'll be there to pick her up in a few minutes."

We got off the phone and Juanita was more than fine with the carpool arrangements. "Si, si. Go. I'll be fine. I was thinking about snatching a double chocolate chip ice cream cone to drown in while I wait anyways. Chocolate is good for the nerves. I'll see chu tomorrow morning?"

"Actually, I have tomorrow off since I'll be working a weekend shift. I'll stop by the hotel in the afternoon though. We will talk more then."

"When chu say 'we'll talk more then' does that mean I'll still be getting paid for the time we spend talking?" she innocently inquired.

I sighed. "Yes, Juanita."

"OK, OK. Good. I was just checking." She smiled and bounced away to the ice cream counter.

Landon popped the trunk of his car, and we both wiggled the moped inside. I rode shot gun while he calmly navigated through the streets of Miami until we arrived back at the house. On the way, I told Landon about Tito getting lost, running into Toni and Juanita, and then the entire warehouse scene. When we pulled up outside of my place, he helped me unload the moped from the car and then walked me inside.

"I'm staying the night." Landon threw his hands in the air as if that were the end of it. "There's no way I'm letting you sleep here alone. No way."

I attempted a smile. "You don't have to do that. Really."

"I don't feel comfortable with you being here alone…well, alone and with that obnoxious parrot. Do you still have some of your ex's sleeping clothes I could borrow?" He locked up the door behind him.

"Sure do." I pulled some out of my closet and gave them to him, so he could change real quickly. Meanwhile I swamped my attire for some overly baggy navy sweat pants and a yellow loose T-shirt. Somehow big, soft clothes made me feel more at ease.

I flipped on the TV and popped a bag of popcorn downstairs. Landon came barreling down the stairs and jumped onto the couch next to me. "Oh, I just love pajama parties! The only thing that would make this complete is a Sex in the City marathon."

"Pop open the drawer underneath the TV. We'll crack open the first season."

I smiled at him. At this, he jumped up with an excited squeal, and Tito leapt from the couch with him. His care-free silliness helped me to relax from the earlier sequence of events. I'd pick it apart with Juanita and Toni tomorrow. Tonight, I chose to be an ostrich with my head in the sand.

CHAPTER FIVE

The next morning, I woke up and put on a pot of coffee. Landon left a note on the couch; apparently he slipped out this morning while I was still asleep. Unlike me, he didn't have the day off.

While the coffee brewed I went upstairs and tossed on a pair of dark blue jeans and a green, loosely-fitted top. I dabbed on my makeup and flung my hair into a carefree bun on top of my head. Thank heavens I had the day off. With all of the chaos from yesterday and the continuous pressure at work to meet our numbers, I felt an irreversible outburst in the making. Last thing I needed was to have a conniption at work in front of all the employees and customers. Definitely would not be professional on my part.

I had an abundance of errands and chores to take care of as it was, so I decided to handle my not-so-fun grown up responsibilities first and then meet with Juanita and Toni at the hotel. I'm still unsure as to why Toni ran off in the opposite direction when we fled the warehouse. Landon and I left Quella's before he arrived to pick up Juanita, so I haven't even seen him since before he took off. On the phone he said he was fine, but knowing men and their macho bullshit, he could have been all beat up from his encounter with those thugs. That is if he even approached them directly.

While I drank my coffee and finished a bagel, I created a mental list of things to do. For starters, I needed to go to the grocery store and restock on food; my fridge was looking rather pathetic these days. Next door was a liquor store, so I might as well scoop up another bottle of Cuervo for Trixie while I'm there. Also, I needed to stop by Lowes to get the materials for the guest bedroom headboard. I've been putting off my do-it-yourself headboard project for too long. The guest room is nearly complete, just the headboard and a few knick knack decorative pieces are missing. I'm not sure if I'd necessarily start the project this afternoon, but purchasing the materials is a step in the right direction. I awarded brownie points to myself for that at least. After errands I would need to make a pit stop by the office to talk with Juanita and Toni this afternoon.

If I was lucky, maybe, just maybe, I'd also be able to squeeze in a little time at the beach to catch a few rays. That might be pushing my luck though.

I geared up Vi's moped and carted off to the local supermarket. Usually I would drive to a further supermarket since the one closest to my place was overpopulated most days. I swear it's more crowded than some of the clubs on Ocean Avenue. However, since I already had so much on my plate I didn't want to take an extra half hour out of my day.

Once I arrived at the market, all of the normal grocery carts were occupied. So I was left standing at the front of the store debating one of those mini grocery carts that you see five-year-old girls pushing around next to their mother's 'big girl cart' versus an automatic cart on wheels.

Unfortunately, an elderly lady with a turquoise cane was eye-balling the same cart, too. Her eyes shot daggers at me when she realized I was her competition. She may have looked more aggressive than me, but I was younger and probably faster.

We concurrently took a step toward the cart and both looked up to glare at one another.

The old one spoke, "The cart's mine, punk."

"Over my dead body, old lady."

"Who you calling old? Why I ought'a come over there and teach you some manners." She started hobbling toward the cart at what was probably her full speed.

I darkly chuckled and whizzed right past her. As I reached for the cart, the old lady smacked me in the back with her cane, and I arched away from the cart. Then she hooked her cane around my ankle and yanked hard so that I tripped, falling fast and mercilessly onto the concrete. I lie there on the floor, rubbing my head as she stepped over me and plopped onto the chair of the automatic cart.

"Old fart," I muttered under my breath, and she whacked me on the head with her cane again.

"What was that youngin'?" she squawked and simultaneously her dentures slid off of her gums.

I scrambled away so that I was at a safe distance from the crazed old bat and that deadly weapon of hers. Geez. She smacked that cane around like it was some kind a light sword from Star Wars or something. A whole new kind of crazy.

"That's right, spider monkey. You can't beat me. I'm quick. 'Quick feet,' they call me. Move like lightening." And that was the end of it. She wheeled off into the store, leaving skid marks on the tile.

I stood up and limped over to the little shopping basket for toddlers. I hunched over it, awkwardly, as I pushed the basket throughout the grocery store, collecting an assortment of groceries.

There, I saw her as I rounded the aisle of apple sauce and prune juice. Granny Quick Feet, herself.

I retreated and scurried around the corner onto the cleaning supply aisle that smelled of rubber and Lysol. Busy listening for the dreaded sound of the automatic motor, I crept backwards, further and further down the aisle until the sound disappeared into the distance.

"Phew," I sighed as I straightened up.

"Hiding from someone?" A cool voice muttered from behind me.

I whirled around in a combination of fear and nerves nearly back handing the man in the process. It would have been a five star bitch slap, but he gripped my arm at warp speed. Ninja quick.

"Sorry!" I gulped. "What are you doing here?" I asked sounding surprised.

I guess I was shocked to see Rafael Mancini, our frequent customer at the hotel, here in the local grocery store. The gorgeous gray-eyed, Italian model-looking one? Yeah, him.

His facial expression was smooth as silk when he answered, "Just collecting a few things I forgot to pack." He cocked his head to the side in amusement as he took in my mini-sized shopping cart. "Got your big-girl cart today?"

I blushed and moved on to the next topic. When I glanced down at his basket I found travel-sized toiletries, some snacks, and headphones. I grabbed the headphones from the basket.

"Forgot your headphones?" I raised a brow. "That must have made for one long plane ride."

He grinned, and his smile was painfully sexy. Did I mention I'm a sucker for smiles? Well, his was incredibly seductive. It made me want to toss him against the wall and strip off all of his clothes here in public. Tempting, tempting.

"Who are you telling? I almost snatched a pair from the little boy sitting next to me on the flight. It's not like he needed them as much." He teased and slid the earphone packet out of my hands.

I relaxed an ounce, but that was about as much as I could bear standing next to him. His mere dominating and intoxicating presence sent waves of uneasiness through me. The tingly, happy kind of uneasiness.

This kind of thinking was dangerous territory. I had to get it together. Quickly, I fished around for another topic, "Well, Mr. Mancini—"

"I'm surprised to find that you remembered my name out of all the customers you have."

I blushed. "Born with a good memory I guess."

CAUGHT! I'm undoubtedly crushing on the guy, and if he didn't know it before by my word-fumbling, palm-sweating, jittery behavior, then he certainly knows now. His gaze made me shift uneasily.

"I see that. But please, call me Ralf."

"Oh, Ralf. Well, how are you enjoying Miami so far?" I decided to redirect the conversation with travel. Travel talk and the weather are always a safe bet.

"If it wasn't in the nineties, I'd be able to enjoy it a little more. This is mostly a business trip, though, so I'm cooped up inside most of the day anyways."

"That's a shame. You don't plan on visiting the beach or Ocean Avenue?" He sounded a bit like a stiff. Who comes to Miami and skips completely over the nightlife?

"I would, but we generally start work early and end late. I'm usually wiped out by the end of the night. Surely you must understand; I have yet to see a day when you aren't busying around the hotel, except for this morning, I guess."

"Actually I'm going back to check on things at the hotel once I finish a few errands. However, I do intend to get some beach time in today." Maybe. Hopefully. God-willing.

"I'm going that way too after I get a few more things. Would you like a ride?" He offered.

I contemplated having him drive me back to my place, showing him around, popping open a bottle of wine and mysteriously leading him upstairs to my bedroom, but then I had a moment of clarity which ruined that idea.

"Thanks, but I have a ride, and I need to drop some stuff off at my house first before I go over. Well, if you get the chance for some free time, you should make your way to the beach. Sunset Cove happens to have a killer view. And who knows, I might even see you out there later this evening for the sunset. That is, if I ever get through my to-do list in time."

He shifted his weight as a gesture to let me pass. "Well by all means, don't let me get in the way of your time at the beach. I wouldn't want to miss the opportunity to see you again later today." Ralf strolled down the aisle and turned toward me to smile. "Hope to see you down by the water."

Oh my. If I didn't know any better, I'd say it sounded like Ralf Mancini actually wanted to see me later tonight. It was an unofficial understanding that now we were both expected to be there at the beach outside the hotel. That means I'd have to do the head to toe primping to look decent before our off-the-record date-ish-thing. Whatever it was.

Knowing this, I hurried through my to-do list, focused on saving enough time to get ready for seeing him again. I can't believe he caught me looking like this, with my hair in a messy bun and pushing around a child-sized grocery cart. Not the impression I wanted to make. Although on the other hand, it must have still made a good enough impression if he wanted to see me again. I could feel my stomach doing cartwheels at the thought of him wanting to see little 'ol me.

I finished collecting my groceries, scanning the aisles in an attempt to avoid the old lady on wheels. When I was all checked out, I stopped next door at the liquor store and bought another bottle of Cuervo for Trixie. The ride back to my house was interesting, balancing shopping bags on the handle bars and looping the bag of Cuervo over one knee. By the time I reached the front of my house, my leg was quivering with exhaustion. This was yet another sign I should hit the gym.

When I entered the front door, I found the booze hound, Trixie, erratically squawking again. Instantly, I replenished her booze and cleaned out the lining of her cage. "You do realize your drinking habits are burning a hole in my wallet, right?" I mumbled to the bird. She tilted her head to the side and then returned to her tequila bowl.

I stashed away the rest of the groceries and then went to Lowes down the street for the DIY project. Instead of discovering a creative way for balancing two stud boards, six boards, bags of bolts and washers, and wood stain paint buckets on a moped, I decided to hail a cab for convenience sake.

At Lowes, I picked through the aisles and added the necessities to my cart. The entire time I questioned why I did these DIY projects to myself. They are always a lot more work and a lot more expensive than it initially seems.

While in the store I got the impression that some of the customers weren't used to seeing women in the store or something because I kept getting creepy stares, like I was a creature from outer space and they were trying to figure out what planet I came from. Or maybe it wasn't so much all the customers as one in particular.

I grabbed the bag of washers from the shelf and quickly turned to peek over my shoulder, from where I could feel a stare radiating. A short man sporting a red shirt and a black goatee was staring at me from between a gap the row over. When our eyes met, he pulled out of sight.

Who the hell was that guy, and what was his deal? My gut wrenched in uncertainty and then in panic when I thought of last night. One of the guys at the warehouse said they could have me followed and kill me or my family if I spoke a word about that night to anyone. Is that guy one of their thug friends? Are they having me followed?

Surely not. We lost those losers in the warehouse. There's no way they caught up to me. No one followed us to Quella's.

When I calmly rationalized the situation, I felt more certain that I was letting my paranoia get the best of me. Obviously I was still shaken up from yesterday, and now my imagination was running wild.

For the remainder of the time in Lowes I didn't see the man in the red shirt, though I thought I felt a heavy gaze from time to time. After the rep finished ringing me up, I hobbled outside with all my materials and called a cab. I was back home in a matter of minutes and simply unloaded the items in the hall closet. That's enough progress on the project to satisfy my quota for the month.

I snagged a tote from my closet and shoved my makeup, black bikini, hair utensils, and beach cover up into it. The time said I still had several hours before I should make my casual appearance on the beach. If I went to the hotel early to meet with Juanita and Toni first, we'd still have time to put together our thoughts about the warehouse thugs and missing girls' events. Afterwards, I could hop in a vacant room and do some much needed primping before Ralf. The thought of Ralf seeing me in my teeny tiny bikini made my face drop in fear. But then the thought of seeing Ralf down to his swim trunks was enough to make my smile reappear.

All packed and ready to go, I locked up the house and rushed to Sunset Cove. Still dressed in my casual attire, the front desk representatives didn't move an inch when I wandered up to the counter. Rose was busy filing her claws while chomping away on a piece of bubble gum. Valerie was too absorbed with texting on her phone that she couldn't chance taking a break and addressing the person at the counter. I folded my arms and leaned closer to the counter. Not a damn change.

"Excuse me." I growled in a voice I didn't know I had.

Both heads shot up with eyes wide in shock. Rose immediately placed the nail file down, and Valerie pulled her phone behind the counter and tried to conceal the text message she was still typing.

"Seriously, Val?" I shot her an annoyed look. "I'm not your high school teacher. I can actually tell when you're still texting on your phone."

At this the phone dropped to the desk behind the counter, and her full attention was on me.

"Now, I don't consider myself a mean boss or anything." I paused waiting for them to jump in. Crickets. "Do you think I'm a mean boss? If you know what's good for you, you'll be careful how you answer that."

"Oh, yes! Yes, I think you're a great boss." Rose plastered on a smile.

Val chimed in, "Like the best!"

I already knew this was an inauthentic response, but I didn't object.

"And being the nice boss that I am, I don't expect you to completely power down your phones or stand at attention for the duration of your shifts. As Front Desk Reps, I merely want you to address the customers as they approach the counters, answer the phone lines, handle customer service complaints, that kind of thing. If it just so happens that the phones aren't ringing and there is no one at the desk, then absolutely you can check your phone or file your nails. That's not a concern. What is a concern is when I walk up to the counter and have to literally wait for minutes before you'll even acknowledge my existence."

Rose nodded in agreement. "You're right. I'm sorry I didn't realize it was you standing there."

"That's just it, though. It doesn't matter if it's me or a random customer or a delivery boy. Your job is to interact and assist with the customers. You are their first go-to person. If they have a problem, who do you think they're going to call?"

"Ghostbusters!" Juanita interrupted as she slid over. The girls looked quizzically at Juanita in confusion. "Oh my God. Val, Rose, please don't tell me chu don't know Ghostbusters?!"

They shook their heads in curiosity.

"Ay, ay, ay. These youngins have no culture." She waved them off.

"You just dated yourself, Juanita. I hate to break it to you, but we're getting old."

"Ay! Don't chu say things like that. We will never get old." She shook her head in denial. "Chu ready to have that chat we talked about yesterday?"

"Yeah, I'll meet you at the bar in just a minute." Juanita nodded in agreement and pivoted toward the bar.

I shook my head and returned to my down-to-business face. "Now, where was I?"

Val added, "You were saying we need to pay attention to the customers and be more service oriented."

My brows shot up in surprise. That was it in a nutshell. I'll say. I was shocked they were actually listening. "Yes, exactly. I don't want to have this talk again. Do you understand what is expected of you?"

"Yes ma'am." they both said in unison.

"Good. Thank you. I'll see you both tomorrow. Enjoy your evening," I said before I ventured to the bar.

Juanita was already plopped on a bar chair with her legs outstretched ahead of her because she was too short for the chair. She was slurping down a frozen margarita. "Want one?" she asked and offered her straw.

"No thanks, I think I'll have Toni make up a new concoction. The last one he created was called Danger Zone, and it was incredible. Although, it totally knocked me on my ass."

"Toni's not here." she said in between long slurps.

I froze a few heartbeats. "Wait a minute. What do you mean he's not here? He was scheduled to work today."

Juanita shrugged not really concerned about anything other than her alcohol. It seemed as though she hadn't grasped the concept of just what this could mean.

"Why didn't he come in today?" I asked trying to pry information out of a steel tight vault. She was being so detached.

"I don't know."

The way Juanita chugged her frozen drink made me want a frozen strawberry daiquiri mixed with a pina colada. I gave Jackie my orde,r and Juanita tacked on a second margarita to the order, too. She was going to be intoxicated for the remainder of her shift; I could already see it.

"Oh wait, Jackie! Do you know why Toni didn't show up today?" I asked before she bounced to the kitchen.

Jackie leaned onto the counter, chomping her bubblegum and chuckled. "No, he didn't even bother to ask me to cover his shift, either. Apparently, he didn't show up at all. I'm waiting for him to text me back, but I figure he's trying to articulate the right words to beg for my forgiveness." She straightened up from the counter and continued toward the kitchen.

"So what happened last night when Toni showed up? Did he elaborate any on what he was doing?" I asked.

"Chu know Toni. He's not going to talk about things he doesn't want to talk about. I asked him where he went and what he saw, but he just said he ran down the neighboring street and tried to divert them so they wouldn't catch onto us. Some kind of distraction ploy."

"So they saw Toni?" I asked. "I mean they know what he looks like?" My heart was pounding in my chest, worried they would track him down.

"I don't know, Señora. He kind of shut down after that, so I didn't push him anymore."

"Well, when he picked you up, did he look any different than usual?" I pried, in attempt to find out if he was wounded or hurt by the thugs from his little distraction number.

"Mmmm, I don't think so. He looked the same to me." She thought hard. "But I guess it was dark in the car, so I'm not really sure. I didn't notice anything."

"I want to know what happened with him back there. Maybe I should give him a call real quick?" I pulled out my phone and dialed his cell. The phone went straight to voicemail. Odd. I left a brief message asking him to call me back, so we could talk.

"He's probably playing hooky and recouping in bed, Señora," Juanita patted my back comfortingly. "Don't think too much into it. We can talk to him when he comes in tomorrow."

I nodded in agreement. "First things first. We need to check the video cameras to identify the group of girls and the two missing friends. As discussed last night, we need to put a face and a name to them if we're going to investigate this any further."

"Si, of course." Juanita nodded in all seriousness. "I'll pull up the check-in history at the front for their room number and get the time and dates of their check-in. I'll pull the cardholder name from the credit card, too."

"Great. I'll be in the back room where we can access the camera records. I'll get it queued and meet you there when you're done." I snatched my drink off the counter and headed toward the back. I stopped, "Oh, and Juanita? Don't mention any of this to the other staff. Including the front desk reps. Just tell them something about me needing the information for a billing request."

"Chu got it." Juanita pointed a finger at me like a gun and threw in a wink.

I hurried to the back room and unlocked the sectioned-off, caged area with the master key. There were several monitor screens displaying various locations throughout the hotel: the front entrance, back entrance, pool patio, bar area, front desk, and elevators. There was one unoccupied monitor reserved for playing back the history of the recordings. I used this to review the recording from earlier this week.

Juanita arrived with a mini notepad and pencil behind her ear. She was out of breath and panting as though she'd just finished a half marathon.

"Phew!" She bent over with her hands on her knees. "We need to have one of those mini golf carts for the ground floor. Chu know how far that is to run from the front desk all the way to here? Dios Mio." She handed the notepad to me, and I reviewed the chicken scribble.

"What is this?" I handed it back to her. "I can't read any of this. Just tell me the date and time frame I need to skip to."

She stared at the page. "It looks just fine to me. Chu are just being fussy now. It says they arrived four days ago. Check in time was at 4:18 PM."

I skipped back accordingly on the front desk camera. When everything was aligned with the proper timing, the four girls appeared at the counter with their luggage. "There we go." I stopped the tape. "These are our girls." I sat back and studied their faces. "If only we knew their names."

"I can tell chu the girl with the black hair in pigtails is the girl with the credit card on file. Her name is Nancy Jennings. We don't have record of the other chicas though. Maybe we should go to their room and ask?"

"And just what reason would we give them for asking?" I raised an eyebrow. "That would be so suspicious."

"Chu're right. I don't know how else we'd get their names, though."

"We could give them a free breakfast coupon and say their room was randomly picked. We could request their names for the coupon distribution. You know, I think we still have a few of them in my office."

"Aha...so chu are the one who's been hoarding all those coupons. I haven't had a free breakfast here for months." She hesitated after she said this.

"I'm not surprised you've been using the guest coupons to your own benefit. And I also wouldn't be surprised if my stash went missing after today." I rolled my eyes knowing I'd have to move them to a new location after Juanita saw their secret location.

"Let's go get their names. We can stop by my office on the way."

I locked up the caged area behind us and ambled to my office. In my desk drawer, I found four breakfast coupons. Quickly I scooped up the mini notepad and pen laying on my desk to take down their names.

Juanita and I rushed to the elevator and took a short trip to their floor.

"This is the room." Juanita pointed at the door and then scooted back from the door with her arms behind her back.

A few sturdy knocks on the door. "I need to speak with Nancy Jennings. This is Nicole D'Angelo, the hotel manager."

A slew of giggling followed by a hissed hushing noise came from the other side of the door. "Coming!" A voice shouted out.

Nancy swung the door wide open. She was sporting the low pigtails again and was dressed in cut off shorts and a pink bikini top. "Hello, I'm Nancy." She smiled somewhat nervously.

"Hi Nancy, it's nice to meet you. I'm Nicole, the hotel manager here at Sunset Cove. How are you today?" I displayed my well-polished managerial smile.

"I'm fine," she glanced around nervously. "Are we in trouble or something? Were we being too loud?"

I chuckled, "No, not at all. Actually I wanted to let you and the other guests staying in the room know you were randomly selected for a free breakfast coupon here at the hotel. We have a drawing every so often, and your room was picked."

"Ooo, sweet! I've never won anything before. Are you sure I didn't win a free convertible car?" she gleamed.

"Nancy, don't push your luck. She just said we all get a free meal, and I'm down for whatever will keep more money in my pocket." Another girl interrupted as she made her way to the door. "Hi! I'm Elane. Please forgive Nancy, here. She's new to the whole broke, college student lifestyle and hasn't quite learned how to be grateful when a crumb is thrown her way."

I smiled. They seemed in high spirits for losing their friends a few days ago. I wonder what's changed from the time Juanita overheard them. "Been there, done that. All part of the college experience." I pulled out the four coupons and handed them to Elane and Nancy. "So we will just need the names of everyone in the room so we can put it in our system to ensure you aren't charged at check out. Nancy Jennings," I pointed to Nancy. "And Elane…" I paused waiting for a last name.

"Connor." Elane added before she turned around to the room. "Get your lazy bums up here and get your free meal coupon. If you don't want it, I could just take them for myself."

I'm sure my face looked more than shocked when I saw two more girls rise from their beds and make their way to the front door. Elane and Nancy moved to the side and distributed their coupons.

"We're not lazy; it's just been a long night." one girl rubbed her eyes groggily.

"A long night? I see you were able to make it out on the town to enjoy some of Miami's night scene?" I winked. Usually I'm not this nosey, but I couldn't figure out what was going on here. The two missing girls suddenly reappeared? Just like that?

"Oh, Jessica and Elle had a long night indeed. The night before, these two decide to ditch us at the club, and the next evening they wandered in doing the walk of shame." Elane shook her head still in disbelief with the two. "Must have had themselves a hell of a time considering they didn't even pick up the phone to tell us they were alive!"

Jessica and Elle simultaneously squinted their eyes. "Oh, brother. Enough with the yelling already. We've got killer headaches today. We already apologized."

Elane muttered something under her breath, "That's what you get for trying X."

The girls looked up in fear that I'd heard her remark, but I pretended that I didn't catch that last part. "OK, now I just need both of your names, and you all will be able to use the coupons whenever as long as it is during our breakfast hours from seven to ten."

"Jessica Halls and Elle Wendale." Nancy answered. "Thanks for the coupons. Let me know if you reconsider that convertible as the prize instead."

"Thanks ladies. I hope you enjoy and call down at the desk if you need anything. There should be a few water bottles in the fridge and Advil packets next to the fresh toiletries if those headaches persist. Enjoy!"

The girls waved goodbye, and I pulled Juanita over to the elevators. Once we were inside there was a group of customers so we held our tongues until we reached the seclusion of my office.

"What…in…the…world?!" I shouted.

Juanita rubbed her hands together nervously. "I know this looks bad, but I promise, I heard what I heard that night. Two of the girls were missing."

"Yes, I know they were missing, but as evidenced by our recent encounter, all of the girls are back in the same place. This is exactly why we don't butt into our customers' business. You invented this whole story based on a conversation that you eavesdropped on, and came to a wrong conclusion based on paranoia." I tossed my hands in the air as I paced back and forth in my office.

"Ok, but they really did go missing. I didn't get that part wrong." She raised her index finger in the air. "Where's my credit?"

"Yes, and remember when you told me that I said to what?"

"Give it more time."

"Exactly. And I said this in case of what?"

"In case it was just a one night stand situation."

"Which it clearly was. Damnit, Juanita. I can feel my ulcers getting ulcers about what it would mean if two girls actually went missing from our hotel. Can you imagine what this would do to our business?" I vented.

"What? If anything it would put our name in the news, right? Even bad publicity is good publicity." she shrugged.

I couldn't go into detail about our financial state and the chance that staff members would be let go, so I just shook my head. "No, Juanita. It would be very bad for the hotel and very bad for me. Just stop." I waved her off in exhaust. "Stop butting into our customers' lives and stop dragging people into it. It only does more damage than good."

I lifted my bag onto the desk and sighed. "You can leave now."

Juanita hung her head low and nearly whispered, "I'm sorry, Señora. I won't butt in anymore." She scooted out of the office and closed the door behind her.

This job was making me old real quick. It was a matter of months before I'd sprout my first gray hair. I was sure of it.

I crumpled my list of names from the notepad and tossed the wadded ball toward the trashcan. It missed and landed in the back corner behind the filing cabinet.

"Of course!" I grumbled in annoyance. Nothing seemed to go right when you needed it. I stood up to go for the wad when I noticed my appearance in the mirror. Geez, I needed to get ready for my unofficial beach date with Ralf. I could not meet up with him looking like this.

I turned back around, opened my bag of essentials, and went to town on my hair and makeup. Once finished my hair was down in beach-styled waves. I went for a natural look with my makeup. The kind where you'd create a soft glow that most men mistook as being makeup-less, but women knew otherwise. I shimmied into my black bikini and threw on my cover up which was a sheer yellow, high-low dress. I kicked my bag to the corner of my office and only took my phone, towel, sandals, and gold rimmed Aviators.

When I had made my way out to the beach there was still a decent amount of afternoon sun before it would be ready to set. A vacant beach chair laid on the beach near the water and on the outskirts of Sunset Cove's property. I settled down into the lounge chair and reclined the back, so it was almost lying horizontal. Just as I closed my eyes beneath my shades my ringtone went off. I answered in a somewhat dream-like voice as I welcomed the warmth of the sun.

"Nicky? Hey, it's Vi. What are you doing?"

"I'm catching some rays at the beach. What do you want?"

"Well, for starters, I'd like my moped back. I said you could borrow it for one night and you still haven't returned it yet."

"Right. I'm sorry. Mind if I keep it for the rest of the week? I'm contemplating buying one. It's so much cheaper than a car, and it gets me from point A to point B."

"See, I sold my car with that exact idea in mind."

Yeah right, she sold her car with a designer dress in mind, but whatever helps her sleep at night.

"OK, but just until the end of the week. Care if I join you at the beach then? I've been scratching to check out the newest meat in town." Such a horn dog.

"Fine with me." I paused remembering Ralf. "Well, for a couple hours, but I'm expecting someone later on. As long as you're gone by then. I don't care."

"Please!" she laughed. "It doesn't take me that long to pick up a babe."

She hung up the phone, and I chuckled to myself. The girl does work fast.

CHAPTER SIX

Vi lowered her Gucci sunglasses and her eyes trailed after a man like a drooling dog would follow a piece of bacon.

"My God, look at the buns on that one." she sucked on her bottom lip.

"Really Vi, have you no shame? I'm sure men don't find that kind of talk appealing." I settled further into my chair, enjoying my free time of baking in the warm sun. I suppose in Miami, 'warm weather' doesn't exist, but we locals have grown accustomed to the blistering heat. It was around ninety degrees or so now, and that's considered pretty mild around here.

"Oh please! Are you kidding? They love that kind of talk," Vi sneered.

A one-on-one conversation with her always resembled a one-on-one sex ed class, in which she was the teacher and I was the student. Vi had an extensive knowledge base on sex and relationships equivalent to Hugh Hefner's knowledge base on Playboy bunnies.

It was a little pathetic on my half. I mean, I'm her older sister, and she's giving me dating advice the majority of the time.

"Seriously," Vi continued, "guys eat up that kind of dirty talk. You should especially try it in bed sometime. It propels their ego and they work that much harder because of it."

"That's not the only thing that's harder because of it," I snorted and chuckled to myself.

Vi's lip curled up as she stared at me annoyingly.

"Well, maybe the kind of guys you go after like that," I suggested. "However, I want a man who isn't looking for a short-lived, spicy kind of…fling." I didn't have the heart to say one night stand, so I decided on the term 'fling'. It's not that I think my sister is a whore or anything, just very, very, sexually active.

"Please," she waved it off, "those are the best kind. No strings attached. No drama. None of the bullshit."

"I can see your angle, but what about marriage? I know you're still young, but I'm looking for something more serious and I surely won't get there with various flings. I need something more mature if I plan to settle down." I wiped a droplet of sweat from my brow, the sun still baking my skin.

She bobbed her head. "True, but my question is why would you want to get married in the first place? I read in an article one time—" She glared at me from above her sunglasses, no doubt in response to my shocked expression. "Yes, I read. Don't tell anyone though, it may ruin my reputation. Anyways, the article said that of the three top stressors in a person's life, first is death of a loved one, second is a divorce, and third is marriage. You might as well avoid all three heartaches and enjoy the single life instead."

Hmm. Touché.

She dug around in her pink and white striped beach bag until she pulled out her makeup mirror. Quickly, she dabbed on some powder and smoothly applied a coral-tinted lip gloss, which complimented her flawless tanned skin. She eyed the same man who walked by a moment ago, perked up her boobs in her white bathing suit and smirked.

"Don't worry about me being here when your little friend arrives. I think I've found my next victim." She winked, and then, she was off. Just like that. I envied the bitch.

She left her pink bag, so I figured she'd left to lay a foundation down. Once she reeled him in, she'd be back to scoop up her things. I dug out her iPod from the beach bag and plugged in the ear buds. I scrolled through the tunes and decided on old school Janet Jackson, blasting it on blow-out-your-eardrums-loud. I hummed along to the music and soaked up every moment of my sliver of peace and relaxation.

Approximately eight minutes later, I was roasting. There was a steady flow of sweat dripping from the dip of my back and between my breasts. I tried to fan my body with one of Vi's Cosmopolitan magazines, aka her Bible, but it wasn't doing the trick. Since I was somewhat afraid that she would catch me misusing her sacred magazine and give me hell for it, I placed it back in her bag.

I reached in her bag for a water bottle. The water's temperature was on its way to boiling by this point because it had been left in the sun for too long. So instead, I decided to cool off by jumping into the water. There were plenty of tourists and surfer dudes out bobbing in the ocean. Of course, many of the tourists hung close to the baby waves, while the locals tended to meander further out toward the big waves.

I dipped a toe into the water, and it felt surprisingly cool. Perfect. Without purpose, I ambled out into the water, past the collection of broken seashells that collectively settled at the beginning of the shoreline and beyond the baby waves that crashed just below my knees.

The water was surprisingly shallow, so I had to trudge through the water for what felt like forever. Finally, when I was far enough out, I completely melted into the water, dipping my already burned shoulders beneath the surface and tilting my head back so all my hair was soaking wet. I guess Ralf wouldn't get to see my hairdo pre-water damage, but I didn't care at this point because the water just felt too incredible.

Mmm, the coolness was so refreshing. Like many of the locals around here do, I surpassed all the tourists and was so far out, I could barely touch the sand anymore. I forced my feet up to the top of the water and floated. Here I lounged on the ocean's surface, soaking up sun beams all the while enjoying the cool smoothness of the waves.

I was relaxed and drifting away from all worries and stress when I felt it. Little droplets of water splashed my face. Even with my eyes closed, I could feel that the sun was still blazing brightly in the sky. I raised my hands and smeared the water off my face and the droplets ceased.

Suddenly, a large whoosh of water practically brushed over my body, and I struggled to cough up the salty sea water. When I opened my eyes, I saw Ralf's stunning gray eyes shining back at me. A beaming grin was sprawled across his face and his large muscular body towered over me as he sat comfortably on a surf board.

When I was finished choking up a lung or two, I turned to him and slit my eyes. "Ralf!" I sounded as surprised as I felt. Take it down a notch, Nicole. "Ahem. Um, what are you doing here?"

"Looks like we both had the same idea to get out here a little early and catch some waves."

"Yeah, though I just like to float on the waves." I gestured toward his board. "I had no idea you surfed?"

Ralf paddled toward me, and I lapped an arm across the surf board for support.

He playfully knocked on his board and then lazily leaned back on his elbows so I could see his incredibly sculpted abs. Goddamn!

"Just for fun when I get the chance. I don't have access to the beach back home, and usually I'm too busy on these trips to squeeze in some surf time. But yeah, I used to surf way back when I was young and in shape."

"As evidenced by your six-pack there, you are so clearly not in shape anymore." I rolled my eyes.

He smirked. "I just meant that I can't surf like I used to. Do you ever surf?"

"That's a negative. I have never been able to stand up on a board without falling in less than two seconds. I'm good to stick with body floating." I raised my feet to the surface of the water as an example.

"That does take skill." he teased. "How long have you been out here? Looks like you've already got a bit of a sunburn going on across your shoulders, Toots." He ran a hand gently across my shoulders as he tilted his head to the side to get a better look.

Tingles ran the length of my body despite his gentleness. The butterflies in my stomach went berserk, and a slow burn of yearning began to tug around the edges.

What is wrong with me? I need to get some action before I jumped on the next testosterone-pumping male I laid eyes on. I melted like pudding from no more than his soft touch? For God's sake, girl, pull yourself together. You are an embarrassment!

"Yeah, I've been cooped up inside too long." I tried to casually pull away from his hands and free float next to him as I lightly treaded water. "Now I kind of get burned easily. You know, I have to build up my tolerance again, I suppose."

"Guess we should get you out and about more. It's good to come to the surface every once in a while and join society." He lifted his hands behind his head and threw a wink at me. "Oh, I know your type, Nicole D'Angelo. You've got 'work-a-holic' written all over you. I'm taking you out after the sunset. Re-introduce you to this little thing we like to call 'fun.'"

His angle allowed me a full shot of his brilliantly tanned body. Without thinking, my gaze slowly travel up his body, beyond a, um, ahem—bulging piece of merchandise—to his rippling six-pack abs.

My eyes traced further upwards (yes, I'm sure I was near drooling) and peeked at his sculpted chest and nicely toned shoulders. "Delish," I slipped up.

Ralf grinned, "What was that?"

"I said 'Swedish fish'." Clearly my lying skills are impeccable. "So tell me, what kind of plans would a visitor have in mind for a local? I'm curious to see which spot you'll take me to have 'fun' that I haven't already been to."

"Oh, I've got a few ideas for tonight. It all depends on you." His face lit up with a devilish grin.

"On me? OK, let me know my options, and I'll choose."

"No, I mean it all depends on what I think you'll be game for. I'm still gauging your sense of adventure. Sorry, you'll just have to wait until tonight. I wouldn't want to give away the surprise or anything." He lowered himself on his back so that he faced the sky on his board. In the process of shifting around, I couldn't help from noticing how every muscle moved in sync with one another.

Now, I can safely say I've never been much of a fan in learning about human science, but right about now I was definitely interested in studying his anatomy.

I shook my head, trying to shake the thought loose. Get your mind out of the gutter, Nicole!

"In your observations, have you learned that I'm not a fan of surprises?"

"I don't find that hard to believe. And no, I'm still not going to tell you where." He chuckled, "You really need to loosen up and live a little. A little spontaneity never killed anyone."

I huffed in defeat, "Well I at least need to know what I should wear tonight. I presume we're not going in swimwear."

"I'm not objecting to the view," he threw a playful wink at me.

My face grew warm, and I knew I was blushing. Oooo, he likes my body!

"Don't worry. I'll be sure to steer you in the right direction as far as outfit selections go."

As we lazily floated on the water, I peered up at the sky and noticed the sky was starting to darken. The sun had not set yet, but it was well on its way.

"Ready to head in?" I asked. "My fingers are getting all pruney from the water, and more importantly it's getting close to shark feeding time."

"Agreed. Here, hold on to the board, and I'll paddle us in."

I gripped the board and started kicking my feet to help move us along. Once we arrived at the shore, Ralf headed toward the left to collect his towel and belongings. I returned to my beach chair. I noticed Vi's belongings had vanished. There was a folded note pinned to my towel. I opened it and Vi's handwriting read:

Don't wait up for me. ;)
By the way, who's the hunk? Hubba Hubba!
-Vi

I rolled my eyes as I crumpled the note. I wrapped my towel around my shoulders and dried off. My hair was lifeless, I imagined, as it was still sopping wet from the ocean. This wasn't quite the naturalistic look I was hoping to go for.

The sea breeze kicked in and although it wasn't cold outside, the combination of the wind, setting sun, and wet skin was enough to send a chilled shiver down my body. I wrung out my hair and dabbed it with my towel.

I was in the middle of shimmying into my yellow cover up dress, arms outstretched above my head when I felt a warm pair of hands skim over my stomach and lightly tug the bottom of the dress down. When my head popped through the top I found Ralf helping me pull the dress into place.

The act of him dressing me was as sensual as the act of him undressing me would be. A strap from my dress slid off my shoulder and ever-so-slowly he guided it back to place. It felt exceptionally intimate, the way his gentle hand barely skimmed across my skin.

My trance-like gaze followed the trail of his hand before I glanced up to meet his eyes. Intoxicated with lust my eyes weighed heavy with desire. How could a touch so simple melt me into butter?

His hand lingered on my shoulder, and I tentatively leaned closer toward him. As I reached for his cheek to invite him in for a kiss, his phone went off. I instantly dropped my hand and pulled back to my personal bubble. He cursed under his breath in annoyance as he looked at the phone. "I'm sorry, it's work. I need to take this real quick."

"Of course," I waved in agreement. Ralf stood up and answered the phone in a somewhat perturbed tone. He trudged through the sand to a distance out of earshot. I rolled my towel over my arms and walked down the beach, filtering the soft sand between my toes.

Ralf trotted over and placed a hand at the small of my back. "Sorry about that. Our business clients lose their mind if you take off for an afternoon."

"Yes, I know how that goes. Does that mean you won't be able to go out this evening?"

"What?" He sounded shocked. "No, it means I'll have to re-introduce them to the concept that we have personal lives outside of work. Just you and me tonight."

"You still haven't given me a clue yet." I playfully nudged him with my shoulder.

"Right. Well, as far as clothing goes, you should wear something that's comfortable. Where we're going doesn't call for fancy attire. Does that help?"

I squinted my eyes trying to think of what he had planned. I was happy about the not squeezing into a skin tight dress, but what exactly did he have in store for us? "Fine, but I need to stop home and take a shower first. I can't go the rest of the evening covered in dried ocean water."

"Same here," he nodded in agreement. While we were walking, the sun hovered a few moments longer before it disappeared out of sight. Seeing as I was preoccupied with Ralf next to me, I can't say I caught much of the sunset.

"Well, I'm going to go home and get cleaned up. What time do I need to be ready by?" I asked.

"Let's meet back up in thirty minutes?"

I baulked at him. "I'm going to need a little more primp time than thirty minutes. Plus, I have a bit of drive time to and from. What about two hours?"

"Two hours?!" He threw his head back in exaggeration. "We aren't going to the opera for heaven's sake. It's casual attire, remember?"

"Oh, you have no idea the lengths we women go through to look like we do." I squeezed his cheeks. "An hour is the best I can do, and that's with you picking me up."

"That I can do." He smiled back. He took my phone and entered his number in my contacts list. "Just send me your address, and I'll be there in an hour."

After I texted my address, he walked me back to the hotel. We parted at the lobby, and I calmly strolled to the exit before kicking up the gear to turbo speed once I was out of sight. "An hour?" I half whimpered to myself as I zipped off on the moped. There's positively no way!

When I arrived home, I hurried inside desperate to hop into a shower. My feet and legs were still sandy from the beach and I felt an uncomfortable accumulation of sand in my bathing suit bottoms. I'm certain I somewhat resembled a baby with a load in their britches.

The first thing to do is take a shower. Ugh, I'll probably be washing my hair for days trying to get all the sand out of it. This is exactly why—

I stopped mid-thought, mid-step, mid-breath.

I looked around me. I was downstairs. But something was different... something was off.

Everything looked in its place, but rather it was the smell. I sniffed the air more intensely. Ick, it smelled grotesquely of...hot sauce and... and... fried chicken? Heavens, I haven't had fried chicken since college when my old roommate practically shoveled it down my throat by pure force.

I silently dropped my things and tiptoed around the corner of my living room ducking out of sight of the kitchen. I felt like the three bears and Goldilocks. Someone's been cooking in my house.

But does that really happen? I mean, who on Earth raids other people's kitchens while they're gone? And who had the audacity to make a batch of some awful smelling fried food? The odor was enough to gag a maggot.

Listening closely, I waited for some kind of clue. Then I heard it. The unmistakable sound of a country twang. It was ear piercing, and yet it was music to my ears.

"I got a six pack, got a single stem rose. My baby's dressed up she's raring to go. I got a Jones for the moon and the jukebox. I like to two-step, she likes to rock. That clock on the wall it rings, it chimes. It's beeeeeeer thirty, a honky tonk time!"

"Emily Pickens!" I shouted in a pretense Texan accent. "I do believe your singing has gotten worst since I've last seen you, as if that could be possible."

She pivoted on her heel and accidentally thwarted a piece of greased chicken across the room. Fortunate for me, I've kept my quick reflexes in her proximity due to her unfailing, accident-prone tendencies. I was able to dodge the flying chicken. The chicken hit the wall behind me and skidded to the floor leaving a visible slimy residue.

And to think, people eat that stuff.

Emily pressed her free hand to her chest and sighed before she took her earphones out.

Emily lingered just shy of six feet. She had wavy auburn hair, deep blue eyes, and the slightest hint of a tan. She was a gorgeous Southern belle, in particular, a Texan, as I have been corrected in the past. She is truly your stereotypical, loveable, Southern country gal. We were college roommates, and I distinctly remember her undying love for country music, soul food, cowboy boots, and two-stepping. She was as sharp as a tack and yet she most certainly had her ditzy moments.

"Whoopsie!" She squirmed as she ran to pick up the piece of chicken off the floor.

"What were you, dare I say, singing?"

She giggled. "You don't remember that song? I'll give you a hint: we used to listen to the band almost every night."

"Correction: you used to listen to it every night. I was simply being punished in the process. Is it that Dirt Betsy or Books and Drums people?"

"Oh, good Lord." Emily rolled her eyes. "It's pronounced Dierks Bentley and Brooks and Dunn. For Pete's sake, Nicky." She glanced around. "I'm just glad you didn't say that in public. What would people think?"

I glanced down at her outfit which consisted of a large night shirt and brown cowboy boots. Yes...what would people think?

I ran over to her and exchanged a big hug. It's been years since I've seen her and yet here she is, the same as ever, cooking fried chicken in her cowgirl boots just as she did back in our college days.

"So what's the occasion?" I asked. "And although I'm thrilled to see you instead of a burglar, I'm still wondering how the hell you got in here?"

"What? Do I have to have a hidden ulterior motive to visit my old college friend?" she shrugged.

I looked at her accusingly.

"OK, OK, so maybe in addition to me wanting to see you, 'cause of course that was my number one priority, I mighta run into a bit of trouble with my ex."

I sighed. "Aren't there any good men in Texas?"

I clearly remember her asshole boyfriends running over her, taking advantage of her humbleness and good nature. She would come to me when things turned out badly, and I would always be there for her. We've sort of seen each other through hard times, and neither distance nor time would change that.

Her eyes welded up with tears, "No, there sure ain't." Her bottom lip drew into a pout, and I knew what was coming next.

"I'm sensing a Bitch Session coming on" I predicted. Then I glanced at the clock, but time was not on my side. "And you already know I want to hear all about whatever stupid thing was done by that son of a bitch."

"You forgot punk ass. By that punk ass son-of-a-bitch," she corrected.

"Yes, of course. That's what I meant. But I have plans for tonight, and I have less than an hour to get ready."

"Not a problem. I'll just finish cookin' my chicken. You know nothin' quite heals the soul like some good ol' fashion comfort food," she winked. "When I'm done cookin' I'll help with your hair."

I debated her bouffant hair styling, which would undoubtedly be the fate of my hair but agreed when I acknowledged there was no way I'd be ready by my deadline with only one pair of hands. "Great! We can catch up a bit then too."

Quickly I rushed up the stairs, hopped in and out of the shower in record time. Wrapped in a luscious bath towel, I sat at my bathroom mirror and blew dry my hair. It was a cloud of frizz, but at least it was to a point where Emily would be able to work on it with the iron. Just as I was turning on the iron Emily knocked at the door.

"Come in!" I yelled. "Are you sure you're going to be able to tame this in the next twenty minutes? I need to put my makeup on."

"Honey. How quickly you forget. Eighteen beauty pageants under my belt, I think I can handle a little hair waving. Now you want those Susie Q curls I'm so good at or you want somethin' with a little more spunk to it?"

"No!" I shouted in horror remembering the last time I let her style Susie Q curls. "Ahem, I mean no curls. Just a very soft wave to it. I want it to be very simple."

"That can be arranged." She picked up the iron and started working on my hair while I started my makeup. "So what is it you're getting ready for?"

"Oh, you know. Just a date." I tried to shrug nonchalantly.

"A date?!" She perked in interest. "What's his name? How does he look? What's he do? Where is he from?"

"Slow down with the interrogation. The date was kind of spur of the moment. His name is Ralf Mancini."

"Mancini? Sounds Italian. I like so far. Does he have the three T's?"

"Tall, tan, and toned. Check, check, and check!" I laughed. "And he sets my skin on fire. He's got that kind of touch where you just know he's amazing in bed."

"Oh?" Emily wiggled her eyebrows in excitement. "Well what have ya'll done so far? Everything but?"

"No," I padded my face with bronzer. "Actually, we haven't even kissed yet."

"Come again?" Emily stopped styling my hair to stare at me through the mirror. "You haven't even kissed, and you jump to the conclusion that he's a God in the sack?"

I motioned for her to keep working and she resumed with the iron. "I know, but I can just tell these things. The way he's touched me, even though it was PG rated, it was electrically charged with sexual tension."

"Or maybe you're just charged with too much sexual tension," she muttered.

I dismissed her remark. "And the way his body moves in perfect synchronization with his suave composure. Not to mention I've seen him half naked. Legit. He has the whole package."

"Now that sounds interesting. Go back to the half-naked part." Emily was eyeballing me suspiciously. "You know you caught my attention there."

I finished dabbing on my eye makeup. "We were at the beach earlier today. So we were both in bathing suits. Like I said, PG rated."

"Shucks." Emily snapped her fingers in disappointment. "I'm goin' to need you to hop to it, girl! Live it up for those of us sworn off the dating world. I need someone I can live through vicariously."

Emily finished my last strand, and I fluttered to my closet. "He said something casual and comfortable," I muttered to myself combing through the hangers. A pair of whitewash denim cut-offs caught my eye.

A toothpick was twirling around Emily's mouth. "Those are cute. The more important question is what are you gunna do in the way of lingerie? I'm thinkin' you should go with a pair of lace trimmed cheekies and a matching bra."

I pulled open my drawer and found a royal blue lace set. "Good thinking." I slipped into both underneath my towel and then discarded the towel on the floor. I shimmied into the shorts I was eyeballing before and stood helplessly browsing for a casual top.

A minute later Emily shouted in triumph. "Aha! What about this top?" She handed me a loose gray, off the shoulder top fit exactly with the look I was shooting for. After I pulled the shirt on I browsed my shoe collection and found a pair of thin strapped charcoal sandals. Perfect.

"Now for some jewelry." I tapped my finger on my lip and heard the doorbell. My eyes met Emily's wide with fear. "I'm not ready yet!"

"You keep lookin' for your accessories, and I'll keep him occupied downstairs. Don't fret. Any man worth his weight knows he'll be kept a few minutes before a gal's ready for a date. You just take your time." Emily tottered down the stairs and invited Ralf in. I couldn't make out what they were saying, but I did hear two sets of voices.

Quickly I decided on a thin, delicate silver chain with a single blue stone at the bottom. I buttoned on a tan leather bracelet and was satisfied with my outfit. Before I ran downstairs, I brushed my teeth and gargled some mouth wash for extremely minty scent.

When I had collected myself and centered my nerves, I descended the stairs with as much composure as I could manage. I found Emily shinning off her pistol with the barrel aimed in Ralf's direction. Ralf's eyebrows were a little further north than usual, but he continued with Emily's discussion about deer hunting techniques.

"Um, what's going on?" I asked with a worried tone.

"Oh, I was just showing ol' Ralf little Mrs. Ball-Clipper, here, and we got side tracked on huntin' stories." She smiled innocently at me, and I knew what she was doing.

"That's right, she named her gun Mrs. Ball-Clipper." Ralf stood and slid in my direction away from the barrel. "Quite an interesting story on how that came to be."

I sighed and headed toward the front door. "If you ask me, I'd say Emily herself is an interesting story. Sorry for the wait. You ready to go?"

"More than you know," Ralf followed behind me.

"Bye now! Don't keep my girl out too late, you hear?" Emily waved goodbye. That girl was a hot mess. We severely had to have a conversation about refraining from bringing Mrs. Ball-Clipper out in front of guests. She was trying to give him the old passive aggressive scare routine, and let him know that any harm done to her friend can be also be done to him.

I locked up the house, and he opened the passenger car door for me. I slid onto the smooth leather seats and secretly admired the sweet ride. When he hopped in and revved the engine it purred like a kitten.

"Nice wheels," I lifted a brow.

"I've got a soft spot for BMWs." he shrugged. "Besides, it's just a rental when I'm in town. My ride back home has a little more of the sporty flare to it."

"Oh," I hesitated. I decided not to mention the neon moped I was currently borrowing from my little sister, as desirable as that sounded.

"So, your roomie back there," he stared at me.

"Former roomie, from college," I corrected. "She's a friend unexpectedly visiting from out of town. I know…she may be little over-protective about her friends, but that's only the first time she meets you or if she doesn't like you."

"I see," he scratched his chin as we pulled away from the house. "And how do I know if she liked me or not?"

"She didn't take you outback and 'accidently' discharge a shot next to your feet."

"Lucky me." His grip tightened on the wheel.

"So are you going to tell me where we're going now?" I pleaded. "The suspense is killing me here."

"I'm certified in CPR. If it kills you, I'll bring you back to life."

I shook my head in resignation. "As you wish."

Ralf switched on some soothing music as he maneuvered through the streets. Shockingly he didn't rely on his GPS to navigate us to where I guessed was a bar of some sort. The wheels suddenly changed friction as we drove from pavement to condensed sand. The car slid a little here and there, but, in general, the car kept its grip. When we reached the softer sand, he drew to a stop and peeked at me. "We're here."

I surveyed the scenery from the window but couldn't make out much of our surroundings. I was certain we were on sand by the tug of the drive. "I don't want to be a party pooper or anything, but if I just spent all this time cleaning off the beach to get all sandy again, I'm not going to be happy about it."

He laughed as he exited the car. A heartbeat later he opened my door and extended a hand to me. "Oh, come on, Nicole, spontaneity, remember?"

"Yeah, yeah, yeah." I grumbled as I took his hand to get out of the car. "YOLO and all that jazz."

"Exactly. You only live once." He popped the truck and handed me two thick blankets. Once he lifted up the big basket, he closed the trunk and headed toward the sound of the waves. I could make out wooden fence posts spaced about a foot apart and the neighboring fields of wild grass.

A few yellow flashes dispersed throughout the fields and I stopped in my tracks. "Do you see that?" I asked in uncertainty. "There, those lights?"

I could hear the smile in his voice. "Yes, I see them too. You're not hallucinating."

"But aren't those..." I struggled for the name of it that was so far back in my childhood memories.

"Fireflies," he sounded amused. "What about them?"

I closed my mouth in shock. "I haven't seen fireflies for as long as I've lived in Florida. The last time I remember seeing them was up North. Didn't even know there were any down this way."

"Interesting. I guess I picked a good spot then," he continued through the sand.

"Speaking of, where are we? I don't think I've ever been to this beach before."

"Now will you look at that? I, the visitor, showed a local a whole new part of town. I should've placed money on that bet." He chuckled and set the basket down next to a piece of drift wood.

"I'd hardly say this is a part of town. Beaches don't count."

"You like to make up the rules as you go, huh? Either way I'm sure we'll manage some fun." He pulled out a metal can and started pouring some liquid on the collected pile of wood. "Take a few steps back for me, will you?"

I did as he said and he lit a match and threw it on the pile. The fire took thrill in the gasoline and instantly created a mini bonfire. Ralf laid the two blankets on the ground with the drift wood positioned to support our backs.

"Do you like red or white?" he asked holding a bottle in each hand.

"Definitely white."

"Typical," he smirked. Once he opened the bottle he handed it to me and then looked around the inside of the basket. "Whoops. Looks like I forgot the glasses. I knew I was missing something."

I shrugged. "I personally think it's just as sophisticated for us to drink straight from the bottle. No?" As a demonstration, I took a chug from the bottle and plopped down on the blanket.

"Keeping it classy."

He opened his bottle and clinked our bottles together for cheers. "To good company," I suggested. At that we drank a few mouthfuls worth before I peered into the basket of unknown goodies.

"What else you got in here?" I leaned over and pried into the basket. He didn't answer me so I glanced over my shoulder and found him obliviously admiring the clear shot of my backside, I snapped him back to attention.

"Ralf!" I teasingly tisked in disappointment. "Here I was thinking you were such a gentleman. And then I catch you shamelessly checking out my ass." I sat back on my heels and eyed him as I took a few more slugs of my wine.

"A gentleman is still a man. I only snuck a peek. I didn't try to touch, now did I?" He pulled his hands back in innocence.

I didn't get all dolled up for looks. If I had it my way he would have initiated the touching. The booze was already making me feel giddier than my typical self. I could feel my playful side peeping through.

I leaned forward and pulled some of the items out of the basket. "What do we have here? A bag of marshmallows, chocolate bars, graham crackers. Uh-oh," I wiggled my eyebrows in anticipation. "S'more time! How did you know about the secret love affair I have with chocolate?"

"Toots, I hate to break it to you, but I think everyone has a secret love affair with chocolate."

He leaned forward and snatched two long sticks from the basket. I pulled open the bag of marshmallows and he held the sticks steady as I pressed the marshmallows into place. After I broke open the packages for the chocolate bars and graham crackers, I placed my stick of marshmallow over the fire. We both continued to drink our wine, and when I felt the lightness of my bottle, I looked down and noticed it was more than half empty. I'd need to get some more food in my stomach fast if I was to drink so much so quickly, or I'd be more toasted than our marshmallows.

I tried to position mine over the fire so that it would speed along the cooking. I desperately needed to get something of substance in my belly; I could already feel the drunkenness creeping on. "The last time I had s'mores," I shook my head trying to remember, "had to be when I was a kid. It had to be well over a decade." When the marshmallow caught fire, I screamed in surprise.

Ralf reeled it back in and slowly blew on it until the fire went out. He raised a brow. "Clearly, it's been a while since you've done this. Rule number one to achieving the perfectly golden marshmallow is to be patient. And by patient, I mean not shoving it into the pit of the fire. That's exactly how you achieve the less desirable, charred marshmallow." He pulled in his marshmallows and exhibited the perfectly golden ones so that I could appreciate their flawlessness.

"Alright, golden boy. I get it." I sniffed my burnt ones and curled back my lip in repugnance.

Suddenly Ralf swapped our sticks so that I was holding the perfect ones and he was holding my…not so perfect ones.

"I can't have you eating that. Take mine." He assembled the graham crackers and chocolate bar around the marshmallows so quickly I didn't have time to protest.

I smiled at him as he obliviously proceeded to make his own burnt s'more sandwich. What a thoughtful guy. I know it's over something as small as a burnt marshmallow, but I haven't seen such consideration from a man in a long time. Bonus points.

"Kudos on the wine and dessert bonfire date tonight, Ralf." I nodded my head in admiration. "I can honestly say I am surprised."

"Surprised you're enjoying yourself tonight? Or surprised that I had a good idea for this evening?"

"Not surprised I'm enjoying myself." I lifted the bottle for another swig and found the bottle empty. Oops! "Surprised by your idea. I have never been on a date like this before. Points for originality."

"Good. I'm glad you like. I'm having a good time here with you too."

We continued talking and laughing as we ate our s'mores next to the bonfire. I'm not sure how he did it, but somehow I felt the excitement of butterflies swarming my stomach. At the same time, I felt inexplicably comfortable lying there with him. I can't explain the two conflicting feelings, but it just felt right.

Ralf had already finished his second s'more, and since I had another bite of mine left, I offered it to him. His brows shot up in pretend excitement. "You mean I get to have a bite of the perfectly toasted s'more?"

I laughed and angled it toward his mouth to feed it to him. He opened his mouth, and I started to bring it to his lips. As he closed his eyes, I couldn't resist the opportunity so completely mine for the taking. I smashed the melty contents all over his mouth and cheeks and his eyes flew open in surprise.

"You little troublemaker!"

He lifted off his elbow, and I burst into a fit of giggles. Quickly I stood from the blanket and took off running along the soft sands of the beach in his opposite direction.

"You smear the perfectly good s'more I gave to you in my face, and now you run away? Oh I hope you can run like lightning woman because when I catch up to you…"

"That's if you catch up to me," I teased. Just then I tripped and fell to my knees in the sand.

"That would be karma," he chuckled as he caught up to me. Playfully he wrestled me to the ground, so I was lying on my back. He was positioned over me on his elbows.

I stared back at him and swiftly licked a piece of the s'more I smashed on his cheek. "Yum," I giggled.

"Yeah, thanks for that." He shook his head. I reached up with a free hand and wiped away most of the s'more. All except a little residue on his lower lip.

My hand steadily lowered from his face and fell to his chest. Our breathing grew into slow, concentrated breaths. My eyelids began to close, and I leaned inward toward him.

Ever so shyly, I moved closer and closer to his mouth, afraid of making the wrong move. A few inches away I paused. I knew myself well enough to know that if I took the next baby step it could very well lead to a whole different level.

I wanted him in the way that every bone, muscle, and nerve in my body ached for him with a relentless yearning. I turned off my inner thinking and just fully tuned into my physical wants. Fuck it. I'm grown.

Finally I closed the gap between us and sucked the s'more remnants off his bottom lip. His full, luscious bottom lip. With this he reciprocated the kiss and relaxed his posture so that he was laying on me. His strong hands crept up my arms, one placed around my shoulder, and the other ran gently through my hair.

The kiss deepened, and I swear fireworks were going off somewhere beyond my eyelids. I wrapped a smooth leg around his side and swapped places so that I was on top of him.

"Interesting," Ralf muttered between kisses. I could feel his lips shaped into a smile. "I should've known you prefer to be on top. The control freak that you are."

"Control freak?" I pulled away, withholding my kisses. He just chuckled and refused to further elaborate.

I grabbed his shirt and pulled him forward so that we were both in a sitting position. We were facing each other, with my legs wrapped around him and his legs angled around me. I hesitated and then slid my hands along his neck, then his jaw, then his ears, then…his body made an involuntary moan.

"Oh…" I titled my head to the side. "You got a soft spot, do you?" I ran my fingers back over his ears, and his body trembled. "That's good to know."

I skimmed my swollen lips to his ear and sucked on his lobe before I teasingly nipped his ear. With this he jerked my hips toward his and showered me with feverish kisses. Clearly his soft spot had a direct line to his downstairs level.

Suddenly his phone went off and we both jumped from the vibration coming out of his front pocket. He licked his lips and shook his head while I combed through my hair with my fingers to collect ourselves. Ralf looked at the phone and rolled his eyes. He declined the call and placed the phone back in his pocket.

"Who is calling you this late?" I asked with a little more defensiveness than planned. Only another woman would be calling him this time of night.

"Work. Again." He grunted. "I already told them once that I'm unavailable tonight."

"Are you sure it's not serious?" I asked.

"No, they just—" The phone interrupted him. "Damnit. Let me take this real quick," he mumbled in aggravation.

"Sure, take your time," I waved him off. I needed to collect myself anyways. Cool down a minute or two. I mean goodness, I was about to jump his bones on our first date. I didn't even know anything about him. Except that he's mighty fine. And sweet. And thoughtful. And adventurous. And he makes me laugh. And he's a damn good kisser.

Phew! Reved back up again. So much for the cool down.

Ralf stomped back, clearly upset. He extended a hand to me, and I used it to propel off the ground. "It turns out this is pretty serious. We just had a major issue with the client, and I'm afraid I'll need to get back to do some damage control. I'm sorry, Nicole. Looks like I'm going to have to cut tonight short."

"I hope everything is OK?" I asked.

He sighed and ran his hand through his hair. "I'll know more once I get back to assess the damage."

"OK, sure. Let's pack up the car." I held his arm on the way back to the campfire, and then we tagged teamed picking up the contents from our bonfire picnic. He smothered the mini fire and led the way back to the car.

We drove back to my place, nearly in silence. I could sense that he was in a mood about work. How annoying it must be for him to dedicate as much of his time to work where he can't even take off an afternoon while visiting Miami.

This brought me to another, darker thought. He was technically visiting Miami. Although he's still a regular and frequently visits the city every other week or so for business, I'm still going googley eyes for someone that doesn't even live in the same city. Ugh. I much rather enjoyed living with my head in the clouds, though it was very short lived. Long distance never works. Why was I even doing this to myself?

When we arrived at my house he parked the car and opened my door for me. I slid out of the car, and he closed the door firmly behind me.

"Thank you for tonight, Ralf. I really did have a wonderful time." I leaned in for a peck on the cheek. His warm hands were rested on my lower back when he tugged me back in for a real kiss.

"What I wouldn't give to have left my phone in the car tonight." he sighed. "I'll call you later?"

"Sure," I smiled, still uneasy about my earlier train of thought. "Goodnight."

He watched me to make sure I got inside OK and then took off toward the hotel. On the inside of the house, I leaned against the front door and sighed. Oh boy, I'm in trouble.

CHAPTER SEVEN

When I rounded the corner of the entry way, I found Emily bundled up on the couch, fried chicken leg in hand, watching G.I. Jane on the flat screen.

"I just love this movie." Emily peeked up at me with a devilish smile. "It's such a kick-ass, independent-woman type of movie. Makes me feel like I could do one handed push-ups right now if I wanted to."

"Easy there, tiger." I strolled to the kitchen and snatched a pint of chocolate chip cookie dough from the freezer. "You wouldn't have happened to bust out the old woman power flicks because of your recent break up, would you?"

I handed her an extra spoon, and we both took turns picking at the ice cream. Emily blushed a little and then smiled. "They always help me in these times. It helps me make a clean break from an ex and keep moving forward with my life."

I nodded. "And what happened with your ex exactly?" I asked. "Jonathon, right? Last I heard you both were about to move in together."

Emily more forcefully dug her spoon into the ice cream. "Ugh, Johnny." She rolled her eyes in disgust. "I can't believe I was ever going to live under the same roof with that sorry sack o' bones."

"What happened exactly?"

"I came home and found him testing out the springs in my mattress with another woman! That's what happened." Emily unconsciously snagged the ice cream from me and hastened her speed of scooping out the ice cream. I decided not to try getting one last scoopful. I didn't want to risk losing a finger.

"Oh, Emily. I'm sorry." I gently patted her on the back. "How long was it going on for?" I asked.

"A couple of months." She shook her head. "I was completely caught off guard. You know how some people say they had a feeling they were having an affair, or when they say things were so rocky that they knew something wasn't right? Well, I had no clue whatsoever. I thought things were moving along fine and that we were doing great until I busted in on him and Medusa."

"Medusa? You mean someone actually named their daughter after the mythical creature with serpents in place of hair?"

"Well, no. Her name isn't actually Medusa. I just call her that because she had an uncontrollable mane of bed hair when I met her. Plus she's the spawn of Satan." She shoveled another spoonful into her mouth and continued. "Her real name is Kelsey."

"Oh. Well if she is in fact the spawn of Satan, then I guess it's a good thing she ended up with such an asshole. I know it sounds cliché, but in reality you're much better off without a guy like that."

"Yeah, good riddance," she huffed. "Glad I found out before we signed a lease together. I just needed to get away for a while, put a little distance and time between us to get some perspective."

I nodded. "I'm glad you decided to come here. You know you're always welcome in my house." Triggering a new thought, I asked, "So just how long are you planning to stay here?"

"Oh you know, just for a little while. I didn't exactly put a time frame on it." She changed the subject, "Hey, how did your date go tonight? Woooweee! He was hotter than Aunt Katrina's homemade seven peppered hot sauce. Hot damn!"

My face lit up with excitement as I folded my legs under myself and thoroughly explained every detail of the night. She looked just as smitten as I'm sure I looked by the end of date breakdown.

"Honey, you've got yourself a winner there. I'm glad my gun speech kept him on his best behavior."

"Your gun speech almost prevented the whole date from happening. He thought you were crazy."

"Hell, I am half crazed by now after all these failures in the dating scene. Johnny was the last straw. I swear I'm turning to knitting. I'm finished with men for good. Done. Done. Done!"

"Something tells me your knitting replacement won't be near as satisfying as men. Give it some time, and the jadedness will start to fade," I offered.

"We'll see about that." She emptied the ice cream container and plopped it on the table. "Oh, I'm sorry...did you want some of this?"

"No, no. I'm good," I lied. "I'm going to call it a night, or I won't be able to function tomorrow at work. Are you already settled into the guest room?"

"Yep. I'm just going to finish watching my movie, and then I'll head to bed too."

"What's on your agenda for tomorrow?"

"Oh, I'll probably spend some time at the beach. Get a little relaxing in. Do you want me to make us something for dinner tomorrow? I've got all the time in the world."

"Yeah, dinner would be great. Make anything you'd like...except for fried chicken." I sighed. "Must be nice to be on vacation. I can't remember the last time I took off from work."

"You see, I'm not exactly on vacation."

"No?" My eyebrows shot up in surprise until I remembered her line of work. "Oh, you're journaling from the road? I am looking forward to your next piece."

"Actually, I quit. Seeing Johnny every day in our office meetings and holding back this strong urge to wrap my hands around his neck was just too much. Anyways, I'm just having a mini break while I'm between jobs."

"I see," I murmured, considering what this would mean for me and the vacancy of my guest room. "And how long is this mini break for?"

"Oh, you know. Just a little while is all," she waved it off nonchalantly. "I'll let you know what's on the menu tomorrow once I have it lined up. Go get to bed. We can shoot the shit more tomorrow."

"OK. G'night, Emily." I wandered upstairs and hopped in a quick shower to get all of the sand off. Once out, I dried off, slipped into a loose T-shirt and boy shorts, and jumped into bed.

It felt as though my alarm went off as soon as my head hit the pillow. I must have been exhausted if I didn't remember having any dreams. Promptly, I dressed for work in a gray pencil skirt, button down blouse, and black peep-toe pumps. My makeup was fully applied, and my hair was styled in voluptuous waves. I felt like a million bucks.

When I flitted down the stairs, I remembered the booze hound, and decided to fill up Trixie's cup with tequila before it ran dry and the squawking began. After I fixed a bagel for breakfast, I wandered out the front door and puttered off to work on the moped.

I found myself singing 'It's a Beautiful Morning' and practically skipping through the lobby. Juanita was in the corner watering the plants when her frumpy expression switched to a curious one.

"Well, well, well. What have we here?" She shimmied toward me with her hand on her hip. "Chu are looking very happy this morning."

"I woke up on the right side of the bed, I guess." I stretched out my arms in delight.

"Oh?" She wiggled her brows. "And who woke up on the left side of the bed? Mhmm…I could tell a man caused all this." She gestured her finger in my direction.

"No." A gigantic smile involuntarily spread across my face. "No one else slept in my bed."

"Chu're right. A smile that big didn't get there from just sleeping all night. Spill the juice, Señora. Who is he? What's he look like? I would ask if he's any good in bed, but judging by your face, I can see that's a yes."

"We didn't do the deed, Juanita. I just had a spectacular time last night on our date."

"Mhmm, and who is this mystery guy?" Her eyes were wide with excitement.

I glanced around and noticed a few bystanders were within earshot. "Come with me to my office."

We both scurried to the office, and I waited until we were behind closed doors before I busted out with, "Remember Ralf Mancini?"

Juanita shook her head. "The name doesn't ring a whistle."

"It's ring a bell." I corrected. "You blow a whistle and you ring a bell."

"It doesn't blow a whistle," she attempted to correct herself.

"Anyways," I brushed it off. "Ralf Mancini. He's the customer that stays with us every other week. He's always in Miami on business." I paused seeing that she still wasn't making a connection. "The gorgeous tall Italian with gray eyes?"

"Ah, si! Yes, with the squeezable ass?" She looked impressed. "Chu two went out on a date?"

"Sure did," I smiled with smug delight. "And he kisses just as delicious as he looks. My God, Juanita, this man sets me on fire. The only thing preventing me from jumping his bones last night was the fact that his job called him about some emergency."

"Saved by the whistle," Juanita shook her head.

"Saved by the bell," I put my head between my hands, exasperated.

She rolled her eyes. "When's the next date?"

"We didn't schedule it yet. Is that bad?" I wondered aloud. I haven't been on many second dates seeing as I usually kick the losers to the curb after the first one.

"Are chu asking dating advice from me?"

"Yeah. You're right. Your husband's in jail." I leaned back in my chair and stretched my hands above my head. "I'm not going to over-analyze it. I like it here on Cloud Nine, so I'm going to revel in the feeling for a while longer."

Juanita tapped the desk, and she stood up from her chair. "I'm so glad everything is going so well for chu, Señora. I was starting to see the worry lines in chur face about work, chur family, chur love life…or there lack of."

I nodded at her unintentional reverse compliment. "Thanks, Juanita. I'm glad things are going smoothly, too."

With that she headed toward the door. "I had better be getting back to work. Plants to water, rooms to turnover, more Mary Jane to find." I baulked at her. "I kid, I kid!" She tucked out of the office, and I stifled a groan.

Once Juanita left, I revved up my computer and dove into work. I needed to rotate staff schedules this week and initiate the auto-generated notifications for their change in shifts. An e-mail pinged with the inventory report for the kitchen and bar records with items that needed to be purchased on the next order. I noticed the message was sent by Jackie who has never been responsible for the report.

I picked up the phone and dialed the kitchen.

"Hello?"

"Hey Jackie, it's Nicole. Just saw the inventory report you sent."

"Yeah, did I send it right? Usually Toni sends it in, so this was my first time taking records. Let me know if I used the wrong format or something?" She sounded nervous, but I wasn't concerned with the report itself.

"Oh, yeah. Sure, it looks fine. I was calling because I wasn't aware anyone else filled out the report. I'm used to Toni sending it in. Anyways, can you put Toni on the line? I need to speak with him."

"That's why I sent it in. We need some items in soon since they're dwindling down pretty quickly. I decided to conduct inventory by myself since Toni didn't show up for work today."

"He didn't?" I breathed absentmindedly.

"Nope, so I'm stuck here covering his shift yet again. Seriously, two days in a row? He's going to owe me big next time I want to play hooky."

Last I remembered calling Toni and leaving a voicemail the day after the warehouse incident to see what happened. I checked my phone, no missed calls or messages from him. An uneasy feeling grew in the pit of my stomach.

"Did Toni call you to let you know he'd be out today?"

"No, Ramona from the kitchen called me when he hadn't arrived as scheduled. She's been trying to get ahold of him, but he must be dodging her calls. I can't blame him. I'd be scared of the verbal lashing she'd bestow on me, too, if I left her high and dry at work."

"I see," I muttered. "Thanks, Jackie. I'll try Toni's cell, too. That doesn't sound like him. I'll put in your order, so it's delivered with the next shipment."

"Great! Call back if you need anything." We disconnected.

I tried Toni's phone and got his voicemail again. "Uh, Toni. Where are you? I haven't heard back from you and I'm starting to get worried. Jackie says you didn't even call in to work today. You just pulled a no show? Call me back ASAP!"

I followed up with a text as well to further emphasize the seriousness of my concern. What else could I do to try to get ahold of him? Send smoke signals?

My hands ran feverishly through my hair as I debated taking a trip to his house to make sure he wasn't dead on the toilet or something. I texted Juanita to meet me in the lobby in ten minutes. She was the last one in contact with Toni. Maybe she'd heard from him at least. While I waited for her to come down to the lobby, I decided to grab Toni's home address from the back room where all the personnel information was locked up.

I dug through the folders until I found Toni's and typed his address into my phone. When I was through, I locked up the files and returned to the lobby.

Juanita was there tapping her foot impatiently while scouting the area for me. Two minutes late, and she acted as though I left her there for an hour.

"Sorry, I had to grab something from the back," I opened before she could get a complaint in edge wise. "The reason I called you down is because Toni missed his shift again, and no one's heard from him since he dropped you off that night of the warehouse incident. Please tell me you've talked with him since then."

"Ay, no. What do you think happened to him?"

"I don't think my thoughts on what happened to him are the best place to start. My imagination has a tendency to lean toward the worst. I'm going to go to his address and see if he's home. I'm hoping there's a logical explanation for everything."

"Ok, what do you want me to do?" she asked.

"You just stay here. Maybe you could try him on your phone, too? He might answer for someone other than me."

"Si, because when I see that the boss is calling, I let it go straight to voicemail. No offense, but chu calling me on my off time always results in me picking up another shift or something."

Precisely my point. "Well, I'm going to run over there real quick, I'll be back—"

"Nicole," Val from the front desk shouted at me and quickly waved her hand for me to go there.

I motioned for the door and tried to communicate that I had to go.

"This will just take a moment. I need your help real quick."

I stifled an eye roll and stomped in her direction. It better be quick. This unresolved business with Toni had me on pins and needles. I couldn't deny the pit in my stomach suggesting something was wrong with Toni.

"What is it, Val?" I asked as I rounded the front desk.

"There's an issue with Room 407." Val clicked through the computer and pulled up the occupancy schedule and calendar.

I took reins of the computer and scrolled down the page. "It was booked by a Jennings, and the check-out schedule was at eleven this morning. What's the issue?"

"Well, the issue is that it's well past check-out time, and the guests haven't checked out of the room yet. We've also surpassed the late check-out time."

"Did you call up to the room?" I asked.

Val nodded. "Yes, but there was no answer."

"Hmmm, it could be that they overslept. Let's give it another try." I dialed the number and let it ring for a minute. No answer. "Maybe they left without checking out. Wouldn't be the first time, especially since their card is already on file. What was the name again?"

Val answered promptly, "Um, I believe the cardholder's name was Nancy Jennings."

I paused toying with the name. Nancy Jennings. Nancy Jennings, why did the name ring a bell?

Juanita was standing on the other side of the desk, peeking above the counter with wide eyes. "Señora, she was the girl who…" she hesitated observing Val. "Uh, she was the girl who got the free breakfast coupon. Remember? Chu hand delivered the coupon to her and her four friends."

The light bulb went off. The room we initially thought two of the four girls had gone missing, which was completely wrong since we saw the four of them unexpectedly in their room that day. "Yes, I remember now. Val, Juanita and I will go check on the room to see what's going on. Try giving the room another call to see if anyone picks up."

Juanita and I rushed toward the elevator and were silent during the ride up since there were other guests with us. We were the only two to get off on level four. As soon as the doors slid closed,

Juanita whacked me on the arm. "See! I told chu. I told chu something was up!"

"We don't know anything yet. They may still be hung over from the other night. You know how college kids can be. Reckless and irresponsible. They probably just missed the check-out time."

Juanita muttered something under her breath in Spanish, and I disregarded it. When we stopped in front of Room 407, I knocked on the door a few times and called out Nancy's name. I couldn't remember the other girls' names off the top of my head.

No one answered the door. Juanita and I glanced at each other.

"Maybe they left without checking out? I am going to check and see if they're all moved out." I ignored the Do Not Disturb sign on the door handle and opened the door with the master key. "Hello, this is the hotel manager. I just wanted to make sure everything was alright. Hello?" I peeked my head through the door when no one responded.

The room was a chaotic mess of clothes, shoes, opened bags of snacks, and dried bathing suits hanging from various knobs throughout the bathroom. Juanita followed in behind me on her tippy toes.

"Looks like they didn't skip town yet. All of their stuff is still here."

I nodded. "This is strange."

I started to reach for a suitcase when Juanita stopped me in my footsteps. "DON'T!" she yelled.

I froze. "What? I was going to see if there was anything lying around to explain this."

"Don't touch anything. Chu don't want to leave fingerprints anywhere. If they really have gone missing, the police will be here to investigate, and chu don't want your DNA at the scene of the crime."

Missing? Police investigation? Crime scene? I could feel my throat tightening around itself in fear. All things Sunset Cove could not afford. If word got out that another abduction had happened in Miami, at my hotel, nonetheless, business would be completely in the shitter. Forget trying to save the jobs of everyone here…I wouldn't even have a job here.

I slid my hands down my face, as the feeling of hopelessness washed down on me. "This can't be happening. No, there's an explanation for this. Surely."

Juanita patted a stubby hand on my arm. "Señora, it's ok. I can call the cops for chu. Let them handle it from here."

"NO!" I shouted louder than I intended. "I mean, no, we can't involve the cops yet. The bad publicity for our hotel would be catastrophic. This here stays between you and me." I struggled to formulate a plan in my head.

"But what about Val?" she asked.

"We'll lie. We, um, we can tell her that the guests earned a free seven-day stay in order to compensate for their bad experience with the hotel."

"What's the bad experience? Chu needs to have all these details planned out in advance."

"You're right." I stared at her quizzically, impressed by her knowledge on the matter. "What about a scheduling error? No, because Val is responsible for scheduling the rooms, and she'd already know something was fishy if it was based on her area of expertise. Hmm...what about the restaurant? The four girls had a free breakfast coupon. What if we say they all got food poisoning, and as such we provided them with the free week's stay?"

"I think that will work." Juanita rubbed her hands together. "So that will give us a week to do some of our own investigating. We won't need to involve the cops until their week is up."

"Yes, good. Now, I need to go find Toni, but while I'm gone I'm giving you permission to go full spy happy with the room. Do whatever it is you need to do."

"Si. I'll get the info on where they were last before they went missing," Juanita said.

"That's if they have actually gone missing. I'm holding on to the chance that they haven't truly been abducted. Just find out what you can. I'll have my cell if you need me."

I jetted out the door and Juanita was right behind me. Curiously I peered back at her. "Where are you going?"

"There are a few things I need to get before I can do my investigating. Don't worry. I know what I'm doing."

I didn't even bother to ask. Right now my faith was hanging by a thread, and I had to believe Juanita was going to handle her responsibilities. I was going to lose it otherwise. I decided neglecting to ask for details would help keep faith alive.

Juanita and I parted separate ways in the lot as we split for our own vehicles. I plopped on my moped and sped away in the direction of Toni's home. The GPS on my phone guided me in the right direction.

To say he lived in a rough neighborhood was putting it mildly. The shutters on the homes hung lopsided and in desperate need of a fresh layer of paint. Trashcans were still at the curb two days after the garbage trucks had hailed away the refuse. There were metal chain fences around each house and I was surprised not to find razor wire wrapped at the top of them. An overwhelming number of pit bulls scrounged around their yards, tortured by the awful heat.

This neighborhood was the last place I expected Toni to live. Perhaps he needed a raise at work. This place was a dump.

I stopped in front of his house and wearily slid off the moped. As I walked up the uneven sidewalk to his front door, I contemplated turning around and bolting for an escape several times. When I finally made up my mind, I knocked a few sturdy taps. Toni stumbled to the door with a 9mm already drawn. To say that I was a bit taken aback would be an understatement.

Once he registered my face, he quickly lowered his gun and apologized. "Sorry, I, uh, didn't know it was you." He glanced around outside suspiciously then creaked opened the door for me to walk through.

"Didn't know it was me? As opposed to whom, a local gang member?" I raised a brow. "First off, why the hell haven't you returned my calls? Secondly, why are you answering the door, guns drawn? And thirdly, what are you doing in a neighborhood like this?"

"It's close to work." he shrugged. "Sorry, I wasn't expecting visitors." He shoved the gun in the waistband of his pants.

"Hell, Toni, do you even have a permit for that thing?" I motioned toward his gun.

"Course."

"Wait a minute. You had me flipping out over here. Why didn't you return my calls or show up to work?"

"Nicks, I meant to call you but I've been busy dealing with some things." He gestured toward the house. "Excuse the mess, I didn't know I'd have uninvited company over today." He eyed me accusingly.

Disregarding his comment, I looked around his kitchen which opened up into the large, spacious living room. The interior of his house was actually quite impressive in comparison to the exterior.

The walls were painted a charcoal blue with white trimmed baseboards framing the dark hard wooden floors. A massive flat screen hung just below a cream colored surf board holstered up by hooks. His couch was a neutral cream, which lacked in frilly throw pillows but instead harvested a pile of grey blankets built for comfort.

A few sand dollars collected dust on the window sill. A tall plant sat perfectly in the far corner of the room, bringing about a sense of hominess to the room. In truth, the place suited him. A nice laid back bachelor pad with a few pieces here and there that hinted at his surfer streak.

"Your place isn't a mess. It looks fine." I said, quite impressed with its cleanliness. I shook my head back to the topic. "So what is it you're dealing with? Why'd you leave us all high and dry? Jackie has a few choice words for you when you get back by the way. Good luck with that one."

He smiled, "That's if I come back." He switched the subject, "You want something to drink? Eat?"

"What do you mean by if you come back? Where are you going?"

He moseyed into the kitchen and hollered that he was going to get us a beer. When Toni did not want to talk about something, he really wasn't going to talk about it. I impatiently paced his living room waiting for him to return. I've learned by now not to force him into conversation. There was a way to approach, and there was the unsuccessful pushy way to approach, which would wind up nowhere useful.

While he was off in the kitchen I glanced around his place. Across the living room was his study, where a dark wooden desk was cluttered with old news clippings of Sunset Beach professional competitions. Clippings of Pipe Masters. Surfer's Paradise off the coast of Australia. Uluwata, Indonesia and reef competitions. I snuck a quick peek around the room and noticed a bookcase mounted with trophies, medals, and ribbons.

They weren't on show as if they were appreciated though. They were sort of jumbled together in a mess with wads of trash that had been pelted at them, squished between little crevices. It was peculiar, but I had the sudden feeling that I shouldn't be in that room. I scrambled out and glimpsed at his bedroom down the short hall.

His bedroom had a Tuscany finish to the walls and it was painted a soothing golden color. A wooden night stand was cuddled up to his bed, California King-sized, of course, and a matching wooden dresser against the far wall. Leaning against the back wall was a stack of flattened brown boxes.

Toni handed me a beer and stuck his hand in his pocket unsure of himself.

"Moving boxes." It sounded more of a statement than a question. "So that's what you meant by if you come back."

"Like I said, Nicks, I've been dealing with some stuff lately. I think I'm going to skip town for a while. Maybe a year or two."

I blinked back my disbelief. "Have I done something to cause this?"

Toni's stance relaxed and the carefree grin that I knew so well slipped into place for a moment. "What? No, absolutely not. Look, me leaving has nothing to do with you. Promise."

"So why are you leaving?" I folded my arms and sat down on the edge of the bed. "I don't understand."

"I know it doesn't make sense, but you're going to have to trust me when I say that it's for the best." He was visibly struggling with the explanation. "Just trust that I'm leaving with good reason."

I shook my head. "So if I hadn't come over, you were planning on packing up and heading out without giving notice. I mean, damn the two weeks notice, Toni. How about a goodbye? I know I'm your boss, but more than that, I thought of us as friends."

He wrapped me into a hug. "Nicks, we are. It's not like that. Somehow my past manages to catch up to me wherever I go."

"What do you mean your past?" I stared at him more intensely. He refused to bring up his past for as long as I've known him. All that I knew was there was some bad history there but not to press him for details or he'd put up a wall and turn on the defense mode.

His jaw tensed and he glared off in another direction.

"I know you don't like to talk about your past, Toni. And I've learned not to ask you about it since you seem to get like this." I gestured at his cold demeanor. "But you have to give me something here to understand what's going on. All of the sudden you stop coming to work, you don't return anyone's calls, you're stashing a pile of moving boxes…I mean where did this come from?"

"I'm not going to get into all of it," he hesitated for a long pregnant silence, "but I ran into some people from my past a few nights ago. People I never cared to see again. People I thought I'd never see again."

"A few nights ago?" The wheels in my brain began to turn. Work faster hamsters, work faster! "Wait. You mean that night at the warehouse?" My heartbeat quickened as I recalled the near death experience with those merciless mongrels.

Toni nodded.

"What exactly happened to you when you pulled your distraction stunt? Did they catch up to you?" My tone tightened. "What did they do to you?"

A low and dark chuckle escaped him. "They didn't do anything to me, yet, at least." He rubbed the back of his neck. "I ran a different direction, making more noise than normal to get them to follow after me instead of following you and Juanita. Anyways, I kept running until I found myself blocked in by surrounding buildings at a dead end. I doubled back to the shadows next to a dumpster and waited for my followers to run past me. Once a few of them ran ahead I rounded the dumpster and snuck out the entrance of the ally."

"So you got away, home free."

"Not exactly. I was foolish." He shook his head, visibly upset thinking back. "I ran back the way I came, thinking that was all of them. Then I ran into the two guys that apparently fell behind to sweep the streets. Caleb and Logan."

My eyes widened. "Who are they?"

"Like I said, people from my past. It doesn't matter anyways. I may have escaped them, but they definitely recognized that it was me."

"But you lost them didn't you? What's the chances you'll see them again?"

"Let's just say I didn't exactly leave on the best of terms. They'll make it a point to find me again and anyone I care about if I don't leave now while I still have the chance." Toni shook his head and sighed. "I know you don't believe what you don't understand, but just trust me when I say you and I will be much better off when I'm out of this city."

"Better off?" I shouted. "Better off? I am about two slices away from losing my shit. Now, not two, but four girls have gone missing – if not abducted – from the hotel on my watch. I've created a total façade to cover up the mess before their absence goes noticed. Sunset Cove is about to be the center of a police investigation, meaning the hotel is going to lose business, during a time when we cannot afford to lose business. So forget saving half of the staff's jobs. The entire facility would be shut down for good. I'm going to lose my job and claim bankruptcy in a matter of months trying to support one monthly mortgage payment for Ma and Vi, and another mortgage for me and my unexpected roommate, Emily. Not to mention, I'm also babysitting a Cuervo-addicted parrot while my neighbor is away."

I was starting to hyperventilate, and patches of blackness were appearing before my eyes.

"Woah, there." Toni leaned me forward with my head between my knees. He took the beer from my hand. "Just take deep breaths for a minute. You're looking a little pale."

I took slow breaths in and out, in and out, until I felt a little more back to normal.

"Before we jump the gun, let's just take it back to the beginning. I remember seeing a text from Juanita that the missing girls were back, though I didn't reply. What do you mean that the four girls have gone missing?"

"Exactly what you said. First two girls were gone and now four girls are gone." With my head still between my legs, I blindly held up a hand with four fingers. "So you picked a hell of a time to jump ship. I'd join you if I wasn't so entangled with the hotel. No turning back now."

I could hear Toni scratching his cheek. When I peered up at him I noticed a conflicted expression. Concern and determination. Finally he spoke, "Let the law handle it. They'll take care of things."

"Have you been listening to a word I've been saying? If the law gets involved all hell will break loose. Sunset Cove will be ruined. I will be ruined. Everyone that works there will be out of work. No, we're not involving the police. We've found a way to stall time for another week. Juanita and I are going to try and investigate it ourselves. If we can just trace backwards maybe we can find them."

"That's if they're even still in Miami. They could be long gone by then. By getting in the way of the police investigation, you're obstructing justice. You could even be charged as an accomplice if you're tampering with anything to cover it up." Toni was standing now. His chest rushing in and out with the words. "Nicky, you need to stop while you can. Those girls' lives could be at stake."

I shook my head. "Toni, I've got a plan. We'll involve the police whenever we have something that doesn't solely lead them back to the hotel. If we are the focal point of this, everything I've worked for is gone." I stood up and shouted. "Gone!"

Toni ran his hand through his buzzed cut hair. "Damnit, Nicky. Don't get involved. I'm telling you for your own safety. You don't know what you're up against."

"Well, it's not your problem anyways so don't concern yourself with the mess I have to clean up. Just do your thing and skip town. I can handle myself." I set my beer on the dresser and marched off.

I could hear Toni calling after me as I powered away, but I was done. I didn't need to hear any more of his judgments. His opinion didn't matter to me. He was abandoning me in my time of crisis. That's fine. Good riddance.

Toni was storming down the sidewalk from his house yelling something, but I gassed the moped and took off.

CHAPTER EIGHT

In a sour mood, I returned to the hotel and hustled straight to my office. When I opened the door, a small shaded figure almost karate chopped me in the throat.

"What in the world?" I gasped.

"Señora Nicole. Chu can't sneak up on me like that. I'm under a lotta stress right now, and I can't be held accountable for my actions." She rolled her shoulders and cracked her neck.

"You're being held accountable, alright." I stared her up and down, "and you can start by explaining your choice of wardrobe."

She was wearing her hair up in a tight bun, slicked back with half a pound of grease. Her eyes were thickly outlined with jet black eyeliner; heavy swipes of what looked like black paint were smeared beneath her eyes.

She wore a black warm-up jacket which was zipped all the way to her chin. Black gloves. Black Puma's. Black spandex pants that stretched over every inch of her thighs. She looked like a wannabe cat burglar.

"I was going to ask chu the same thing." She disapprovingly examined my work attire.

"What do you mean? This is what I've been wearing all day," I said a little defensively. "You're the one that looks like a nut. Did you just get released from a movie audition or something?" I motioned toward her ensemble. "What's with this?"

"Esssscuze me?" She pressed her hand to her chest. "No, no, no, no. I," she heavily emphasized, "am dressed like a spy. We are mid-spy investigation here. The question is what are chu wearing? Chu don't even look like chu are ready to do some sneaking around. We are not on the clock anymore. We are investigating a potential crimery."

"Crime." I corrected.

"Crime. Whatevers." She slid a judgmental glance at me. "Amateur hour."

I just shook my head. "If you are dressed like a spy, and if you act like a spy, and all the while you really are trying to spy; then guess what happens if people are suspicious?"

"What happens?" she asked, uninterested.

"They catch on. And you get caught spying," I answered.

"But at least you'll go down with style," she grinned and her tongue poked out between her two front teeth.

She was impossible. "So is this what you have been doing for the past few hours? Going home to change into your spy gear? I thought you were going to do something useful with the time. What exactly is the game plan, mastermind?" I waited for her reply.

"I changed clothes and already scoped out the girls' room. Found some things we might be able to use. I figured we could set up shop around some of the places that I believe they went to last. Check out the pyramiders and see if we come across any funny business."

Pyramiders being translation for perimeters, I presumed.

"OK, show me what you found."

Juanita lifted her black body bag onto my desk and opened it up. She pulled out a few folded pieces of paper, receipts, torn wrist bracelets, and an iPad. I looked at the iPad and back to Juanita.

"Chu know how to hack into a computer system, right?"

"What?!" I shouted. "No, I'm not a hacker. How in the world am I supposed to do that? I don't even own an iPad, much less know how to work it."

"I dunno. I just hear the people in the movies talk about computers and hacking and stuff and thought I'd try it on for size. My bad." She shrugged it off. "It's password protected but it's ok, we can take it to an Apple store to unlock it. We can skip that part for now."

"I have no desire to go through someone's personal e-mails. I don't see what the point of that would be."

Juanita picked up a heavy object from her mysterious bag of tricks on the desk. "Not to access her e-mails. To gather information from her web history. It may tell us more places they were looking up. Here." She motioned for me to hold out my hands.

A walkie-talkie the size of a boom box plummeted into my hands. I nearly dropped it on the ground from the weight of it.

Juanita went back to searching her bag and shouted over her shoulder. "Latch it onto chur hip and keep it with chu at all times. I'll communicate with chu when we split up to scout an area."

"Juanita, what is this?" I stared at her, still traumatized by the idea of carrying around a walkie-talkie.

"Um Señora Nicole, it's a walkie talkie. Hello!" She snorted. "Chu must have had a deprived childhood."

"No, I mean I got that, but why are we using these? We have cell phones."

"Our phones could be tapped. They might try to listen to our conversations, or they could trace our phone calls and try to pin down our exact location. That would be no good." Juanita shook her head. "Trust me. I know these things," Juanita patted my back. "I watch CSI."

I wasn't sure that would be necessary, but I was more interested in the items she found in the room. "So what are all these receipts for?" I grabbed the different receipts from the table. "We've got several for local restaurants. A few bar tabs. Shopping receipts. Cab fare."

"Si, we can trace back their steps starting with the most recent time stamp."

I snatched a paper clip from my desk and pinned them together. We'd go through and sort them out next. I grabbed two torn off wrist bands and read aloud the words "In addition to their earlier night out at Chic, it also looks like the girls went to Mansion and Rooftop Lounge for a bit more of the Miami night life."

"And here is a list of activities or daily excursions they must have researched before they got here." Juanita unfolded a piece of paper with a list of touristy activities with the locations and pricing listed.

I set the paper back on the desk. "My these girls were busy."

"I know. It makes me tired looking at everything they've done over the past few days. Do you remember their names? I know there was Nancy, and I think there was an Elise."

"I wrote them down." I groaned in frustration. "And then I threw it in the trash when I found out the girls were back."

"That was a little premature. We need all of their names."

"Thank you, Captain Obvious. I got that. At the time I thought the issue was resolved, so I wadded it up and tossed it." I glanced in the direction of my trashcan. "Actually. I thought it didn't go in."

Juanita crinkled her brows in confusion.

"If I remember correctly," I hurried to the corner and saw the crumpled wad of paper next to the cabinet where it bounced off the rim of the can. "Thank goodness I'm a lousy shot." I unraveled the paper and found all four names. Nancy Jennings, Elane Connor, Jessica Halls, and Elle Wendale.

"OK, now let's go to the Apple store to see if we can crack this password on their iPad. I'm sure we'll get a lot more from their web browser history."

I snatched the iPad out of her hands. "No, I don't feel right taking something like an iPad from their room. In the event that they do come back, whatever the reason is that they went MIA, this hotel will be in serious hot water if they return and their iPad has been stolen. We need to put it back and see if there's another way to unlock it from here."

"But Señora…"

"No buts. This is going right back to the room."

"OK, OK. Before chu goes out there we need to review the code names for communication." She waved her walkie talkie in the air.

"I think we should just stick to our actual names and our cell phones in all honesty."

"Well chu are not the brains of the operation here. I have more experience with these things, so I think we should follow my line of thinking," Juanita exhaled. "Alright, chu are' Black Hawk'."

"Black Hawk," I repeated. "Got it."

"Si. I am 'Red Sparrow'. 'Marilyn Monroe' means trouble."

"Right, but what kind of trouble?"

"Trouble, like abandon ship! Run like hell!" she continued, "I'm talking high tail it out of there. Don't look back. Leave me behind because there's no use coming after me."

"Alright." I nodded.

"Seriously. Just go ahead and leave me in the dust. I no care. I sacrifice myself for the team."

"Let's not get dramatic," I rolled my eyes. "That's the end of the code names right?"

"And then there's 'the eagle has landed' which means that you've found the girls, and they're safe. 'Code turquoise'—"

"Turquoise? About that one, can we just make it 'code blue'? It's easier to say."

"No!" She snapped. "We don't want to try switching things up now. It's too late. We're in too deep."

Oh, brother.

"As I was saying," she slanted her eyes at me. "'Code turquoise' means I'm surrounded by them, and I need a diversion."

"Anything else?"

"I think we covered it all. Now, return the iPad to the charger on the wall, and I'll wait down in the lobby. If I need you, listen for a message on the walkie," Juanita whispered. "I'm going to put together their receipts by order, so we can work backwards once you finish with the iPad."

Then she vanished. She was a mini Speedy Gonzalez, especially considering her compact size.

I headed for the elevators and pressed the up button at the same moment someone else reached for the button.

"Nicole?" Ralf's voice rose in surprise. "Coincidence, I was just thinking of you. Debating the play-it-cool card and whether I should engage in the charades of waiting two days after our first date." He shook his head. "But guessing by your unresponsiveness I guess I should've waited the forty-eight hour rule."

I was taken aback by his honesty, but confused by his comment. "Unresponsiveness?" I asked curiously. He motioned toward my phone and I skimmed my texts. Unread message from Ralf Mancini, asking how my day was and looking forward to our next adventure.

I smacked my forehead. "So sorry, Ralf. I didn't even see that you sent a message. After the day I've been having, I've just been a little distracted."

"No worries." He shrugged nonchalantly. "That work issue I had to resolve last night took up the better half of my sleeping hours. I'm practically running on empty today."

"Oh yeah, so everything worked out OK?"

"I managed a temporary plug on the situation, so things will settle for a few weeks, Overall it's far from being completely resolved. I'll be happy when these clients move forward with the new contract. It'll make my life that much easier. Certainly won't have to spend so much time in a hotel."

My eyes lowered at the thought of it. "So that means you won't be visiting Sunset Cove as much?"

Ralf peeked over at me and was about to reach for my face when the elevator doors opened for a few stragglers to get off. Both of us boarded the elevator and selected different floors. "I mean, yes, things will be different in that I won't stay at the hotel every other week or so, but I am still going to visit. I'm not worried about the distance thing, if that's what you look so down about."

The doors opened, and I exited my floor. Ralf held the door open and waited for my reply.

"No, of course not. We're just having fun anyways, right?" I waved it off. "Go catch up on your sleep. I'll see you around!" I managed the best nonchalant tone I could bear. We'd only gone on one date. There's no way I'd confess that I was already concerned with the distance factor. That's crazy talk.

He titled his head and was about to say something, but Juanita's loud, piercing voice projected through my walkie-talkie speaker, interrupting him.

"Black Hawk. Black Hawk. Come in. Do chu read me?"

I mentally rolled my eyes and silently cursed Juanita to the high heavens. As I unclipped my walkie-talkie, I mouthed to Ralf, "Sorry." I turned my back to him and quietly but sternly spoke into the walkie-talkie.

"Juanita—"

"RED SPARROW!"

I refrained from banging my head against the nearest sharp object.

"OK, Red Sparrow. I'm in the middle of something. Give me one more minute."

"No can do, Black Hawk. The time to strike is now. I repeat. The time to strike is now." Her voice blared through the speaker.

I glanced back at Ralf and did a nervous chuckle. Returning back to the conversation with Red Sparrow, I asked, "We never went over that code name. What is the time to strike?"

She sighed. "Are chu equipped enough to handle this assignment, or should I send you back with the little ones to play in the kiddy pool? I feel like that was pretty obvious." She took on a new tone of an improperly-speaking Cuban sergeant.

"What did you say?" I snapped.

"Oh, uh. I sorry. I kinda got into character back there. Lo siento, lo siento," she apologized.

"Mhmm, I'll be on my way in a moment."

When I turned back to Ralf to tell him that I had some business to attend, the elevator doors were closed and he was gone. Just like that.

When I continued down the hall to 407 I found the door was propped open and several deep voices came from within the room. Oh thank heavens! The girls were back! I knew there was an explanation. I just knew my luck couldn't be that bad.

I held the iPad behind my back and flung the door open. Before I spoke my voice caught in my throat at the sight of two men carelessly tossing items into the suitcases. Silently I pulled the door closer and peeked through the crack. This was the same room, but these definitely weren't the guests checked into the room. It should have been extended a week for the girls.

Though the items thrown into the suitcases resembled the property from the four girls, it didn't make sense what these two bulky men were doing in here.

Both men resembled each other with short buzzed hair styles and broad shoulders. One had a few inches on the other guy, but they each had a hook nose and thin lips. They weren't twins, but maybe they were related. Like brothers or cousins even. The shorter one blindly tossed a frilly bikini behind him and it accidentally landed in the face of the taller one.

"Dammit, Ronnie. Watch where you're throwing things."

The shorter one grabbed a pair of undies and jokingly tossed it onto the taller guy. "Oh, Donnie. Don't get your panties in a bunch. It's just underwear. You act like you've never seen a pair before."

Donnie crumpled up the pair and forcefully threw it into a suitcase. "Quit playing around. You know he doesn't like us to waste any time. We need to get in and out. One of the girls said their check-out was today so we already dropped the ball on this one."

Ronnie snorted. "Jesus. Lighten up. What do you think he's going to do if we're a few minutes late? Just how would he clean up the clean-up crew?"

"I'm sure he'd think of something," Donnie answered solemnly. "Hurry it along, and I'll meet you in the car." He zipped his few suitcases and rolled them toward the door.

Quickly, I backed away from the door and bolted for the stairs. I started down the stairwell and unclipped the walkie. "Juanita?"

"I don't know a Juanita." Her voice replied.

Seriously! "Red Sparrow!" I snapped. "There will be a tall man coming down the elevator with several large suitcases. I want you to keep a safe distance back and follow him to his car."

"But Señora, why?"

"I'll explain later, but he's somehow involved. Saw him and his buddy packing up the girls' room from 407. We need their license plate and car information. Then we need to follow them."

"Chu got it." She disconnected, and I continued down the stairs. When I arrived on the ground floor, I rushed to the lot to power on my moped. I prayed they had no intention to leave South Beach since my ride didn't go above 40 mph.

"Señora, I got the license plate number, make, and model of their car. I wrote it down under notes in my phone. Come to the back lot, and I'll wave you down. Are we going in your ride or mine?"

I debated this for a moment. I don't recall being in Juanita's ride. "Perhaps it would be best to take yours since I am riding a neon yellow moped. Doesn't exactly blend in." I puttered around to the back lot at a slow and quiet pace.

"Stop. I see chu." I glanced around and found Juanita crouched between cars vigorously waving her hands. I pulled into an empty space and crept between cars to where she was squatting. She pointed in the direction of the car, and I saw a sleek black Audi A5 running with the headlights on.

"Great, he's still waiting for the other guy. I think the tall one in the car is Donnie and the other one is Ronnie? Let's hop in your car and wait to follow them once they leave. Where's your car?" I asked.

I glanced over at Juanita, and she was already pulling her car keys out of her satchel.

"At the front of the lot. So we can wait for them to pull around, and we'll slip right in behind them."

Still crouched between cars, I followed her to the front of the parking lot. When she stopped next to her car, I did a double take and then blinked.

"Why are we stopping here?" I asked her.

She opened her arms as if presenting a rare piece of art. "It's my car." She smiled her gap-toothed smile.

"Quit joking. For real, where's your car? We don't have time for jokes."

She manually unlocked her door and then reached across the seat to pull up my lock. I hesitated.

"Get in, get in. Come on, we've got some stalking to do."

"Yes, but…what if people see us in this?"

I was still gawking at the '75 AMC Pacer. A machine that seemed as though it had been to the brinks of hell and back. Several times. Once upon a time it might have been a pale blue, but now it was covered in rust and deteriorating flakes of paint so that the color was now debatable.

As evidenced by her entry ritual, it was clear that it wasn't power locked. A side mirror had been, what appeared to be, duck taped to the car door. In the wrong location.

I tried to open the passenger door.

"Come on already!" Juanita rushed. "Get in."

"I'm trying." I grunted as I squeezed the handle and tried yanking the door open again and again. "It won't let me open the door."

"Chu has to jiggle it a little bit. Put some elbow juice into it."

So I jiggled it. Harder and harder until finally it moaned and released itself, creaking all the way open. I closed the door, but it didn't shut right.

"Chu kinda has to slam it. Come on, don't be shy."

I pulled it toward me with all my strength and it locked into place.

"That's nice," I said.

"Isn't it?" she smiled. "I gots this baby for a great deal."

"Really? How much? 'Cause anything over thirteen dollars was a waste of money."

"Three hundred buckeroos. Plus they threw in two Butterball chickens for no additional cost."

"I hope those chickens were worth two hundred fifty bucks then, because if you paid over fifty for this hunk of junk, you were ripped off."

I set my purse down on the floor and it disappeared.

I screamed. "Your car ate my purse!" I looked down at the floor of the car.

"Oh I forgot to tell chu. Make sure to keep chur feet lifted so they don't get tore up on the pavement.

There was a gaping hole in the bottom of her car where the passenger floor mat would have been located, but I'd bet it fell through the hole at one point, too.

"What in the—your car's missing a key detail, don't you think? What happened to the floor?!"

"The past owner told me it was a freak accident of some sort. He didn't go much into details. I've lost a many of personal items that way. They'll shift and fall off the seat and roll to the ground, making a quick escape. I like to call it my fire exit!"

"I feel like Fred from 'The Flintstones'. What's next? Am I supposed to stick my feet through the hole and push the car forward, too?"

I snatched my purse from the ground and pulled it through the fire exit positioning it on my lap along with the iPad. Juanita did some kind of routine where she punched the dashboard, pounded the brake pedal, and used her other hand to crank over the engine. It was actually rather entertaining to witness.

The car stalled and sputtered for a few seconds. Puff! And then it revved to life. The space behind the car was filled with black smoke, and there was a sudden back fire noise that startled a few innocent bystanders, causing them to cover their heads.

"Arriba, that's my little sustantivo!" she shouted over the gurgling and grinding of the engine.

"Sustantivo?"

"Si, my survivor."

Suddenly a seat belt strap jumped to life following a track and was about to stop in place over my right shoulder, but jammed. It made a hideous churning noise and once defeated returned back to its initial resting place.

Her car's name, Survivor, somehow felt appropriate. Cockroaches were also considered a species of survivors, but it still didn't mean they did not deserve to die.

"I'm beginning to rethink the subtlety of taking your car versus my neon moped. Yours seems to draw enough attention as it is," I muttered glancing around for any onlookers.

The black Audi drove past us toward the exit, and we both froze.

"Game time," Juanita rubbed her hands together mischievously and shifted her stick to drive. The gears released a metallic screech as they grinded together.

We followed them out of the lot and Juanita managed to tail them from a few cars back.

"Looks like you've done this before." I suggested.

"I may have done a little stalking in my day when I thought Alonzo was cheating on me with other women."

"It shows."

"Si, for this to really be effective, it's best if you have two cars tailing one person and chu can switch off between the two so they don't catch on. Why don't chu call Toni and have him help us out?"

I strummed my fingers impatiently on my purse. "Toni's not in the picture anymore."

"What do chu mean? He's been looped in on everything from the start. Whatever it is chu're pouting about, get over it. We need more hands on deck."

"He's leaving us, Juanita. When I went to his place today I just so happened to discover that he was skipping town. Didn't even bother to put in his notice or tell me face to face. He was just planning on sliding out of Miami without so much as a goodbye."

Juanita broke contact with the road and stared at me appalled. "I don't believe chu. Toni would never do something like that."

"Apparently we both don't know Toni very well because it's the honest-to-God truth. He tried to explain why, in the best way Toni could verbalize his reasons. Something to do with two guys from his past showing up the night of the warehouse. Caleb and Logan, I believe? Anyways, he was excruciatingly vague. Big surprise there."

"Chu mean that chu actually got Toni to open up about his past? Señora, chu know that's a pretty big deal for him. It must be serious if he's letting you in."

"Define 'open up,'" I snorted. "That man is so guarded."

"Maybe he has his own reasons for it," she offered. Since when did Juanita represent the voice of reason?

"Bottom line is that he's leaving, and he is dead against us investigating things on our own. Doesn't matter. We can handle ourselves."

"Chu will regret it if chu both part on those terms. Chu both need to smooth things over before he leaves."

I decided not to acknowledge her wisdom by sitting in silence. The Audi rounded the corner a few blocks ahead and Juanita took a left to follow them to what appeared to be their final destination. Juanita continued driving and passed the parked Audi before she turned a corner into a dark side alley. She cut the engine and the thing died instantaneously with a sigh of relief.

"Now what?" I asked feeling my nerves spike to a new level.

"Now we set up shop outside and scope out the place from afar. We're merely doing surveillance tonight."

I nodded. "A safe distance away from any danger. I'm good with that."

Juanita opened her car door and eased along the edge of the brick wall until she was at the corner of the building. I was stuck in the car still trying to dislodge the passenger door from its fixed position. Finally I decided to hop across the seats and exit the driver's side. Quietly I tiptoed to Juanita's position and peered above her head. Fortunately, we had a clear view of the building while our position remained hidden by the shadows cast around us.

Donnie and Ronnie stepped out of the car and heaved the girls' bags from the trunk and from the back seat. "You'd think these chicks were visiting for a month with how much shit they pack. I'm getting my exercise in for the day," Ronnie mumbled.

"Hurry up. He's waiting on us." Donnie gave Ronnie a shove. "And don't mention shit about us missing the check-out date. The last thing we need is for him to be all over our case after the last incident."

"Funny how we get in trouble for being sloppy when we're the ones who have messes handed to us to clean up. I think we should have a talk with him about that. Guy needs a reality check."

Donnie glanced around them. "Mind your tongue. You never know who's around, so stop talking crazy like that. You'll find yourself in a heap of trouble, if you don't. Now come on."

Both of them lifted the suitcases up the ramp and disappeared into the building.

"Should we follow after them?" Juanita was preparing her short stubby legs to make a break for the door. I grabbed her shoulders and slammed her back against the wall.

"What are you crazy? What happened to surveying from a safe distance?" I hissed.

"Fine, fine, fine." She folded her arms across one another in a pout. "We'll stay here. Wish we stopped and picked up some donuts first."

"Considering this was kind of last minute, I don't think we would've been able to schedule a donut stop while maintaining a tail on our only lead to the girls." I folded my legs underneath me and sat on the pavement which I'm sure was covered in germs.

"And now we wait for an hour," I sighed. If there was no activity by then we could check out the surroundings if it seemed safe.

Two minutes and fifty-seven seconds later.

"So, how are the trout biting these days?" Juanita amusingly eyeballed me.

I stared at her with a perplexed look. "I don't fish, so I wouldn't know."

"No, it's an American saying, right? Like for dating," Juanita said.

I thought for a second longer. "Oh, you mean fish?"

"Si. That's what I said."

"No, you said trout. Trout is a type of fish."

"Right."

"You know you don't have to specify an actual type of fish. The saying is a general statement. You see, it's 'how are the fish biting?'"

"Look here, Señora. I know what I said, and what I said was fish. Why are chu all up on my case?"

I glanced at my watch hoping we had miraculously talked about fish versus trout for the remainder of fifty-seven minutes and three seconds.

Unfortunately, no miracle work today.

"You're right." I raised my hands in surrender. "Well anyways, one fish in particular has caught my attention."

"Oh? And how is Ralf? Don't think I didn't notice chur glow."

I felt my cheeks flush, and I was grateful that the shadows camouflaged it.

"I ran into him on my way up to Room 407, and he informed me that he sent me a follow up text after our date. I totally missed it due to the whirlwind from today, and I think he was a little offended." I pressed on in my defense. "It truly was a mistake."

"Si. It has been a loco day. So did chu text him back?" I slowly shook my head. She leaned back and lifted her hands. "Ay, ay, ay. He's not going to take another hit to his ego and tell chu again. Chu better text him back, right now! Don't give up that sexy man because of this drama. Chu might miss chur one and only chance."

I slid my phone out of my purse and aimlessly played with the screen.

"What's the hold up?" Juanita lifted a brow.

"I'm really into Ralf, but the whole distance thing is really posing a problem for me. Yes, he's here in Miami enough now, but he said his business deals would come to an end soon enough. I don't want to keep seeing him and start to get attached. I can already tell he's the kind to grow on you real quick. Part of me wonders if I should keep my distance, you know?"

"No, I don't know." She shook her head between her hands. "Chu needs to live life in the moment. If chu are into him and he is into chu, chu should not be worried about the what-ifs that may or may not come later down the road. Chu don't have a crystal ball. Chu never know where things will end up."

"Easier said than done. That sounds great in theory, until I wind up moping around the house in my PJs, eating a gallon of ice-cream by myself once he's gone."

"YOLO." Juanita said as if to end her argument. "And I'll tell chu something else. If chu don't go after that man, I will see to it that he doesn't go to waste. God sends a gift like that, and chu won't have to tell me twice to take it." She licked her lips. "I will not be held accountable for my actions."

"I'd be curious to see what Alonzo has to say about that remark." I raised a brow.

She backpedaled. "I kid, I kid. Just a joke."

Humph.

I switched on my phone and pulled up Ralf's text from earlier today. I apologized again for earlier today on the elevators and asked him how his day was going. Once I sent it I anxiously awaited for his response. I hope he wasn't pissed off from our last encounter. He took off on the elevator without any kind of notice.

In the time span of an hour, Juanita must have stretched her legs at least fifteen times. That woman could not sit still even if her life depended on it. When both my patience and my curiosity had run its course, I brushed off the debris from my legs and stood up to leave.

"I don't think much is getting accomplished out here. Perhaps we should call it a night?"

"But, but, we're not done yet. What about our lead and the missing girls? We can't just abandon them." Juanita tried to hurriedly get to her feet.

"Nothing is going on out here." I muttered. "We haven't seen a body enter or exit the building since those two initially walked in."

"That's because we're sitting on the sidelines. Let's have a closer look and see if there's any other activity going on."

"I don't know Juanita. It doesn't feel safe."

"Of course it doesn't. Sometimes we have to step out of our comfort boxes though to get things done."

"Yeah, and we really need to find these girls and get them on a plane and out of my hair. My ulcers can't take much more of this stress."

Juanita motioned with her walkie, "OK, I'll take the left side of the building, and chu take the right. We'll connect around back, but do not go inside."

"Oh, I thought that was a given. No, I'm definitely only staying outside. And I can already tell you I'm leaving the walkie behind."

Juanita began to protest. "Wait, but why?"

"For one, it's too bulky. It's messing with my balance. Secondly, it's not subtle. If you decide to blare across the speaker anyone around me will be able to hear you. I'm not going to get busted because of your loud mouth. So if you want to bring yours you can but I won't be on the other end of it. Text or call my cell if you need me. I'm putting it on silent but I'll continue to check it."

Juanita unclipped her walkie with a huff and took the set back to the car in defeat. We parted ways and approached the building from different angles. She skirted along the outskirts of the building we were surveying from, so she could pass several blocks away and creep back to the left side of the building. I on the other hand had a much more hidden route due to my proximity on the right side of the building.

Fortunately, there were a few dumpsters and large plastic trash bins I could sneak behind, along the outskirts. The street was poorly lit which allowed me to blend in much easier with the shadows. When I reached the brick of the building I held my breath and listened for any sign of life. The windows above my head were blacked out, and I gathered that no one was positioned in that room.

As I kept my breathing shallow, I tiptoed around the borders of the place. My hands traced the crevices along the brick wall as a guide through the darkness. When I rounded the rear of the building I paused to hone in on the muffled voices from a room off the back entrance.

The back door was cracked open an inch due to the rusty hinges that prevented it from closing properly. Quietly I leaned closer so that I was able to peek inside. The room looked like an oversized storage closet with dim lighting that reflected from underneath the door. I listened closer and was able to make out a few muffled words and chopped sentences, but it was still impossible to piece the conversation together.

"Boss says...price for...mistakes. Perpetual fuck up." Then it sounded like there was some kind of shuffling around and the air escaping lungs. I couldn't quite make out all of the sounds, but it didn't seem like it was a pleasant conversation.

Juanita emerged from around the other corner of the building. I almost didn't see her in her total blackout outfit, but she lit up her phone screen and gave it a quick wave so I'd know it was her. She took a few steps toward me and then made a quick retreat back when we heard the sudden staggered footsteps move from inside toward the back door.

I spastically shuffled backwards toward the yard and aimlessly bolted for some type of cover, anything I could hide behind. When my legs connected with a short, rigid bush I accidently toppled forward and did a flip onto my back. I choked on the air that caught in my chest and blinked back a round of tears.

The back door flung open, and I scurried to the thickest section of the bush to blend in better. One man stumbled first into the yard and a second man followed, shinning a harsh bright light in the other's face. The man tripped over the grass and sat on his behind for a moment before slowly crawling to his knees.

"Get up," the man with the light ordered. "I said get the fuck up, Ronnie!" His voice was low and sharp.

Ronnie chuckled as he rose to his feet. "So what, we can't have an opinion now? I make one small comment about fairness, and this is what I get? Kicked around like some kind of mutt."

"The problem isn't that you had an opinion, Ronnie. The problem is that you questioned his orders. Then you proceeded to undermine him in front of his team." He made a tisking noise and shook his head. "I thought you were smarter than that."

Ronnie spat out some blood from the beating he must have taken inside. "A little blood never hurt nobody." he chuckled. "Fine, I'll go in there and apologize. He can take a cut from my check."

The other man sighed. "Don't think that's gonna fly this time."

Ronnie's tone became more serious. "Come on, Bruce. Tell me what I gotta do. Whatever it is, consider it done." Ronnie began taking bigger, more calculated steps backwards and right toward my hidey spot behind the bushes. Not good.

"What you gotta do?" Bruce repeated. "Well you know what owners have to do to a dog that refuses to be broken?"

At this, Ronnie turned and sprinted as fast as he could in my direction. I ducked lower, waiting for him to pierce through the shrubs when...

POW. POW. POW.

Followed by a groan and a thud to the ground. I felt a spray of warm substance spackle my face and chest but dared not move a muscle.

The light grew closer until it was shining down vertically, a few inches away from my fingers on the other side of the bush. If Bruce moved just a smidge over with the light there's no doubt he'd see my figure between the limbs. I inhaled a sharp breath of air and waited as Bruce leaned down toward the ground.

He hovered over Ronnie's limp, dead body and held two fingers to his neck. Satisfied, he dusted off his hands and added, "That's right. They take them out back and shoot 'em."

When he reached into Ronnie's pocket and pulled out his wallet, I noticed some familiar markings on his inner wrist. A tattoo with a skull encased in a heart with the words "Love Kills" beneath it.

It was almost like deja vu when I read the writing. My limbs began to quiver with fear as I realized Bruce was also one of the guys from the warehouse, the one who pinned me down and threatened to have his way with me before he killed me.

Holy shit.

The sound of a cat screeching in the distance caught Bruce's attention as he whirled the flashlight around toward the building. His light searched the wall from one end to another before he stood up and headed back to the back door.

As he approached it a few more figures hustled out of the door and glared over at the dead corpse in my direction.

Donnie shoved through the front of the crowd and stopped in his tracks, clearly torn to go to Ronnie or to hang back with the crowd.

Donnie decided not to go to Ronnie's body. Instead he grumbled, "He never did listen to me. I warned him about that mouth of his. Do you need help moving the body?" He asked with an edge of bitterness.

"Nah," Bruce slapped Donnie on the back. "What kind of man would I be if I asked the cousin of a dead man to help move his corpse?" He spat a spew of tobacco. "I'm not that heartless. One of the guys will help me take him to the pit to be burned. We'll wait until he stiffens up a bit. Come on, let's grab a few cold beers."

Donnie stiffened and ambled back inside with the rest of them, not given a moment to grieve or a minute alone with his cousin. He was forced to keep up a disengaged façade by going with the flow, or he'd be lying there just as cold as his cousin.

The rest of the group moseyed inside, and I remained frozen in my position until I could no longer detect any noise from the group. Crouched low to the ground, I scurried along the side of the building as fast I could without making a sound. A thin man was puffing on a cigarette near the front entrance of the building. Not wanting to risk it, I anxiously shifted my weight from one foot to the other, antsy to get as far away from this place as possible.

Finally, thin man took one long, final draw before blowing out a steady stream of smoke. He flicked the remains at the wall and strolled back inside the building. I took this as my opportunity and hauled ass back along the same route I used in my approach. A quick blur caught my attention from the other side of the street, and I felt my heart stop while my feet continued moving. My heart resumed once I realized it was Juanita making a dash to safety from the opposite side of the building.

When I reached the car I was visibly trembling and breathing short jagged gasps. I attempted to slow my breathing and collect my nerves by the time Juanita returned from the route, which had a few extra blocks than mine. She shot toward me like a lightening bolt.

"Times to go!" she hurried. When she opened the driver door I jumped across to the passenger side. She mimicked her routine from before to start the car and with an obnoxiously loud kick start, the car stirred back to life. Juanita and I flew back against our seats as she threw the gear into drive and pressed the pedal to the metal. As I learned from experience, I held my purse and the iPad in my lap.

Once we were back on the main streets, she resumed a normal speed, and I kept looking for any potential tails. It seemed no one was chasing us, which meant no one knew we were there. I slid my hands through my hair and let out a huge sigh of relief.

"I am speechless." My eyebrows shot to the top of my hairline. "Did you see what I saw back there?"

She nodded in silence. "What do chu think caused that cat screech back there? I was so nervous that Bruce guy was going to see chu. He was so close that I saw an opportunity and took it to pull him away from chu. There was an alley cat next to where I was standing so I stomped on its tail and hid out of sight. I figured that would take the heat off chu for a little while."

I fanned my face with a hand. "I thought I was a goner, when Ronnie was running for me and Bruce came to take his pulse."

"And his wallet. What a scumbag."

"I know. It was pure luck, and of course, quick thinking on your end with the cat diversion, that kept me safe tonight."

Juanita shook her hand. That was close. Too, too close. Tomorrow we'll start by looking at the places they went to last. Maybe we can find more clues in a less intense environment."

Shock was beginning to rush over me. "Juanita, we just witnessed a murder back there. I don't exactly know much about this Ronnie character, but we just saw him purposely murdered in cold blood."

"I know." Juanita's tone was solemn.

"I mean, that does something to you. I don't know what I'm feeling in the moment, but I can tell you that I don't feel like me."

"I feel dirty, but the kind of dirty that won't wash away with soap and water."

I shook my head, just wanting to get back to Sunset Cove. I needed to get away and process everything on my own. My brain was too overwhelmed.

My body began to react to the recent series of events. My heart felt as though it was going to explode in my chest as the sound of my pulse grew louder in my ears. In fact, I could barely hear Juanita announce our arrival at the hotel. She was pulled up next to the curb near the front entrance. I muttered something and struggled with the passenger door before it finally released.

When I slammed the door shut, I lugged myself toward the front doors and continued through the lobby. My body felt weak from the prolonged adrenaline rush. My mind was clouded with the scene that replayed over and over in my head. It felt so surreal that I debated whether it even happened in the first place. I could feel the stares of others around me, yet somehow their bewildered facial expressions regarding my muddied attire, wasn't at the top of my priorities.

One woman's eyes nearly popped out of her head and a disgruntled "Woah" slipped out.

"What the fuck are you looking at?" I growled, and she backed away in a rush.

A warm arm wrapped around my shoulders and I hadn't realized how much I needed support. My knees buckled, and I swooped down before the arms turned into a stronger embrace.

I peered up and found Ralf's smooth expression shift into one of panic. "Jesus, Nicole! Are you OK?" he asked in an alarmed tone.

"Yeah, I know I've got a bit of dirt on my clothes. Why is everyone acting like they haven't seen a little mud before? Must be another debutant weekend gathering." I whispered between us, "You know how they get about those things."

"Nicole," Ralf turned me toward him. "You've got blood stains all over you. Are you hurt?"

I glanced down and simultaneously wiped my cheek discovering blood spattered stains on my shirt, on my chest, and residue on my hand from my cheek.

I screamed. "It's all over!" I flapped my hands in disgust. The last thing I wanted was to be covered with the blood of a murder I witnessed. I feverishly started smearing the blood off my face and began to unbutton my blouse. "I have to get out of these clothes," I whispered before I repeated it louder, "I have to get out of these clothes now!"

Ralf smiled at the bystanders. "I told her paintballing gets messy even if she brought a change of clothes." He wisped me away toward the elevator. "Let's get you out of those clothes and send them to the cleaners."

When we reached his floor he continued with me in his embrace toward his room. Once he opened the door, I started clawing at the buttons on my shirt, visibly frustrated by their stubbornness to stay buttoned. Ralf calmly lowered my hands and began to unbutton them starting from the top and working his way down.

When he reached the last one he turned around and started a hot shower. "You may want to shower off the blood. Once it's cleaned off we can plug the tub and start a bubble bath, or whatever it is you need to do to relax."

"Who said I'm not relaxed?" I snapped. Ralf just scratched the back of his neck. "I'm sorry," I added. "You're right. I am a little tense."

"I'm going to get something to take the edge off." He didn't know what to do to help. "Wine?"

"Something a little stronger. I have some brain cells to kill." I went into the bathroom and finished undressing before I stepped in the steamy shower. I washed the blood and dirt from my body. After three rounds of rinsing I stopped the tub and started a bubble bath. When it filled near to the rim, I stopped the faucet. My body eased into the deliciously warm water and sunk to the bottom of the tub so the only things exposed above the layer of bubbles was from my shoulders up. Slowly, I laid my head back on a folded towel and closed my eyes for a moment.

There was a light tap on the door. Ralf cautiously entered the bathroom and left the door open. He brought a few selections from the mini bar. I snatched the tequila bottles, and he took the whisky. He settled down on the bath mat next to the tub with his legs outstretched in front of him,.

"Do you mind?" he asked before he made himself too comfortable.

I shook my head. "I'm sorry, Ralf. I was trying to make it to my moped out back so that I could have a meltdown at home instead of in the middle of the lobby. I had no intention of boarding the crazy train, and in front of you," I sighed. "This has been the day from hell."

"I'm getting that," he chuckled. "So do I need to ask?"

"It wasn't my blood. I'm not hurt, other than a few bumps and scratches from a little tumble I took."

"That explains the dirt. Whose blood was that and what happened?"

I took a deep breath and debated telling him the truth. Nah, I think my traumatic breakdown was enough crazy for one evening. "I took a tumble outside and took down an innocent bystander. She broke my fall into a patio glass table and got the worst of it. They took her to the ER, and I stayed behind to pay for the damages with the owner of the place. I feel terrible about it, so forgive me if I don't care to elaborate much further on it. I've been dealing with this all evening."

"Say no more," he raised his mini whisky bottle, and I raised my tequila. We both downed the equivalent of a double shot and scrunched up our faces at the bitter taste.

"Would definitely go down better with some salt and lime." I winced. "So tell me about your day?" Anything to keep from replaying the violent images from earlier tonight, over and over again in my mind.

"It's been busy but productive. We've made some headway with negotiations for our contract terms, but we've still got a gaping canyon between both parties. It will take some time with the bureaucracy of both ends. Anytime the risk management and legal department get involve, you can usually bet around a three week turnaround time." He shook his head. "I consider myself a patient man but I've been courting these clients for months on end and won't get commission until it's official."

"Yeah, you mentioned you'd be closing the deal soon enough, which means I won't be seeing you here as much." I nodded and opened another tequila mini bottle.

He smirked. "Yes, I'll finally get to sleep in my own bed again. Not that anything is wrong with your hotel beds. It's just all this traveling…I'm ready to close this chapter in my career."

I took a swig of what would now be the equivalent of my fourth shot. "And where exactly are you from Mr. Mancini?" I was positioned to shoot the bottle into the bathroom trashcan but then thought better of it. "Actually, could you toss this for me? Knowing me I'd probably miss."

"We wouldn't want another glass catastrophe in the same night," He grabbed the bottles and leaned over to throw them away.

"Another glass catastrophe?" I mumbled leaning my head back on the folded towel.

There was a pregnant pause before Ralf answered. "You said you and some other woman fell into a glass table earlier."

I peeked open one eye at him. Oh, yeah. "Yes, of course! No more accidents. Sorry, the booze is making my mind a little woozy. Hey, you never answered my question," I accused, trying to distract him enough to wipe that suspicious look off his face.

Ralf resumed his relaxed state. "Oh, I'm from Houston."

"Houston?" I repeated in disbelief. "No way. Houston?"

He smiled amused. "Yes way. Why do you sound so shocked?"

"No offense, but I've lived with Emily throughout college, and I just assumed all Texans would be as loud and gun-happy and country-oriented as her."

Ralf pursed his lips. "Miss D'Angelo, are you admitting to your prejudice based on a stereotype? We don't all wear cowboy boots, twiddle straw around our mouths, and ride horses to work."

"No, I didn't think that exactly," I scoffed. "Emily already confirmed that people don't ride horses in the city."

He laughed. "No, we certainly don't. I've lived there for a few years, but I wasn't born and raised there as I presume Emily was."

"Yes, she was. Has the 'Made in Texas' tattoo to prove it." I studied him more thoroughly. "I just never pegged you for a Houstonian I guess. So what things do you notice are different from Houston to Miami?"

Ralf finished his second mini bottle of whiskey and tossed it in the bin. "Not much difference temperature wise. Both are unbelievably hot. Enough humidity to make it feel like you're swimming instead of walking. People seem about equally friendly, although you'll see a mean side to Houstonians when they're driving. I have a working theory, that road rage there runs rampant due to the insane amount of rush traffic. It's enough to make you crazy."

"Does everyone listen to country music there? Their night clubs are all boot scootin' dance halls, huh?"

"Seriously? I thought you'd have a more realistic perception of the city since you've known Emily for so long."

I shrugged. "I can't openly ask Emily some of these things. She gets so defensive about her home."

"The answer is no. Country music does exist as does all the other genres of music. And there is a mixture of night life which does not strictly involve two-step. It's the fourth largest city in the nation. It truly is a melting pot. I'm surprised that you haven't taken a trip with Emily."

"No, I never have."

"Well you should plan a trip sometime. I could show you the sites."

"Have you ever thought of moving?" I asked. "Or do you intend to stay there?"

"I'm not tied to the city. Truthfully, I'm tied more so to my career. For me to get where I want, I need to bite the bullet for a few more years and go where I'm needed."

"Well you've been needed in Miami a lot recently. If this deal goes through would there be a chance of you moving to Miami?"

He tilted his head to the side and leaned over to pull a wet strand of hair out of my eyes. "Why are you interested in where I plan to live? Earlier on the elevator you said this was just a casual thing not going anywhere." He lifted a brow. "By the way, that's always nice to hear."

I cast my look to the side and gnawed at my lip. "I didn't mean it that way. I just meant we're in two different cities, and whatever it is that we're doing here isn't toward anything serious because of the distance."

"I see." He pulled his hand back to him.

"I don't do the long distance thing, and I'm betting you don't either. It's so much work, and I have enough on my plate that I don't have enough energy to give it the effort long distance would require."

"Well, to answer your question, Houston is where my job is based. I may be able to relocate in a few years, but I have too many things in the works where I'm at now."

My small ounce of hope crumbled and demolished into broken pieces.

Gently I tapped on the tub as acceptance settled in. "It is what it is. So let's just enjoy whatever it is we're doing now and not think into it. Keep things fun and light."

Ralf rose and snatched an extra towel from the rack above the toilet. "Keep it light? Like how your sheet of bubbles are lightening? Not that I protest to the view or anything."

I shot up from my resting point on the towel-made pillow and for the first time took regard to my bubble coverage. Only a few clouds of bubbles remained over my prime real-estate. I'm sure he was enjoying the view.

"Towel, please!" I demanded. "Couldn't have mentioned anything earlier?"

"I didn't want to interrupt our conversation."

"So polite. Just being the gentleman that you are."

He held the white towel outspread in front of him with his head turned and eyes closed. I lifted somewhat awkwardly from the tub, covering my front with both hands in case he tried to sneak a peek. When I stepped out of the tub and into the towel, he wrapped it around my shoulders so that my body was covered. And he didn't even attempt a glimpse.

When he opened his eyes I was wrapped in the towel facing toward him. He rubbed my shoulders and arms with the towel still covering me to help dry me off. The motion felt soothing, and naturally my body leaned into him. Our bodies were flat against each other. I tilted my head to the side and slowly traced a visual line from his chest to his eyes. The intoxicating tug of desire in full effect.

His eyes drugged with the same pull. The motion of his hands slowed until they nearly stopped. Deliberately we leaned closer as the sexual tension between us intensified. Merely a layer of air between our lips and Ralf shifted to pull away.

My eyes flew open in surprise at the abruptness of his departure.

"Clothes." He pointed a finger and then left the bathroom. I blinked in confusion. Ok, I guess we were on the hunt for clothes.

"There's no way I'm putting those back on again. You can trash them for all I care." I secured the wrapped towel around me looking around for anything I could wear. "Not sure what exactly I'm going to walk out of here with, but I could call Emily and ask her to bring me something to the hotel."

"No need to bother her this late. I'm sure I have some extra clothes. They may be a little big on you though, if you don't mind."

"I'd rather walk through the lobby in oversized clothes than stark-naked. Whatever you got will be great." I plopped on the edge of his bed while he rummaged through his suitcase. He grabbed a faded navy shirt and handed it to me. You can use this as a shirt."

"As a shirt?" I held it at arm's length in front of me. "And here I thought I'd wear it as a dress. You may be underestimating our height difference."

"I know I have some gym shorts I haven't worn somewhere in here." He continued digging while I slipped the shirt over my head and slid the towel off beneath it. The length was mid-thigh and smelled like him, a mixture of laundry detergent and cologne. Clean and sexy."

Ralf grabbed a pair of black cotton shorts from his suitcase. His eyes trailed my body from bottom to top. Being barefoot with nothing on but his T-shirt, I couldn't figure out what he was studying for so long.

A growl in delight escaped him. "Keep it. That shirt never looked as good on me as it does on you."

I blushed. He handed me the shorts and I slipped them on. The shorts shimmied their way to the floor, refusing to stay on my hips. "Shorts might not work." I shrugged. "I have dresses that are shorter than this shirt. I should be fine in it."

"Driving commando in a shirt on a moped?" He raised a brow.

"No, you're right. I'm not that brave." I admitted.

"Come on. I'll give you a ride home." He headed toward the door.

"That would be great. I owe you one."

A devilish grin spread across his face. "Careful. I collect on my IOUs."

CHAPTER NINE

I was dreaming. I knew it was a dream because I was picking dandelions with Al Pacino in the sand dunes on a cool summer afternoon. Not long after, Ricky Martin appeared...dangling from a string of yarn from the sky wearing a speedo and singing "Living la Vida Loca." A personal show performance just for me and good ol' Al.

Like I said, definitely dreaming. I mean let's be real...when has Miami ever had cool weather in the summertime? Come on now. Summer temperatures here are either blistering hot, or melt-the-skin-right-off your-bones hot.

Ricky's song became louder and louder until I opened my eyes. I found myself at the foot of my bed, head hanging off the side, with a numb right arm. How did I end up in this position?

Since Ricky was still whining in the background, I lifted my head and searched for the source of the ruckus. On my phone, the screen displayed a small picture of none other than—the infamous Juanita.

Sorely, I straightened out my arm and contemplated throwing my phone across the room. Fortunately, I reconsidered that idea. Instead, I settled for silencing my phone and cuddling back into my comforter.

When I woke up this time, the sun was burning heavily through my windows. I glanced at the clock.

"Nine o'clock?!" I grunted and pulled the covers over my head. "I just want to sleeeeeep!"

A few moments later, Emily bounced through the door, all smiles and sunshine as usual.

"Mornin' there sleepy head," she twanged in her Southern Belle accent. She sounded a little too chipper this early in the day for me.

"Let me go back to sleep," I moaned. "I'm worn out."

Emily lifted the covers and set a tray on the bed. "Come on, now. Up, up, up. I cooked you breakfast."

I opened my eyes to find a plate piled with eggs, bacon, sausage, and French toast. It was as though she was trying to feed an army. It was absolutely, horribly fattening, and I completely loved her for it.

"You are truly my best friend," I said before I dug in. She nibbled on the corner of the French toast.

"So, Ralf huh?" She wiggled her brows. "Don't think I didn't hear him helping you in the door last night and putting you to bed." She observed my all-too-big navy shirt. "That's his shirt, isn't it?"

"Maybe," I managed in between bites. "Before you ask, no, we did not have sex."

Emily's face dropped into one of disappointment. "Dagnabbit. I'm gonna need you to hurry it along already, so you can give me the juice."

"Over-involvement in other people's love life is a warning side effect of unemployment. You should focus your interest on something more productive, like finding yourself a job."

Emily rolled over on the bed, so she was lying on her stomach. "Pish posh. And FYI I am lookin' at gettin' into the journaling market in Miami, but it's not that simple. You can't just waltz in based on your mediocre career history and expect to land a respectable job. You either have to have the right connections, which I don't, or pitch a story worth telling, which I also don't have."

"You'll find something to write about," I shrugged. "You've always had a flare for it."

"Well thanks, darlin', but it's not my writing I'm stumped on. It's what to write about. I need a story that's a career-changer if I'm going to land my dream job with one of the big companies," she sighed. "I need to put my ear to the ground and see of any potential stories in town. It's Miami, for crying out loud. Crime Central."

I licked my lips once I finished my last bite of heaven. "There were those unresolved abductions a few months ago. You should look into those. No one has been able to report much on the incidents."

"Meh," she waved it off. "Great in theory, but anything that far outdated will turn up nothing but cold trails. I'd have to strike while the iron's hot. While there's still time to follow leads."

I chewed on my lip and looked away. Should I tell her our suspicions with the resent missing girls? I hated keeping secrets, and especially if this could help her get her career off the ground. I didn't want to hold her from that. But then, I didn't want her shouting it from the roof top and having the story lead back to Sunset Cove, which could put us back in the line of fire.

"What are you not tellin' me," Emily asked studying me as though she could read my thoughts.

"Nothing," I plastered on a smile that looked as forced as it felt.

"Nicole D'Angelo, don't you lie to me. I've known you long enough to know when you're holding something back. You got that look. Spill them beans."

I sighed. "Emily, I may be able to give you a hot trail on that story. I mean I don't know for sure. It could be related, or it could just turn out to be a coincidence."

Her eyes widened like a kid's on Christmas morning. "Well go on then. Tell me what you got!"

"The thing is," I scratched my head. "This hits a lot closer to home than I'd like. Some recent events occurred that could lead to bad publicity, which could result in a negative reputation. Lots of innocent people would be severely impacted by this if a certain minor detail about the story got out."

Emily rolled over and sat upright on the bed, intrigued at the idea of a breaking story. "What certain minor detail?"

"Well if I tell you, I need your word that you would exclude any information from the story tracing back to the minor detail. Can you give your word?"

"Depends on how minor it is, Nicole. Just tell me, and I'll let you know."

"Sorry, Emily. I need your word first. I would love for you to bust this story in the nuts, honestly, I would! However, I need confirmation of immunity regarding this detail before I give you anything. This would hurt me too much."

Emily's expression turned into a serious one. "It would hurt you?" She heavily weighed her options. "Fine, Nicole. You have my word."

I sighed. "Recently four girls went missing from the hotel. From *my* hotel, Sunset Cove. No one knows except for you, me, Juanita, and Toni." Emily's eyes widened in horror as I continued. "It started with this stupid hunch Juanita had when she overheard that two girls went missing one night. Her and Toni attempted some amateur investigating and got nowhere for lack of brains. Next day we find out the two girls are back and think nothing of it. You know, like they just had too much fun for a night. Anyways we thought that was the end of it, until yesterday when they missed their check-out deadline. We found their hotel room with all their belongings in there, but they were nowhere to be found."

"Are you sure they didn't have another night of too much fun and just miss their check-out?" Emily was entering journalism mode.

"That was one of my thoughts too, so we took extra precaution. Juanita did her snooping thing with the room to get some information on where they could have gone last. She even snatched their iPad. When we connected later that evening I went to return the iPad in case they came back to the room. But Emily," I leaned forward with a hand pressed on the bed, "when I went to the room to drop it off I found two guys in there raiding through their things and packing up all of their belongings."

"Were they robbing them?" she asked.

"There was no sign of forced entry," I shook my head. "They had a key to access the room. I don't know how they got it, but I do know it couldn't have been a coincidence that they were there cleaning up the room. That's what they called themselves, The Cleaners."

"Holy shit." She held up a hand. "Stop!" She sprung from the bed and rushed out of the room and down the hall. She was back in less than ten seconds with a notepad and pencil in hand. "Please, keep going!"

I explained the rest of the events from tailing Donnie and Ronnie, to stake out across from the brick building, to Ronnie being shot by the man with the Love Kills tattoo.

"Wait a minute. What do you mean by the same tattoo as the guy from the warehouse? You never mentioned a warehouse." She glanced up from her notepad.

"Oh, it was from a few nights ago. It was before shit hit the fan, and prior to seeing the tattoo I had no idea the two were even related." I went on to explain the incident at the abandoned warehouse and what I recalled seeing and hearing in that back room.

Emily was feverishly taking notes when I finished the breakdown.

Finally Emily stopped and placed the notepad and pencil next to her. "Nicole, do you know how big this could be?"

I nodded feeling an uncontrollable wave of emotion scratch at the surface.

"I mean..." Emily shook her head in amazement. "I mean...shit."

My head planted between my hands and a tear fell down my cheek. "I know! I'm completely fucked. If this story gets out that they were taken from my hotel, I can just call in my bankruptcy claim right now." Going over everything with someone else and realizing the degree of danger in all of this was overwhelming.

Emily patted my knee to soothe my anxiety. "Sunset Cove is not going anywhere. It is just a detail in the story. Not a make-or-break point. I won't mention anything regarding your hotel's name."

I attempted a smile in appreciation.

Emily shook her head in disbelief. "But imagine if y'all are right? If the abductions from several months ago are related to the four girls that were recently abducted then we've got a lead back to the culprit that no one else does. And if what you're telling me about the warehouse incident and the events from last night are connected, then we've already got some intel on the activity underlying the abductions."

"What do you mean activity?" I asked confused.

Emily picked up her pencil and abruptly stood from the bed. She paced the room as she twirled the pencil between her fingers. She spoke with incredible speed as she thought aloud. "Look at the big picture. Someone, or by the looks of it, some crew has been abducting tourists in Miami. Pieces we don't understand yet..."

She listed them off one at a time, "We don't know how long it has been going on for. Are they really isolated incidents, or is it connected? I'm betting on the latter. And we don't know who is at the head of this. We have a few names like Donnie, Ronnie, and Bruce, but we don't know who this *boss* is that they report to. More importantly, we don't know why these people are being abducted."

"Couldn't the reason just be that the abductor is mentally unstable? Untreated psychiatric problems can lead people to do all sorts of twisted things, right?"

Emily slanted her eyes at me in agitation. I see I've disrupted her journalism groove. "It's not because of an undiagnosed disorder. That might explain it if it were an individual behind the disappearances, but this is organized. There's even a designated clean-up crew. If they've assigned roles and responsibilities, then it's a pattern. If it's a pattern with this level of structure, then likely it is for a collective purpose. The question is 'what's their purpose?' I have a few ideas, but I'll need to do some investigating first."

I lifted my finger to ask her ideas but thought better not to interrupt her again. We could discuss her ideas later.

"Now, what facts have we witnessed during these interactions?" Emily asked. "We know that there is some type of process to proving one's allegiance to the boss. At the warehouse that ponytail guy you mentioned was trying to get in front of the boss, but his little minions wouldn't allow any meetings until he proved himself. Ponytail was bringing in some hot shot client to bring in more cash flow with more business opportunities."

Emily paused in her pacing. "What business opportunities though?" She looked deep in thought when suddenly she resumed her hasty pacing and out-loud ramblings. "To be continued later once I research the why aspect, since the two are undoubtedly related."

I could already see her obsessive wheels turning. I do the same thing when I can't think of the name of an actor from a movie. I can't stop trying to figure it out until the name comes to me, or until I simply breakdown and Google the answer.

"If we wanted to get to the bottom of their business, a good person to follow would be that ponytail guy since he's more on the front end of the business opportunities. Guess that's a moot point since we don't know his name or have any identifying factors about him. You know what would be great?" Emily suddenly turned and pointed a pencil in my direction.

I pressed a hand to my chest and looked around in disbelief. "Oh, me? I wasn't sure I'd been given speaking privileges."

Emily pressed a hand on her hip. "It would be great if we had an actual connection to someone inside. I mean we can still work back from the receipts and iPad that Juanita snatched, but it's going to take longer. Time is the worst enemy for hot trails. We'll need to start following up on these places, stat. I can work my magic and hack the passcode protection on the iPad." I looked at her in shock. "Well it ain't my first rodeo, dearie."

"Never cease to amaze," I muttered. "Yeah we have the car information and several of the meeting grounds for Donnie and Ronnie since we tailed them. I guess for just Donnie now. I still feel bad for him. Watching his own cousin murdered by one of his crew members? I understand he had to play detached for the sake of his own safety, but if I were him I'd want to make them pay. First, the boss for ordering the murder and second, Bruce for pulling the trigger."

Emily grabbed the sides of my face and shook me until my eyes bounced around in my brain, "Nicole, you're a goddamn genius!"

"What?" I asked peeling off her tight grip.

"You just bought our ticket in. Why didn't I think of that? Donnie! He's just seen his cousin murdered in cold blood which means he's emotional. Betrayed by his own crew, which means he's vengeful. The ultimate recipe to turn an insider into a source of information."

"Hold on a second. Are you proposing that we approach Donnie and expose ourselves on what we know in hopes of him wanting to side with us? What in heaven's name makes you think he's going to betray his crew for someone who wants to expose all the criminal activity he's ever been associated with?"

"For starters, I think his concept of loyalty has been shot in the ass all thanks to his own crew members. The concept of turning him isn't the issue here, though you're right on our approach of turning him. We can't walk up and say we are investigating the crimes they've committed and please cooperate with us so we can then have you put behind bars. That wouldn't go over well at all."

"You think?" I shouted.

"But," Emily continued, "we could approach with a different cause that may speak more to his emotional state."

"Like what?"

"Well, you could approach from a vengeful stance which would be far more relative to him, given his recent experience. We could give you a cover that you're looking to find your sister who went missing several months ago. You are seeking vengeance on the boss who had her taken in the first place."

"And what the hell am I going to say when he asks me how I found out about him and his whole crew? That I just stumbled across the information at Sunset Cove? I don't want this leaking back to my life."

"Oh, a cover is the easiest part to put together. I'll do some digging on the information about one of the missing girls from a few months ago. I'll put together a profile for you to study. Where you're from, family dynamics, education, blah, blah, blah. You will have all the details to align accurately with your alleged sister. In regards to the information you found leading to Donnie and his gang bangers, no, you didn't just stumble across the information. You have been working your ass off trying to find your sister for the past few months. The recent approval you received to gain access to her phone history and bank accounts has allowed you to put enough clues together to find where she was last before she went off the grid."

"When you're making a cover story you'll need to do better than that. That's far too big of a gap for my comfort which means he'll be uneasy with it too." I held out my index finger. "Another thing you haven't addressed. So let's just say that whatever profile you throw together, and whatever excuse you have for me finding Donnie, fails. What then if he decides I'm a liability and elects to *off* me like a cleaner would normally take care of a loose end?"

Emily scrunched her forehead deep in thought. "You're right. We would need a failsafe in case things took a turn for the worst. I mean, you already know I'm great with a gun."

"Uh, no ma'am! You are not going to have a gun aimed at him if I'm within twenty feet of your target. Besides, you just escalated to murder. This is getting out of control! What about some form of blackmail?" I suggested. "I could say I'm working with a few people, and they are one keystroke away from going viral with our evidence if he doesn't help me gain access to my sister or the man in charge."

Emily nodded. "Yes, the threat of prison is a great motivator. Problem is, we don't exactly have evidence, but those are just details."

"If he's guilty, the uncertainty is enough. And at least I have the names of the girls he recently took. He'll know I'm legit when I relay the details that haven't even hit headlines yet."

"I like how you think!" Emily was wiggling with excitement. "OK, game plan...I am going to do some research and put together a cover profile. Once you send me the vehicle information you pulled from his car last night, I'll do some digging in the databases, so we can get a last name and find out where to find him."

"If worse comes to worse I suppose we could just wait for him to make an appearance at the brick office building."

Emily was already leaving my bedroom. "Lots to do, lots to do! Don't forget to send me his car info. We won't be able to act until everything is in place. Hopefully by tomorrow we'll be up and running."

Great. I just found myself getting deeper and deeper. I'd loop Juanita in later when we actually had a game plan.

My phone started ringing Landon's ringtone. I answered, "Landon? What's wrong?"

Landon squeaked, "Wrong? Why would you assume something was wrong? Other than the fact that we made brunch plans for Jasmine Café weeks ago in advance and now I've been sitting at this table by myself for five minutes?"

"Brunch!" I smacked my hand on my forehead.

"I mean I do love me and all, but keeping my own company in public doesn't do much for my reputation."

"Who wouldn't love you," I stalled, trying to hop into a pair of cut off shorts. "And your reputation?" I huffed frantically shifting through my tops. "Landon, you're a legend. And when do legends rely on reputations. Look at Einstein? His rep was that he was bat-shit crazy, but generations to come will forever know him as a genius. Look I'm on my way there now; I'm in a cab as we speak."

"No, you haven't even left your house. You know how I can tell? You're smothering me with flattery for one, which we will definitely continue when you get here. And secondly, I can hear you going through your clothes in your closet."

Busted. "Be there in ten."

"Another lie." He sighed. "You never leave the house with your hair a mess, so you'll try fighting your untamable hair for five minutes before deciding on a hat. You'll try on at least two to three tops before you're satisfied which will take another five, including review time in the mirror. And then—"

"And then if I listen to you anymore I am going to waste an additional ten minutes. So I'll see you soon. Bye!" I hung up my phone and returned to the closet.

After I had tried on three shirts, I finally settled with the white striped blouse and a pair of gold dangling earrings. I damped my hair in the sink and tossed in some mousse to keep the form. Nothing was working so I tied it into a low side braid and covered the top with a white fedora hat. Once positioned in place, I cursed myself. I hated it when Landon was right.

I snatched a cab since my moped was still at work, and was in front of Jasmine Café in no time. There I found Landon lazily waiting beneath a white umbrella at a table for two on the patio. Quickly, I swooped in and gave him a surprise smooch on the cheek. He wasn't expecting my speedy arrival.

"Sorry, I'm late," I apologized. "Brunch completely slipped my mind."

"Not to worry, sweet cheeks," He smiled and appeared much too calm considering our previous interaction. "I was just enjoying the company of this fine, young man." He leaned over to the man at the table next to him. "I don't believe I caught your name."

"It's Charlie," he smiled.

"Charlie," Landon repeated in a flirtatious tone I'd heard him use so many times before. "The name is Landon."

Oh boy. I took this as my chance to part from the table for a brief moment to let them wrap up their undeniable flirting. Landon was such a hottie magnet. His current victim had black cropped hair and dreamy green eyes. He wasn't wearing anything spectacular, just a faded orange T-shirt and some casual white shorts, but his face and build made me wish he played for my team.

"I am going to go to the bathroom real quick. Be right back," I said before I rushed off. Landon nodded in agreement and understood he needed to exchange their digits in less than five minutes, so we could start our brunch date.

When I returned, Charlie was already gone. As I sat across from Landon, I couldn't help but laugh at his smitten smile. "You're glowing. I take it you got his number?"

"You know it. And we set up a date to grab drinks after work next week."

"Of course you did. The dating department has never been an area of improvement for you."

"It's a gift! That and fashion make-overs." He looked me up and down. "And as your dear friend, I still don't understand why you won't let me dress you. I could put together a whole closet for you based on your style preference, if you'd only let me."

Giving his offer more thought than I typically did, I actually considered having him put together a wardrobe for my cover profile, then shook it off. My cover was to be a concerned sister looking for revenge. I'm sure Emily would put something together, but regardless, it wouldn't call for high end fashion like the clothes Landon had access to.

"I think I'll pass. Maybe some other time," I shrugged.

"That's what you always say," he rolled his eyes. "One day, I'll break you down, and you'll be begging me to be your stylist." He picked up his menu. "Now let's figure out our orders by the time the waiter comes by. My stomach is growling from not eating brunch as planned."

He eyed me accusingly, and I stuck my head in my menu pretending that I couldn't see his heated glare. When the waiter came to the table, Landon ordered what sounded like the left side of the menu, and I took a small side salad. The breakfast Emily made me this morning was still digesting, but I wasn't going to dare tell him that.

Over brunch, or more like lunch, we caught up about his work and his little rodent dog, Tito. I filled him in on Ralf, and purposely omitted any of the abduction investigation. Some things were just too big to trust with Landon and that gossip-happy mouth of his. Of course, he was much more interested in my love life anyways.

"OK, we need to devise a plan to get you laid on your next outing." he pondered aloud while stroking his chin.

"Is it always about sex with you?" I asked.

"Duh! What kind of question is that?"

"I'm sorry, what was I thinking?" I laughed. "I don't know what to think of it all anymore. I thought he was as into me as I was into him, but then at the hotel when he helped me out the tub, I thought we were going to kiss…and then who knows what else. When suddenly an internal switch must have flipped, and he abruptly pulled away from me. No kiss. Nothing. It came out of left field."

"Mhmm," Landon was listening intently, quietly dissecting my story with his expert analysis. "So things were going smoothly, you leaned in for a kiss, and he leaned in too right? Or were you hanging out there solo?"

"No, he was leaning in too, but we never made contact."

"I see. Then it's not a matter of if he's interested in you. I think that much is obvious. Maybe he was trying to respect you by keeping hands off after the day you said you had."

I shrugged. Maybe. He was a gentleman about everything else, so it wasn't a farfetched idea.

"Don't let that little voice in your head over-analyze it. He's into you. I know these things. Now, the question is what do you have planned for your next date?"

Exhaustedly, I leaned back in my chair. "I have no idea, Landon. How do I top an intimate beach bonfire with smores and wine? That's a pretty original idea. I mean, I was contemplating seeing a movie or having dinner, but that's so boring compared to what he planned."

Landon nodded in agreement. "This is true. You do not want to follow up with some lame movie date. Uck, snoreville."

I pouted my lips. "Well, what would you suggest? You have to help me out here. What would you recommend?"

Landon's eyes squinted in concentration. "You need to have some sort of activity-based date, obviously. At the same time you want it to be in the proper setting to instigate some physical progression, if you know what I mean?"

"It's you, Landon. So yes, I know exactly what you mean, you horn dog."

He made a nonchalant shrug of indifference. "What if you took him to a paint party? Cocoas is throwing one tomorrow, if memory serves. Oh, that would be so much fun! It'll be just like the college days!"

Landon seemed more enthusiastic about the idea than me. I thought through my memories, back to the club venue where everyone was playing around in glow-in-the-dark paint. The scene could get pretty wild, but I guess that's to be expected when you combine messy paint, lowered inhibitions, and alcohol all under the same roof. "A paint party?" I contemplated, not yet sold on the idea. "But then we'll both get all sticky with the paint, and the atmosphere is so loud in there that we wouldn't be able to hear each other…I don't know if that's the environment I'm going for."

"Look Nicky, here's why you want to do this. He's going to get so turned on when he sees you wearing nothing but a pair of little white shorts and a cut off tank, covered in glow in the dark neon paint. You won't need to hear each other because you'll be too busy shoving each other up against the wall while groping in all the right places."

I lifted a brow amused by the image.

"Trust me, sweets. It's just the right environment."

"Oh, Landon you're a dating genius."

He propped an elbow on the table and sighed. "This I know. Now, as payment for my dating advice, you can cover our brunch bill. Besides, you were incredibly late. It's the least you could do."

I rolled my eyes, "If I hadn't been late, Googley Eyes from the next table wouldn't have grabbed your number," I protested as I pulled out my card to pay for the meal regardless.

Landon tapped his hair in a snobbish manner and laughed, "As if that would've stopped him."

CHAPTER TEN

After Landon and I wrapped up our brunch, I took a cab to Sunset Cove to collect my moped which was left in the lot from the previous night. When I arrived, I peeked around for Juanita in the lobby and saw her near the front desk. I tried to grab her attention, but she zipped out of there to the hospitality closet before she could spot me. Since her cart was still behind the counter I knew she'd be back shortly.

When I approached the front desk, Rose, one of the teenage front desk representatives, was absent-mindedly clicking away on the computer. She must have stumbled across something funny because she managed a horn-like chuckle in between her loud, exaggerated gum popping. As she chomped away on her bubble gum, a spontaneous image of a grazing cow flashed into my mind.

Silently I peered over her shoulder and discovered a Facebook page was displayed on her screen.

"What is this?" I pried with a strong edge to my tone.

"I was, a, just sorta checkin' my comments is all. I just pulled it up before you got here. Swear." She had that deer-in-the-headlight look and was five seconds away from breaking out into a sweat.

"I see," I nodded. "Don't mind if I use your computer for a moment," I stated more than asked. Once Rose stepped aside I exited out of the page and another window revealed itself, Instagram. When I glared across at her, the skin in her cheeks turned beet red. I closed the window out and was confronted by yet another window, Twitter.

"Are you serious?" I growled. "Maybe I'm missing something here. Is social media included under your job description?"

"Well, no. Not quite, but it was kinda like extra labor. You know, like I was doin' additional work, stuff I wasn't required to do, but I took the extra effort to do it. If anything I should get a gold star or a raise?"

"Oh, so you want some kind of reward, huh?"

Her perfectly aligned white teeth gleamed as her smile broadened. "Yeah, exactly. Can you really give me a raise?"

"Well not a raise, but we do have something that would be even better. We can award you personal vacation time."

"Wow, really? That would be awesome."

"Uh-huh, keep up the Facebook, Instagram, Twitter shenanigans, and you'll get your reward time. It's otherwise known as unemployment." Then Rose's smile wasn't so bright anymore. "Now go answer phones, or welcome our hotel guests, or at least something that is covered under your job description."

She vigorously nodded and disappeared to our office supply room. I think I made my point. I strummed my fingers absentmindedly on the granite countertops and waited for Juanita to return, so I could speak with her about my conversation with Emily this morning.

"Señora," Juanita whispered as she tapped my shoulder from behind me. I spun around in surprise and gasped under my breath.

"Dangit Juanita!" I clutched my shirt. "What's with the sneak attack? You should know better than to creep up on me after what we went through yesterday."

"I'm sorry. Si, I can see chu're a little jumpy. Me? I slept like a toddler last night."

"It's slept like a baby," I corrected her.

Juanita snarled. "Please, why would it be baby? Everybody knows babies don't sleep. I think it's supposed to be toddler."

Why do I even bother? I shook my head and my gaze swept over the bar area. Immediately I did a double take. Did my eyes deceive me? I heard the unmistakable sound of his voice and confirmed it was no hallucination.

Hastily I marched over to the bar and slammed both hands on the counter with such force that I caused the few bystanders to lean a few inches away. Toni continued wiping the glass in his hand and raised a brow in disinterest. We paused for a few moments in tense silence.

"Well?" I growled.

"Hi, Nicole," he returned in a formal tone.

"Hi, Nicole?" I mimicked. "That's what I get? Just a 'hi, Nicole?'" I could feel the vein in my neck bulge. "Why don't you start with telling me what in the hell you're doing here? Last time we spoke you said you were essentially walking off the job and deserting us because something came up."

Toni put down the glass and picked up the next one. He maintained eye contact as he spoke with a clipped tone. "Something did come up. I have every intention of leaving, but due to a very stubborn person who refuses to remove herself from a dangerous situation, I now have to stay and babysit until the threat is eliminated."

"So you're not leaving?" I softened my tone, still confused.

"And how am I supposed to do that when you're here trying to figure out a way into the lion's den. Jesus, Nicks I could never abandon you, not knowing that you're getting yourself in some serious shit. And since you refuse to heed my warning, there's obviously no stopping you."

I fiddled with my fingers and cast my gaze at the ground as he continued to lay into me. Why did I suddenly feel like a scolded child?

"Now I'm obligated to stay to make sure you don't get yourself killed, at least. But I'm telling you, like I said the other night, I know those two guys from the warehouse, and they are involved with some dangerous people. Don't ever underestimate them."

I felt a chilled shiver roll through my body, at his grave expression.

"Dun, dun, dunnnn!" Juanita added in. "Toni, we got it, OK? Message received. Now let's talk about our next move. I've been thinking of ways to work back from the most recent receipts."

I held up a hand to stop her there. Bystanders were still sitting around us, all eavesdropping on the conversation. I shook my head. "Let's go to my office to discuss. Toni, take a fifteen minute break and have the chef hold down the fort until you get back."

We scurried to my office, and when Toni caught up, he closed the door behind him. I reviewed the previous discussion I had with Emily about the new game plan. Our idea was to approach Donnie with a cover story and work that angle so we had a man on the inside.

Juanita was excited and practically bubbling over the brim with eagerness. Toni, on the other hand, looked wary with concern written all over his face. "I don't like it. There's too much at risk having you expose yourself like that. What if shit hits the fan? Are you so willing to put your life at stake like that?"

Juanita jumped in, "What about the other lives that are already at stake now? It would be selfish for us to sit on our hands while these little girls are being taken. Who knows what they're doing with them?"

"I get that, but why can't we let someone else do it? We aren't trained for negotiating and finding abducted people. We are completely inexperienced and unequipped to handle this."

"And you tell me how that's ever going to happen while saving the reputation of this hotel and keeping it in business so that we all still have a job to come back to? You know the press eats up this kind of stuff. No stone will go unturned. No detail will be left out. Sunset Cove will be destroyed by the harm it will do to our customer flow. I am not willing to hand my livelihood over so easily. I'm sorry, but I have worked too hard to get here. I have people counting on me for employment. This is the only way, Toni. So either you're in or you're out… there's the door."

Toni folded his arms in aggravation. "I think we've already established that I'm not going to leave you to fend for yourself. So you can take that option off the table."

"OK then. You both think you'll be able to make it to my place tomorrow, say noon? Emily is putting together a game plan as we speak, and it should be ready by the morning. We'll address an approach from there. Which reminds me, Juanita, do you have the car information from the other night?"

Juanita whipped out her phone and texted me the details. I forwarded the information to Emily per her request so that she could do some more digging.

"I was thinking of going back to the brick office building tonight to see if I could follow Donnie to his house. If we're going to approach him we will need to know where else we can find him. I don't think we want to meet him for the first time at that building. We need a neutral, safe zone away from his trigger-happy companions," Juanita suggested.

"I agree," said Toni.

"Si, and I'll need a big strong man to be with me for back up." She peered over at Toni and batted her eyelashes seductively. "Good thing we got one of those in stock."

Toni huffed but agreed to join her with her investigating.

"Great, now let me know what you find—" I was interrupted by the office phone ringing. I glanced over at it and silenced the ringer. "Officially, I'm not in today, so I'm definitely not answering—"

My cell started going off, the caller ID read Ma. I declined the call and resumed with Toni and Juanita, "Let me know what you find when you follow him. Send me the address, so I have it for the record. Be certain to give updates on where you are so if something goes wrong, I'll be able to find—"

My cell went off. Ma was calling me again. I declined the call again and finished up. "Well, keep me updated, and I'll see you both tomorrow. Please approach with caution tonight. Don't do anything that your gut doesn't agree with."

"Si, and just so we're clear, we are getting paid over time for these 'off the clock' runs."

"We'll figure something out," I patronized her.

"AND I want reimbursement of gas money. It's beginning to get expansive."

"Expensive? Yeah, we can make that happen, too."

Juanita continued down her mental check list. "What about food? I need extra personal fuel from all this running around. And did I ever tell chu that I had to personally cough up extra cash for my spy clothing?"

I sighed, "Why don't you just send me a bill, OK?"

We exited the office and parted ways. I was headed to the lot to grab the moped and head back home to see what Emily had put together so far. On my way through the lobby the phone rang again. I was about to answer it when I heard my name called behind me. I turned around and found Ralf sporting a pair of dark jeans, a gray shirt, and a black blazer. He looked as though he'd just stepped out of a J.Crew magazine.

I dropped my phone by accident, caught up in his good looks. Clumsily, I scrambled to pick it up and decline Ma's call.

"Hey," he smiled. "I was just about to step out for a bite. Would you like to join?"

Technically, I didn't have anything scheduled. As incredibly sexy as he looked, the thought of looking at him longer over dinner was compelling. I appreciated his good looks, which only reminded me of my quick assembly this morning, and that I was definitely not dressed in my A game. "Yeah, I could go for some food."

We angled toward the parking lot, and he opened the passenger door. I slid into the seat. Southern hospitality never gets old.

Once he sat down, he revved the engine and pulled out onto the street. We were headed to a little seafood restaurant a few blocks down and over, when my phone rang yet again. I was about to ignore the call when Ralf chimed in, "Why don't you get that?"

"It's my neurotic mother. She's been blowing up my phone. This woman is excessively persistent," I rolled my eyes.

"Maybe it's important?" he suggested.

I sighed not wanting to answer the call. "What, Ma? I'm in the middle of something."

Her voice came blaring through the speaker, and I held it away from my ear a few inches for the sake of my eardrum. She wasn't making much sense. All of her words were jumbled together, but what was clear was that she said she needed help at the house now. I hung up the phone and stared over at Ralf.

"What was that about?"

"I don't know. Something's wrong. That was my mom, and it sounded like an emergency. I'm sorry, Ralf, but I can't eat dinner. I have to go. Could you drop me off at the hotel, so I can pick up my ride?"

Ralf gripped the wheel. "How do I get to your mom's place from here?"

"What? No, Ralf you don't need to drive. Really, I already feel like a big enough inconvenience by having you drive me back to the hotel. Seriously, I can drive myself."

"It's an emergency, Nicole. Don't be ridiculous. I'm taking you there. Now what's my next move?"

"Left at the next light." I motioned with my hand. "Thank you, Ralf. I owe you." I added.

"No worries, raincheck our date, and I'll consider your debt paid." He winked at me before he revved the engine and burned some rubber.

I gave him directions throughout the ride as I replayed the panic in Ma's voice. Each time her tone caused an uneasy nauseous feeling, and I silently prayed that she didn't somehow set the curtains on fire. Again.

When we arrived at her house I noticed several cars were parked out front. I recognized Ma's friend, Wanda's car, but I had never seen the other vehicle before.

I flung the back door open, Ralf by my side, and frantically scanned the kitchen. Wanda was lighting candles on the kitchen table. She peeked up and shot a wink at me in greeting. I didn't see Ma, so I trotted through the house, trying to find her. I rounded the upstairs landing and spotted her next to the wall of family portraits in the loft.

"Ma," I was panting, a little out of breath. OK, so maybe a lot out of breath. I'll run a couple of laps later. "What's—what's the problem? You said there was an emergency?" I gasped between breaths.

The man standing next to her turned around and shot me a slick smile. "You must be Nicole. I see you've grown into your buck teeth nicely." He motioned toward the portraits behind him.

I stared open-mouthed at the hideous school portrait behind him. "Yeah, I couldn't decide whether I should have brown bagged it that day or not. Guess I should have chosen the bag," I paused. "I'm sorry, who are you again?"

"Travis Wattner. I've heard such great things about you from Wanda and your mother."

"He also goes by Dr. Wattner," Ma hinted.

"Doctor?" my eyes widened in fear. "Ma, what's wrong? Are you hurt? Sick? Is it Vi? Where is she?" A slew of questions came streaming out at once. Ma appeared fine on the outside, but maybe there was something much, much worse going on internally. But why would she have a doctor make a house call to have this discussion with me?

Ma cocked her head sideways. "Nicky, I'm fine. So is Vi. She's around here somewhere."

"Well, what the heck is the emergency? You said on the phone…"

"Oh, yes. Did I say it was an emergency? These damn cell phone connections are terrible sometimes, aren't they? No, honey. There's no imminent danger. I was calling you to invite you over for dinner. Sorry it's a little unexpected."

I had to give my body enough time to catch up to the situation. My heart was still pounding. Now whether it was pounding on account of running up the stairs or because I was anticipating an emergency, I wasn't entirely sure. But when Ma's words began to register my heart resumed its normal pace, and my breathing slowed accordingly.

"So there's no emergency?" I repeated. "What was with the bugaboo phone calling then?"

"Well I wanted to invite you to dinner since I knew you wouldn't want to miss it. Then when you didn't pick up I started to get worried. I was beginning to wonder if the wolves had eaten you or something. Where've you been? You don't answer my calls, or my e-mails, and you never stop by." Ma instantly went into lecture mode.

"If someone doesn't call you back in five minutes, it likely means they're busy." I placed a hand on my hip. "So aside from your array of calls within the last hour, when else did you call?"

Ma smacked her gum before answering. "Well, aside from that I haven't called, but the phone works both ways you know."

"And what e-mails? You don't even know how to start up a computer."

"Hey," She blew a bubble and sucked it back in. "That piece of junk, computer, or whatever you call it, has more to it than you think. Don't judge."

Well let's see. There's one button that turns on the laptop. It's not rocket science.

"Besides, I was here a few days ago. Things at work and at home have been a little busy lately. I'm sorry."

"Mhmm," she glared at me with arms folded over one another and nearly burnt a hole in my stomach with her laser-beam eyes.

"So why is there a doctor here? Jesus I thought you were going to tell me you were dying." I peeked back at him still puzzled.

Ma smiled her mischievous smile and placed a hand on our backs to guide us closer.

"Sorry, what was your name again? Doctor…" I asked extending my hand for a handshake.

Instead he cradled my hand and raised it to his lips for a kiss on the hand. "Dr. Wattner, but please call me Travis."

My mouth opened in surprise as the light bulb turned on. First of all, who kisses on the hand anymore? We are not in the 1800's. And secondly, what was my mother thinking? Trying to play matchmaker with some stuffy doctor without even giving me the heads up? Such a meddlesome old woman.

His touch lingered a second too long, so I ripped my hand away and backed up to where Ralf was standing.

"Nice to meet you, Travis," I muttered. When I glanced up at Ralf his expression was blanketed in amusement.

To prevent this from getting any more awkward, I broke the dating 101 rule and made the introductions, "Travis, this is my boyfriend, Ralf. Ralf, this is Travis." I squirmed at the term since I know guys get wigged out about it, especially when you've only gone out once or twice. I just needed Ma and Travis to back off their matchmaking attempt since it would make things pretty uncomfortable if he tried to pursue me with Ralf right there.

They both nodded a curt greeting, and Ma's eyes about popped out of socket. I was shocked that she was able to refrain from squealing in delight.

"Now wait a minute, who is *this*?" Ma was eyeballing Ralf like a wolf seeking out a piece of raw meat.

"Hello," Ralf extended his hand and shook Ma's hand in greeting. "I'm Ralf Mancini. Nicole's…boyfriend."

"Nice to meet *you*." I think I saw her flex her boobs. Great. My own mother is after him.

Ma picked up on the awkwardness of all four of us huddled around the upstairs loft. She grabbed Travis by the wrist and led him down the stairs. "Travis, be a dear and help me downstairs. I can't decide if I should serve red or white wine with our dinner tonight, so I need to borrow your taste buds. Help me pick the wine for the evening?"

"Sounds great," he quickly followed her, gracious for an escape.

"Ma, I think we're going to head out then since there's no emergency. We were actually on our way to dinner already when you called." I turned toward Ralf for only him to hear, "Come on, let's get out of here."

Ma called out, "I'm finishing a batch of lasagna in the kitchen and have bruschetta appetizers on the table."

I popped my head over the banister. "Lasagna? Well…maybe we could stay for a little while."

CHAPTER ELEVEN

When I straightened up I found Ralf staring back at me with pursed lips. "I'm just learning all sorts of new things today. One, that you have an apparent weakness for lasagna. Two, that we've gone official without my knowledge. Make sure you let your mother know that I am not fond of her pimping my *girlfriend* out to random men. That's just not going to fly in this relationship," Ralf teased.

"First and foremost, it's not just any lasagna. It's my Ma's special lasagna. A recipe that has been passed down from generations of Italian women. Don't under estimate the power of the pasta." I peeked over his shoulder to make sure no one was around. "And secondly, I'm sorry! I had to lie and say we're a couple or else this would have gotten weird quick. Just fake it for an hour or so. It'll be one quick meal, and then we can jet. We'll never speak of this again."

He chuckled at the predicament and pulled me closer so my hips were flesh with his. "Since your mom's busy downstairs, maybe you can give the tour of where little Nicole D'Angelo spent her time as a kid." He leaned in for a kiss but pulled away at the last moment, tantalizing me with the desire to be kissed.

"A tour?" I pulled away and teetered at the edge of the doorway. "Why don't we start with the bedroom?" I beckoned him over, and he eagerly made his way toward me. When he reached me I pinched the fabric of his shirt and tugged him closer.

Hungrily he slid his fingers under my shirt and grabbed the skin around my waist as he pressed his mouth down to mine. I wrapped my arms around his neck and reveled in the feel of his body. He stepped forward until I was pressed against the wall. His body followed mine until the lengths of our figures were melded together. A perfectly airtight unit. My horn-o-meter jump-started to one hundred in a matter of seconds. The way his hands molded to my body here in this moment, made me want to rip off our clothes and get down to business. The fact that we were at my mother's house made it feel like we were two lustful teenagers. The breaking the rules…the sneaking around…it certainly magnified the exhilaration of it all.

Suddenly Vi flung open her bedroom door which was a few feet over from where we stood. "Hello!" she shouted in a disgusted tone. "Sis, please. Get a room, you animals." Then she paused in thought. "Oh, wait. You don't have a room here anymore. I needed more closet space, so I had to do some expanding and remodeling."

Immediately when he heard Vi's voice, he pulled away and resumed his charming composure. "You gotta do, what you gotta do." He smiled a heartbreaking grin. "Clothes need their space. I'm sure Nicole will understand."

"You've got a smart one here," Vi swayed in captivation, "and a handsome one, too."

"The name's Ralf Mancini." He met her hand with a shake. "I'm the new boyfriend."

Vi sighed a little taken off guard. "I mean usually I don't jump into relationships with men I've just met, but I could just make an exception for you." She winked in flirtation.

I corrected her misunderstanding. "By *the* boyfriend, he means *my* boyfriend."

Ralf rested an arm around my shoulder, and it clicked into place for her.

"Right, right. Of course." Then she blinked her eyes at me in shock. "So *you* have a boyfriend? I bet Ma is in seventh heaven, huh?"

I just rolled my eyes at the thought.

Vi was quite the vision in her little number. Her skin still tanned to perfection, her hair neatly straightened and slightly rounded inwards at the bottom. Her nails were trimmed and manicured. She was wearing a light weight peach summer dress which simply made me envy her long legs even more. The kid was a Barbie doll and I looked a disgrace standing next to her.

"What are you so dressed up for?" I asked. "Another date I presume?"

"You remember that beautiful man we saw on the beach? We're going on a second date. He wants to take me to Table 8 for a late dinner."

"So you're planning on having lasagna here and eating again at the restaurant? That's quite an appetite."

"Sacrilegious!" she baulked. "Everyone knows you aren't supposed to eat more than a fist size of food on your first three dates. Hello, it scares them off. So I have to eat some real food before I go, or I'll pass out."

"I never got that memo. I used to eat a supersize Big Mac combo in front of my dates," I shrugged.

"OK, I don't know what's worse, the fact that you supersized a combo on a date, or the fact that your date actually took you to McDonalds."

I diverted back to our initial topic. "So you and…" I paused for his name.

"Alex."

"So you and Alex plan on going out again tonight. Did you two, you know, last night?"

"Have sex? Of course, I didn't want to waste my time with other dates if he was horrible in the sack."

"Right. I mean, of course." Ralf chimed in with a light tone.

"Wish I had that philosophy, don't you?" I turned my head, eyeing him in judgment.

"I see I've picked the wrong sister," he teased. In response I smacked him on the side and returned to Vi.

"Well, I'm happy Alex passed the test then."

"Yeah he was pretty good. A little too much tongue in his kisses, but he made up for it later."

Ralf's eyebrows shot upwards a few inches surprised at my sister's willingness to discuss sexual relations in front of strangers. I, on the other hand, already knew that she had no boundaries when it came to sex.

"Oh, I see." I nodded, hoping she wouldn't get lost in details again with Ralf here. A normal, boring first impression is all I asked of my family. Miraculously, if there was a second meeting, they could reveal all their craziness then. Just one normal meeting, please! I silently begged in my mind.

"Although, now that I think about it, we did queef a lot. It was actually starting to get on my nerves," she recalled from her memories.

"Queef?" I asked in curiosity. What in the world is a queef?"

Ralf scratched his neck and intentionally avoided eye contact. Vi just shook her head. "Sometimes I can't believe you're older than me. A queef is when you're having sex and your vajayjay makes a farting noise."

"Vajayjay?" I repeated idly, entertained by the nickname.

"Yeah, that's what Oprah calls your goodies." She gestured down south.

"I see. Wait, your goodies can fart?"

"Sure. You've never had a queef before? Oh, the first times a doozey. Sort of embarrassing if you don't know which hole it came from," she winked.

"Who's hungry for dinner?" Ralf interrupted and gestured toward the stairs. "Ladies first."

Vi led the way and began to descend the stairs. "By the way, Ma and Wanda are trying to introduce you to some doctor. You may want to shoot that down when you meet him."

"We've already covered those grounds. Thanks for the delayed heads up. A text in advance would've saved us the headache, so feel free to send me a message next time."

She lazily waved it off and proceeded to lead us to the kitchen. Immediately Vi charged toward the kitchen table and grabbed a bruschetta slice in each hand. Ma pointed a tomato-soaked stirring spoon at Vi and was holding a big gulp glass of wine in the other. "Vi, where are your manners? Guests get the first serving. Now pick up the plate and serve the bruschetta to everyone."

Vi froze with the bruschetta nearly engulfed in her mouth and painfully refrained from taking a bite. She growled under her breath as she placed it on her bread plate. Vi picked up the platter and made her way around the kitchen making stops at Wanda, Travis, and Ralf first before she returned the platter to the table.

"Yeah, don't worry about me. I am actually the only human in the world that doesn't need food to survive," I shrugged nonchalantly.

"Get one yourself. You don't qualify as a guest," Vi answered. "So what's the status of the lasagna, Ma? Will it be ready soon?"

She was positioned behind Ma and staring intently over her shoulder.

"Lasagna will be finished in five more minutes. Go and sit down at the table, child. Your hovering is making me crazy."

Vi started for the table, and Travis rushed to pull a chair out for her. When she sat down she eyed him with a newfound interest and leaned forward with her flirtatious charm kicked into full bloom. Travis sat across from her and smiled back in mutual interest. I'm glad this night wasn't a total waste for him.

I reached in the cabinet for the dinnerware and started to pull down six plates. A pair of strong, warm hands met mine as Ralf helped to lower the heavy stack of plates to the counter.

"Thanks," I breathed not expecting his presence behind me. The feel alone of his hands over mine left a tingly sensation in my fingers.

"How can I help?" he asked with a subtle expression that nearly masked his charged longing. Apparently he was also reminded of our little rendezvous upstairs when his hands brushed mine.

I stuttered for a moment lost in that same desire when I locked eyes with his. "Well I, uh. I'll get the silverware if you could take the plates over?"

He nodded and went to set the table with the plates, and I prepared the silverware. Once everything was arranged and everyone was seated, Ma placed the lasagna dish on a hot plate in the center. By this point, everyone had a glass of wine they'd started and eagerly took turns serving the lasagna.

As we all chowed down on dinner, Ma dove right in to the crazy talk.

"So, Nicky, Ralf? How long have you two been keeping your relationship a secret from us? Do I need to set a date with the church?"

Ralf and I both simultaneously choked on our wine. I coughed and set my glass down. "Ma! We just started dating. I think we'd both agree that you can hold off on the wedding dress measurements."

Vi smirked. "Yeah, Ma. You know Nicky likes to take things slow. They haven't even had sex yet. I don't know how she does it because if I had *all that* to myself for a full twenty-four hours, I don't think I'd be able to walk for a week straight when I got through with him."

Ma and Wanda took an oversized gulp of their wine. Like I said, no boundaries in matters of sex.

"I mean, he is easy on the eyes." Wanda giggled from behind her wine glass.

Travis was casually looking around for the nearest escape route. Vi noticed Travis's bruised ego and included him in the mix too. "Don't worry Travis. If it were you and me, we wouldn't be able to walk right for two weeks." She winked and his eyes widened in enthusiasm before he returned to his polite composure. I'm sure his excitement by her promiscuous banter was conflicted by reservation due to their audience at the dinner table. The poor kid didn't know what to do with himself.

Ma returned to her previous topic, her gaze shooting from me to Ralf. "Nicky, from one woman to another, you better quit dawdling with this one. You can bet your ass he'll get snatched up as soon as you give him reason to leave."

"In other words, you ought to treat me like gold," Ralf beamed a smug smile.

"No, in other words, I mean you better get knocked up before he breaks it off with you." Ma tipped her glass toward me then finished it off. "Chop, chop now. You need to seal the deal."

I flew into a fit of coughs at the sound of this. When I glanced across the table at Ralf, I noticed that his jaw practically dropped to the table.

I managed to choke out, "We haven't discussed the topic of kids yet, but thanks for your suggestion."

"You haven't even discussed children?" Ma gasped. "Jesus, Nicky this is why you've been single for so long. You kids need to quit playing games. In my day this was the second question out your mouth. The first was to find out his name."

"Times have changed," Vi chimed in. "Thankfully. You start off with that doozy of an icebreaker and you'd find yourself at home with a bucket of ice cream each night." She mumbled more silently to herself, "I'm surrounded by amateurs here."

Quickly I changed the topic, "So Wanda, how have you been?"

Wanda peeked over from the top of her thick black framed glasses. "Oh, I've been just wonderful, dear." She flashed a warm smile. Wanda was always my favorite of Ma's friends, and she was probably the nicest member of the Delightful Daisies club that Ma was involved with. I sometimes wondered why a person as calm and sweet as her would ever be friends with a person as wild as my mom. I was grateful Ma had at least one stable, grounded friend in her life. The same couldn't be said for the rest of the Daisies.

"What about you, Nicole? Has life been treating you well?" she asked in a soft voice.

"Sure has," I smiled back. "Just a little busy with work-related matters, but nothing that can't be handled," I lied.

"Oh, well that's good then. You were always such the busy bee, even before with school when you were a teen," Wanda reminisced.

"So you need to unwind from work a little?" Ma grabbed for the wine bottle and filled the wine to a centimeter below the rim. "Here, this will help." She handed me the glass.

My eyes bulged. "Perhaps just a little less," I suggested as I poured three-fourths of the drink into Ma's glass. Ma and I had different ideas of proportions.

"Anything new in the Delightful Daisies' gossip arena?" I pried. Ralf and Travis were looking at me perplexed by the name. "Sorry, Delightful Daisies is a gossip cult that my mother and Wanda have been initiated into."

"Ahem. It is a member-only social group." Ma corrected. "And the Delightful Daisies are encouraged to keep matters of the circle confidential."

"So naturally that means you're going to give us an update anyways," Vi added before she took her final bite of lasagna.

"Naturally," Ma continued. "Well, do you remember Mr. Wallace? You know, the man who had an obsessive, rather odd, foot fetish?"

"Hard to forget a man who spends most of the conversation drooling over my feet rather than making eye contact," I nodded.

"Yes, well he passed away. The dear old thing," Wanda shook her head finishing Ma's sentence.

"As I recall he wasn't that old," I thought back on the graying man. He couldn't have been much older than Ma.

"He was in his early sixties," Wanda explained. "Apparently, he left a pretty hefty amount of money to his only son."

"I didn't know he had a son." I shrugged.

"Oh yes. A very handsome, striking young man," Wanda eyed me for a moment. "In fact, he's only a couple years older than you."

"Single?" Ma pried.

"And single."

"Hmm, and recently turned wealthy." Ma was rubbing her hands together in a devilish manner.

Ralf muffled a cough and interrupted Ma's line of thinking. "If I didn't know any better I'd say the wheels in your mind were starting to turn at the idea of introducing this single, strikingly handsome, millionaire to your daughter." He continued, "Unfortunately for him, Nicole is no longer on the market."

Ma shook her head in forgetfulness. "Ah, yes, of course. That would be inappropriate since you two are an item now." She chugged a few more gulps of wine. "I'll just hold onto his card for safekeeping and make introductions if you both don't work out."

Ralf's eye twitched, a sign that his endurance regarding my family was beginning to diminish. Any soldier would've cracked hours ago. I slipped my foot out of my shoe, and secretly initiated a game of footsie with Ralf under the table. Ralf only managed to drop his utensils once when my foot accidentally ventured too far north of his thigh. Whoops.

"So what's this I hear about some woman moving in with you?" Ma waited, "Care to explain why I had to hear all this from Patti Siegler next door?"

"Patti? How does Patti know about my house occupants?" I was baffled.

"I know! It's an embarrassment. I find out that you have a new roommate, not through you, but through the lonesome hermit next door who never leaves her house. Did you ever stop to think how that makes me look? If the girls suspect that I'm not on top of my gossip game, I could get kicked out of the Delightful Daisies."

"Poor thing," I patronized. "Just how did Patti know?"

"Patti found out through Annabel, who was notified by Franny, who overheard Ginger talking to Victoria, whose younger daughter Rachael noticed an auburn chick has been staying at your place for a while."

I debated popping a few Advil from my purse. Her breakdown of the gossip process was making my head spin. "No, Emily is not my new roommate, but she is staying with me for a while until she is able to stand on her own feet again. She ran into a little bit of boy trouble."

"Emily Pickens?" Vi regained interest in the conversation. "From college?"

"The one and only."

"Oh, I love that firecracker," she giggled. "Ralf, you have to meet Emily, she's so much fun."

"Oh, we've met," he smiled recalling the memory of Emily showing him her hand gun. "So much fun."

Vi's phone on the kitchen counter began to sing Marvin Gaye's "Let's Get It On."

"Hmm. Interesting ringtone," I cocked my head to one side. "I wonder who that could be?" I asked innocently knowing that was likely Alex calling for their date. Travis appeared confused. You know, for a doctor, I was surprised at how frequently he exhibited that dumbfounded expression. Guess the ringtone selection didn't perk any alarms in his mind.

"Oh, it's just my friend. We have matching ringtones," she squinted at me and rushed out of the room to answer it.

When I glanced over at Ma I realized she was well on her way to slosh town. She was slumped in her chair and started humming an out-of-tune number from the Sound of Music.

"Ma, why don't you go to your bedroom and take a nap." I suggested.

"Yes, but the dishes," she slurred.

"I've got the dishes. You should rest your eyes for a few minutes and then come out and join us afterwards," I encouraged.

She nodded and leaned over to pat my cheek in satisfaction. She stared aimlessly across the table and smiled. "Such a doll this one. You see why she's my favorite?" When she stood from the table she staggered a few steps, and I wrapped her arm over my shoulder to stabilize her.

Ralf and Travis rose from their seats about to come to my aid, but I stopped them. "No, please. We've got this down to a routine."

I braced Ma with my other hand around her waist, and we headed toward her bedroom. "It was nice meeting you Travis. Wanda, if you'd be a dear and make Travis a container of leftovers before you show him out, I'd appreciate it."

"Oh, of course," she hurried into the kitchen with him, and Ralf waited at the table not knowing what to do with himself in this situation. "Ralf I'll be right back. I'm going to clean up the dishes, and then we can go."

Ma muffled a protest against my shoulder as we shuffled toward her room. "Don't worry, Ma, I think everyone is feeling a little tired, so we're going to get you to bed and then we're all going home to sleep too. Your meal was so rich and filling that we're all about to go into a food coma. Our Italian ancestors would be so proud."

"Eat, sleep, breed," Ma slurred with pride.

I laid her on the bed and tucked her beneath the covers. She smiled a thank you before her eyes closed and her breathing slowed. I was well acquainted with this scene. After Dad passed, this became a routine that I had mastered by the age of sixteen. Ma was a wino, a gambler, a chain smoker, and a whole slew of other issues I didn't even care to think about tonight.

When I meandered back into the kitchen Vi, Travis, and Wanda had already parted ways for the evening.

"Great," I muttered to myself anticipating the mountain of dishes that were waiting for me. I was shocked and exceptionally grateful at the sight of Ralf scrubbing away at the dishes in the sink. He wore a pair of yellow rubber gloves and had already worked through the bulk of the dishes.

Sneakily, I crept up behind him and slid my arms around him and up his chest. He paused and craned his head so that he was peeking over his shoulder at me. I rested my chin on his back and looked up at him.

A smile spread across my face, "You're a good man Charlie Brown. You really are."

He chuckled at this. "So does that mean I get some kind of award or special recognition for enduring an entire evening at the D'Angelo house?"

"Oh, your brave endeavors have not gone unnoticed." I slowly traced my fingers down his torso and made teasing circles over the skin on his hips before I ventured further down beneath his jeans. "And without a doubt, will be rewarded."

The wine glass he had been washing fell in the sink. The unmistakable sound of glass shattering shortly followed.

"Shit," Ralf cursed.

"I'm sorry!" I pulled back and hurried in search of a mini dustpan for the broken glass.

"Don't apologize," he darkly chuckled. "Please, don't apologize for that. The broken glass was on me."

I mentally patted myself on the back for triggering his excitement before even getting to the good stuff. It's always good to know that he's as hot for me as I am for him. When I found the mini dustpan and rushed back to the sink, I noticed a cut on his palm where he tried to collect the bigger chunks of glass.

"Are you OK?" I asked setting the pan down. "Here let's take care of this, and then I'll finish here in the kitchen. I turned the faucet to a mildly warm temperature and washed my hands real quick so that I could then guide his hand under the spout for cleaning. Gently I rubbed some soap around the cut and the rest of his hand to prevent an infection. I turned off the water and reached for a paper towel before I dabbed his hand dry.

"Nurse Nicky to the rescue." He smiled down at me. "I've always had a thing for nurses."

"Oh yeah?" I pried as I grabbed the first aid kit from the cabinet and began to dress the cut. "Remind me to show you my nurse costume from a college Halloween party sometime."

His eyes widened in anticipation. Once I finished he turned his hand over to inspect my handiwork. "Well, kid...it looks like you're going to make it after all."

He laughed, and I returned to the sink to sweep up the rest of the broken glass. I finished the few remaining dishes in the sink. When it was all done and the kitchen had been restored to its natural order, we turned out all the lights and locked up behind us.

On the car ride home, Ralf turned on some soft background music, and we both sat in comfortable silence.

"Thanks again for tonight," I mentioned as we pulled into the hotel's parking lot. "You were seriously great back there. I know my family's a lot to take in, and you jumped in like a pro."

"Your family's not as crazy as you think," he said. I stared at him knowingly. "OK, I mean they are crazy, but they're not as bad as you think. Your Ma is a bit of a wild child, but it's obvious she loves you. And your sister...seems to be friendly with the boys, but it's evident that she admires her big sister."

"Yeah, Ma is definitely a filter-free, rebellious bag of mental instabilities, but she didn't always used to be this way. She has always been a tough bird but was much more responsible before my dad died."

"Hey," Ralf pulled the car into a spot and parked the car. "Your mom packed up her life and moved to a new city where she managed to raise two kids by herself. She may have developed some issues along the way, but raising two kids under those conditions sounds responsible to me."

I leaned my head back against my seat. I guess I never looked at things from that angle. "OK, wise one. You're getting deep on me here."

He chuckled and shrugged it off. "Just saying you're harder on your family than anyone else. They have a good heart, which is also apparent to the people around them."

His understanding about my family baggage was refreshing. I smiled and leaned in for a sweet kiss. "I promise, the next date will just be the two of us."

"Next date? Who said we're going on another date after you dragged me to that circus back there?" he teasingly mocked before he pulled me back in for a long, sizzling kiss. In between kisses he murmured, "So when is next time?"

I laughed and pulled away. "Whenever you're free next."

"Tomorrow evening it is. Surprise me with whatever you want to plan for the evening. Just tell me where I need to be and when."

"You got it, dude." I smirked.

"You got it, dude? Did you seriously just quote Teenage Mutant Ninja Turtles? I have the best girlfriend in the world," he teased.

I smacked him on the chest. "I already apologized for boyfriend/girlfriend charade, but I had to use the term or their matchmaking intentions would have turned the evening into a very uncomfortable one."

"See? Always looking out for her man," he continued.

"Goodnight, Ralf!" I rolled my eyes and hopped out of his car.

"Goodnight, my honey-bunches-of-oats, darling-baby-bug-a-boo, cupcake."

I laughed and slammed the door behind me. Always got jokes. I powered up the moped and hurried back home. The food coma from the lasagna started to settle in. My eyes were heavy, and I was looking forward to plopping into bed.

CHAPTER TWELVE

When I finally awoke the next morning, I rubbed the sleep from my eyes and lazily stretched my arms and legs in the bed. I trudged down the stairs to find that the house was eerily silent. This was unusual these days since either Trixie was squawking in the background, or else Emily was twangin' to some old country song. But today there was nothing.

As I rounded the stairs I almost slipped on the floor when I spotted Emily curled up on the couch, staring straight ahead. She was so still she could've been mistaken for a statue.

"Well, hello there," I said. "Creep much?"

She broke her daze and glanced up at my face before returning her focus to its place of origin. "Howdy." An uncomfortable silence fell around us.

"Why are you so quiet? That's not like you. Not get enough sleep?"

"No."

"Then what are you doing?" I asked again.

"Thinking."

That's unusual. "About what?"

She didn't respond, which I took as a very bad sign. "What did you do?"

She shifted her gaze toward the kitchen.

Uh-oh.

I flew into the kitchen, first checking for any fire damage. I know how Emily loves to experiment with fire. No soot or destruction. Check. I made sure the water from the faucet was still working. Check. She didn't try to fix the plumbing again, thank God. I inspected the booze rack. Humph. The bottles were empty.

"Trixie must have been thirsty."

Emily didn't comment. I slid a glance toward Trixie and noticed something was different about her.

When I reached her, the first thing I noticed was that her booze bucket was empty. Not good, yet she wasn't making any noise. I looked harder at Trixie and much to my surprise she was breathing. Phew!

"What's, what's wrong with Trixie?" I asked.

Emily shuffled to the kitchen doorway. "What do you mean?" she said as she looked down at the floor.

"I mean, why do her eyes look like that?"

"Like what?"

"Like they're about to pop out of her head." They did. Trixie's eyes were bulging out of socket and nearly skimmed the bottom of the cage. Highly unusual.

"Oh that," she sighed. "Well, I didn't mean to. I swear it was an accident."

"What, did you try to strangle the noise out of her or something?"

"No, nothin' like that. I was sorta makin' my special, spicy jalapeno omelet. You know, the one with the peppers, on the peppers, on the jalapeno omelet?"

"Who could forget? Those things damn near burned a hole in my tongue."

"Yeah, well, Trixie was gettin' antsy again, and I guess we ran low on tequila or somethin' because the bottles were empty."

"How did that happen? I just restocked the liquor."

Emily's cheeks turned pink. Guilty.

"I had to unwind from all this investigating somehow. But regardless, the how doesn't matter. It happened all the same, and since I didn't know what to do, I gave her some grub. Figured maybe she needed some human food."

I shook my head. I'd already tried crackers, and it was a no-go. Let's face it, Trixie needed help.

"It didn't work quite as I intended," Emily continued. "She got quiet alright. Too quiet though. Her eyeballs nearly shot out of socket."

"And she's been like that ever since," I concluded.

"Maybe she just needs some rest," she said.

I feared that if she got some rest, she may never wake up.

"Well, I'll check on her later in the day," I said crossing my fingers hoping she wouldn't bite the dust on my watch. Mrs. Guerreza would kill me.

"I made some extra for you, if you want some jalapeno eggs?" she offered.

"I'm really in the mood for some cereal," I lied. "Thanks anyways though. So, what did all your alcohol-impaired investigating discover last night?" I poured a bowl of cereal, and then joined her at the table.

"Well, first off, the alcohol didn't start until after the bulk of my researching was complete." She pointed her fork at me before proceeding with her breakfast. "Now, if I'm right, I think I've found some important pieces of this puzzle yesterday."

"What did you find," I asked with a hint of anxiety slipping through my voice.

"Well, I called up club Chic where two of the four girls went missing that first night, and I asked the lady if Donnie and Ronnie were there."

"What?!" I practically sprung out of my seat.

"Don't worry. I didn't use my name obviously, and I used a pre-paid phone that I paid for with cash. Totally untraceable."

I sat back down in the chair and resumed my composure. I needed to have a little faith in Emily and her journalism skills. Remember Nicky, she knows what she's doing.

"Anyways, I said Donnie and Ronnie to get some street cred since I didn't know their last name, but figured if they're frequents, they'll know the duo. They weren't there, so I asked if any of the 'guys' were there. The lady said that no one was there yet, but that Diego would be there that evening."

"Diego? Who is that?" I asked unfamiliar with the name.

"Well, I couldn't ask who it was or else I'd raise flags. So I went to Chic myself to do some snooping in person. I dressed the part of a club hopper, so I didn't look suspicious. Sure enough, I found him amongst his posse."

"Did you find out what his job is for their crew?" I asked. "Is he another cleaner?"

Emily laughed. "The way everyone else bent to his every need, I'd guess he's a key player. I'm thinking he's the boss man they keep referring to."

"Did you find out why these tourists are being taken?" I've been trying to guess this since Emily first vaguely mentioned she had ideas about this.

"No. They didn't talk about business there, but it's safe to say it's bad whatever it is."

"Crap," a sudden light bulb went off in my head. I rushed up the stairs and unplugged my phone. When I hurried downstairs I reviewed my call history. No missed calls from Juanita. She said she'd let me know the address they found for Donnie when she and Toni tailed him from the office building. I checked my text messages. There was a text from her stating his home address. "Let me text her and make sure she's OK still."

It made me nervous thinking that Donnie may have picked up on their obvious pursuit. Juanita herself wasn't exactly a subtle person. I asked if they were alright and told her they should come over earlier than noon to discuss the game plan.

Emily continued to tell me about the digging she'd done on Diego and her observations on how the crew seemed to operate. Apparently this Diego guy had a ferocious attitude. Easily agitated. Paranoia to the extreme. Not one to be tampered with by the sounds of it.

Emily continued on, "Fortunately, we can sneak around this unstable Diego character by using our route through Donnie. Donnie is going to be our safest course to getting deep enough inside the organization to get what we need. We'll manipulate him into showing us the back door to see the missing tourists… that is, if they're still alive…and that is all we'll need. Diego and Bruce though are wild cards, and wild cards are dangerous. We don't want to actually put ourselves in their line of fire. You get what I'm sayin'?"

"You don't have to tell me twice. I'm all for the safest bet on this one," I nodded.

Before we could proceed with the next steps, a loud banging came from the front door. Both of us jumped in our seats in surprise. Clearly the topic put us on edge.

I peeked through the peeping hole, and saw Juanita vigorously fanning herself. Toni was behind her with his arms crossed, not looking in the best of moods. I opened the door and welcomed them inside.

"Ay, ay, ay. It's too hot to leave people out on your doorstep for hours on end. What took chu so long?" Juanita gruffed.

"It wasn't even thirty seconds, Juanita. Quit exaggerating." I locked the door behind them.

"Juanita? Exaggerate?" Toni mocked.

"What's with the grumpiness guys?" I asked. "You two are just a ball of sunshine this morning."

"The problem with that phrase is *morning*," Toni emphasized as he plopped down on the living room couch. "You know I'm not a fan of mornings on my days off, let alone after we played stake out until the wee hours of the night. I need sleep."

"How about coffee?" Emily suggested.

Toni cut his eyes to the kitchen where Emily stood in a pale cotton pajama set, hair around her shoulders in perfect auburn waves, and bright blue eyes smiling back at him. Suddenly, his demeanor changed all together. His eyes softened, and he tossed on a charming smile.

"Coffee sounds great. Sorry, I didn't see you there." He straightened a little on the couch.

Emily just waved it off. "You sound like Nicky when she doesn't have her coffee. No worries. I'm Emily, by the way."

"Toni," he replied. "So you're the brilliant mind behind this whole operation they're trying to pull off?"

"*We* are trying to pull off," I corrected him. "Don't forget you're in this too."

"Well, Emily," he resumed his conversation with her, ignoring my comment, "Is there any way you can talk this stubborn ass out of going through with this? Nicole doesn't listen to me when I tell her she's playing with fire."

"Nicole is going to be fine. We're going in with a solid game plan," Emily returned with his cup of hot coffee and sat down next to him, suddenly turning up that Southern charm. "And from what I hear, she's got a big, strong man looking after her just in case." She handed him the cup then lightly squeezed her delicate hand around his bicep to test the muscle. "Yes, I trust she's in very capable hands."

Toni's cheeks flushed a hint of pink before returning to their normal state. "Well, I mean, I have been through one or two fights before," he shrugged.

God, I wish I had her raw talent in flirting. She could make them worship her if she wanted. It wasn't fair.

Juanita crossed her arms on the chair and interrupted, "Ahem. Scuse me! Are we gonna get down to business here or what? If we came here to watch a love story unravel, I could've stayed in my bed and finished The Notebook instead." Juanita appeared a shade of green with envy.

Emily pulled away and led the group meeting. "OK, I've put together our cover profile for the assignment. Our goals and our tactics on obtaining those goals. I've also put together a basic person of interest list for the connections I found with the organization. I repeat, basic list, because I need at least several days to conduct a comprehensive background check and criminal search."

Emily handed out folders to each of us and all three of us stared back at her. We were impressed with her structured presentation. "Now, you can go over your list of crew members on your own. Right now we need to focus on the actual plan of action for how we'll approach Donnie. Nicole is going to present herself as the sister for one of the tourists that disappeared three months ago. The only one that we could manage a sister profile for is Maria Ortega. The other two didn't have any family left."

I read my profile from the folder. "My name is Gabrielle Ortega, and I'm Maria's older sister. Wait a minute." I paused. "It says I'm supposed to be twenty-two years old. I haven't looked twenty-two in five years."

Emily just sighed. "Heavens, Nicole! You're young, you're gorgeous, now move off the age thing. We'll style you in a younger look for the cover anyways, so they won't know the difference."

I frowned but continued to read my profile. "I am a third year photography major at Santa Fe University of Art and Design. Our parents passed away in a fatal car accident three years ago and we've lived modestly off our inheritance. No connection with extended family." I set the paper down. "Is this even real?"

"You bet your ass it is." Emily squinted her eyes at me. "I pulled her information from the news articles and found her on social media. She's taking off this semester so if they wanted to check in on our story it wouldn't conflict with the real Gabrielle."

"Alright," I muttered. "So I'm Gabrielle Ortega. And just how did a photographer college student find out about this secret underground organization? Doesn't sound like I'd be able to come up with all of this on my own."

"Which is where Juanita comes in." Emily shifted toward Juanita. "You, my dear are going to be Gabrielle's lead private investigator. Gabrielle hired you after an exhausting month of looking for Maria on her own. Finally she got you and your team of investigators involved for a very hefty fee, and they had enough experience and connections to lead you to their organization."

Juanita was ecstatic as she learned her role in all this. "I like that. I'm the one in charge of the investigation. What's my name?" She asked as she read her individual profile. "Ooo, Veronica Rocco. That sounds sexy. Si, I think a name like that suits me well."

"Yes, become familiar with your profile. You need to be in character when you present in front of Donnie."

"Wait a minute there!" Juanita stopped. "Chu mean I need to actually meet Donnie for the first time with Nicole? I don't know...I think the first meet sounds a little risky from what I've heard. We don't know if he's going to whip out a gun when he hears the story or not. Maybe just Señora should go to the meeting herself? I'll go to the second one...well, if she's still alive to go to the second one."

"Thank you for your words of comfort, Juanita." I snorted.

"It'll be fine," Emily soothed us. "Everyone needs to take a step back and breathe. I swear he is not going to try to kill you once he hears the story. Have I ever steered you wrong, Nicole?"

"There was that time you thought it'd be a good idea to shave my eyebrows instead of plucking them." I stared at her knowingly. "That didn't turn out so well."

Emily huffed. "OK, fine. Fine! Let's just scratch the whole thing then. Shall we? Let's just go tell the cops about it and hope the press doesn't reveal Sunset Cove's name in the process. I do love a good gamble, don't you?"

"I get it," I growled.

"Do you?" she raised her hands, "because for a second there it sounded like y'all forgot what was at stake here. I mean aside from the innocent lives of the girls who were just taken. We don't know if all the tourists are even alive or being held captive somewhere, but if they are…their imprisonment is on you. Since you won't jeopardize the business of your hotel or the employment of your workers, it looks like this is the only way. You will need to get the details of their organization, the location of the abductees, and the proof to warrant a raid or else the cops will look to Sunset Cove as their most recent connection with the abductions. They will turn Sunset Cove inside out, not only interrogating the employees and hotel guests, but also attracting news media and press in the meantime."

I ran an aggravated hand through my hair and groaned. "Just get the information and proof needed, so I can hand it to the law and let them handle it from there without ever crossing paths with Sunset Cove. We can do this." I nodded looking around the room.

Toni appeared as though he was biting his tongue and Juanita peeked up at me knowingly. "OK. Let's just bite the knife then."

Toni and Emily were perplexed, confusion written all over their faces.

"It's a bullet," I corrected. "You bite the bullet."

"Nonsense!" Juanita laughed. "Who can catch a flying bullet with their teeth? It's impossible."

"You're hopeless!" I shook my head. Toni and Emily's face lightened in understanding.

I stood up and made my way up the stairs. "Um, where do you think you're going missy?" Emily perched a hand on her hip.

"I am going to take a shower, and then I think I'm going to pay a visit to Landon. He was just asking about styling me the other day. I am going to get him to dress me like a twenty-two year old college student from New Mexico."

Emily liked the idea. "Great, yes! Ask Landon for a few different outfits since this could take a couple of meetings before we get the information we need. Study your profile in the meantime. I'm going to work with Juanita and Toni some more."

"What is Toni's role in this?" I asked not recalling his profile.

"Toni will be a shadow," Emily stated. "He won't have a profile because he is going to be invisible to the enemy."

"I'm merely going as a last resort back up if things get messy," Toni filled in the gaps for me.

I rushed up the stairs and freshened up with a hot shower. Once I brushed my teeth and hopped into some form fitting athletic wear, I laced up my royal blue sneakers and tossed a ball cap over my damp hair. Landon would want to start with the basics, so I left my face naked of makeup and hair un-styled. I texted Landon to meet me at his office on the hour.

CHAPTER THIRTEEN

As I pulled into the parking lot, Landon squealed with delight, "Ah, omigod. I heart you so much." He gestured a heart with his hands. "It's so not you to step out of your comfort zone and try something different, but this new attitude is so edgy and fresh! I'm digging the change of heart to let me style you."

Landon eyed me suspiciously, "What's gotten into you? Or should I say, *who* has gotten into you?"

"Landon!" I elbowed him in the ribs. "I just wanted to try a new look, none of it has to do with a boy."

"Mhmm…" He nudged me toward the garage exit as we headed to go inside the building. "How about we continue this conversation in my office? It's too hot out here; I'm practically melting." He did an overdramatic fanning motion.

"Somewhat similar to the wicked witch of the west," I mumbled.

Landon rushed me inside and tapped the elevator to go up. He worked in the corporate building for some gigando fashion clothing line. It's been his dream job since day one, as he tells me. He not only gets to be surrounded by beautiful, magical pieces of fabric flown in from all over the world, he also gets to take part in the design process, or as he calls it, the creation of life. Drama queen? Perhaps a little.

Of course, along with his job there were numerous little perks. For starters, he gets to boss other people around and has a personal assistant who is required to bring him warm vanilla lattes on his command. He also has a closet stuffed with designer clothes and accessories thanks to his prestigious position. Not to mention his salary. They paid him a fat sum of money each paycheck because he's amazing at what he does. Now, I don't know much about the fashion world, but I do know it's a fiercely competitive field and for him to be as desired as he is, speaks highly of his talents.

"So how's work?" I casually asked which felt odd on my tongue since less than thirty minutes ago I was talking about my incognito profile to approach a bunch of sociopathic thugs. We drifted higher in the dimly lit elevator. Soft elevator music daintily hummed in the background.

He shrugged, "Fine. It would be even better if half of these interns around here knew what they were doing," he sighed. "Clearly some of these dim-wits have been skipping basic fashion one-oh-one class, because they're lacking in complete style."

"That bad?" I raised a brow.

"You have no idea," he snorted. "You can see their lack of skill not just on their projects, but even how they dress at work. I mean, one intern came in wearing a violet purple sweater dress, brown pleather sandal heels, and black vintage lace gloves. Hello, I mean, who would wear a sweater dress in midsummer. And what kind of amateur would pair a winter dress with sandal heels? Totally opposite ends of the season. Oh, oh, and what's with the gloves? Is she Michael Jackson reincarnated?"

I nodded my head in silent confusion. What did I know about fashion?

I glanced behind us and noticed a young girl, maybe nineteen at best, wearing a purple sweater dress and brown pleather sandals. And as if I needed more confirmation, I found that she was quickly trying to pull off her black laced gloves in a subtle manner.

Landon followed my stare of focus and suddenly realized she was in the corner of the elevator with us. His back stiffened, and then he plastered on a bright nervous smile, "Hey Leslie. I, uh, I didn't see you there."

Leslie nodded, her eyes still glued to the tiled floor of the elevator.

This was awkward and slightly embarrassing. Sometimes when I feel uncomfortable I accidentally say the wrong thing at the wrong time. I rocked on my heels a few times and then finally broke the painful silence.

"So, uh, Leslie, right?" I did a nervous smile. "I like your gloves."

Landon shrugged before we exited the elevator.

Back in his office, Landon giggled, "Well *that* wasn't awkward at all." He plopped into his leather, over-sized, premium-quality black chair. I plunked down in the egg shaped chair across from his glass-top desk.

I glanced around the room; it was mostly decked out in black and white pieces of furniture with the occasional dash of an accent color that seemed to be changed out on a monthly basis. This month, the accent color was mango yellow. It seemed to brighten up the place more than usual.

"You think?" I asked. "But don't worry; I'm sure those were just tears of joy near the end of the elevator ride."

Landon pressed the intercom button to connect to his personal assistant. "Hannah," he paused. "I said Hannah!"

A timid, mousey voice replied, "Oh, hi Landon. It's uh, it's actually Rebecca."

"Right. Hannah, could you bring me a venti, java chip frap with extra whipped cream?"

"Yes sir. Coming right up."

Landon disconnected and massaged his temples. "I'm surrounded by imbeciles. She has the audacity to try to say I'm wrong? I know her name. Don't try to correct me."

I raised a brow. "My, oh, my. Aren't we cranky today? What's wrong with you? Boy troubles?"

Landon laughed a humorless laugh. "Hardly. When have I ever needed help in that department? It's Tito."

"Tito?" A moment of confusion. "Oh, right. The rodent."

He nodded. "He's been pissing and crapping all over my couch and throw rugs at home. Everywhere I turn, he's making a mess. I just don't know what to do with him anymore."

"Did you ever potty train him?"

Landon stared at me as though I had asked him to brush his teeth with a toilet brush. "Potty, what? Oh no, no, no, no. Landon Pressley does not deal with such matters. Do you see these hands?" He gracefully lifted his hands, palms facing him. "They are freshly manicured and they certainly do not pick up dog shit."

"Then what have you been doing about Tito?"

"I have to hire a cleaning crew every time he makes another mess. He's beginning to run up his bill. A few grand more and the dog is out."

"Take him to a dog school or something. They will potty train him for you. It's not that expensive either."

The light bulb over Landon's head turned on, and he jotted the idea down on a sticky pad. I assumed he was going to look into it further after we were done.

"So what's new with you, my love?" He batted his lashes. "Anything you care to share with me?"

I shook my head. "Working is all."

"Uh-huh. Sure. Would you care to explain your previous date with some tall Italian lover boy? I heard all about you taking him home to meet the family for lasagna," he giggled. "Vi told me everything!"

"You both are junior Delightful Daisies in the making. Always excited to gossip."

"Why, of course," he gestured innocently. "It has been a dual effort on our part to get you hooked up with a man. I, the king of dating, and Vi the queen, are utterly embarrassed that our little girl here can't get it together in the dating scene. Truly it's humiliating."

"I'm so terribly sorry for your hardship."

Landon leaned across the desk on his elbows. "So tell me," he winked. "How was the sex? A-may-za-*zing*, I'm sure. You were holding a record there for a while. How long had it been? You just might have become re-virginized considering the length of time and all."

"No sex." I growled. "Why is everyone so interested in my sex life, seriously?"

He eyed me, "You've got too much pent up, hun. You could definitely stand for some sexual release. And now you've got a sexy Italian man within your grasp? You need to make this happen and stop farting around.

"Actually, I have a date lined up tonight, if you must know." I crossed my arms in a smug manner. "Plan to take him to a paint party like you suggested."

"Oh that's fabulous! Simply fabulous!" He clapped his hands together in a fast repetition. "So let's get you something saucy for your resurrected dating life. I think we should go for a sexy, feral look and really accentuate your raw sensuality—"

"I'm going to stop you there. Actually, I want to be styled like an innocent, twenty-two year old woman who's more in touch with her artistic side."

Landon raised a lip in disappointment. "I'm not dressing you like a hobo, Nicole. Rags are not my specialty."

"Not rags, but I just want that type of vibe. Kind of like the young girl next door look, you know?"

"Baby steps," he sighed. "One day we'll get you into some sexy numbers, I swear it. But for now, fine. I'll pull some outfits for the look. Meanwhile, let's get you acquainted with our on-call makeup artist and hair stylist. In the photo shoots, we'll usually have our consultants create more of the *out of the box* look, but they'll be able to tone it down accordingly."

Landon pressed the intercom button and shouted. "Hannah!"

Silence. Landon rubbed his temples again. "Hannah! I've always wondered what it would be like to fire someone over the intercom. Say nothing if you'd like to share that moment with me?"

"Hi sir. Sorry about that. The name didn't register at first."

"Well make yourself a damn name tag and stick it upside down so you can read your own name should you forget it again, or else you'll be packing up your desk."

"Sorry, sir."

"Assist my guest to the studio and send hair and makeup for styling. I want her finished by the time I get there with the wardrobe selections."

Almost immediately after they disconnected, a tall and slender redhead came through the door and guided me to the studio. When I arrived the duo was already waiting for me, blow dryer and face cream in hand. Nervously, I sat down in the chair and told them the look I was going for. They instantly went to town, and I closed my eyes angling my head as directed. As soon as they stopped, they assembled their tools and were out of the studio in record timing.

When I opened my eyes I was alone with a reflection I hardly recognized. I turned my head from side to side, never peeling my eyes off the mirror. Strange how I appeared younger and more rejuvenated with a few flicks of a paint brush here and a bit of hair tossing there. My skin was flawlessly smooth, and somehow they softened the number of years evidenced by my face. The rosy pink cheeks they created looked natural, and somehow they managed to remove the darkened circles from under my eyes.

"Not only do you look young," Landon startled me as he silently emerged from the hallway, "You also look innocent." He made his way to me and hung the piles of hangers on the stationary rack. "And that might have been a good call, actually. A lot of men dig the whole innocent, virgin-like woman. If your Italian lover boy is into that, then I understand your tactics now."

I secretly hoped Ralf wasn't into this look, or else it might not work out after all. It would be impossible to maintain this look without scheduling his team of artists to style me every morning. I certainly couldn't work this magic on my own.

Ralf! That reminded me. I whipped out my phone and texted him the details for our date tonight. I sent him my home address and the time. Then I added that he should wear something that could get dirty. I figured we could drive to Cocoas together for the paint party.

Landon grabbed my hand and shuffled me over toward the rack of outfits.

"Here we go. Now, I've arranged ten outfits to get you started. They have already been pieced together from head to toe, so don't deviate from it. Jewelry is included on the inner pouch and your shoes can be found in the bottom of the hanging bag."

"But I already have a million pairs of shoes. I'm sure—"

"What did I just say, Nicky?" Landon pressed a hand on his hip. "Don't deviate. The best way to ruin a style is to cut it off prematurely by omitting the predetermined items. A style must be expressed from the tip of your head to the tip of your toes. Just let me do my job."

I saluted him. "Yes, sir."

"OK, now I need to get back to work. It may be the weekend for you, but some of us have demanding jobs that require sacrifices. Fashion, my dear, never sleeps."

If he only knew just how demanding Sunset Cove really was. "Thanks again, Landon!"

He kissed me goodbye on both cheeks and shouted at me on my way out of the studio. "Please don't forget to do something about those chipped toenails of yours. And for heaven's sake, shave your legs. No man should have to witness that."

I flipped him the bird with the free hand, which was not carrying the hanging bags. When I reached my moped, I played with the positioning of the bags until I finally discovered that I could wrap them around my waist like a belt by hooking the hanger to the tiny loop at the bottom of the bag. The entire ride home I looked like I was sporting black tires around my torso. I'm sure Landon would be proud of my out of the box fashion statement.

I rushed into my house and found Emily, Toni, and Juanita sprawled across the living room. Stacks of folders, papers, and maps laid atop of the hardwood floor. The three of them peered up at me when I entered the front door.

The pencil in Emily's mouth fell to the floor when she saw my handcrafted inner tube attire. "I knew fashion would destroy Landon's mind someday. Now he thinks it's fashionable to dress up like an inner tube? He's clearly lost his touch."

I started unhooking the black hanging bags from my waist. "Hardly. I had to get these home somehow. The moped isn't much for storing things." When I unhooked them their faces exhibited a sigh of relief. Clearly they thought the same thing.

"I am going to get ready for my date with Ralf tonight. I need to shave my legs and touch up my nails. Landon's orders."

Toni made a visible shiver at the thought of women with unshaved legs. I noticed he was sitting rather close to Emily, and Emily didn't seem to mind it. Interesting.

"Wait a minute," Emily called out before I ascended the stairs. "We need to go over the details. We're going to address Donnie tonight."

"Tonight?" My eyes bulged. "Don't we need more time before we dive head first into the danger zone? I thought we were supposed to be practicing our profiles for a few days first."

Juanita vigorously shook her head. "No, Señora. We need to move on this pronto. We have his home address from following him last night."

Emily elaborated, "Juanita and Toni have Donnie's home address from when they followed him last night. We need to strike while the iron is hot. The four girls were taken from Sunset Cove recently enough that they are likely still alive or still in the area. We need to go to his house this afternoon so you and Juanita can introduce yourselves and form an allegiance with Donnie, while he's still feeling the pain of his cousin's murder."

I nodded. "I wish someone told me we were doing this tonight. Would've been good to know. I definitely need to study my profile more. And now I'll have to cancel my date with Ralf."

"No!" Juanita and Emily shouted simultaneously, already leaning out of their seats.

"Nicole, don't cancel with Ralf. We can just work around your plans," Emily stressed.

Toni baulked. "Is anyone else worried about Nicole's safety here? She's never done anything like this before, and she's confronting a treacherous killer. I think it would be wise if her head was one hundred percent in the game. She can always reschedule some date."

Emily glared at Toni, "*Some date*? Um, have you seen Ralf before? The muscular, Italian, gray-eyed hunk of meat? No, she most certainly cannot reschedule. A man like that doesn't come around very often. She needs to get her nails in him and lock it down."

Toni made a disgusted noise. "Look, I may not know this Diego or Donnie guy very well, but I do personally know Caleb and Logan from years ago. If Diego and Donnie are anything like them, they should not be taken lightly."

"Nobody is taking anything lightly, Toni. But Nicole can't drop everything in her personal life. She's a multi-tasker by nature. She can handle this. It's just introductions tonight."

Toni stood from the ground and made his way toward the downstairs bathroom. "It's your choice," he huffed as he passed me.

When the bathroom door had shut, Juanita and Emily were silently clapping their hands in excitement. "So the game plan is for you and Juanita, or should I say Gabrielle and Veronica, are going to make introductions at Donnie's house before he's surrounded by his gang members for their nocturnal festivities. Once you present the deal, to help get your sister back and draw Diego out for Donnie to seek revenge on, then we'll see if he's willing to be our inside man."

"Where will you and Toni be?" I asked.

"Toni will always be on the perimeter whenever you and Juanita are interacting with Donnie or anyone from their crew, but he's going to be invisible to them and act as one of the crowd. Toni will only intervene if it's a matter of safety. He can act as a distraction or as muscle if needed for a quick escape," Emily explained. "I, on the other hand, will be operating from Toni's SUV. I will be monitoring each of you and your surroundings. Think of me as the centralized brain for the operation. I will be able to hear, see, and even talk to each of you while you're in the field."

"And just how do you intend to do that, 007?" I teased. Emily's imagination was ridiculous sometimes.

"With these," Emily crossed the room and plopped two plastic bins on the coffee table. She uncapped the first and pulled out four small boxes. She opened one up and slipped out a tiny translucent ear piece and a delicate black pin to place on a shirt. She placed both in my hand with a smug smile. "The ear piece will allow me to talk to you while you're on site. I can guide you through any sticky situations that might arise. The other is a pin for your blouse so that I can see everything you're seeing."

My mouth dropped in surprise. "I'm officially impressed. So journalists are actually glorified spies."

Emily snatched the items from my hand. "Yeah, the good journalists, at least, are pretty badass. Now, I need to sync these to the primary before anyone can use them. So go get ready for tonight's meeting. By the time you get done, these will be set and ready to go."

"What time are we leaving for Donnie's?" I asked with a wave of nausea.

"In a couple hours, so you should be back with plenty of time to meet with Ralf afterwards."

I nodded, no longer nervous about my date with Ralf. I was much more preoccupied with my concerns about meeting Donnie. When I hurried upstairs, I hung the outfits in my closet and returned to my bathroom to draw a hot bath so I could shave my legs. I didn't want to mess up my hair and makeup so I clipped my hair off my neck.

Deep in thought as I silently rehearsed my Gabrielle persona, I slowly slid off my shirt and began to shimmy out of my shorts.

"Nicks, are you sure you want to go down this road?" a low voice warned from behind me.

I turned around and saw Toni with his arms crossed, leaning against the bathroom doorway. Quickly, I jumped back and stifled a scream. My shorts were only a few inches off my waist, so I pulled them back into place. I attempted to cover my bare stomach with my arms. Toni stared at me, unflinching, when he noticed my unease.

"Do you mind?" I growled, but Toni just walked closer to me.

He grasped the sides of my face and stared at me with unspoken pain behind his eyes. Something had him rattled. It wasn't just about us meeting Donnie and potentially diving further into those ties. There was something else that he was worried about, something even darker that had him shaken to the bone.

"Are you sure, you want to go down this road?" he repeated in a grave tone.

"Toni," I reached for his hands. "You're starting to scare me."

"There are things that you can't come back from. Things that will change you and your life forever. So I ask you…one. more. time. Are you sure, you want to go down this road?"

Goosebumps crept up my spine at the severity of his words. I saw a new edge to Toni that I had never witnessed before.

I nodded. "I have no other choice at this point," I hesitated. "Yes, I'm sure."

The muscle in his jaw tightened, and he looked away for a moment. When he returned his stare, I felt my blood run cold. A darkness to Toni surfaced and for the first time I actually felt unsafe next to him. He reached into his back pocket with the other hand still grasping the side of my face.

Before he could reveal what was in his hand, Juanita threw open the bedroom door and Toni pulled away from me resuming total composure. Toni backed out of the bathroom into the bedroom in a façade of embarrassment. "So sorry, Nicks! I should've knocked before I came in. Just wanted to let you know that once you're done Emily is going to dress you with the technological gadgets for tonight."

Juanita hurried Toni out the door. "Shoo, shoo! It's time for Señora and I to practice our cover together while she gets ready. Chu don't need to see her half-dressed. Out!" When Toni stumbled out of the room, Juanita closed the door and shook her head at me. "Men!"

I absentmindedly nodded still processing the sudden shift in Toni's demeanor. It was so brief that I debated whether I'd imagined the whole thing.

"Get to town on those legs," Juanita guided me to the bathroom to resume. "I'll be outside the bathroom here so chu still have chur privacy, and we can practice our profiles together for this afternoon."

"OK," I agreed, still absorbed about Toni. I hurried into the tub and shaved my legs while Juanita gabbed away about our presentation for this evening. Once I dried off, I painted a nude pink nail polish on my fingers and toes. We continued to rehearse until I no longer hesitated when I'd say Gabrielle Ortega's information as my own.

Hastily, I slipped into outfit number one from Landon. A white tank top covered by an unbuttoned striped jacket with clumsily ripped jean shorts. There was a matching brown leather belt with a multiband leather bracelet and a pair of cream Converse shoes.

"Wow," Juanita mouthed as she sat on the bed watching me emerge from the closet. "That's how I would picture Gabrielle Ortega. Chu looks the part."

"Yeah, it's a little hipster, huh?"

"Si, but chu pull it off well. Come on, let's go show everyone and get this damn thing over with. All this waiting around is making me anxious."

I couldn't agree more. When we hurried downstairs, Emily and Toni looked shocked. "Alright, Gabrielle," Emily emphasized handing me the earpiece. "You're all hooked up and routed to my lap top so I can sit in the car and manage the show and remain mobile. Just don't venture out a hundred feet from me or I lose the signal."

"Got it," I said. I adjusted the ear piece in my ear and Emily conducted a test run. I heard nothing. She dabbled with some controls and tried it again. Instantly I shouted and ripped the thing out of my ear. "Shit. You almost blew my eardrum. Turn that thing down!"

She adjusted the settings again and spoke. "Perfect," I mumbled still agitated from the earlier test run.

Emily helped Juanita with her earpiece and hollered for Toni to help me with the pin. Toni grabbed the pin and started to prep it for my shirt.

"No," I shouted. "I'm fine. I got it." He cocked his head to the side and furrowed his brows confused. I snatched the pin from his hand and placed it myself. I didn't want him near me after the scene upstairs.

When we were all suited up, Emily and Toni loaded Toni's SUV, and Juanita and I drove separately. We didn't want them to trace the plates of the moped or Juanita's ride if they decided to do some digging, so we both took a cab to Donnie's place.

The sun was starting to set by the time we arrived. I noticed Toni's SUV parked a few houses down. We exited the cab and paid the fare. Suddenly, Emily blasted into my ear. "Toni is already positioned behind the bush on the side of the garage. You have the green to proceed as planned."

Nervously, Juanita and I scooted up the sidewalk toward the front door. My heart was chaotically beating within my ribcage. I licked my lips and extended a hand before knocking loudly on the front door. We waited, and waited, anticipating the next scene of events. No one came to the door. Juanita and I looked at each other and were in silent agreement to turn and walk away.

As we retreated, the door swung open, and we were met by a towering man with a hook nose and freshly shaved buzz cut. Donnie glared from me to Juanita. "I don't do Girl Scout cookies."

Juanita baulked, "Who doesn't do Girl Scout cookies? Everybody loves the little chocolaty peanut butter ones."

My palms started to sweat. I jumped in before Donnie could respond. "Hi Donnie, my name is Gabrielle, and this is Veronica. We're not actually selling Girl Scout cookies. I just wanted to talk with you about a business arrangement I think you'd be interested in."

Donnie approached with caution. "Something tells me we're not in the same line of business, doll face." He started to close the door, "Not interested."

I shoved my foot in the door and added, "Well, technically, no. I may not be a cleaner like yourself, but I do think we have some things in common. You see, your boss, Diego, had my sister abducted by your crew a few months ago. Maria Ortega ring a bell?"

The door eased open and Donnie's expression was torn between shock and hostility. He stuck his head out and glanced from side to side. "Come in. I don't talk business outside."

We entered and he slammed the door shut behind us. He led the way to the living room, and we sat on the couch opposing him. "Would you like a drink?"

Juanita and I vigorously shook our heads no. He must have thought we were idiots if he seriously believed we'd consume anything he handed us. He stood up anyways and crept toward the free standing bar across the room. "Don't mind if I have a drink. I can already predict this conversation will call for one."

As he began constructing a concoction, I talked. "Donnie, I've been desperately trying to find my sister since she vanished several months back. I have been tracing back her steps, and I finally hired a team of private investigators." Donnie stopped pouring and glared across the room at me. Quickly I continued, "The team lead is Veronica, who has accompanied me today to coordinate some kind of arrangement."

Juanita cut in, "Si. Several factors pointed us to chu and chur colleagues Bruce, Ronnie, Caleb, and Logan. We are not trying to play cops here or anything, we just want to make a deal to get Gabrielle's little sister back."

At this point, Donnie had not said a word. He was merely listening to our proposal. I resumed the conversation. "We know Bruce was ordered by Diego to kill your cousin, Ronnie. And we know that probably didn't sit too well with you. If you're willing to help us get Maria back, then we're willing to help you avenge your cousin. You scratch my back, I'll scratch yours."

Donnie set the bottle down and reached for his drink and something else beneath the bar. When he returned to his seat he set the glass on the side table coupled with a gun. He propped his feet up and swirled the booze around in his glass. Juanita and I were both visibly trembling.

"And you think you two are going to help me avenge my cousin?" He smirked before taking a swig of his drink. "You think the three of us are going to take down Diego, and that I'm simply going to hand over your sister just like that? I think you're full of shit, or possibly down right delusional."

I explained, "I think you loved your cousin and would want the person responsible for ordering his murder to pay for it. Maybe I'm mistaken though? It's not necessarily true that what he'll do to others is the same that he'll do to you."

Donnie tossed another mouthful back. "You know where I'm from, killing one's own boss is treason and is punishable by the highest means. It's not something I can be associated with, so it doesn't really sound like we have a deal here."

I added, "All the more reason to have a third party, like me, take care of it. If you can deliver Diego without any protection or any of his bodyguards, I can take care of your problem. Your hands are completely clean. You can rise in the ranks, or whatever your heart desires. And I get my sister back alive with full immunity from your crew for both of us. I take my sister and run, and then we never see or hear from any of your crew members again."

He scratched his chin in contemplation and then idly began spinning the gun around on the table. I clenched my jaw and felt my chest tighten.

"I can hold up my end if you can hold up yours." I concluded.

"Yes, yes. I hear your proposal, and although it does sound tempting, I'm also torn with the idea that you are not who you say you are."

Juanita choked, and I stopped the nervous tapping in my left leg. "What do you mean? Of course, we are. I'm Gabrielle and this is Veronica." I gulped and it felt like a rock was lodged in my throat. He was onto us. He knew we were imposters.

"Congratulations, you can recite two names." He stopped spinning the gun. "Two names which don't mean shit to me. How do I know you're not a Fed or someone hired by Diego himself? How could I trust a complete stranger?"

Donnie picked up the gun and twirled it once in his hands before aiming at us. Juanita and I raised our hands slowly. I began to speak in a slow, measured tone, "I guess you don't have much to go on but our word. You're between a rock and a hard place."

Donnie cackled a dark laugh, "I'm the one holding a gun to your heads, and you think I'm the one in a tough situation?"

I continued, "I say that because currently the rest of the team of private investigators are ready to go live with your information and all your illegal activities to the public, and inevitably the authorities, if we don't come back alive. If they don't hear from us at predetermined time intervals, then they've been instructed to air all of you and your crew's dirty laundry. So yes, I'd say you're up against a rock and a hard place too. If you kill us, you'll undoubtedly face incarceration, possibly death depending on the court's ruling. On the other hand, you would be releasing a captive and run the risk of exposing the plan to murder Diego. However, in regards to your latter option, should everything go as planned, you would be rid of us, Diego would be gone, and you would be free to take over the entire organization. Of the most rewarding choices, I'd say your best bet is to take our deal."

Donnie grit his teeth and pulled his gun back. "That's some insurance policy you put in place."

I shrugged and relaxed an inch when he placed the gun on the table again.

"Well, in that case I'd say the second option sounds most appealing. If you're fucking me over, Gabrielle, you should know that betrayal is the gravest offense. To deceive me would be the stupidest mistake in your life."

"Betrayal? I'm not interested in anything other than getting my sister back alive." I countered.

"Well you need to understand that your sister may not be in the same condition as when you last saw her." He explained. "Did your team of PI's ever elaborate about the line of business we're in?"

"Pieces." I lied so we didn't lose credibility. "Why don't you tell me your view of the business before we discuss our next plan of action?"

"Trafficking." He shrugged and struggled with something lodged in between his teeth.

I waited for him to expand on that. When the silence continued, I pried. "Care to elaborate? What does trafficking entail exactly?"

Donnie sighed. "Trafficking. We profile certain targets who are essentially orphaned or without many family ties, and we use them for trade. Some are used for forced labor, others are used for sex. There are different needs in the business, and we simply farm them until they are sold to clients. The clients then decide what their purpose will be."

"Jesus Christ!" I clutched a hand to my chest. "Jesus Christ." I stood up and quickly sat back down when Donnie reached for the gun.

"Hope you're not getting cold feet about our arrangement." Donnie cocked his head to the side.

Juanita patted me on the back, "No, of course not. Gabrielle wants her sister back, end of story. I think she's just worried that her sister has already been sold?"

Donnie warily set the gun down and returned to his drink. "Maria is still here. She isn't due for auction until another three months. She has more work to be done."

"*Auction?*" Emily repeated disgustedly from my ear piece. "We need to hurry this along. You both have been in there for too long. Make plans to meet Diego tomorrow."

Juanita asked, "What kind of work needs to be done to Maria exactly?"

"Let's just say we need to recreate a certain mindset to develop the best product."

I had no idea what he meant by the mindset part, but I knew we had to wrap things up. The sun had completely vanished and Emily was right, we had been here for too long.

"OK, so let's set up another time to meet. Will you be able to get us in front of Diego tomorrow?"

Donnie laughed. "Diego is a little paranoid bitch. It takes months to get in front of him."

I balled my fist. "We're going to need to expedite this process then. My sister can't wait that long."

He looked me up and down. "No offense, but someone like yourself doesn't have any reason to cross paths with Diego. Now, if you were of someone with status or importance regarding his business, then he may make an exception." He paused for a while. "We could present you both as a potential business opportunity as someone who is already established in other areas. Diego is always interested in growing his business. I can't see him turning down a potential lucrative business deal."

"So who do we need to be?" I asked.

"There's the illusive Sasha Harris, one of the few well-known female distributers who's expanding nationally. I know for a fact, Diego has been trying to get an audience with her. No one has seen her, but everyone knows of her. She's incredibly connected in the black market. Word on the street is she's looking to cut a percentage of the local sales for an established organization to run the Miami unit. An added thirty five percent to our income would be too tempting for Diego to pass up."

"Nicole!" Emily blasted through my ear piece again. "You've got company. Some black car just pulled into Donnie's driveway. You and Juanita need to get out of there now."

I nodded, trying to move things along. "Sasha Harris. Do you think you can arrange a meeting tomorrow night? Maybe at the same place he's holding my sister? You could sneak her out, and I could handle Diego when we're alone discussing the business proposal?"

Donnie looked unsure. "Let me see if I can talk him into a meeting for tomorrow. He may not be susceptible to showing their housing quarters on the first meeting. Like I said, he's obscenely paranoid, so we have that working against us."

A booming noise came from the front door. The three of us turned to each other in a panic. "Come on Donnie, open the door. It's hotter than hell out here."

I pulled out a pen and paper from my purse. "Your number?" I rushed.

He gave me his digits and I jotted them down in a hurry. "Call me tomorrow, and we'll talk more then. You two slip out the back. My guys can't see us together, or the whole plan is shot to hell."

We nodded and hurried toward the back door. I struggled with the handle until I realized it was locked. We heard voices in the front foyer, and Juanita tapped me on the shoulder in a frenzy, trying to hurry me along. Finally, I yanked open the door, and we slid out the back. We ducked, once a light flickered on, and we hugged the wall until we rounded the side of the house.

Looking back to ensure we weren't being followed, I took another step and bumped right into Toni. I started to scream, but he covered my mouth before a note slipped out. When I realized it was him, I swatted his hand away and smacked his chest.

"Move it!" I silently mouthed and he led us away from the house, so we were all out of sight. Emily turned the corner and pulled up next to us.

"Get in!" she hollered, and all three of us squinted in pain because of the volume from our ear piece. "Whoops! Let's turn that off," she said as she selected a button on the controls. Emily peeled out on the street and sped on the ride back to my place.

"What did you find out?" Toni asked tone slightly anxious. He apparently didn't have the same access as Emily had to our video feed since he was on the ground.

Emily gripped the wheel in rage. "They are human traffickers. Those filthy, disgusting, grotesque varmints!" she growled. "I don't know how you kept your cool in there. I would've reached out and wrung his goddamn neck like a water-soaked towel. Just horrible!"

"It was disturbing! Did you not see how I almost blew the whole thing? If Juanita hadn't intercepted like she did, this may have gone down a whole different way." I shook my head. "Those poor girls."

"I could barely stand to look at him when he told us what they did. Did chu see how he didn't even flinch? No regard for how he helped ruined those girls' lives. I can't wait to see the look on his face when we bust his ass."

Toni was unusually quiet in the passenger seat. "Don't worry, Toni." Emily squeezed his hand. "We're going to make sure nothing happens to those girls."

Toni nodded and stared straight ahead in front of him.

"What did Donnie mean back there about recreating a mindset for their product?" I asked still trying to grasp an understanding.

Emily sighed as though she were mentally exhausted by the revelation of tonight. "It means they are brainwashing, possibly torturing their hostages until their minds are so warped that they actually think they need to work off their freedom. It's a common tactic amongst traffickers, to distort their perception of reality, so they mold them into compliant slaves. Mental and emotional re-programming at its worst. Sometimes trafficking survivors don't really ever recover from it. There's a certain point when just too much damage, too much trauma, has been done to the mind. We're flexible to a degree, but beyond that we can become broken."

I shook my head in utter sincerity, "How can anyone be such a…such a monster?"

"Greed." Toni finally spoke up, "It's the eternal hunger for more. More money, more domain, more power. You say they're the monsters, Nicole, but the truth is we all have a monster within us. The only difference is you haven't met yours yet."

I stared at Toni in surprise, but his eyes never left the window. He was physically in the car with us, but he was clearly somewhere else in thought.

CHAPTER FOURTEEN

The rest of the car ride home we sat in an awkward silence. Toni's oh-so-enlightening philosophy on inner demons put us all in a funky mood. When we arrived home, Toni took off with his car and Juanita, Emily, and I went inside my house.

Juanita and I plopped down on the couch in exhaustion. Our adrenaline must have finally shut down from our little face to face meeting with our new gun happy ally, Donnie.

Emily strutted into the kitchen and shouted across the bar at us, "Y'all want me to whip up a salsa casserole? We need some brain food after the kind of evening we just had." She started clanking the dishes, crumpling pasta bags, shuffling the spices, and chopping chicken. Juanita and I graciously accepted her offer to make dinner.

I plopped my feet up and sighed. "You know, after the disturbing evening I've had, I honestly don't even feel like going out tonight. I think I need to cancel with Ralf."

"What?!" Juanita popped up from the couch and Emily poked her head from around the corner.

"Absolutely not!" Emily lectured. "If anything, you need to get out and away from this. You should spend it with someone who'll take your mind off things. Ralf, is just the distraction you need."

"Actually sex is the best distraction. Now, if chu could get Ralf in the sack, then chu would be completely distracted. Hell, chu'd probably be distracted enough that chu'd forget chur own name."

"I don't know. I'm not feeling it. Getting knee deep in a trafficking fiasco kind of takes away the dating mojo. Call me crazy!" I pulled out my phone to reschedule with Ralf when there was a knocking at the door.

This started a frenzy throughout the room. Juanita and Emily were frantically trying to collect the scattered papers from earlier and hide them.

"Who is it?" I called out as I helped pick up the stacks of paper.

"It's Ralf." He answered through the door. "Were you expecting someone else?"

"What?" I called out trying to grab a few more stragglers.

"Nicole, are you going to let me in, or did you just want to have a conversation through a wooden door? Personally, I'd much rather talk face to face so I can see those adorable dimples."

Juanita and Emily stopped and clutched their stacks of paper to their chest as the whispered, "Awwww!"

I rolled my eyes and shooed them out of the room. When I opened the door, I found Ralf casually propped against the doorway, amused smile across his face, and intense gray eyes staring back at mine. How could I have ever thought I wouldn't be in the mood to see him. The mere sight of him still made my heart skip a beat.

"Hey," I grinned taking him in. When I noticed he was wearing black slacks and a button down shirt my smile dropped. "Are you sure you want to wear those? They're going to get messed up."

He reached for a bag behind him. "I got called in to work last minute, but I did bring a change of clothes. Mind if I change real quick?"

"Uh, sure," I opened the door for him to come in. "Don't judge me on my place though. We've been working on a project, and it's a little messy."

When I followed him into the living room, the paper trail from earlier had vanished. Juanita and Emily were nowhere to be found.

"We?" Ralf asked.

"Well, earlier today I was working on some things with Emily and Juanita. Anyways you can change in my room." I bolted up the stairs, and he followed behind. I didn't see the girls down the hall or in my room. I still wasn't quite sure where they disappeared to.

"Here you go!" I showed him into the room. "Let me know if you need anything." I started to leave him in the room but then I made a quick turn for my closet. "Actually I need to grab some clothes to change into too."

In my closet, I flipped on the switch and went for a pair of raggedy cut off shorts that were already in bad condition. A hand lifted the hanger and handed it me, and I just about shit my pants. When I peeked around the shorts I saw two pairs of eyes blinking back at me. Juanita and Emily were hiding in the closet trying to stay out of site from Ralf while he was here. I threw a silent temper tantrum to show my surprise and frustration. Why would they pick here of all places to hide? These two were a mess.

I shot them the look of death before snatching the shorts from the hanger. I shimmied out of the striped cover and picked up a pair of paint-splattered Toms. When I stepped out of the closet, Ralf was standing there with his shirt off and was stepping into a pair of black gym shorts. Apparently, my sexy Ralf Mancini was a boxer's guy. A subtle sound of delight escaped my lips, and Ralf turned to meet my gaze.

"I'm going to just get out of your way here," I skirted along the perimeter of the room and was about to leave when he caught my hand in his. "Nicole, you've been in my way since I first laid eyes on you at the hotel. Why stop now?"

Ralf pulled me toward him and met me with a slow, warm kiss. He wrapped his arms around the small of my back and lifted me onto the bed. Gently he crashed down on top of me and intertwined his fingers with mine. He pressed them into the sheets and slid them over my head so I was pinned beneath him. God only knows I would've kept going had I not seen two pairs of wide eyes blinking back at me from the cracked closet door. I wasn't about to have peeping toms watching my most intimate moments. Immediately, I wiggled out of his hold and whipped him with his shirt that was already tossed on the bed.

"Get dressed," I teased. "We have a schedule to keep."

"Playing hard to get, are we?" he smirked.

I shrugged and hurried out the room. I went to the downstairs bathroom and changed. I left the white tank top on since it was just a tank and could stand to get some paint on it, but I did take off the designer shorts and boots and swapped for the items I selected from my closet. When I opened the door I found Ralf in the kitchen opening the microwave where the casserole dish was beeping. "Oh, so you do cook?" he asked.

"Cook is a strong word." I cautioned. "But I do microwave, yes."

We dished up a plate for each of us since we'd both be doing some drinking and thought it wise not to do so on an empty stomach.

When we finished up I offered to drive the moped, though I'd never driven with anyone bigger than me on the back of it. The visual was rather entertaining, but I didn't think the seating arrangements would operate well with the moped's design to distribute weight. We ended up taking his car, and I gave him directions until we found ourselves in the parking garage for Cocoas.

"You're taking me to a club called Cocoas?" he inquired. "From the outside it looks like a strip club."

I shrugged. "Well there is usually a bit of stripping, but it's not technically a strip club. Come on," I hopped out of the car and looped my arm through his.

"I thought it would be fun to kick it old school for a night. Don't you remember neon paint parties from the college days?"

Ralf drew his brows in curiosity. "Neon paint party? No, never."

"Wait, you've never been to one before? Not during college?" My eyes were wide in disbelief.

"Can't say that I have. What is it exactly?"

I hurried him toward the entrance. "Well, this will be a new experience for you."

When we passed the bouncer, we headed inside to the front desk, and I ordered several small buckets of neon glow in the dark paint. Pink and purple for me and blue and green for Ralf. They had paint guns that could squirt tubes of paint so naturally I got one for each of us and a round of paints for the guns.

We ambled across the floor which was already congested with people that were engaging in bizarre movements. "Dare I say dancing?" Ralf hinted at the pair next to us as we maneuvered through the crowd.

"God, I hope not," I laughed. The couple was doing a swanky, swaying type movement with their arms cascading around their heads. "Maybe drugs?" I suggested.

When we made it to the bar, we ordered a few rounds of shots and downed them in minutes. "So, first things first," I opened my miniature bucket of pink paint. "I love a man that wears pink." By the time he started to process my intentions, I had already smeared a glob of pink on his cheek.

He was holding his mouth open in shock by the feel of cold paint on his skin. I grabbed his chin with my painted fingers and planted a kiss on the bare cheek. His expression settled down as the initial shock started to wear off. "So this is a paint party?"

I giggled. "Well there's a lot more artistic expression than that. I was just getting warmed up." We took our third shot, and I stood from the seat, nudging Ralf to follow. "Now, it's tradition for one to decorate their date to inform other's that you're not available for the night."

"Oh?" he smirked. "So you have your own, separate mating calls here too, I see?"

"Don't get sassy with me." I plopped a dab of paint on his nose. "Or I'll paint you into a girl." I grabbed my bucket and started drawing little pink hearts and arrows sporadically across his arms. "Hmm," I strummed my fingers on the counter. "I think you could totally pull off knee high socks. What do you think?" I drew on a pair of ribbed knee-high gym socks on his bare legs.

When he glanced down at the finished product he protested. "Nope, definitely can't pull those off."

"I know, you're right. You're still missing something." I snapped my fingers. "Ah yes, a spiked choker. That will definitely offset the nerdy looking gym socks." I began to outline a purple choker collar.

As soon as I stepped back to admire the masterpiece, he leaned toward the bar and order two more rounds of shots. "I definitely need to be drunk for this," he shook his head. When the bartender delivered the four shots, we each tossed one back.

Feeling a wee bit fuzzy, I kept on with my work of art. I stared him up and down. "Ah yes, he wore an itsy bitsy, teeny weeny, yellow polka dot bikini," I sang in pure drunkenness, and I drew on a rather squiggly bikini top and bottom.

"I think it's my turn at the chalkboard now, if you don't mind," he jokingly huffed.

"Wait!" I stopped him. "One last touch."

He rolled his eyes, "What?"

I dabbed my right hand in paint and smacked him hard on the ass. "There. Now that you've got my pimp hand marking, you're officially my bitch." I grinned in delight.

"Oh you think you're cute, don't you?" He cuddled up to me and smeared his paint from his nose onto mine. "Well isn't that fitting? Cute as that bunny nose of yours. Let's pair some whiskers to go with that."

He steadily drew on three whiskers on each cheek. "Perfect. Now we need a little bow tie." He bent down and planted a gentle kiss on my neck. "Here we go!" He softly drew a blue bow tie on my neck and added green polka dots to it.

"Some whiskers and a bow tie?" I asked. "I certainly got the better deal out of the two of us."

"Shh!" he mocked. "Never interfere with an artist and his canvas." He grabbed my shoulders and traced his way down my curves, stopping at the hips.

I lifted a brow at him and he proceeded down to my knees. "I think we should turn your kneecaps into smiley faces." He doodled on my ticklish knees, and I had to refrain from bursting into a fit of giggles.

"Is that a ticklish spot I found?" he teased with a few extra strokes than necessary.

Before he turned me around he grabbed the last two shots and handed one to me. This would have to be my last one, or this night would take a turn for the worst at some point. We chugged it down, and Ralf directed me to face the opposing direction.

Immediately he started drawing something on both of my shoulder blades. "What is that?" I asked. "Are you drawing me a pair of wings?"

He chuckled, "Wouldn't you like to know?"

Once he finished I turned around and feigned his pretense annoyance. "Are you finished yet?"

"One more thing," he splattered both hands in blue paint and reached around to smack my ass on both sides. He grabbed me and lifted me a few inches off the ground for emphasis. "Two cheeks trumps one. Looks like you're my bitch tonight after all."

He set me down, and I grabbed his shirt leading him to the middle of the crowd. I'll show him who owns who with my moves on the dance floor. I wanted to see what kind of moves he had.

Out on the floor, our bodies moved perfectly in sync with one another. He knew how to lead, and I knew how to follow as though we'd been dancing together for years. I have never had that kind of chemistry with a dance partner. You know what they say…a man that can dance is just as good at the horizontal tango.

After a few rounds of dancing I fanned my face and told him I had to cool off. We exited the club and found our way back to his car. Fortunately, he had some car blankets in the trunk, which we covered the seat before we sat down.

"I'm burning up," I kept fanning myself. "I need to cool off."

"It's the alcohol and the dancing," Ralf replied. "You should probably take a cold shower."

"How about a late night dip instead?" I suggested. "Take us to the hotel!"

He shrugged. "Your wish, my command."

As soon as we arrived we snuck through the back gate and checked for any of the other guests or staff members. The coast was clear. I stripped down to my panties and bra and slipped into the cool, refreshing pool. Ralf peeled off his clothes, with the exception of his boxers and plopped in after me. We lazily floated along the water and just goofed around being in the drunken state we were in. I was more affected by the alcohol than he was, but he was certainly feeling the effects too.

The water slid over my skin like a layer of soft silk as I floated on my back and breathed steady breaths. Oh, what a night it turned out to be.

CHAPTER FIFTEEN

First thing I noticed was my head. It felt like someone took a jackhammer, to put it lightly. It throbbed with every subtle movement. My brain felt like it was trying to squeeze out of my skull. Pain. Lots of pain.

Though it wasn't as painful as the aching in my thighs, the muscles felt sore and completely exhausted, like I had just had a work out after several months of being dormant. I glanced around the room.

Uh-oh.

I know this room. It's familiar and yet still disturbingly foreign. You know that feeling when you wake up and at first you forget where you are, but it eventually comes back to you after a few heart beats? Well, a few minutes had passed, and it wasn't getting better. I was drawing a blank here.

I heard a ruffle next to me and a soft snore. My eyes widened as I leaned up on my elbow and found Ralf lying in bed next to me. Naked, from what I could see. He was on his stomach, face toward the opposite direction, and his body was sprawled out nonchalantly.

I would have thought he looked cute asleep, only I was still busy panicking about last night. Did we have…sex?

I peeked under the covers and saw that I was missing my panties and bra from last night and had some big T-shirt pulled on. Ralf's shirt, I guessed. I didn't remember changing.

To be honest, I was tempted to stay in bed, cuddled up beneath the plush white comforter, with the thick black-out curtains pulled together. Ralf's soft snore was kind of soothing. And I was awfully tired.

Wait a minute. Focus. Comfy, but small room. The walls a soft blue with occasional accents of white and dark blue scattered throughout the room. It looked like—

Damn, it was. Apparently we had sex last night and under the same roof of where I worked. Super classy.

What will the maids think? I had to get out of here. I needed to recollect and try to piece together the evening. Last I remembered we went swimming, but I had no idea how I wound up in his shirt. Did I shower last night after the paint party? More importantly, who showered me last night? Everything was a blur. I had to leave before the staff saw me though. Oh, the horror. I rubbed my temples.

Carefully, I crept out of bed and tiptoed to the corners of the room, looking for any sign of my clothes. I wasn't finding them. I debated making a dash from the hotel in just Ralf's shirt, but then I'd have to wait to hail a cab. I wouldn't want to be spotted by someone I knew.

I peeked over my shoulder to check if Ralf was still asleep, which he was. I ran into the bathroom to assess my morning hair and stifled a yelp. It was atrocious, and I desperately needed some makeup. As most women do the first morning they wake up with someone new in their bed, I decided to primp and hop back into bed as though it were my natural state. I frantically searched for my purse and lugged it into the bathroom with me.

I prayed Ralf wasn't a light sleeper as I turned on the hot water in the shower. Once I hopped in, I quickly switched the temperature to cool when I felt the alcohol-induced nausea begin to surface. Cool showers managed to keep the alcohol remnants at bay. When I finished the teeth-chattering shower, the nausea had subsided, and I felt like a whole new woman.

Since I didn't carry a toothbrush on me I just used my finger with the toothpaste that was already sitting on the counter. I smeared on some facial lotion then pulled out the basic beauty utensils I carried around in my purse. After I applied the base, I dabbed on some sheer pink eye shadow and shaded the edges with a soft brown. The eyeliner and mascara only took a few minutes. A dash of lip balm here and a dab of gloss there. I pinched my cheeks to create a natural blush since I didn't have any in my purse.

As for my dripping wet mane of hair, I combed it out with my fingers and pulled it to the top of my head for a messy, casual bun. It's the best I could do without the noise of a blow dryer.

When I tiptoed across the room, I gently slipped into bed beneath the covers. I gracefully angled an arm above my head and the other one across my stomach. Not only did a girl have to look decent the first morning together, she also had to present like a dainty sleeper…which typically is not the case. Ralf would see a whole other side to my morning glory on the third morning we woke up together. I just didn't want to scare him off quite yet.

As soon as I had snuggled back into place, Ralf rolled over and smiled. "You know, Toots, you didn't have to get all dolled up on my account. You look great with and without makeup."

My eyes fluttered open in laughter. Dammit. He was onto me. "How did you know?" I chuckled. "I was super quiet."

He wrapped an arm around my hips and pulled me into him so my back was aligned with his front.

He nestled his face in my neck and planted a soft kiss at the base. "Well, I'd be worried if you woke up with lips that glossy each morning. Besides, when you crashed last night you looked a lot less graceful than you do this morning," he shrugged. "No need to be modest about it. I like my women to be real."

My face flushed red. "Just didn't want you waking up next to Medusa hair. That kind of visual can give someone a heart attack."

"Oh I'm sure you've got potential for issuing heart palpitations, though I'd bet it would be for different reasons." He outlined my curves through sheets. "Simply magnificent."

My eyes had already grown drowsy again cuddled up next to him. I muffled an inaudible reply, which trailed off near the end. Ralf just rubbed my shoulders and whispered, "Go back to sleep. We had a late night."

At this, I sprung up to a sitting position. "Late night? Yes, so what exactly happened last night? Please tell me we, at least, used protection."

Ralf's eyes widened as he turned over in a fit of laughter. "You must have been having sex dreams about me then because we didn't do anything that required protection."

My eyes widened. "Are you sure? I mean, I woke up practically naked, minus your shirt. And you are down to…" I lifted the covers to examine his attire. "Down to your knickers."

"Yes, I sent our clothes for cleaning on account of all the paint and chlorine from the midnight swim. They should be delivered this morning." He checked the clock. "Matter of fact, they might already be here. I had them expedited."

"So no sex?" I clarified.

"No sex," he grabbed my chin and planted another delicious kiss on my neck. "Yet, at least." He added with a mischievous grin.

Oh…I liked the sound of that.

He rose from the bed and meandered toward the door. I had to cock my head to the side to enjoy the view of his departure. That was one good looking man, I will say.

Ralf swung open the door and found a bag hanging on the handle. He pulled out his clothes and tossed them on the suitcase. When he handed the bag to me I deliberately threw it back on the bed. Not much interest in putting on clothes, but rather the removal of them.

I toyed with the bottom of the shirt and began to tease him by drawing the shirt further north at an achingly slow pace. The excitement between us climbed at exponential rates. Ralf's eyes grew hooded, and he carefully approached me similar to a predator stalking his prey. Oh yes, he definitely knows what to do in the bedroom.

As his hands came in contact with my waist, he raised a brow with his hungry eyes assessing my attire. "You really do look incredibly sexy in my shirt."

His phone rang, and I could visibly see that he was torn between answering it or staying in the sexually-charged mood we both fell victim to. He ignored the first two calls, but when it rang for a third time in a row, he pulled away from me in frustration. Ralf snatched the phone off the table and answered with a hiss.

I almost felt sorry for the person on the other end of the line, who was clearly receiving a verbal whipping for interrupting Ralf's important current engagements. Ralf was staring me up and down longingly. When his expression changed to a serious one, I knew play time was no longer a possibility.

I slid into my panties, shorts, bra, and top from last night and Ralf balled a fist in annoyance that our moment had been taken from us again. When he got off the phone, he hurried to the bathroom and turned on the water for the shower. He returned to the room and sighed. "Damn this job!" he growled. "Something's come up again, of course. I'm so sorry, I need to get with this guy and redraft our sales pitch. We just found out that we lost a deal, and we need to take things back to the drawing board to see if we can regain our ground. It could be a total loss at this point. Fuck." He ran his hands through his hair.

"No, I totally get it. Jobs are important. Yours sounds pretty demanding."

"Incredibly. Since no one knows how to maintain an already-established deal, I get to play janitor and clean the mess they've managed to create. Sorry, let me get cleaned up and I can drop you off before my meeting."

"Don't sweat it," I shrugged. "I'll call a cab. Maybe some other time we can pick things up where we left off." I planted a kiss on the mouth and slung my purse over a shoulder.

"You are some kind of woman," he smirked. When I scurried out the hotel and hailed a cab down the street, all I could think about was the next time I'd get to see him again. The girls were right. Ralf was quite the distraction.

I arrived at my place and crept inside hoping Emily might still be asleep.

Emily poked her head out of the kitchen entry way and grinned. "Say um, Nicky, why are you walkin' like you have an exercise ball between your thighs? Did you get some work outs in at the gym last night?"

"Yep, sure did." I lied as I tossed my purse and keys on the front table.

Emily giggled. "You're so full of it. I'm telling Vi. She'll be so proud."

"It's not what you think." I said, "I'm just sore from pulling out dance moves I haven't used in years. Still no sex." Unfortunately, I thought to myself.

"Right," she winked before she disappeared into the kitchen. "Get you some eggs and bacon. You'll need to recover your strength for today."

I sat down at the table and dug into Emily's freshly-cooked breakfast without hesitation. I was starving.

By the time I had finished a plate, Emily shoved a prepaid phone in front of my face and ordered, "Call Donnie and get the game plan for tonight. I've been doing some research on this Sasha Harris character but haven't found much about her on the web. She must be pretty damn good at keepin' a low profile if even I couldn't get my hands on anything of substance."

I took the phone. "Emily, I don't think I can keep track of these multiple profiles. What if I slip up and refer to myself as Gabrielle, or what if I slip up and reveal myself as Nicole? What if I can't pull off this Sasha Harris persona? I'm not much of an actress. It is already becoming confusing."

"You got this, hun. Remember I'll be in your ear to guide you through whatever sticky situation you run into. You handled the last encounter wonderfully. I only chimed in when it was time for you to get a move on. Aside from that though, you're a natural."

I sighed. I certainly didn't feel like one. The whole thing was too messy for me. I like structure, and order, and familiarity. These unchartered waters were giving me stomach ulcers.

I dialed the number from the paper and waited for Donnie to answer. A groggy voice answered the phone, "Yeah?"

"Hi Donnie, it's me Sasha." Crap! I stammered for a comeback. "I, uh, was just testing the name on for size. It's Gabrielle from yesterday."

"What are you doing calling me this early? It's not even noon yet."

"I know, I just wanted to get the details for tonight so I could plan accordingly. You said I'd have to present as Sasha Harris, but I know nothing about her. What should I look like? How should I act? I've never done this before, but I imagine I have to get into character."

He yawned, and I pulled the phone away from my ear at the loud noise. I could detect some type of scratching in the background too, though I didn't want to imagine what exactly he was itching. "Well, you need to look like a glorified slut, act like a sophisticated business woman, but be a little mysterious. Do that and you should be fine."

"I'll work on that," I shrugged at Emily who was listening close by. "What kind of arrangement were you able to work out?"

"You'll need to get a section at Velvet Lounge. I've already arranged for our section to be on the patio. Their host knows to coordinate your section next to ours, so make sure you book under the name Sasha."

"So Diego decided to meet at a club?" I asked.

"It's a lounge," he corrected me. "And no, he doesn't know you'll be there. You just so happen to be in the neighboring section at one of his favorite spots, and when he discovers that you're Sasha Harris, I'm certain he'll make his introductions. Trust me."

"OK," I shrugged. "What time should we arrive?"

"Get there at least twenty minutes after we've arrived. More of an entrance that way. Order a bottle or two. The hoorah with the sparklers will catch his attention."

"So is it OK if it's just me and…" I snapped my fingers at Emily trying to remember Juanita's cover name. She whispered it to me, and I jumped back in. "and Veronica? Or do I need a whole posse?"

"Two of you should be fine. I think Veronica can go with her name, but lose the last name. We'll be there at eleven." He abruptly hung up.

"Ugh did he just hang up on you?" Emily snorted. "It drives me crazy when men can't say a simple bye on the phone."

I shook my head. "Well, let's call the crew over for another round of plotting. I'll see if I can dig up something slutty in my closet."

Emily dispatched for Toni and Juanita to drive over this evening for the meeting. Meanwhile, I prepped for my Sasha Harris impersonation based on the little information Donnie provided.

In a moment of distraction, I texted Ralf to see how his issue at work faired out. He didn't respond, so I presumed he was still occupied.

Later that evening, Juanita showed up wearing an air-tight, spicy red dress that, in my opinion, appeared to be a smidge painful to wear. Toni was sporting a Ricky Ricardo look with black slacks and an ice blue button down top that complimented his crystal eyes. I noticed Emily was playfully nudging him throughout their flirtatious bantering. Previously I would have thought that they'd make a cute couple, but there was something dark in Toni's eyes lately. Honestly, my intuition was warning me about him. I planned on keeping my distance until this trafficking madness was put to bed. I didn't want him in the field with us, but I know Juanita and Emily would never go for it. They thought we needed his muscle as a backup plan, but I had the creeping feeling that he wasn't really there to help.

Toni glanced over at me and smiled a dazzling smile. "I've never met such a little firecracker before. Where have you been hiding this one?" Toni asked me as he gestured to Emily.

I made a non-committal shrug. I don't know. Maybe I was just imagining things. This whole mess has set my paranoia into overdrive. "I'm going to get ready," I announced looking at the time. We had an hour to spare before we needed to leave.

I rushed upstairs and changed into a white, slinky silk dress which almost looked translucent in certain lighting. There was a slit from the ground to the top of my thigh, and the dress showed an abundance of bare back, which went perfectly with my current temporary tan. I waved my hair and pulled it to one side. My lips were glossed, and my smoky eye-shadow was dabbed on to create a smoldering look.

OK, OK, so maybe I went to further lengths than necessary but I've only worn the gown once. I was a little excited that I was able to rescue it from the closet once again.

Emily poked her head around my bedroom door, "Oooo, don't you look purdy," her eyes widened as she took in the outfit.

"Thanks," I smiled as I squeezed into my caramel leathered pumps. "Let's get this show on the road." We hustled downstairs and loaded the Tahoe.

Emily was driving and pulled onto a side street, so Juanita and I could walk up to the lounge without being spotted. Toni found his way to the building through a different route. When we arrived at the lounge, I introduced myself as Sasha with the reserved section.

The host led us to a section on the patio, and I brushed past Donnie who was drinking in my new transformation while he sipped on his beverage.

"Veronica," I looked at Juanita. "Your dress looks…new," I offered. "Go shopping recently?"

"Gracias," she slid off her pea-sized red jacket with a little trouble and sighed when it was off. As she exhaled, a sequin from her dress popped off and hit me on the forehead.

"This damn thing must have shrunk," Juanita shrugged as she stared at the material of her dress stretched out to the maximum strand.

"Happens to the best of us." More quietly I whispered, "Which one is Diego?"

"My guess is he's the pack leader with all the hoochie mamas hugging each arm."

I glanced over and spotted him. Diego was laid back on the white couch in the corner patio with two provocative looking women embracing each arm. Several men in suits sat stiffly around him. Donnie being in my direct line of vision.

Toni strolled up to the bar and ignored us completely so that there would be no suspicions. He acted like a typical customer who was just taking a trip to the local watering hole. Emily whispered into my earpiece. "OK, Toni is in position now. Order a bottle like Donnie said."

When the waitress popped by I told her to get us a bottle of Belvedere vodka. The thought of more alcohol after last night's drinking binge forced me to physically suppress my gag reflex.

Juanita turned to me, "So chu wants me to lean over and do some batting of the eyes? I mean we all know that I'm the looker of the two of us. And I do know how to ignite a man's sexual arousal. What chu want to do if his plan for the name dropping approach doesn't work out. We need a backup plan."

"Stop it, your flattery is too much, really."

Juanita made an angelic smile and then stopped suddenly. Emily must have tuned into Juanita's earpiece because Juanita startled and then made a curt nod. I'd have to thank Emily later for keeping Juanita's wild plans under control.

When the waitress returned with a bottle displaying a sparkler on top, she set it on the table while the flares continued their flashy statement. Juanita leaned over and tried to blow out the sparkler like it was a birthday candle, and I shoved her back against the seat before she embarrassed herself any further.

I opened the bottle shortly after the flares died down and poured it into two cups paired with pineapple and cranberry juice. I noticed Diego and his section were casually spectating, so I made a toast that would be just within earshot of Diego.

"Cheers," I smiled. "To a successful business. May our empire continue to grow faster than we can count the money. And may we—" I abruptly interrupted my toast and pretended to answer a call. "Sasha Harris," I answered. I made a dramatic sigh. "I already told you, Phillip, cross Rodriguez off the list. No, I don't like how he handles his business. You'll need to come up with something better." I hung up the phone with a reserved expression.

"Señora," Juanita played along. "Why don't chu turn off your phone for the night. It's time to celebrate, not worry more about work."

"It's done!" I agreed and slipped my phone in my purse. "Where were we?" I asked.

"I don't know exactly, but I do believe we were about to get drunk." Juanita clinked her glass to mine, and we threw one back.

Out of the corner of my eye I noticed that Donnie had leaned over to Diego, and Diego instantly ordered his arm candy to get up and shake it for him on the dance floor. The sex-craved twins wandered out on the dance floor and started grinding anything that had a pelvis.

We poured another round of drinks and my stomach churned at the scent of alcohol. It was too soon for me to start knocking these back. I'd need at least two weeks before I could even say the word alcohol without cringing. What's a girl to do though?

Diego stood up and straightened out his jacket before strolling to our section.

"You ladies celebrating alone over here?" he asked and gestured as if to see if he might sit down with us.

"We could always use some more company," I responded with the same caution.

"Si," Juanita said twirling her hair around her finger. "So long as chu invite that cute friend of churs over, too." She pointed at Donnie and wiggled her finger in a come-hither motion.

"Diego." He extended a hand to mine. I shook it and noticed his hand was rough with calluses.

"Sasha Harris." I nodded. "And this is my assistant, Veronica Juan."

"Sasha Harris?" he replied in surprise. "It's nice to finally put a face to the name. And what a pretty face at that."

I faked innocence. "I'm sorry, do I know you?"

He titled his head. "Not yet, though you'll find I'm someone you'd do well to know. It seems we are in the same line of work."

I pulled my hand out of his going with the cautious sham. "I'm sorry, Diego, but I'm afraid I don't know what you're talking about."

"Well I won't dive into the nitty gritty details of our career paths, but I will say that I've heard through the grapevine that you're looking for someone to run the local trade while you're expanding your other establishments throughout the country. I'd love the chance to discuss that opportunity with you."

I slowly nodded. "I don't talk business with people I don't yet know. How about we share a few drinks and get to know each other before we dive into anything further."

Diego smiled a slick smile and snapped his fingers behind him without removing his eyes from mine. He announced, "You boys hear that? The Señorita here wants to get to know us. How about we drop this place and venture out to something more lively? I'm thinking La Cama, if the ladies are interested."

The other men chuckled, and Juanita's eyes widened. "La Cama?"

Diego turned around and wrapped his finger around Juanita's chin. "Ah, I can already tell that she's a spicy one. Wouldn't doubt it if you've taken a trip there once or twice before, too?"

"No, but I'll try anything once," she breathed as her pupils dilated a centimeter. Once again getting caught up in sexual attention. Focus!

"Veronica," he repeated her name. "Sort of just rolls off the tongue, huh?"

Juanita winked at me.

"So, you ladies interested?" Diego turned back toward me.

"Sure, let's see what this place is about."

Juanita tensed a little at the name of the place we were going, but I couldn't understand why. Guess 'La Cama' is a bad word in Spanish? Hell if I knew.

Diego stood up and extended a hand to help us to our feet. He grinned at me and added, "Tonight's on us." He ordered the waitress to add it to his tab, and we slipped out of Velvet Lounge to follow the black suits toward their cars. There were four black sleek Mercedes and everyone dispersed to their own Benz while Juanita and I glanced at each other in uncertainty.

Diego opened his door and grinned, "You coming?" That's our cue.

Juanita and I sunk into the plush leather, and Diego climbed in after us. He yelled "La Cama," to the suit in the front seat, and he peeled away from the curb at 170 mph. Donnie climbed into the car behind us. It was unsettling not to be able to talk to him throughout this encounter. I wanted to ask him if this place was where they were keeping the girls, but I imagined tonight would be strictly about fun.

"So, how do you ladies feel about sex on the beach?"

My jaw dropped, and I made a quick recovery. "I'd have to say it's a first."

Goodness! He wants to screw already? What a horn dog! I hope Toni is tailing us. He may need to step in earlier than expected.

"Yes, this place makes the best sex on the beach drinks according to all the women. Their cosmos rank a close second, I presume, judging by how often they're ordered."

Phew. "Oh, then I'll have to see for myself. You go to this place regularly?"

"Eh," he shrugged. "From time to time."

When we arrived at 'La Cama,' we instantly skipped the line and passed through the bouncers. The giant wooden doors shoved open, and we drifted into the dimly lit hall. It opened up into a spacious room that consisted of half-naked men and women that were sprawled across couches and velvet-covered beds.

It was like one giant orgy party. The club had a huge wrap-around bar where bartenders were kept busy with limitless drink orders. Toward the back of the space was a curved staircase that led to a second level with open ceiling-to-floor windows. That's probably what kept ventilation circulating. Surprisingly enough, with that much sex in one room, it's amazing the place didn't reek of dirty ass.

We followed the others up the stairs, and Juanita whispered in my ear, "Now look what chu got us into. I'm gunna have nightmares because of this place."

"Calm down, Mrs. I'll-Try-Anything-Once," I mimicked her. "We're fine."

"I was caught in the moment, OK? Do you even know what 'La Cama' means?" Juanita squinted her eyes.

"Sure I do. It means 'The Sexy.'"

"See, chu didn't even know where they were taking us. No. It means the bed. guess it explains all the furniture around here. I thought he meant he literally wanted to take us to his bed." She shook her head. "Chu better be glad he didn't try that crap, or I would've been out of here like lickety split."

"Yeah, yeah. We're fine." I glanced ahead of us at Diego's followers climbing the stairs. "We just have to act the part. Disregard anything that comes out of my mouth tonight. It's all an act."

We sat down next to Diego close to the edge of the seat where an innocent strip pole was being raped by a floozy, thong-ridden dancer. The poor pole.

Over the next couple hours, conversation became more relaxed as the drinks were knocked back. I kept telling myself that all was OK though, I'm Italian. I was created to hold my liquor.

Unfortunately, contrary to my heritage tolerance, the alcohol got the best of me at some point in the night.

"So tell me," I slurred, "Why La Carmas? What do you like about this place so much?"

"La Cama," Diego corrected me as he grabbed the bottle from our table and poured me another shot of vodka. "I mean what's not to like? The atmosphere is quite appealing."

"Of course," I hiccupped. "You're a man. Anything related to boobs and booze is a winning ticket for men."

"To boobs and booze," he raised his glass to mini cheers and gulped down another drink.

The burly man dressed in a black suit to his left leaned closer to me and flashed a blazing smile. He chimed in, "Yeah, it's also a great place for business. We meet a lot of our clients here."

"Business?" I pried. "And is this the type of setting that you actually exchange your business products? Certainly not how I run things with my business."

Diego replied, "Eh, no we just bring clients here for wining and dining. The transitioning of products actually occurs in a more discreet location, of course."

"Señora," Juanita hiccupped. "We should consider some corporate changes. We should have our own brigade of Mercedes filled with hunky men waiting on us hand and foot, too," Juanita said as she ripped the suit off the man sitting next to her with her eyes.

"Veronica," I lectured. "We've been over this. You know I like to keep a low profile. We're not drawing that kind of attention to us."

Diego chuckled, "I think attention is inevitable given that dress you have on."

I blushed and twiddled with my straw. "Flattery will get you everywhere, Diego."

Juanita grabbed her head and started leaning over in a haphazardly manner. "Oh no, Señora. I think those last two martinis are catching up to me."

The men in the suits all crouched away from her in fear. Amazing that the threat of vomit can cause bodyguards to run for cover, whereas they'd happily dive in front of a bullet. Some logic.

I turned to Diego and sighed, "Guess we'll have to call it a night. Looks like Veronica here had a little too much to drink. Tell you what though, I like what I've seen so far. Let's set up a meeting for tomorrow evening, and we'll talk shop. You can tell me what you're looking for from the deal, and I'll relay my expectations. From there, if we can work out some kind of agreement, I'll want to check out your facility to see if the conditions are as I see fit. You can review mine as well, so we have an understanding of the partnership."

Diego shifted uncomfortably in his seat, "I would love to discuss a potential business opportunity, but I'm afraid I'm not available tomorrow. I'm meeting with a distribution vendor to work out shipping arrangements for future deals. What about the day after?" he proposed.

I took it upon myself to decide that it was too far away so I lied. "Diego, I'm free tomorrow, or I'm free on the first of next month. Those are the only availabilities. I'll be on the West Coast for work and won't be back until then. I pushed another meeting behind yours, but if you can't work it into your schedule, I will proceed with other options."

Diego finally grinned. "Tomorrow it is then. Donnie will coordinate the schedules." He yanked Donnie over and explained, "Exchange numbers and schedule a meeting on her terms. It will need to be tomorrow evening, so try to move around our conference with the distribution vendor."

"I think I'm going to hurl," Juanita motioned with her stomach, and I pretended to jot down Donnie's number.

Diego nodded. "Of course, I understand. They say Miami drinks are often twice as strong. Rest up dear," he patted Juanita on the back. "Tomorrow we'll meet at a wonderful underground salsa joint. Delicious food, fabulous music, and plenty of dancing. We'll talk business afterwards."

"We'll be in touch. I'm dialing a cab to pick us up so no one runs the risk of ruining their upholstering because of this one over here," I nodded at Juanita.

Diego raised one of our hands and kissed each. "You ladies enjoy the rest of your evening."

Once they left, I spoke into my camera pin and told Emily to meet us on the side of the building to pick us up. I had to make a pit stop at the bathroom on the way out though. I vigorously scrubbed my hand with steaming water and sterile soap as I tried to scrape off the skin Diego touched with his lips.

Disgusting. Who knows where those lips have been.

CHAPTER SIXTEEN

When Juanita and I emerged from the club and rounded the dark alley, we found Emily in the car idle at the curb. We scrunched into the back, and Toni was already seated in the passenger seat with a vicious scowl across his face.

"This is stupid," he growled. "Absolutely and completely stupid. I think we should stop this tonight. This will only end badly."

"It's OK," I tried to calm him down. "Nothing happened. We just set the stage for tomorrow where we'll actually learn the location of the hostages. We can hand it over to the authorities once we get confirmation."

"Uh-huh. And what about Caleb and Logan? I told you there was some bad history between us. Caleb was one of the guys wearing the suits. Do you know how difficult it is to keep an eye out for you two while simultaneously dodging Caleb's line of vision?" He glared over his shoulder at me. "If he spots me and ties us together, this whole thing is shot to hell."

I glanced away as we continued the drive home. "What in the world are you so worried about? A blast from the past? Wear a damn disguise if you're so worried about your own neck. For that matter, why don't you just scat, we all know you were going to anyways when we first started this thing."

Toni frowned and turned back around to face the front. He loudly cracked his knuckles in aggravation. "Once we find the damn location, amateur hour is done, you hear me?" He asked the entire car. We all nodded in agreement. "Or so help me I'll go to the press myself and destroy Sunset Cove's reputation."

I gasped. He wouldn't dare.

The rest of the ride home was a charged silence. Emily and Juanita could feel the tension growing in the car too, and when we arrived at the house they fled the car in seconds. Emily hurried inside to the safety of my house, and Juanita waved goodbye before she scurried into her car.

I exited the Tahoe and slammed the door shut with excessive force.

He rounded the car and caught my arm before I could angle for the house. When I turned to face him his expression was no longer full of rage but was filled with another emotion…fear, sadness, anxiety? I couldn't quite pinpoint it.

"Nicks," he spoke more gently. "I don't know if I can pull tomorrow off. I can't do my job if Caleb or Logan are there. You just have to trust me on this."

"If you can't do it," I shrugged, "don't go. Nobody is twisting your arm."

He groaned. "Hop off the defense, goddammit. I'm trying to be real with you here. I am not telling you to stop because I want to control you. Lord knows you only do what you want to do anyways. I just couldn't bear to see anything bad happen to you. I don't like this. I cannot stress it enough to you."

I wiggled my arm free and gave him my full attention. "I don't want anything bad to happen to any of us either. But I've told you, there is no other way. I just need the girls' location and a bit of proof, so I can take it to the authorities to arrange a rescue mission for them. I'm not trying to be a hero here. I do like having all my limbs intact, you know? But this is going to happen, Toni. So you can either help us or get out of the way."

The veins along Toni's neck were bulging beneath his skin. I knew he was frustrated, but there was too much risk exposing this prematurely.

"Sleep on it," I suggested. "Things have a way of brightening up when you reevaluate in the morning." I dragged myself into the house and closed up shop for the night. My legs felt like jelly from the prolonged adrenaline rush, not to mention these shoes were killing my feet. I slipped into a comfy shirt and boy shorts before I plopped into bed. Immediately I checked my phone for any missed calls or texts from Ralf.

One voicemail from Ralf. When I listened to it I felt my stomach do a few cartwheels. He was apologizing because of the abrupt departure this morning, and wanted to go on a date once he muddled through his work crisis. He suggested later tomorrow evening, although that wouldn't work with Diego's salsa plans. I'd text him in the morning. Right now the call from my pillow was just too much to resist. I drifted into a heavy slumber.

The next morning I woke up without any kind of interruptions. I stretched lazily in my bed and for a split second had the fleeting thought that I was grateful I called in to work for a few days off. Then the recent events caught up, and I remembered I was only on 'vacation' because I needed time away from the office to sort out this trafficking debacle. My phone was charging on the nightstand, and when I flipped it over I blanched at the time.

"Emily!" I shouted. "Why in the world did you let me sleep until three in the afternoon?!"

Emily came trotting down the hallway. There was a light knock on the door before Emily pushed it open. "Technically it's twelve after three but whatever helps you feel better about wasting your vacation day."

I rolled my eyes and plopped my head back on the pillow in frustration. "I can't believe I slept so late. I haven't done that since college."

"Your body and your mind are tired, Nicky. Sleep is a very important function that helps reboot and rejuvenate the brain. You've had a lot to take in lately, so I didn't want to disrupt the process."

"Well now I've missed breakfast," I pouted, "and lunch." That was probably what I was most upset about. Sigh. Fat girl problems.

"I'll make you a batch of blueberry pancakes, what do you say?" she offered.

I nodded my head and gave her the puppy eyes like a spoiled child would do after they got their way. Thankfully, Emily loved to cook almost as much as I loved to eat. With these kinds of living arrangements, I'm sure we could work out a long term residential situation.

She departed for the kitchen, and I slowly rose from the dead. I pulled on some fuzzy slippers and a cotton robe before I met her in the kitchen. She was finishing a round of pancakes when I moseyed into the kitchen. She set the places and served the pancakes while I managed the laborious task of pouring two glasses of milk.

We sat and ate our long overdue breakfast in peace. I glanced over at Trixie who was now showing signs of life again.

"I see Trixie survived, after all," I motioned toward the cage.

"I know. It was touch and go for a while back there." Emily breathed easy. "Strangest thing though, she won't go near the booze in her water bowl now."

"She probably doesn't trust anything you serve her. As far as Trixie knows, the last thing you gave her nearly killed her. I can understand the trust issues there."

Emily disregarded my comment. "Well I figured aside from some extra sleep, you'd also need to unwind a little with some Cosmopolitan love, homemade mani and pedis, and a sappy chick-flick."

I wiggled my brows in delight. "Tempting, but I just need to keep my head in the game before tonight."

"Aw come on, Nicky. You can still ruminate about all your anxiety-evoking thoughts, which I know you'll do regardless. How about one teeny tiny distraction at least?"

I added, "Pedicures then, but that's it!"

Emily slapped the table and then shot up in excitement. She snatched up her bags of nail polish and returned to the kitchen table. We each sorted through the colors, and I selected a summery coral shade. Once I had finished my nails, I let them dry for a few minutes while sparing some extra time for boy talk with Emily. It was obvious she was crushing pretty hard on Toni. By the looks of things, it seemed like he was interested in her, too.

Although, I can never quite be sure with Toni. He's definitely the cryptic type. I always assumed a lot of it was centered around his mysterious past that he was so tight lipped about, but these days I'm not so sure. Lately, I've been getting the feeling that he's up to something. The way that he's been acting recently is so…suspicious. I almost got the impression that he had an ulterior motive for being involved with our little undercover investigation.

I couldn't put my finger on what exactly, but my intuition was sounding the alarms. Emily, of course, wasn't picking up on the same queues that I was, as evidenced by her continual doting and pining over his charm and good looks. Obviously, Emily was interested in him, so I didn't want to be the neigh sayer and rain on her parade based on a gut feeling, especially, given the awful break-up she just survived.

So I left her on her cloud nine and kept my concerns to myself. Once our nails were dry, I grabbed my purse and decided to step out for a breather. I desperately needed some alone time to think about tonight. I started my moped and puttered off to the best place where I could clear my head. The beach. When I stepped into the warm sand, I found a quite spot on the sand away from the crowd and plopped down on a rock lodged into the ground.

I thought I would feel better if I called Donnie and made the arrangements for this evening. First, we would meet at Francescos, which was an underground salsa club for a few drinks, and then we'd move to the housing facility when we were ready to talk business.

"So when are you going to grab my sister?" I asked slipping into the Gabrielle persona. "I need to know how this transaction is going to work."

Donnie whispered. "Now isn't exactly the best time. We'll discuss when I meet you there. I'll text you the address, but make sure you're there by ten."

"I'd really prefer it if we could discuss the game plan now if—" I started to say but he'd already hung up. "Ugh, I hate when men do that!" I frowned at the phone.

I played with the sand between my toes trying to develop a new approach to work out the details of tonight's exchange since I didn't want to draw attention to us in front of Diego. It would look much too conspicuous if I were to ask Diego to hold on while I had a side bar powwow with Donnie. I suppose I could have Juanita intervene and force Diego onto the dance floor while I discussed the break down with Donnie from the sidelines. That wouldn't draw any negative attention.

I called Juanita and Toni to tell them to come over dressed for a Salsa club. I explained the distraction game plan to Juanita briefly over the phone, and she understood her responsibility in the exchange. Strangely, I wasn't able to connect with Toni though, so I settled for a voicemail.

By the time I felt mentally and emotionally equipped for tonight's events, the evening was beginning to approach. Since the sun was starting to set, I supposed it was time to return home and get all dolled up.

"I'm going to get ready for another lavish night of seduction," I groaned to Emily as I entered the house. Getting this dressed up, although fun from time to time, is still an exhausting process. I hurried up the stairs and took a hot shower. After I dried my hair, I went over it with an iron to create soft, luscious waves. I carefully applied my smoky eye shadow and liner. The base, the blush, the mascara were all whipped into place in no time.

Now for the dress. I strolled to the closet and inspected the dresses. Finally I settled on a vibrant royal blue number that had exposed my skin down to the base of my back, and the front barely dipped into my cleavage. The dress length was mid-thigh in front and skimmed the floor in the back. It was a smooth free-flowing layout along the bottom of the dress, and was a curve-hugging bodice north of the hips. I slipped into my snakeskin pumps and was ready to take this outfit on the floor for a spin.

When I descended the stairs, Juanita and Emily made sounds of approval. Juanita was dressed in a black leather dress that clung on tight for dear life. She had a pair of black leather stiletto boots that climbed above her knees and gold accessories to go with the outfit.

"Juanita," I stared her up and down. "You just upped your game a few notches with that outfit."

I glanced around and noticed Toni wasn't there. Before I could say anything there was a knock at the door, and when I opened it Toni strolled in wearing a black fendora hat with an all-black ensemble.

Emily swallowed hard next to me and then coughed. "You, uh, you're lookin pretty sharp there, Toni. Thought the goal was not to draw attention." A hint of jealously slipped through her tone.

"Can't exactly go to a salsa club in sweats. Don't worry though," he grabbed Emily's hand and pulled her into a spin. "I'll be saving the last dance for you."

She giggled, and he spun her back out. "Let's get these on everyone." She stumbled on her giddiness induced by Toni's seductive dance moves. Emily handed the pins and earpieces to everyone, and we arranged them accordingly.

"We should get going," I motioned toward the door. "Donnie warned us not to be late. Juanita and I can just take a cab and meet you guys up there." We grabbed our purses and phones and hailed a cab.

On the ride there I remembered to text Ralf back about tonight. I let him know I couldn't meet tonight since I had a previous work engagement, but suggested the day after. By the time we arrived to Francesco's I hadn't heard any response yet, so I turned it on silent and slipped it into my purse. We made our way through the line and ventured to the bar once we were inside.

"So, where is Diego and his crew?" I asked peeking around the bar.

Suddenly, Diego leaned over my shoulder and whispered in my ear. The touch of his breath made my stomach churn. "Why, hello ladies. You both look," he paused and raised a brow, "sexy."

Juanita winked, "Back at chu."

I mentally shook my head at her. I turned around toward Diego and slid a my hand into his for a business-like handshake. "How about a drink? A scotch on the rocks would do the trick." Definitely not my favorite drink, but I figured it sounded slick and gave that down to business vibe.

"The good stuff, huh." He slipped the bartender a fifty and ordered a round of scotch on the rocks.

We moved through the club to the V.I.P. seating in the back corner. Not even a minute passed before the table was swarming with various gifts of Cuban cigars, bottle service, and gorgeous women with dresses so tight I wondered if they were sewn into the fabric.

Juanita was graciously accepting the cigars and free booze as she bounced around in her seat like a little school girl on the last day of classes before summer. This was her heaven.

I selected another scotch and sipped on it slowly, silently swearing off alcohol for the next three months after these back to back drinking excursions.

"So what made you pick this spot?" I asked.

"Francesco's? It has the best music. Exclusive accessibility to a particular *elite* crowd. It is the real heart and soul of Latin dancing." He stared me over, up and down, to the point that I had to check if my clothes were still there. "And it's also mine."

"You own this place?" I asked inspecting the ambiance. "Well, I'm one for dancing though I can't say I've ever tried salsa before. I may need some lessons."

"Oh, the things I could teach you," he mumbled, as he rubbed a finger down my arm.

Bleach. Bath. The first two words that popped into my mind. All I could muster up at the time was a half-assed smile. I was too creeped out to encourage that kind of talk.

"You may get asked to dance a lot, so if any guy comes up to dance with you, I'll take care of them."

"I think we should dive into work first, and then we can play," I glanced at my watch as if in a hurry. "If we're going to set up a business arrangement, we'll need to talk numbers and management expectations first."

"Sasha Harris," he ran a finger across a wisp of my hair. "Your reputation precedes you. I see how you've managed to climb so ferociously. All business all day."

"Let's get out on that floor and get our salsa on." Juanita interjected. "These boots weren't just made for walking, chu know!" She jumped onto her feet and beckoned for Diego to take her for a spin, creating the distraction we initially planned. She politely tugged at his shirt, trying to seduce Diego from his chair, but despite her attempts, he didn't budge an inch.

Donnie removed her hand from Diego's shirt and held it between his. "She's right, Diego" Donnie shrugged. "Let the poor girl dance already. Mind if I steal her for a round on the dance floor?"

Juanita baulked and glanced at me for guidance. I motioned for Juanita to do whatever she wanted.

Emily whispered into my earpiece. "OK, not exactly as planned, but this can work too. Let Juanita dance with Donnie. She can talk with him while they're dancing and no suspicions will be raised. I'll relay the plan to you once they've discussed. Go talk business with Diego."

"Alright then!" Juanita breathed in ease at the new plan. "Dance we shall. Come on chu! Let's go!" She touched Donnie's hand and wiggled her other finger in a come-hither manner.

Diego slightly tilted his head in amusement as he watched her bounce toward the floor.

I tried a cigar and nearly gagged. OK, no more for me.

"So, Diego, we can join Veronica and Donnie on the dance floor once we've covered some matters. Remember, this is my last night in Miami before my trip. If we're going to do this, we should really get down to business."

"Agreed," Diego snubbed out his cigar and rose from the table. "Let's see what kind of deal can be made so that we can continue to play in the same sandbox without stepping on each other's toes. Perhaps we should discuss this in a more appropriate setting. I'll show you to the back office." His teeth gleamed off the lights' reflection.

"Sounds great," I managed a false smile. "Let's talk business."

CHAPTER SEVENTEEN

"Please," Diego motioned toward the metal chair. "Have a seat." He led me through the dark, damp hallways in the back of the club which was marked as 'Do Not Enter.' The back room was dimly lit with a continuous drip in the corner furthest from the door. It smelled rancid, and the metal table and chairs were rusty, in which I was confident that it was a death trap for hepatitis.

Nonetheless, I took a seat in the chair and scooted up to the table which released a nails-on-a-chalkboard type of screech. Juanita was still on the dance floor with Donnie, and Emily would be relaying the game plan shortly.

I interlaced my fingers together on the steel table in front of me and leaned in. "So, what kind of business arrangement are we talking here?" I asked with a smug pretense. "What can you do for Sasha Harris?"

Diego turned his chair around and straddled it with his arms crossed over the back. "Well, doll face, we've got a large, functioning organization already in operation. We've got the distribution down to an art. One piece of the formula we've recently had to re-address with distribution transportation, but I've rescheduled that meeting later this evening. What's your experience been in that area? Any suggestions?" Diego tilted his head.

The hair on the back of my neck started to rise. Something about his stare in the dim lighting struck me as eerie. His eyes had a certain gleam to them I hadn't quite noticed before until now.

"Yes, well," I hesitated, "Rule 101 to business is to ensure your parts don't exceed the whole. If you're looking for a reasonable vendor, I could send you some names we've used locally in the past. Typically, my assistant tracks the books, so I don't recall them off the top of my head."

Diego scratched his chin. "How often do you schedule your auctions? What kind of clients do you permit? Any trades outside your scope of work? All things we need to be on the same page with before we can draft an agreement."

"Feels like an interrogation, when, in fact, you are the one who sought me out for my business opportunities. Why don't you start by answering some of your own questions, and I'll decide if we're truly on the same page or not." I glanced toward the door and noticed one over-sized, beefy guy waiting outside the door.

Diego chuckled and suddenly reached across the table for my hair. He smashed my face down onto the metal table and kept me there while he rounded the table to lean over me. "I've done about all the ass-kissing I can stand. Let's get something straight. You're in my world now. So you'd better start with the truth, or you're going to find yourself in a whole world of pain."

He slipped out a knife and twirled it around in his hand. Finally, he let up and sat on the table still fiddling with the knife.

I lifted my head from the table and rolled my jaw. I'm sure there would be bruising later.

Diego lowered his voice, "Why don't you start with your name?"

I shuddered and straightened up more forcefully. "What do you mean? Sasha Harris. I thought we were here to discuss business not play games of interrogation."

In a flash, he swung his hand toward me, and I leaned back in my chair to dodge contact. It became apparent that I moved too slow when I felt the sudden stinging across my collarbone. When I looked down, I saw that he'd sliced me with the knife, and I was bleeding a slow, but steady stream of warm blood.

I grimaced and made tight fists in pain.

"We can do this the easy way, or we can do this the hard way." He wiped the blood from the knife on a white towel.

I cursed the heavens. Where the fuck was Emily with the plan? I haven't heard from her since we were at the section in the club. Now would be a good time for some guidance. Where was Toni and Juanita?

I waited and waited, until Diego's voice broke the silence. "Let's try this again. You can start by telling me your real name."

My voice caught in my throat, and I shrugged my shoulders to repeat my statement from before. "Sasha Harris."

He sighed and leaned in for another lashing. This time he cut my cheekbone, and I screamed out at the sting. I reached for my cheek, but Diego had whirled behind me and pounded my face onto the metal table again. He held me there and leaned in so his front was against my back.

"Now look what you made me do. I was fine to just have a normal conversation with you, but then you had to go be a stubborn woman. You know you're nothing like some of these floozy women around here." He rolled his eyes. "They're trash and deserve to be treated as such. No, you're a rare, sophisticated breed. I find it rather intriguing, actually."

Diego began to outline my face. Only a thin layer of air remained between his fingers and my skin, yet it left a cold trail in its place. I involuntarily shivered and eyed the door contemplating whether there was the slightest chance I could bolt for it.

Diego slowly followed my gaze, and his eyes snapped back to mine.

"Since you refuse to cooperate and give me what I want, I suppose I could find good use for you elsewhere." He teasingly twirled the end of my hair around his fingertips. Diego waved over the big suit that was standing outside.

"Yes, boss?" he answered.

"Get this bitch to the holding cell. Hands bound."

The man grabbed me so that both hands were trapped behind my back. He maneuvered me through the dimly-lit concrete hallways, and I struggled to get free. I was no match for his P90X build. At last, I succumbed to the realization that I wasn't going to escape his grasp and slumped forward as he shoved me toward the isolated holding cell.

As soon as we arrived, I noticed Juanita was tied up by her wrists, suspended a few inches off the ground. She was already bruising from the trauma she endured across her arms and face. Her right eye was nearly swollen shut. To her left was Donnie, beaten to a bloodied pulp. He, too, was suspended in the air in the same manner. He certainly looked like he got the shit end of the stick compared to the beatings we'd endured. However, something told me more pain was to come.

The man in the suit bound my hands, and I decided to make one last attempt to free his grasp, but he socked me on my cheekbone that was already cut, and split the seam. Now the blood was pouring more ferociously. I flopped my head back in complete agony. My body went slack as he pulled me up so I was in the same suspended position.

I cried in pain at the tug of my arms begging to pull out of socket. When the suit finished, he chuckled darkly at my pained expression. He intentionally bumped me on his way out, so I'd sway forcefully back and forth. I felt the stress of the motion on every tendon, muscle, and ligament all threatening to detach with each swing.

"Fucking shit!" I wailed. When the swinging slowed I called out to my neighbors who weren't responsive.

"Veronica." I called out to Juanita. No answer. "Veronica!" Nothing.

Donnie slowly lifted his head. "She's been knocked out since they drug her in here. Sometimes the body's response to handle extreme pain is to go into an unconscious state. I think our girl here hit that point a long time ago. She'll come to when her body is ready."

I nodded still processing the shock of the situation. "I can't believe this happened." I shook my head. "What the hell went wrong? Why was Diego asking for my real name?"

Donnie inhaled a sharp breath, which visibly caused him discomfort. "Diego found out we were working together. I tried to slip to the back to grab your sister, and Bruce caught us trying to flee. Didn't even make it out of her cell. I'm sorry, Gabrielle, I tried."

A tear rolled down each cheek. "They're here? They were right here under our noses," I sniffled. "We're completely screwed. Beyond that, we're dead."

Donnie tried to shuffle out of his ropes but failed to make any progress.

"Well, what about your back up plan? Or your insurance policy as you called it? Surely that team of private investigators will come for us when they don't hear from you as planned."

"What?" I drew my brows together in confusion.

"The PI team that Veronica leads? Will they come rescue us when they don't hear from you? When was the next call?"

More tears fled from my eyes. "Oh, Donnie. There's no team of private investigators. I made it up. There was no real rescue plan. No insurance policy. I made it up to get access to Maria," I sobbed. "The only rescue plan we had was Toni who was here on standby, but even he can't move around freely because he can't be seen by Caleb or Logan. Some guys from his past or something. It doesn't matter. All that matters now is that we're fucked."

Donnie's eyes widened in realization. "Wait a minute. There's not even a real insurance policy? Are you kidding me?"

I shook my head from side to side. "Do I look like I'm kidding you? We got nothing."

Donnie growled in pure rage. He wiggled more forcefully, and then slipped right out of the ropes that were secured around his hands. My face lit up like a Christmas tree. "Oh, hallelujah. I knew this couldn't be the end." I tried to wiggle free of my ropes but lacked the upper arm strength to maneuver such a trick. "Help me with this, will you?"

He hobbled over and took a moment to catch his breath. Once he straightened up he grabbed for my hands and fiddled with the rope.

Suddenly he stopped and retracted his hands. I looked up at my hands still wound in the rope's knot. "Is it stuck?" I whimpered. "Do you have a knife or sharp blade?"

Donnie patted his chest and then his pant pockets. His face looked panicked. "I thought I had one on me." He pulled it out of his back pocket and flicked open the blade. "Aha!"

I wiggled in excitement. "Great, cut me down. I'm about to pop something out of socket."

Donnie ambled backwards and placed a hand on his chin. "No, no, I don't think I will."

I stared at him in confusion. "Quit dickin' around, and cut me down already. We don't know when they're coming back."

Donnie leaned back against the opposing wall, flicking his knife blade in a casual demeanor. "Actually, I know exactly when they're coming back." He started cleaning the groove of his nail with the knife. "They'll come back once I've collected the information needed. Honestly, I was prepared to hang up there for an hour or so until I either gathered information on who else knew about our little operation here, or until we drew them in using you as bait."

"But, but..." I stammered. "You would betray me, so you could stay in your little club? The one that beats you to a pulp and murders your family members?"

He threw his hand back and laughed. "Nobody laid a hand on me except to help apply the body paint and makeup," he smeared his face and revealed the façade. "And as far as Ronnie goes, yeah they had him killed. But not before I approved it. Nice try though, to try and turn a disgruntled member against his own crew by appealing to his vengeance. Guess the problem with your plan is that you didn't study your subject thoroughly enough. Ronnie was a pain in my ass. Caused more harm than good. He had to go."

"Heartless," I whispered still in shock by his detachment.

"You misjudged my degree of affection for family. Big mistake on your part. But then, I also misjudged your ability to bluff. Had I known you were bullshitting the whole time, you never would have made it out of my living room. When you said you had that go live plan on the back burner, I knew we'd have to pull the information out of you to eliminate the threat. Turns out there was no threat at all." He shook his head. "Brains and beauty. A rare combination."

He snagged his phone and dialed Diego. He angled the phone in the air searching for a signal. Frustrated he shoved the phone back in his pocket. "These damn tunnels have awful reception." He headed toward the door. "I'm going to inform Diego, and then we'll return. Diego mentioned some interesting plans for you. Don't go anywhere." He laughed as he exited the room.

Once he was gone I struggled some more to get out of the restraints with no luck. "Juanita," I yelled. "Juanita, wake your ass up!"

She raised her head and peeked open the one good eye at me. "Are we alone?" she asked.

"Yes, you must have passed out from the shit they did to you, but I just found out—"

"Si, I know. Donnie is bad. I heard the whole thing. I was only pretending to be out, so nobody would try to do anymore hitting or punching."

Playing opossum. It was a brilliant idea.

"How are we going to get out of here?" I asked. "Are you able to connect with Emily on your earpiece?"

"No, we don't have reception here. I think it's the tunnels."

Suddenly a dark figure rushed past the door and Juanita and I stirred in fear. The shadow returned and opened the door.

"Toni!" we cried out together. "Donnie's bad. He is going to tell Diego that we don't have an insurance policy, and now they're going to kill us. Get us down, please!"

Toni wheeled Juanita down first and unknotted her ropes. Then he wheeled me down and untied my restraints as well. His face was grave.

"Somehow...*somehow*...'I told you so' just doesn't do the trick."

Juanita and I leaped for him and hugged him in relief. "Thank you, Toni," I started to sob.

"We can get to the blubbering and graveling later. We need to bounce, now."

We nodded and hobbled along behind him. He checked to make sure the coast was clear and then led us down the corridor to the right in the direction of the club music. Almost home free.

Sometimes I just wanted to slap myself for jinxing our luck. Two men strolled out of a side room and spotted our hasty escape. At first Toni continued toward them fully prepared to muscle a fight. When the men stepped into the dim overhead lighting recognition fell over Toni, and he faltered back a few steps. "Caleb. Logan."

The two cocked their head to the side, "Toni. O'Connor will be happy to see you again." They took a few cautious steps and began to approach at full speed.

Instinctively, Juanita and I began to run in the opposing direction. We rounded a corner and Toni shouted for us to split up. Before I could run down a different hallway, Toni caught my arm in his and handed me a folded envelope.

I glanced down and up at him again. "Toni, what is this?"

"I've been trying to give it to you from the start. Keep it safe, keep it hidden. As long as that remains, I'll still have a pulse. Go!"

"But, wait!" I yelled, but he had already pushed me forward and lunged in a different direction. The two men were completely focused on him.

I continued running in the opposite direction, completely clueless where the tunnels would spit me out. I spotted a man lurking in a doorway at the far end of the hall.

He did a double take at me and then started marching in my direction. I turned and ran the opposite way down the hall. At the end of the hall I made a sharp right turn and tried the third door on the right. Locked. Fourth door on the right. It opened.

Quickly I toppled into the room and closed the door behind me. When I glanced at the door handle, I didn't see a lock.

"Don't panic, Nicole," I whispered under my breath as I searched the darkened room for a shred of light from a window or lit up exit sign. I could hear the footsteps outside in the hall. They slowed in pace and were followed by the sound of doors opening. A pair of voices shouted to one another.

As I hurriedly scanned the room I saw a small shifting light toward the back corner. I couldn't quite make out the shape, but I figured I couldn't wait in front of the door with Diego and his lunatics scouting the back rooms for me. I would have to find a hiding place or find a way out, and find it pronto.

A few times I stumbled over the unknown clutter on the floor as I felt my way across the darkened room toward the light glow. When I stubbed my toe on something metal I had to muffle a yelp. As I inched closer and closer to the subtle light I realized it was moving. It was as if the light was playing peek-a-boo with me.

Hand extended, I reached out to touch it but instead my fingers found a damp, mildewed cloth. I bit my lip and grimaced as I thought of the numerous sorts of bacteria I was touching.

The cloth was thick and heavy; I suspected it was a curtain. Still in a hurry to find an escape, I pushed through the curtain and entered into a dank tunnel. The sides of the walls were brick. It was slippery and coated in a slimy residue.

Barefoot, I hurriedly tip toed down the tunnel. It was dimly lit with more visibility than the last room, but it was still difficult to see more than several feet ahead. When I rounded the corner, I suddenly froze. A sound.

I anxiously glanced around waiting to hear the noise again. It sounded like shuffling or footsteps. I froze in silence for a few seconds, but the sound was gone. I continued down the narrowed tunnel.

Then I heard the sound again, only it was louder, much closer. I whipped my head around so fast I wondered if I'd get whiplash. No one was behind me, or so I hoped.

Metal clanked against metal, and I heard a moan. My heart was pounding so hard I could have sworn it was going to burst through my chest.

Between the lights on the wall I pressed against the slime-covered brick in the shadows. Like agents seen in the movies, I inched closer to the opening of the tunnel from where the noises were coming. The wall's thick coating seeped into my dress as I clung to it for the only coverage I had.

At the edge of the tunnel I poked my head into the room, my mouth agape and eyes bewildered. I found it.

Unfortunately, it wasn't the exit I was staring at, but rather the women. There were metal cages formed into several rows. Women were lying down in filth and grit. A few of them were sitting up in their crates swaying in a nonchalant manner, but most of the women were crumpled beneath their ragged sheets.

They were drugged, obviously. Their eyes were glazed over and their movements were sluggish. How could a human being be capable of this? How could anyone live with themselves treating other people like this?

It was heart wrenching to look at and from that feeling, grew anger. Lots and lots of it. The mere sight of it had my adrenaline pumping, revved, and ready to go. I didn't know how, but I was going to get these women out of here.

My feet barely keeping up with my new shot of energy, I kept fumbling over myself to find some sort of key or gadget to unlock their cells. When I neared the back of the room, one of the women reached out and grabbed my ankle causing me to slam into the ground head first.

Instantly I reached for my cheek. "For the love of GOD!" I bit my tongue to stop from yelling. When I looked at the woman who made me crash and burn I recognized her face instantly. It was Nancy Jennings, one of the four college girls from the hotel. She was holding a finger up to her mouth as if to shush me.

Her eyes were wild with fear and her mouth drew into a tight line. Her hair protruded out in all different directions and slightly reminded me of a level-four tornado.

I mentally smacked myself on the hand. I'm sure the hairstyle's not voluntary. She whispered to me, "Help us, please!" She started silently crying. "Please, don't leave us here!"

I nodded and pressed a finger to my lips. "I'm here to help," I reassured her. "How do I get these things open? Is there a key?"

She nodded, "Yes, but the man has it. He walks up and down the hall. The keys are on him."

Great. Plan B. "Let me see if I can find something to pry it open. Wait here."

As I stood up from the ground, I searched the room for something strong enough to break open the cage. Near the back corner of the room, I found a crowbar shoved behind the cluttered debris.

Lady luck was on my side. Once I reached Nancy's cell, I placed the crowbar between the hinges and heaved with all my force. The bars shook, but nothing.

I tried again using short spurts of force. "Open. You. Son. Of. A. B—"

Clink! The door flung off and crashed to the floor making a loud clattering noise.

The woman hurled out of the cage and almost knocked me over as she hugged me. "Thank you, thank you, thank you! Oh my God."

I nodded and took her by the hand and led her toward the tunnel. "We have to get out of here fast," I said in a hushed voice. "I'm sure they heard us and are on their way. We need to be quick."

Before we rounded the corner, Nancy snatched me back toward her. "No, what about everyone else? We can't just leave them. They're my friends."

I shot a glance over my shoulder. "Look, we will come back for them, I promise. But if we get caught before we even get out of here we won't be able to help because we will both be locked in cages. We can go straight to the cops after this, I swear."

"Promise?" she stopped.

"Of course. I promise. Now let's get the hell out of here before they catch us."

She began to haul me in the other direction. "They'll find us that way. We have to go the back way. Come on, follow me. I've seen them use it before."

I followed closely at her heels praying she knew this maze as much as she seemed to think she did. Near the back of the room, she plummeted straight into what I thought was a wall at first, but turned out to be a shadow that flowed into another tunnel.

What's with the tunnels? Was Diego a mole, for crying out loud?

We passed several closed doors as we sprinted down the tunnel.

"This way!" the woman nearly cried. "We're almost there!"

I saw what I presumed was the exit, and we both picked up the pace. I could feel cold wet tears streaming down my cheek. I hadn't had time to take it all in yet, but as we neared the exit, it hit me. Life as I've known it could have been over. I might have been added to their sex trafficking collection back there, or worse... killed.

Gulp.

Unexpectedly, a dark figure emerged from the last door on the left and stepped into the hall. The woman and I tried to screech to a halt, but we were too close to prevent from crashing into the person.

At first Nancy was on the top of the dog pile with me in the middle and a stranger beneath me. Nancy rolled off and yanked my hand with her as she made a dash for the door. I scrambled to my feet and bolted forward with her. She vanished through the doorway, and I leapt after her until an arm hooked around my stomach. A body tackled me to the ground. The man was tall and strong, easily pinning me to the ground while I squirmed under his hold.

"Let me go this instant or I-I-I" I shouted.

The man pulled back and stared at me, looking as confused and bewildered as I did.

"What are you—" We both started to say at the same time and then stopped.

I craned my neck so that I could see more clearly in the dim lighting. He got a look at my face, and his mouth dropped open in shock. "Jesus Christ, Nicole? What, I mean, your face..." He was completely mortified by my beating. "Look at you. What the hell happened? Who in God's name did this to you?" Ralf gently outlined my face and I flinched when he got to my cheekbone.

"The guy that owns this place, Diego." I said looking around still dazed by a mixture of fear and confusion. "Ralf, we have to go. And I mean now. I don't have time to explain!" He helped me up, and I started to pull us toward the door Nancy exited.

"Wait, I just went that way. It's a dead end," he added.

I looked at him more intently, suspicion tearing through my thoughts. "What exactly are you doing here again? I thought you had a business crisis come up? Yet you're at a salsa club."

Ralf's expression was unflinching. "I did, but we tied things up early. My business partner decided we should blow off some steam with a few drinks. This ended up being the place he picked."

"Bizarre coincidence." I eyed him doubtfully but didn't take the time to grill him any further. My primary concern was getting out of this place. This must have shown on my face, too, since he caught my arm in his hand and started down a different path.

"You said you're trying to get out, right? Come on, the exit is actually a few doors down." He started to lead and stopped abruptly, looking me over with care. "Do you need me to carry you? Can you walk OK?"

"Always a gentleman," I murmured with a bite of sarcasm. My mind was still processing the unlikely chance that he was here on coincidence. "I can walk. Hell, I can run if that will get me out of this place." I just needed to get away from these suffocating tunnels.

Ralf led the way with my hand now in his. I was torn with confliction. His warm hand wrapped around mine felt so comforting and gentle, taking me back to our previous more intimate moments from our past dates. Yet at the same time I couldn't shake the undeniable knot in my stomach that he wasn't merely here for a drink with his buddy. If that were the case, why was he roaming around the back tunnels of Diego's club where he handles his illegal business deals? Surely someone would have seen him by now, but why wasn't he being escorted out by Diego's thugs? Does he associate himself with this type of crowd on weekends? Does he have a history with Diego? Maybe he knows some of the people from Diego's crew, but doesn't know what their line of work. He did say he was only here for...business.

By the time my brain went round in a full circle, I was about to yank my hand from Ralf's and demand some answers. But just as we hooked a turn at the next door, my interrogation questions completely deserted my mind.

We both came to a screeching halt, and all the blood in my body ran cold.

"No!" I shouted. Ralf's posture stiffened, and he glanced over to see why I tensed. "That's the guy," I whispered.

A few feet shy of the exit, Diego sat, hands crossed, at the far end of a red oak table. A large blank screen hung behind him. A short burly man was standing with his hands behind his back. On the opposing side of the table, another face glared at me across the room and burned a hole into my skin with his eyes.

The man had a blonde, greased back, slick pony-tail and wore a pressed collared button down with blinding cufflinks and black slacks. The man nodded ever so slightly in my direction, and Ralf's grip tightened on my arm.

I looked from my arm to his face. Ralf stared straight ahead, unfazed. "What are you doing? We have to go!" I tried tugging free of his grip, but it was unyielding.

The rust-covered wheels in my head began to turn as alarms started going off. So it was true after all. That voice of reason I had been secretly trying to deny. I was hoping that maybe there would be another reason that I overlooked about why Ralf was in the tunnels too, but I see now this was merely a fool's hope.

"Ralf? No, no, no, no, no...Not you." I shook my head in denial, but the truth forced itself upon me with no mercy. "You work for Diego."

"Not necessarily," Ralf continued to look forward at Diego.

Diego continued reviewing his papers. "No, Mr. Mancini and I are still in negotiations. The important business meeting I had for a distribution vendor? The one I almost missed because of your stupid charades?"

"You disgust me." I spat at Ralf but it dribbled back on my chin.

Great way to make a statement.

Diego's stare transitioned from the papers before him to my face. Our eyes held, and I silenced the burning desire to run. Diego stood from his seat and smiled with a welcoming gesture.

"Gabrielle, welcome back, my dear. I do hope you enjoyed the tour of our office." His eyes roamed the room in a theatrical manner. "Some of the rooms desperately need an interior designer, but it's such a big decision to make. I can't have this place looking like a pig's sty."

"I don't see why not. There are nothing but pigs here, as far as I'm concerned." I straightened my shoulders. Ralf gave me a threatening glance.

Diego slowly clapped. "My, oh, my. You did always have the promise of sassiness to you, didn't you?" He slowly rounded the table and surpassed the other men. Once he reached me, he stood but several inches from my ear, lingering.

Diego smiled and leaned in further to kiss my neck. In that same moment, I rotated and took his ear between my teeth, yanking my head back with full force.

When I realized I successfully tore off half of his ear, I spit it out onto the table. I suppressed my gag reflexes and took his vulnerability as an opportunity to head butt him in nose.

Diego yelled, "Stupid bitch. Oh, you're going to regret that!" He was holding his ear with one hand and his broken nose with the other. Diego's sidekicks looked to each other in a panic while ponytail raised an amused eye brow.

By this point, Ralf had seized my hands and angled them painfully behind my back.

Diego was now a few feet in front of me, a mess of blood and blind rage.

Diego motioned toward the bulky guy. "Well Whitey, don't just stand there, you dip shit. Give me my fucking gun." Diego snatched the gun out of his hands with one palm still pressed to his ear. "And get me a damn aspirin. What, you think this feels good? Go, hurry!"

Whitey buzzed out of the room, and Diego cursed under his breath.

Ralf's body tensed as Diego raised the gun eye level. Ralf was too close to the target for his own comfort. I knew he'd have to let go of my hands at some point if Diego was going to take a shot. That might be my small window of opportunity.

"Ralf!" Diego barked. "Get out of the way. I'm gunna show our little princess here what it feels like to miss a body part or two."

Ralf glanced at Diego and then to the man with the ponytail who only responded with a glare.

"Christ, Ralf!" Diego tilted his head. "I said get out of the fucking way."

Ralf pulled away from me as he approached Diego.

Diego was staring at him confused. "What, what is it?"

"Well, I was just thinking," Ralf stood next to Diego and turned toward me. "She bit off one of your ears, right?"

"Hence the blood and the other half of my ear perched up on the table there, genius."

Ralf slipped a gun out of the back ban of his pants while Diego kept the gun pointed at me and eyed him cautiously.

"Well, I was thinking, since she took one of your ears, why don't we take both of hers? A little sense of irony. A piece of tradition from my hometown, really; why settle an eye for an eye when you can make a clearer statement with two for one?" Ralf raised and aimed his gun at me.

Diego, half crazed, laughed. "I love it. Yes, yes, two-eyes-for-one-eye kind of deal. I'll take the left ear, you take the right. Though I must warn you Sweets, my aim is a little rusty these days."

My knees wobbled unsteadily beneath me. I gulped loud enough for Diego to hear me, as evidenced in the slight thrill he got out of it. Game plan was to duck on two and a half count and then bolt for the exit. It may have been risky, but it was the best I had at this point.

"Count of three," Ralf smiled a wicked grin I'd never seen before.

"But it's so fun to see her shake in her boots. Let's draw out the suspense a little and make it ten. Yes, on the count of ten." Diego grinned and his eyes nearly turned to slits.

Ralf started the count off, "One...two...three..."

Then the sudden sound of gun fire rung loudly in my ears. I dropped to the floor and held my ears. Next there was screaming and hollering; the sound of people struggling against each other.

I didn't even want to look up; I was too busy assessing my still-attached ears. No blood, no chunks missing. I sighed a quick breath of relief. Still intact, thank heavens!

Once the relief wore off, I crawled under the table. Diego was beside me on the floor, but he was holding his knee to his chest and rolling with pain. He was shot.

When Diego was able to pull himself together enough to register that I was right beside him, he stretched over his head aimlessly reaching for his gun. I intercepted him and pressed on his already broken nose with one hand while grabbing for the gun.

Diego moaned in protest, but I didn't let up. My fingers intertwined with the gun, and I pulled it toward me accidentally firing off a round into the air.

I screamed out of fear at the same time Ralf yelled out of pain. He clutched his arm and leaned against the wall.

"Fuck, Rodger! I'm shot. Why didn't you secure things over there; somebody just shot me!" Ralf growled at the pony-tailed man.

"What are you talking about? I always secure weapons. Look, the two I pulled off are right here." Rodger angled toward the confiscated weapons.

Ralf frantically eyed the room to find the source as I avoided eye contact. "Are you shitting me? Nicole, put that thing down before you shoot me again. What do you think you're doing?"

Ralf's business partner, Rodger, leaned over and whispered something inaudible into a hidden device. I wasn't sure what he was doing over there, but Ralf's sudden movement as he shifted his weight brought my focus back to him.

My hands wobbled as I held the gun in front of me, pointed at Ralf. "Easy now," Ralf soothed.

"Stay away from me." My arms began to tremble. "Y-Y-You tried to shoot off my ears! No sir. Not my ears, do you know how many pairs of earrings I'd have to throw away if I didn't have any ears?"

Ralf's eyes glinted in caution. "Nicole, it's Ralf. Come on, we had something special going on here. We can move past this. Just put the gun down, Toots."

"Toots?! Don't even think about calling me Toots, after you just held me at gun point. No, just stay there. Stay right there while I get the heck out of this hell hole. This is too much crazy in one night for me." I half-sobbed, half-snorted.

I backed away toward the door and turned around when I heard heavy wheezing at the door entrance. Whitey was back with a Walgreens bag filled with aspirins and a bottle of water.

His brain caught up with the scene before him: his boss rocking in pain on the floor, Ralf rested against the wall with a gun wound to his arm, and Rodger over the burly fellow.

Whitey placed his hands on his knees and exhaled as if he were still recuperating from the jog next door, then snapped up with a gun from his waist band. Instinctively, I pulled the trigger.

The sound echoed in my ears, and Whitey's body crumpled to the ground. His hand clasped his chest and pressed against the wound. My eyes widened in horror.

"Ohmygod. Ohmygod. I'm a murderer. I killed him. I'm going to prison." I started to hyperventilate. "Screw that, I'm going to hell. Damn, ass, shit, fuck. Damn, ass, shit, fuck."

"You should probably learn the art of cussing because words just strung together like that really don't hold much meaning." Ralf chuckled a dark laugh. "That solves two problems I guess, gets rid of Whitey. That guy was such a creep. And now we have leverage in the event you ever try to open your mouth about this."

I wheeled in his direction, and he stiffened. "Why don't you take a second and take your hand off the trigger, at least?"

I half nodded still traumatized that I just shot a man in cold blood. Who does that? I dropped the gun unconsciously trying to deny my recent actions by ridding the gun. OK, so clearly I was still in shock because on a regular day, a day that does not include guns and sex slaves and secret tunnels, I would know that you never, ever drop a gun because it could misfire.

And misfire it did.

The sound made me jump, followed by agonizing pain when I discovered that I'd shot myself in the foot. My nostrils flared, and I yanked my foot up to me. "You. Have. Got. To. Be. Kidding. Me!"

I hopped around on one foot. "Who does that? Who really shoots themself in the foot?"

Ralf was nearly rolling on the floor laughing while gasping in pain as he held his arm. "You are something else, Toots, you know that? You really are something else."

Rodger moved from the corner where he was waiting with caution so that he was now next to me in a matter of three bounds. He scooped up the weapon and simultaneously shouted to the device under his shirt. This time I had better visibility to the mechanism than previously. Before I had the chance to open my mouth in protest, men came busting through the door with guns blazing. "MIAMI POLICE! DROP YOUR WEAPONS NOW! I SAID, EVERYONE!"

The guns were already on the floor, so I just lifted my arms and showed my hands. I was so happy to see the police that I almost cried. Diego's crew, on the other hand, was swearing every which way as the cops placed them in cuffs.

CHAPTER EIGHTEEN

It was after six in the morning by the time the police had finished interrogating me at the station. I was tired, and I was anxious because I hadn't been able to contact Emily or Toni or Juanita. And to make matters worse my foot was throbbing through the bandage the doctor had wrapped it in. The doctor said I'd have to schedule a follow up appointment with my primary care physician later in the week for additional care instructions pending my progress. Apparently the bullet grazed the inner arch of my foot, but the doctor placed a temporary bandage on the wound. The doctor informed me that I should be able to walk without much assistance.

So with my bandaged foot and my too-short, temporary crutch, I hobbled to the pay phone in the police station lobby and dialed Emily.

She cautiously answered the phone with hesitation in her voice.

"Emily, it's Nicole. I'm at the police station." Her voice came blasting through the phone, and I had to hold it a few inches away from my ear.

I resumed. "I'm fine, but I'm out of the earpiece distance. Tunnel reception was crap. Have you heard from Juanita?"

"Yes, she is here with me. She found –"

The pay phone ran out of time. "Ah, give me a break!" I shouted at the phone and smashed it repeatedly on the receiver.

A few bystanders were looking at me in fear. I glared at them and hobbled closer to their judging eyes. "Oh, I am allowed to have a moment of insanity given the kind of day I've just had. OK? Keep those eyes to yourself unless you want some of this." I motioned for them with my busted leg and bruised face. As threatening as I looked, they didn't flinch.

Ralf was being shown out of a separate interrogation room and shuffled near a door across from me. Undoubtedly, he just finished with his interrogation, too. Seeing him carelessly roam about the police station had a startling effect on me. It became apparent that he completely had me fooled this entire time.

Ralf leant out a hand for me to stable myself, but I smacked it away. I continued to pathetically hobble back to the couch on the opposing side of the lobby. "What are you doing here?" I grumbled in pain and agitation.

"I just got done with 'em, too." He yawned and stretched his hands in front of him. "I'd kill for a donut right about now." He wiggled his brows in interest. "You want to join me on a donut run down the street? All this excitement gives me an appetite."

I glared at him. "All this excitement?" I mimicked his term in annoyance. "I'd say that's an understatement. I'll pass." My arms were folded, and my body was angled away from his.

"Oh come on, Nicky. You've been dealing with this since what time? I know you must be hungry. Let me get some food in you." He looked at me almost pleadingly.

"No, I'm not hungry," I lied as I endured another sharp pain from my stomach. "Regardless, I really don't want to go anywhere with you right now. I mean, I feel like I don't even know you anymore. I'm still trying to wrap my head around the fact—"

An officer had crossed the lobby to reach us just as I was about to dive into my line of questioning.

The badge read 'Officer Boone' and his thin lined lips spread out into a broad grin as he slapped Ralf on the back. Ralf winced.

"Giovanni!" Officer Boone laughed. "It's about damn time. I saw what the cat dragged in at the beginning of my shift."

Ralf nodded. "Thanks, Boone. Finally brought the son of a bitch in. Diego and the rest of the crew. Though we couldn't get his clients since shit hit the fan a little earlier than expected. Almost had the job too. I mean we were this close."

My brows furrowed at their interaction which seemed foreign to me since I was still processing the fact that the Ralf I previously thought I knew, was a fake identity. Ralf mistook my expression as one of neglect.

Ralf cleared his throat and tilted his head toward me. "Well, actually she helped some, too. This is Nicole."

"Morning," Boone shook my hand. "So you kids brought all the chumps in, huh? Good. It's about time they rot behind bars. Were there any casualties?"

"Officer," I gasped, "Did you not see my statement? This man here almost shot off my ears! If anything he deserves to go to trial, too. Badge or not!"

Boone pouted his lips inquisitively, "What's this about, Giovanni?"

Ralf nonchalantly shrugged it off. "It was to distract Diego from shooting her. Boone, I would never, you know that. I had to distract him long enough and get to a point where I could turn and pull the gun on him. Besides, if anyone got hurt in the crossfire it was me."

Ralf motioned to his arm in the sling. "Nicole shot me in the arm."

Boone's eyes widened. "Ma'am, you shot him in the arm?"

This was so being twisted around. I put my hands on my hips. "It wasn't on purpose," I sighed. "It was an accident."

Ralf agreed, "Yeah it was. Fortunately the bullet only hit meat. You know, she accidentally shot herself in the foot, too. In fact, she even gave the clean shot on Whitey."

Boone stepped back and rested his hand on his gun's handle. "I see. Someone's a little trigger happy, huh?"

I gave up. Ralf was purposely trying to make me look like the bad guy here.

"Yeah, keep a close look out for this one," Ralf winked.

"Noted." Boone eyed me. "Well, Giovanni, good ops. Chief will be happy to see that you're settling into the field work just fine. You did well."

"Appreciate it," Ralf nodded. Boone patted him on the back and then whizzed out of the lobby talking to dispatch on his walkie.

"Field work?" I repeated before turning back toward Ralf. "That sounds like something we should address."

Ralf nodded.

"So, obviously you weren't part of Diego's crew," I acknowledged.

"Nope. My cover was that I worked with Rodger, and we had to secure our business as a vendor in order to gain access to Diego and the hostages. We were also hoping to shut down some of their big clients through our new role, but as evidenced by tonight's sequence of events, that's no longer an option."

"Uh huh. I was taking it all in."

"Now that that's out of the way, you said some pretty rude things to me back there. I can't believe you actually thought I was affiliated with Diego. The cover, all of this," he gestured toward the station. "It's a job and only a job at the end of the day. But you and me...that's real. This has been real from the jump." Ralf's stare burned a hole into my false bravado.

I wanted to believe him. I did. But I couldn't disregard the little voice in the back of mind telling me that I couldn't trust him anymore. I felt vulnerable as it was. There was no way I could just let that go so easily. Despite wanting to believe him, my mind refused it. Anything that came out of his mouth was now tainted with a shadow of doubt. At this I felt my defensive layer form, sealing any capacity of exposing my vulnerable side.

"Well unfortunately I just can't trust your authenticity anymore. I get that you have a job and that it comes with confidentiality baggage, but that doesn't change my distrust in you. Your words hold no validity for me anymore, Ralf." I faked a shrug of indifference.

He shifted uncomfortably in his seat. "Toots, not that I want to add any more fuel to the fire or anything but you should probably call me by my real name. Ralf was a fake identification."

A vein pulsed in my neck. "Wait, you mean Ralf is not even your real name?!"

"The name's Mario. Mario Giovanni."

Ralf, or I guess, Mario, leaned in, slid his uninjured arm around the back of my neck, and pulled me into him for an unexpected kiss. I felt the butterflies take flight in my stomach, and just as I was starting to melt into his delicious kiss, a loud crash from the front of the lobby jolted the both of us back.

Who could it be? None other than the infamous Juanita. Her eyes were wild and eagerly scouted the lobby. I pulled away from Mario and stood up to get her attention.

"Señora Nicole! Señora Nicole!" She charged the lobby knocking over magazine racks in the process.

"Oh boy," Mario scrambled to get up. "I can't take anymore crazy tonight. I'm out of here." He tenderly pecked me on the cheek before he rushed off.

"Señora," Juanita hunched over and gulped in gallons of air. "I'm so glad I found chu! We've been scouting the police stations looking all over for chu! Oye!" She bent over gasping for air. She caught her breath before she continued, "Emily's in the car. It's no good, Señora."

"What? What is it?" I asked her more impatiently. "Is everything OK?"

"No. No, it's not OK." Juanita swallowed. "It's Toni. And it doesn't look good."

"What happened?" I asked between clenched jaws.

"Those two guys from his past, Logan and Caleb? Emily picked up Toni's reception when they herded him out of the tunnels. She tried to follow him, she tried. But eventually they were too far out of range. The last thing she heard was him being brutalized by them. Searching for something that he had. Something very important that they've been hunting for a long time."

"They've taken him," I answered knowingly. Horrified, I pressed a hand against my chest. There I felt the envelope Toni slipped me the last time I saw him. I recalled his final words. *Keep it safe, keep it hidden. As long as that remains, I'll still have a pulse.*

***

Thank you to all of my readers for taking a chance on a first time author! I hope that you've enjoyed Miami Confidential so far. Stay tuned for more…the sequel is already in the works! I would like to also announce that **ten percent** of the book's proceeds are donated to Montgomery County Women's Center. MCWC is a wonderful agency located near Houston that is dedicated to helping victims of domestic violence and sexual abuse. Thank you for your contribution toward the cause!

Acknowledgements

I feel so blessed to have all of the encouragement and support I've received from my friends and family during the fun process of creating Miami Confidential. I owe a big thank you to my editor, Brandon DeHoyos. I am extremely grateful for all of the hard work and help you've contributed along this journey...you are truly one of a kind.

Mom, Dad, Mitch, and Allissa, you are my heart. I could not have asked for a better family than if I'd picked you out of a catalog. Thank you for your support and persistent cheerleading! You are my boost of courage whenever I stand in my own way.

To the girls, Courtney Patterson, Christina Brown, Kristina Gee, Brandy Parratt, and Paige Hajdik, who have rooted for me all the way to the finish line. I'm so fortunate to have you ladies in my life. I couldn't imagine girls' nights, happy hours, or bitch sessions without each and every one of you.

Thank you to the teachers who fueled my love for reading and writing: Ms. Lucia, Mr. Arcement, Ms. Darroh, and you too, Ms. Kendall, though I still object to that B.

To Shelia Bailey, the most warm hearted friend and mentor; there will always be a special place for you in my heart.

An enormous thank you to Michele Timmons for your shared excitement over Miami Confidential. Your enthusiasm and interest mean more than you realize.

And last, but certainly not least, I would like to thank God. Without those gentle hands guiding me toward my path to happiness, none of this would be possible.

About the Author

MEREDITH WARD with her background in psychology, inevitably found herself drawn to the undeniable pull of her desire to write. Starting at a young age, her love for literature manifested as lighthearted short stories scribbled on notepad paper which she then read tirelessly to her parents. She now lives in Houston where she continues her innate passion for writing with her dog, Kodah, snuggled next to her.

www.miamiconfidential.net

Made in the USA
Lexington, KY
16 June 2015